"Do you de ☞

Stefan choked. "What kind of question is that?"

"One that requires an honest answer."

He nodded. "Aye, I desire you."

"Why? Because I am handy?"

He smiled and touched her hair. The soft thickness felt like spun silk beneath his callused fingertips. His blood, already heated, quickened. "Because you are brave, and passionate, and beautiful."

"What if I were not brave, or passionate." She yanked her hair from his grasp. "What if my face were that of a hag but I had this body. Would you still desire me?"

"I would desire your body."

"What is the difference?"

He smiled slowly. "A man can find release between any willing thighs."

"Is it the same for women?"

"I know of some women who soften only for one man's touch."

She peered at him hard, and slowly said, " 'Tis where I am confused. My betrothed's kisses were warm and tender. I did not mind them. But you?" She pressed her hand to his chest, and his heart slammed against it. "You do something else to me entirely. It distresses me that your touch evokes wantonness from me when my betrothed's does not."

"If you've been waiting for the perfect medieval series, this is it. Karin Tabke does for Norman knights what J. R. Ward has done for vampires, with hot alpha heroes and the fiery heroines who tame them."

—*New York Times* bestselling author Monica McCarty

ALSO BY KARIN TABKE

KARIN TABKE

MASTER
of
CRAVING

Pocket Star Books

New York   London   Toronto   Sydney

Pocket Star Books
A Division of Simon & Schuster, Inc.
1230 Avenue of the Americas
New York, NY 10020

First Pocket Star Books paperback edition June 2009

POCKET STAR BOOKS and colophon are registered trademarks of Simon & Schuster, Inc.

For information about special discounts for bulk purchases, please contact Simon & Schuster Special Sales at 1-800-456-6798 or business@simonandschuster.com.

The Simon & Schuster Speakers Bureau can bring authors to your live event. For more information or to book an event contact the Simon & Schuster Speakers Bureau at 1-866-248-3049 or visit our website at www.simonspeakers.com.

Cover design by Lisa Litwack.
Cover illustration by Franco Accornero.

Manufactured in the United States of America

10   9   8   7   6   5   4   3   2   1

ISBN 978-1-4391-0257-2
ISBN 978-1-4391-2734-6 (ebook)

To Rhianna and David:
May your deep love for each other conquer all.
I love you both with all my heart.

MASTER
of
CRAVING

THE BLOOD SWORD LEGACY

Eight mercenary knights, each of them base-born, each of them bound by unspeakable torture in a Saracen prison, each of them branded with the mark of the sword for life. Each of their destinies marked by a woman.

'Twas whispered along the Marches that the demon knights who rode upon black horses donned in black mail wielding black swords would slay any man, woman, or child who dared look upon them. 'Twas whispered their loyalty was only to the other and no man could split them asunder, nor was there enough gold or silver in the kingdom to buy their oath. 'Twas well known each of them was touched not by the hand of God but by Lucifer himself.

'Twas also whispered, but only by the bravest of souls, that each Blood Sword was destined to find only one woman in all of Christendom who would bear him and only him sons, and until that one woman was found, he would battle and ravage the land . . .

. . . but the darkest secret whispered was that there was one amongst them whose violent craving for the one woman he could not have would be the spark that would set an entire region on fire, and nearly bring down a kingdom, with the aftermath to be felt for the next thousand years . . .

Push, milady, *push*!" Jane the royal nurse urged.

Princess Branwen gritted and bore down with all her might, praying to the Goddess and to her Lord Jesus Christ that this time she would see a live child come for all her labor.

"I see a head as crimson as the Beltane fires!" No sooner had the words left Jane's mouth than the lusty squall of a babe filled the small, stuffy chamber. Another painful contraction gripped Branwen as she forced the child from her body. "'Tis a princess!" Jane cried.

Branwen collapsed back into the straw mattress, and though she had prayed endlessly for a son, she could not hold back a smile of satisfaction. "Let me see, Jane, show me my daughter," Branwen said softly, her strength, after three days of hard labor, nearly depleted. She held out her trembling arms for the squalling child, barely able to manage the gesture, but was glad for the effort when the mite of an infant lay in her arms.

Branwen peered down at the fiery thatch of hair atop the most angelic face she had ever beheld. The babe quieted the instant Branwen took her from the nurse. With her fingertips, gently she smoothed away the blood and caul from the babe's eyes, and was rewarded with a calm, penetrating stare. She gasped, and her heart filled even more. She glanced up at the nurse, ignoring the frown lines furrowing her brow. "An old soul, Jane. She has been here before." Branwen gazed back at her daughter, and pride filled her so completely she felt overwhelmed with emotion. The hot sting of tears blurred her vision. Though the babe was not a son, Hylcon would be so proud of her. After so much heartache, they had finally been blessed with a live child.

Jane clucked her response. Ignoring the child, the nurse pursed her lips as if she had just sipped vinegar. "One more push, milady, to rid your body of the afterbirth."

Barely able to muster the strength, Branwen bore down, and, almost as forcefully as the delivery of the child, she felt the afterbirth leave her. She sank back into the damp pillows and hugged her child close, pressing a kiss to the warm forehead. Closing her eyes, satisfied with her chore, she laid the child to her breast and took several deep breaths.

Without a word, Jane pressed her sturdy hands to her lady's belly and began to knead. Slowly Branwen opened her eyes and peered down at the creation in her arms. So enthralled with her beautiful daughter was Branwen, she did not give much concern to the continual flow of blood from between her thighs. 'Twould pass. It always did.

Branwen glanced up at the nurse from her daughter, who rooted at her breast. Perspiration beaded the servant's brow as she continued to massage Branwen.

When she refused to look up and meet her gaze, a

tremor of fear iced Branwen's sultry skin. "Jane?" she whispered, her arms trembling, almost dropping the babe.

The midwife slowly looked up from her task, concern lacing the deep lines around her dark brown eyes, and by it Branwen knew a prickle of fear so chilling that she choked back a breath. In that moment of clarity, Branwen's entire life, a life full of love and laughter and goodness, spun in a slow endless circle before her eyes, and she knew with a sinking realization that she would not see her daughter other than this one time.

"Call my husband," Branwen whispered. At her command, the ancient tiring woman assisting Jane hurried from the chamber.

Branwen pressed the child tightly to her, then closed her eyes, praying once again to the Goddess, for the old ways still lived in the heart and souls of the Welsh Celts. She prayed the Goddess would protect her daughter, and give her to a man who loved her above all others. A man who would sacrifice all for her; a man who would protect her as her own dear Hylcon had protected her.

Jane worked feverishly, her experienced hands kneading Branwen as she would a round of dough. Branwen felt no pain. How could she with such a perfect gift in her arms? Closing her eyes, she tightened her arms around the mewling piece of humanity. Her chest tightened with the combined excitement of love and the jarring pain of despair, of knowing that all that she held dear was lost and there was nothing but a divine intervention that could stay it. She expelled a long tired breath, and with each wave of blood that flowed from her body, Branwen felt her strength ebb.

"Branwen!" Hylcon called as he burst into the birthing room, rushing to her side. Turning her head toward her husband, Branwen managed the barest hint of a smile. Fear twisted his noble features. Did he sense her end?

"My love, I have given you a daughter."

He grasped her hands wrapped around the babe, his wide silver eyes giving no acknowledgment of their child. He had, since the day they first met, had eyes only for her. Her heart twisted in bittersweet pain. Prince Hylcon, every maid's dream. He was so handsome, a mighty warrior and a good husband. A most worthy prince to their people.

"My love," he whispered. Then, ever so gently, with his fingertips, he pushed the tendrils of her hair from her damp brow. "Do not speak, you will need your strength for later."

"My apologies, my lord, for not giving you a son."

Vehemently he shook his head and gently pressed his lips to hers. Just a brush, just enough to remind her he put her above all women. "Next time, Bran, next time."

She could not tell him there would be no next time. But she saw the fear in his eyes when he burst into the room. Aye, he would mourn her passing, and for that she had some satisfaction. Not because she wished him pain, but because she was the source of it. For their love was uncommon. It had grown from just a tiny seed, when they met for the first time on their wedding day some nine years past, into a blossoming garden. But he would need to take another wife.

She caught a sob, as her chest tightened. She had failed him miserably as a wife. While he had given her all, she in return could only, after six stillborn daughters, give him a live daughter and one that would take her life. She choked back another sob, wishing with all her heart 'twas she who could give him his heart's desire. But it was not to be.

"My love," she softly said, "take our daughter, call her Arianrhod after the moon goddess, and give her all that you would have given me."

Shaking his head, Hylcon dropped to his knees beside her, still refusing to look upon the child. He pressed his big hands to hers again, his silvery eyes not looking anywhere but at her, his wife whom she knew he loved more than his own life. "Do not leave me, Bran, I forbid it!"

With what little strength she still possessed, Branwen held her ground. She loved her husband with all her heart, but she would not take the chance that he would cast their child aside in anger at losing his wife. "Swear it, Hylcon," she breathed. "Swear you will not cast her aside." Her eyes beseeched his, and it was not until he nodded that she felt peace. She smiled and closed her eyes. "I will await you at the gates, my love. Take your time, for our daughter will need you. Give her only to the man of her choosing. And make him swear he holds her life more precious than his own." She slowly exhaled, and barely audibly whispered, "Then come to me."

"Nay!" he roared. "Do not leave me!"

But it was too late.

ONE

Thick air settled like a sodden mantle upon the rising heat of the summer morning. The dusky blue sky above hung low and heavy, promising rain. Great black buzzards sat patiently high up in the oak and ash trees, as if summoned by the banshees to come and collect the dead. And there would be many souls to collect this day.

From where Stefan de Valrey sat upon his mighty warhorse Fallon, he had a clear view of the valley below, the forest that edged it, and the Black Mountains that rose behind it like great slumbering giants. Behind him rose the gray stone of Hereford Castle, not yet complete. Before him, a respectable showing of soldiers worked feverishly, fortifying the castle defenses. Behind the castle walls, a greater force stood, several garrisons of ready Norman soldiers, and surrounding them, high upon the ramparts, hundreds of seasoned archers.

Far off in the distance, a sea of standards mingled in a tapestry of colors, as both Welsh and Saxon, unified against Normandy, marched in a steady cadence straight toward them. Though they were leagues away, their intention was clear. Like a swarm of locusts, they burned a wide swath of destruction behind them. Their destination: Hereford Castle.

But they would be hard-pressed to breach the stalwart fortress and the seasoned knights who waited behind the stone walls. Of that Stefan was sure. 'Twas for that simple reason he and his men were summoned by William fitz Osbern, the Norman Earl of Hereford. He had insisted that his cousin the king, William the Conqueror, send his most highly trained guard, *les morts*, to fight beside him against the defiant Saxon, Earl Edric, and the two Welsh kings, Rhiwallon and Bleddyn, who came with hopes of slaying Normans, plundering the countryside and sending a message to Normandy that they would never submit.

Stefan's lip curled in a snarl. Fools! All of them! The Conqueror could not be defeated! The Welsh would regret their decision to ally with Edric. William dealt harshly with any man who thwarted him. Stefan checked his anger as his wrath mounted. For he learned years ago never to go into battle any way but completely composed. It had kept him alive all of his eight and twenty years; it would keep him alive this day.

In a silent salute, he touched his mailed fingertips to his helm and nodded ever so slightly toward the encroaching horde. A worthy opponent, no doubt. But there was no doubt in Stefan's mind who would be the victor at the end of the day. And the day, but a handful of hours old, promised a worthy exchange. Even now, despite the vastness of yonder army, and the activity that accompanied them, it was eerily quiet. 'Twas a sensation Stefan relished: the deadly calm before all hell broke lose.

"The Welsh and Saxons grow bolder each day!" Stefan called to his brother Blood Swords. His eyes narrowed beneath his helm as he turned to his left. Rohan, Warner, and Thorin, the bastard son of the late Norse king Harald Hardrada, nodded in unison, their narrowed gazes focused where his had just been. Stefan looked to his right, to Ioan, Wulfson, Rorick, and Rhys, their faces mirroring his own. Each of them sat astride a great black warhorse, each of them mailed in black, each of them weaponed with bow, arrow, sword, and lance, and Thorin, as always, fondled the handle of his great battle-ax, Beowulf.

Stefan himself fondled the leather-wrapped hilt of his sword. Aye, many would die upon its honed edges this day. Instead of apprehension, excitement filled him as it always did before battle. 'Twas what drove him, 'twas his life, his purpose. He was not a gentle man, but then, neither was war gentle, nor the men beside him he called brother. All warriors at heart, they would die as they lived, by the sword.

He turned his attention back to the oncoming force. Most men would have realized they were outnumbered and fled across the drawbridge, calling for the portcullis to be dropped and prepared for a siege, but not Stefan, nor his brothers-in-arms. His gaze swept just ahead to the wall of Norman soldiers, then over his right shoulder to the high ramparts of Hereford Castle, to the archers who stood at the ready. Fitz Osbern himself would command from above, while Stefan had been given the command of the knights. When the enemy was within the longest range of the archers, a hailstorm of arrows would rain upon them. Once they had been softened, the archers would adjust and continue their barrage into the forest, whilst the foot soldiers marched forward flanked by a wall of steel and horseflesh. Then, and only when the heat of battle reached its zenith, hell's fury would be unleashed when the Blood Swords gave the command to their destriers to engage. Once afield, any living soul that crossed their path would pray for a quick and painless death.

It was a familiar routine, and one Stefan enjoyed immensely, for when it was the Blood Swords' turn, they faced what was left of the enemy's elite, and though there were none more fearsome than they, Stefan never felt good about slaying an ill-matched opponent. So, he was content to await his turn.

Fallon tossed his head, champing on his bit. Stefan patted the great horse on the side of the neck. "Patience, lad, we shall play soon enough."

"Richard is a fool of an overlord here." Warner seethed, "His heavy hand has brought this upon us today."

"Aye," Stefan agreed. "His greed has set this war into motion. Had fitz Osbern paid more attention to his ambitious vassal, we would not be in such a precarious position."

"Despite Richard's arrogance," Rohan rumbled. "Edric is a madman to thwart William! He will lose all."

"More hides for William to take for his loyal vassals, eh, Stefan?" Wulfson asked.

Stefan's heart thudded in excitement against his chest at the mention of land. He nodded. "You and Rohan have done well for yourselves. 'Tis land we all seek, Wulf. With mine, I will breed the finest horses in Christendom!"

"Hah!" Rorick chortled. "What of a wife?"

Stefan scowled. He preferred the company of his

horses over women. Horses were loyal to their master. Women were not. He'd learned the lesson well as a young man, from a noblewoman who had not only given her body to him but pledged her undying love and then her troth, only to take it back at his sire's refusal to acknowledge him. The day she married a wealthy Saxon noble had been the day he sold his sword to the highest bidder and swore that the day he took a wife it would be on his terms alone. "Nay, I am not like Wulf and Rohan. I prefer my solitude. And well you know I have no trust for the fairer of the sexes."

Rorick reached over and slapped him on the back. "Aye, I feel your pain, brother. But you must admit, there is no sweeter ride than between the soft thighs of a maid."

Stefan smiled: a rare gesture. "Agreed." He focused back on the gathering army below and scowled. His heart continued to thud against his chest, but not because of thoughts of a soft ride on a fair damsel. "More swarm."

"Look." Thorin pointed toward the western horizon and the great billows of black smoke that rose up into the thick air behind the encroaching army. A sultry breeze rose up and caressed Stefan's cheek, like a woman after a robust session of lovemaking. He grunted at the thought.

"They are scourging all of Herefordshire," Wulfson muttered.

Stefan nodded, and leveled his lance. "Aye, and they will pay handsomely for the privilege." He turned his horse and gestured for his men to follow. "If we are to beat the Welsh we must do more than soften them with arrows and charge them in the open. If we wait for them to come close to the castle walls, by their sheer numbers they can pin us and hold us at a gross disadvantage. A siege is not in our best interest. We must find a way to destroy them *en masse* before they reach the outer limits of the castle grounds."

The Blood Swords nodded and came together as one, and as they were wont to do, they devised a treacherous plan of action.

Several hours later, Stefan stood with his brothers high on the rampart walls of Hereford Castle. "If your plan does not work, Valrey, your men will die this day," William fitz Osbern said flatly.

Stefan turned to the Norman cousin of the Conqueror and curbed the sneer from his lips. Greed, not honor, drove the bastard. "Time will tell." And as the words left Stefan's mouth the first standard poked through the wood at the edge of the wide meadow surrounding the castle. He smiled tightly and softly said, "Now watch and learn."

Fitz Osbern moved to the edge of the stone rampart and stood with Stefan and his brothers, watching as Welsh and Saxon approached.

When the wide swath, more than thirty men deep, cleared the forest edge and marched into the open field, Stefan raised his hand and a loud horn blew. All at once, score after score of shallow blinds popped up from the meadow ground and Norman soldiers burst onto the field, stabbing and hacking the enemy taking them completely by surprise. Confusion reigned amongst the Welsh and Saxon forces. Stefan grinned.

Lying low in the grass farther back, a deadly band of archers stood and let loose on the enemy, then dropped back to their hiding places amongst the tall grass. Stefan raised his hand again, the horn sounded, and the Norman soldiers dropped and rolled, disappearing beneath the thatched blinds just as quickly as they had popped up. As the Welsh army scattered in confusion, the nearly two hundred Norman archers facing the battlefield just outside the castle walls let loose with another hailstorm of arrows. Screams and curses tore across the field. Another barrage of arrows followed, the reward more screams and, now, wild panic. Stefan raised his hand again and the horn blew once more. The blinds opened up, the soldiers emerged, stabbing and hacking at the enemy. And as before, just as quickly as they appeared, they vanished, and the ground was still. The scene replayed itself out repeatedly until the enemy was able to stabilize themselves and pull back.

Stefan frowned. Before they regrouped, for every Welsh and Saxon soldier who fell, three replaced him.

"Lower the bridge and send the first wave of soldiers!" Fitz Osbern called down to his captain, who waited in the bailey. The huge gate slowly lifted and the heavy bridge lowered. Nearly half of the garrisons charged out to meet the enemy.

"Send the first cavalry group!" Stefan called out. He watched as the archers continued to land their arrows just ahead of the Norman foot soldiers. As the regrouped Welsh and Saxon army came into view, Stefan cautiously watched, and his concern grew. Despite the scores of knights engaging alongside the foot soldiers, and the continued onslaught of arrows into the forest, the Normans on the field began to falter.

"Instruct the archers to shoot into the forest, to stay the flow!" Stefan called to fitz Osbern .

Fitz Osbern scowled, not liking Stefan's interference.

"Do it now!" Stefan commanded.

The command was given, and the result was immediate. With the flow of soldiers staunched, the Normans, sorely outnumbered, gained the time to do what they did best. Fight.

As the battle raged, Stefan watched, his hand gripping and ungripping the leather hilt of his sword. He smiled as he noticed each one of the Blood Swords fondle their hilts as well. They could not help it. 'Twas in their blood.

Stefan turned his attention back to the battle scene playing out before him. The archer's cache of arrows had grown dangerously low, and so the hailstorm into the forest edge was not so quick or heavy. The Welsh took advantage of it. They broke the Norman line, and when they did, fitz Osbern 's men began to break ranks.

"They falter!" Stefan cried. "To horse, men!" The Blood Swords followed him down the narrow stone stairway to the bailey where their horses awaited them.

" 'Tis too early!" Fitz Osbern yelled after them.

Stefan turned on his heel and looked up at the Earl. "If we do not go to rally the men and show them we can win the day, *all* will be lost!" He turned and hurried to his horse.

When the portcullis slowly raised, the creaking sound of the turning chain on wheel overriding the din of battle, the eight knights sat astride, four abreast, a most fearsome sight. Stefan, flanked by Thorin on his left and

Rorick and Warner to his right, was followed up by Wulf-son, Rohan, Ioan, and Rhys at his back.

The heavy bridge lowered, and before it hit dirt, the eight black knights, with lances at the ready and battle cries booming across the field, thundered out to meet their enemy. As the Red Sea had for Moses, so the soldiers before them parted. In a tight formation, they rode out, and with each stride in practiced precision, they moved an inch further apart until they fanned out in a tight semi-circle. In that formation, they began to hack a swath across the field. As bodies fell, a renewed fervor swept through the Norman army.

Each time they regrouped, the Blood Swords raised their battle cry, and like the plague, they destroyed every living being in their path. But as the battle raged, the Blood Swords became the focus of the Welsh kings Rhiwallon and Bleddyn, who watched from the forest edge.

Over time, the tight formation loosened; and when Stefan hacked off the arm of the soldier who would have done the same to him, he cast his gaze to his right, then his left. His brothers were so heavily embedded in the thick of battle that he could not distinguish them.

He turned in his saddle, and with a mighty arc and swipe, separated yet another English head from the shoulders it had rested upon its entire life.

Sweat ran in rivulets down his face, stinging his eyes. He blinked, and spurred Fallon deeper into the fray. His hawk-sharp gaze swept the field of battle, locating then resting on the backs of his fellow Blood Swords up ahead, and he saw they too were as deep into the combined forces of Welsh and Saxon as he. He did not allow the fact that they had become separated to deter him from the task: secure Hereford Castle by any means necessary.

He watched as Wulfson, Ioan, Thorin, Warner, Rohan, and Rorick hacked their way through a gantlet of foot soldiers. As Stefan urged his horse forward, he narrowed his gaze. More Welsh erupted from the surrounding forests to swallow them up. Concern gnawed at his gut. He called to Rhys to his right, and pointed with his bloody sword toward the descending hordes running with the velocity of the wind at his brothers up ahead.

Rhys reined his horse around to flank the right column as it raced forward, while Stefan circled around the left. Both men sheathed their swords and drew their longbows and let loose, one after the other, scores of arrows on the attacking men. Stefan did not have the time to admire his work, as one man fell for each arrow he notched. He did not look to see if Rhys was as accurate, for he knew from years of riding and fighting together there were few who could best the young knight.

Once his quiver was depleted, Stefan reined up the black and drew his broadsword again, and with his other hand he grasped a deadly pike and pulled it from the carcass of a downed Welshman. He twirled it around in his large hand until it fit comfortably in his grip. Then he scanned the horizon for his brothers amongst the hordes. When he could not locate them, for the first time since the eight of them had fled that hellhole of a prison in Iberia, Stefan knew that Madam Death lurked on the horizon for not one of them, but for all of them.

Rage infused him. They would not fall to these cowards!

Stefan cast a quick glance over to Rhys, who had moved in, and as Stefan had, grabbed a pike from a dead man. In his other hand he held his sword at the ready. Each of their mounts was as highly trained in the art of war as were their masters. With both hands free to wield weapons, the knights controlled their mounts with their legs and body movement.

"To the Blood Swords!" Stefan yelled above the din of battle. As they came together, a force of nature to be reckoned with, they let loose their battle cry. The buzzards that waited patiently in the trees above scattered high into the hot summer sky.

And as his brothers came into view, Stefan watched in horror as they were swarmed by scores of Welsh. He roared his fury that he should lose any one of them, and as he hacked his way toward them, the sharp burn of a blade sliced into his thigh. He turned in his saddle to see the flat end of several swords flash before his eyes. Pain seared his face, and then the world went black.

TWO

Dinefwr Castle

Lady Arrrreeeeeeaaaaaaannnnn,"Jane called from the chapel door."Hurry, child, the Jarl's train comes!"

Arian's heart thumped in her chest, and she suddenly felt nervous. From the small graveyard not too far from the chapel, she nodded, acknowledging her nurse's command. Letting out a long breath, Arian patted the spray of late bluebells resting next to the ones her father had left just that morning on her mother's grave. Papa told her they had been her mother's favorite, and every time the sweet scent was taken up by a breeze and passed beneath her nose, it reminded Arian of the woman she would never know.

The stone cross that marked where her mother lay gleamed white, like the seashells on the beaches under the clear August sun. For a long moment, Arian stared at it, and mourned the loss not of her mother, but a father who, so saddened by the loss of his one true love, lived with bouts of such despair she feared for his well-being. Of late, his bouts of darkness came more frequently. He roamed the dark halls of the castle, and could be found late at night and in the early morning fog, sitting here as she did now, tears glistening on his cheeks.

In all her score of years, Arian had tried to pull the man who was responsible for her life out of his dark moods. Gone were the days when he strode robustly through the castle, calling for his daughter to race the wind upon the Dinefwr stallions. Gone were the days when she accompanied him to far-off lands to trade for silks and spices and exotic baubles. And while those luxuries were most coveted in her land, the true treasure they sought in their travels was discovering another hotblood to strengthen their renowned stable's line.

Since their return last spring from King Murchad's court in Dublin, if she came too close, he would stop and stare at her as if she were a phantom. She loved the man who looked at her as if she were a ghost. 'Twas not so easy to convince him, though. For all his distance, she was, with each anniversary of her mother's death, in his eyes Branwen reincarnated. And she knew she was the reason for his deepening despair.

"Arian!" Morwena, her stepmother, called sharply, coming toward her from the bailey. "Get thee in the castle now!"

Arian sighed and gave one last glance to the cross and slowly stood. Morwena. 'Twas not a more unhappy woman in all of Wales than her father's wife. Arian sighed again, and slowly swept the dirt from her emerald and saffron kirtle. She shrugged, and looked over her shoulder to the woman who stood ramrod stiff in the middle of the bustling bailey, her hands on her narrow hips, her dark brows dipped in a V above her noble nose.

She could not blame Morwena. Though the woman tried, she could not, even with the birth of a son, make

Hylcon of Carmarthenshire happy. And it was her father's great sorrow that tutored Arian well in the lessons of love. While she looked forward to marriage with Magnus the Tall of Norway, she would never love him. The life her father led, having loved so deeply only to lose, was not what she wanted for herself. And the misery Morwena suffered daily because her husband would not let go of a ghost did not settle well either.

Nay, Magnus was a good man, nephew to the young King Olaf of Norway. But there were no guarantees he did not have a mistress or two tucked away in his holdings. 'Twas the way of men, was it not? Friar Wythe called her pragmatic, and she took it as a compliment. She would be a good wife to Magnus, and give him sons, but she would never give up her heart only to have it broken. And she was not so naïve to think her husband would never turn from her to another. She understood the ways of marriage, and she was prepared that should he turn away from her as Hylcon had from Morwena, she would be content to raise her children and run the numerous households as one of her station was expected to.

"*Now*, child!" Morwena beseeched. "Get thee up here before he sees you in those rags!"

Arian hastened her step, if only a little. Her clothing could hardly be construed as rags, even soiled as they were. They were fit for any princess. Hylcon was rich, and his vigorous trading with the Norse paid off handsomely. She was better jeweled and garbed than most queens. She smiled as she made her way to her stepmother. Aye, she might be pragmatic in the ways of the heart, but she possessed a frivolous side as well. She was a woman after all! One who appreciated fine cloth and jewels and rode upon the most coveted horses in Wales. Not only did King Rhiwallon, her mother's cousin, and his brother King Bleddyn ride the finest stallions bred from the Dinefwr-Castile line, but kings and emperors brought their mares to stand under the great Spanish stallions of Dinefwr. Aye, she rode with the ease of a breeze upon her cheeks and cherished that time when she galloped like the wind, her chaperone left behind in her dust calling for her to slow. Arian laughed aloud as she thought of poor Oswain, her father's squire, just yesterday. They had ridden west and she had him convinced she was going all the way to the Irish Sea to meet Magnus when he landed!

He had turned as white as the swans that glided along the Tywi just below the steep slope the castle was built upon. Once returned, the upstart informed her father that she was a hellion and she would break her neck and that of any escort who chased after her. Hylcon frowned and forbade her to ride again unless he accompanied her. What good would she be with a broken neck to the Norse jarl, he demanded when she argued. His mandate only reinforced her decision to marry. She could not wait for Magnus to claim her as his bride. And she could not wait to be gone from Dinefwr and her mother's ghost.

As Arian came closer to Morwena, she watched her creamy cheeks redden. Morwena was slight, with long dark hair and big bright heather-colored eyes. She was, for one so slight, full of vigor. "If you were my daughter I would box your ears so soundly you would hear bees buzzing in your head for a fortnight. Come, get thee to your chamber. You must bathe and dress for your betrothed. You do not want him to see his future lady with dirt on her face and mud on her dress. He will re-think his offer."

Arian let Morwena prattle on as she dragged her from the bailey past the dark castle walls and through the great hall that bustled with activity. In two days' time, she would be a married woman, and a great celebra-tion would follow. She shivered at the thought of the marriage bed and hoped that Magnus would be gentle. Her mood settled when she thought of her husband-to-be. They had met in Dublin this spring past. Upon their first introduction, Magnus made known his interest in her. He was a large, gentle, handsome man with a noble heart. He had asked but for a kiss to seal their contract. When she left Dublin, she left with his promise to come to her by summer's end and wed her.

Morwena must have felt her apprehension. "Jarl Mag-nus is a good man, Arian. He promised Hylcon to put you above all other women. He gave his oath he would never raise a hand to you."

"Papa made him swear that?" Arian asked, genuinely surprised.

"Aye, 'twas your mother's dying wish he give you only to the man of your choice and who placed you above all other women."

Arian stumbled at the words: not that Magnus had pledged such an oath, for he wanted a princess bride and would tell the prince he would dance on his head and swallow fire if that was what it took. She came with a large dowry of gold, lands, horseflesh, and the bluest blood in all of Wales. Nay, it was that her mother even on her deathbed had thought of her future.

"Did Papa tell you this?"

Morwena shook her head, and then gently pushed her ahead up the wide stone stairway leading to the upper chambers. "Nay, Jane; one night after too much honey wine."

Arian smiled. Jane. Though she was aged, she was spry and could still keep up with Arian. That she was going to Norway with her greatly calmed the girl's nerves. Jane was all wise and would be able to guide Arian in all things wifely.

As they entered the chamber, Arian expected to see Jane, but did not. "Did not Jane come up from the chapel?"

"Aye, but I sent her on an errand. I would have you fitted one last time in your wedding gown before the wrinkles are smoothed." Morwena spun Arian around, and not waiting for her to undress, began to untie the back laces of her kirtle.

"I am hurt at your eagerness to rid my home of me," Arian softly said, standing still as her stepmother lifted the fabric over her head.

Morwena paused in her chore, the fabric stifling Arian. Then she pulled it all the way off and said, "Do not be, Arian, 'tis not you I want gone but the memories you stir."

Arian let out a long breath and nodded. If she were waspish she could hurt Morwena, but she was not. In her own way, Morwena had been a good mother, and was a most doting parent to her brother Rhodri. He was just ten-and-seven, and so much a man. Where Arian was told she was her mother's image, Rhodri was their father's.

"I pray, Arian, that once you are wed and gone from here, Hylcon will begin to see me as his wife."

"I pray it as well. You both deserve happiness."

Morwena made a soft sound deep in her throat, but when Arian turned to look at her she turned away and motioned to the steaming tub. "Come, the water grows cold as you dally."

As she sank into the warm velvety water, Jane bustled into the chamber, followed by two maids. It took the three of them to carry the length of a sky-blue velvet and gold-embroidered wedding gown. Arian frowned. Though beautiful, 'twas not what she had charged the dressmaker with.

Her heart began a soft steady thump against her chest. " 'Tis beautiful, Jane, but not what I was to wear on my wedding day."

The old nurse looked up and a frown wrinkled her brow. " 'Twas your mother's."

Morwena and Arian gasped in unison. "But—"

Jane shook her head and looked sadly at Morwena before she looked back at Arian. "Prince Hylcon insisted you wear it on your wedding day. When I voiced my concern he cut me off with those silver eyes so much like yours and said, 'She will wear her mother's dress or there will be no ceremony!'"

" 'Tis not right!" Morwena cried. "He will lose all composure when he sees her dressed in Branwen's gown! I forbid it!"

Jane shook her head and looked at her lady with something akin to pity. "My regrets, milady, but he was most adamant."

Morwena choked back a sob and flew from the

chamber, slamming the thick door shut behind her. Jane shooed the maids from the room and set about bathing her charge. "In three days' time you will leave here a wedded woman, Arian. Leave the sadness here, do not drag it with you. 'Tis not yours to bear."

Despite her nurse's words, Arian's heart weighed heavy in her chest. If only her mother had survived her birth, how different life would be. "You have not changed your mind? You will go with me?" Arian asked. For as brave as she was, and as much as she was looking forward to life in Norway, she could not bear the thought of Jane staying behind.

"Aye, I go where you go, just as I did with your mother."

And so, with that peace of mind, Arian was ready to greet her betrothed.

Just as Jane was weaving the last golden ribbons into a braided crown, Morwena burst into the chamber. Her abruptness startled both Arian and Jane. "Jarl Magnus has sent a proxy groom!"

Arian's cheeks chilled. "He did not come himself?"

"Nay, he is caught up in some political strife in his homeland. He will travel to his estate in Yorkshire in two months' time to wed with you there."

"But we were to sail to Norway. Does he mean me to travel across England?" The thought terrified her. With bloodthirsty Normans ravaging the countryside, she would not be safe.

"He sent a large contingency escort and his nephew Sir Dag as your proxy groom. Their ships were attacked by Irish pirates. Only three boats survived. 'Tis too treacherous to sail with so few. With his train and the men Hylcon will provide, you will be safe crossing England."

"But Father supported Harald! And Magnus's great-uncle attacked York less than a year ago! William is no fool. He will see no ally in Wales or Norway!"

"Lord Dag seems to think safe passage in England would be guaranteed with the Jarl's gold."

A buzz started in Arian's belly, as if a single bee sought escape. "What does my father have to say on the matter?" she asked.

Morwena paled a few shades, wringing her hands. "He does not know. He took to his horse along the river path when Lord Dag's outrider arrived."

Arian snorted. "I will see my proxy groom. But if he does not sit well with me, I will wait until Yorkshire to say my vows!"

"Nay, Arian, you will say the vows regardless. Lord Dag has no husbandly rights to you, he only stands in Magnus's stead since he could not be here. 'Tis a common practice," Morwena assured her.

The buzz in Arian's belly intensified. A dark foreboding took hold of her. "Nay," she breathed. "He will not see to my welfare as Magnus would have." Her head began to pound, and she knew that if she said the vows, she would never arrive in Yorkshire intact. The guarantee of her virginity was part of the marriage contract. Magnus had been adamant that his bride be untouched by any man before him. She closed her eyes and pressed her fingertips to her temples, then slowly shook her head. She opened her eyes and said flatly, "I will not say the words."

"But you must go to Yorkshire!" Morwena cried.

"I will go to Yorkshire, but not as a wife wedded by proxy."

Morwena grabbed Arian's hands and squeezed them. "You make no sense, Arian. There is no reason *not* to wed this way! Even if Lord Dag is a lout, he cannot touch you!" Morwena pleaded. When Arian would not relent, Morwena slowly exhaled, and more calmly continued, "If you do not go as a married woman, Hylcon will never permit it." Tears filled Morwena's eyes. "Please, Arian, marry Magnus by proxy, and go."

Arian's back stiffened. "I will find a way to convince Papa. But I will not say the words to Lord Dag if he does not appeal to me."

Jane and Morwena looked askance at each other and they both paled. Arian nodded, her mind set. They both knew her all too well. She had a way of getting what she wanted, even when it went against the grain.

When she swept unannounced into the hall, and she first set eyes on the tall bald-headed Viking with the short golden goatee and ice-colored eyes, Arian shivered. Lord Dag's piercing gaze stabbed her, but only briefly did they meet her bold stare. Instead, his gaze dropped and lingered at her bosom, then traveled slowly down her waist to her hips, where they lingered longer, before returning to her bosom. Arian bit back a sharp barb. His insult was most outrageous. Her gaze traveled up to her father, who sat upon a high dais, Morwena beside him, and while she should have been happy that he scowled deeply at the bold Viking, she was not. Her father's face reddened as a storm gathered within. Abruptly he stood and pointed an accusational finger at Lord Dag.

"How dare you look upon my daughter with lust in your eye? She is a princess promised to your blood kin! Not a mare to be purchased at market!" he boomed.

Dag had the decency to pale and quickly bowed. He kept his subservient posture and said, in a deep accented voice, "One thousand pardons, my lord, I was but awestruck by her beauty. My lord Magnus did not do her justice in his descriptions of her." He bowed lower as he turned toward Arian. "You are most beautiful, my lady. Please forgive my boldness. I am at your service."

Arian did not believe one of the Viking's words. 'Twas lust, not admiration, that filled his bold eyes.

Hylcon turned and sat angrily upon his throne. "You are quick with your words, Lord Dag, but I am not a blind man. Return to your master and tell him that until such time he comes in person to claim my daughter as his bride she will remain here."

Arian gasped, as did everyone else in the hall. Lord Dag stood upright, and though his face had reddened and it was obvious he was alarmed, he kept his composure. He bowed again and when he stood, he took a step closer to Hylcon. "My lord, please, allow my scribe to read the words my lord Magnus would have had me read to your daughter in a private moment. Mayhap it will soften your mood."

Hylcon scowled, but waved his hand. Dag motioned to his scribe—a tonsured monk—and handed him a sealed document. He broke the seal, and as he unrolled the parchment, he cleared his throat.

"My dearest, Arianrhod,

"I pray this missive finds you healthy and happy. It is my sincere regret that I cannot come to you myself, for I have thought of naught but your smile and sweet voice since we first met this spring past. Nary a night goes by that I do not dream of you.

"Whilst your good father made his concern for your welfare clear, I was most happy to assure him he has nothing to fear. For you see, my love, I have refused many noblewomen in my pursuit of the perfect wife, but when my eyes landed upon you that glorious spring day, I knew that instant you were to be my lady. I place you and your heart's desire above my own.

"Please accept my nephew Lord Dag as my proxy. He, as I, has only your best interests at heart, and if I could, I would not wait another heartbeat to come to you. But my king has requested my presence. Whence my affairs for my king are concluded, I will rush to your side. So until we meet again, please, give Lord Dag your hand as if you were giving it to me, pledge your troth to me, sweet Arian, as I, through him pledge mine to you.

"I eagerly await your arrival at Moorwood, my estate in Yorkshire, and promise to come to you, my wedded wife, at my first chance.

"Your faithful husband and servant, Magnus."

Arian stood rooted to the floor. Warmth filled her belly. No one had ever put her wishes before their own. Magnus's words rang true, and it was because of his clear heart that she had agreed so quickly to wed him. For, as he, she had many suitors vie for her hand, but her father had left the choice up to her. And 'twas Magnus of Norway she chose. He was handsome and kind, and they had from the moment they met fallen into an easy camaraderie. Her gaze rose to the icy eyes of Dag, and a hard shiver rent her entire body. "I will not say the words to you, Lord Dag, but I will go to Yorkshire and await my betrothed."

"But my lord Magnus wishes it!" Sir Dag countered, clearly distraught.

Arian smiled. "Aye, he does, but he places my wishes above his. Did he not say it there in his letter to me?"

Slowly Dag nodded.

Arian's smile widened. "Then it is my wish, Sir Dag, that I do not say the vows with you or any other man, but to my betrothed in person."

"Nay!" Hylcon bellowed, coming to his feet. "You will not travel through England an unwed woman, and even were you wed, 'tis not safe, not even with an army as escort!"

Arian stood her ground. She would not remain here. She could not! "Papa, I *will* go to Yorkshire and marry Magnus!"

As Hylcon strode furiously down the steps toward her, she strode just as furiously toward him. She would not back down. She could not! His heartsickness was so great for her mother that he could not see that she was not Branwen. So long as she remained in Dinefwr, his dark periods would grow closer together and any chance he had with Morwena would be gone. She would go, and never look back. To save them all, Arian refused to back down. She would leave immediately.

As Hylcon's face reddened, his breathing became labored; his wide silver eyes looked as if they would pop from his head. Arian halted her approach to him. He grabbed at his collar and pulled the fabric away from his neck. He opened his mouth and his lips moved, but no sound came forth.

Dread filled Arian. "Papa!" She rushed toward him just as he collapsed at her feet.

"Hylcon!" Morwena screamed, coming from her seat on the dais.

Arian sank to the stone steps, and with Morwena's help rolled him over, and was relieved to see that he breathed. Rhodri, never punctual unless it pleased him to be so, burst into the hall, no doubt having come from dawdling with a maid or two.

"What goes on here?" he demanded, rushing to their side.

"Papa has had an attack. Help me get him to his chamber," Arian said.

And so it was that Hylcon fell from a fit of temper into a deep slumber. He was taken to his chamber and tended by his wife and a host of scurrying physicians. Arian stood off in the shadows watching the comings and goings, and felt as if the weight of Wales pressed upon her shoulders. 'Twas her fault. Hylcon made ridiculous demands on her, refusing to let go of the last vital part that was a part of his dead wife. There was no question in her mind as to what she must do.

"Rhodri," she called to her brother, as he strode into the chamber. He came to her, his eyes so much like her own, questioning. She could not help a warm smile. He was a good head taller than she, which was not short for a woman. Whereas she had the sunburst-and-honey-colored locks of her mother, Rhodri was dark like their sire. He was most handsome, and could wheedle a mouse from the talons of a hawk. The people of Carmarthenshire adored him, and were most anxious for the young prince to take a bride. Her smile widened despite the dark mood of the chamber. There were plenty of bastards running about with the same silver eyes she and her brother possessed. Arian knew that as she had her own reservations concerning true love, Rhodri did also. 'Twas a topic they spent many hours pondering: while both desired a spouse, they did not desire love. She took his large hands into hers and pulled him to a quiet corner.

"I must leave here before Papa awakens. As you are master here while he is ill, I beg your permission to go." Rhodri's silvery eyes darkened and he opened his mouth to argue. She shook her head and pled her cause. "By my staying, your mother will never have a chance at happiness, and for me the same applies. If I do not go now, Rhod, when he awakens—and he will, for he is as healthy as our stallions—he will never allow me to go." She squeezed his hands. "I *must* go, Rhodri. I must go and live my own life."

His eyes beseeched her; she could tell he was afraid that if he allowed her to go while Hylcon slept there would be hell to pay when he awoke. "All I ask for is a contingent of soldiers to escort me to Yorkshire along with Lord Dag's men."

After several long moments, Rhodri nodded and squeezed her cold hands. "I will accompany you to the English border myself."

Arian nearly collapsed in relief, but instead she drew strength from her choice, and as the eldest sibling, she did have a say in some things. And she would not have her brother whom she loved above all others put himself in peril for her. "You will be Prince here, Rhodri, if he does not survive. 'Tis not wise to go so close to England now."

He cast an angry glance at the man they both called father. "I have no loyalty to him, only to my mother and to you, sister. If he should awaken and find me gone, 'twill not be the first time, and, as all the other times, he will not care."

She placed her fingertips to his cheek, where dark stubble shadowed the chiseled lines of his handsome face. "Do not make the same mistake as he, Rhodri. Find a worthy wife, but one you can live without."

He smiled a tight, crooked smile. "As have you, sister, I have learned that lesson well." He looked over his shoulder to their sire. "Prepare to depart at first light. I will handle him when he awakens."

THREE

The droning buzz of flies was Stefan's first conscious thought, but the intense pain along his right cheek and right thigh soon overshadowed it. Something heavy pressed upon his chest, and the stench of death clogged his throat and nostrils.

He coughed, and tried to move his legs, but they were pinned by a greater weight. He opened his eyes, only to be met by darkness. Alarm filled him when he could not make out his surroundings. His burning body twitched. Had he lost his sight? He stilled the wave of confusion. Closing his eyes, he took a deep breath, and slowly he opened them again. Inhaling deeply, he exhaled slowly. "Thank the saints," he muttered hoarsely. From where he lay on his back, he could see the slight twinkling of stars above.

Carefully, Stefan absorbed his surroundings, and as his gaze moved across the darkened field he knew where he lay. On the battlefield at Hereford. Low voices far off carried over the still, sultry night. He attempted to move his right leg, but fire burned white-hot in his thigh. He raised his hand to his cheek and winced. His gauntlet was gone, and his callused fingers touched an open wound, sending the flies from it.

"God's blood!" Was he in hell? And his brothers, where were they? Had they fallen? Had they been left for dead as he? In a great surge of strength, he pushed the body from his chest and tried to sit up. But his legs too were pinned. He scowled, and his heart stopped for a brief moment and he felt it constrict. In the soft glow of the moon, Fallon, his stallion that he had raised from a colt, lay dead at his feet, his great head resting upon Stefan's shins. A hard knot of emotion clogged his chest, making it difficult to breathe. The steed had given his all for his master, and had asked only for love and respect in return.

Stefan lay back down on the trodden grass, and as he mustered his thoughts, the voices from afar came closer. Saxon voices. Laughter, and the sound of clanking steel. Looters.

Setting his jaw, ignoring the pain, with great effort and precision, Stefan maneuvered his legs from beneath his steed's head. He was close enough to the forest's edge that if he could drag himself there, he could observe and wait. Taking a full skin of wine from his saddle, Stefan tied it to his sword belt, then he dug in the rear saddle-bag for the small sack of dried venison he always carried, as well as several pouches of healing herbs, salves, linens, and a needle and sturdy thread. As the horse master, he was never without a balm or herb to soothe his or his brothers' horses before, during or after a battle.

Once fortified, under the cloak of darkness, with what strength he had left, Stefan slowly, with only his arms and one good leg to aid him, half crawled, half dragged himself over the bodies of Norman, Saxon, and Welsh alike, into the protective shroud of the forest.

In his gut, he knew Normandy had lost this battle, and when he thought of the loss of his brothers, his heart could scarce stand the pain. He had failed them. He had been given the command and he had failed them!

It took everything Stefan had to crawl to the forest edge. His strength sapped, he leaned against a fallen oak and took great deep breaths. When he gained a normal breath, he carefully prodded his damaged thigh. He could feel the separation of the snug-fitting circlets of steel, and, beneath, the sticky blood. He winced as his fingers went deep into his thigh. He unlaced his boots, kicking them off, then pulled off his mail chauses, the chore costing him more strength. Sweat erupted and rivulets poured down his face, but he pushed through the pain. He ripped the bottom part of his woolen chauses from his right leg and scowled. In the dim light he could see a long deep slice that ran horizontally across the front of his right thigh. At least the wound was not to anything so vital as to prevent him from ever walking again. As deftly as he could manage with what he had, Stefan cleaned the wound with wine from the skin, crumbled up several herbs, mixing them with a balm, then smoothed the mixture into and across the wound. Almost immediately, some of the heat lessened. As he labored, the wound on his face began to ooze, and with only his fingers to guide him, he cleaned the gash, then rubbed the soothing balm into it. He dug through one of the pouches and grunted in satisfaction. His needle and sturdy thread.

In the dark of night, with only his fingers to guide

him, Stefan sewed his own thigh closed. Nearly exhausted from the pain of the injury, he did the same to
his face.

Once he could do no more to help his body heal, Stefan ate. Slowly, for it pained him, he chewed the dried
venison and washed it down with the wine. Exhausted
and barely able to move another muscle, Stefan lay
down, wedging himself between a fallen oak and the
damp ground it rested upon.

He closed his eyes and thought of his brothers, wondering how they fared, and hoping that with the sunrise,
he would find them. Alive.

Bright rays of sun speared his eyes. Stefan squinted, and
as his mind awoke his body did as well. Unbearable pain
jabbed and speared his thigh and face. His body was
warm, and his joints ached. His arms, when he lifted
one to shield the sun from his eyes, felt as if they were
made of lead. He tried to move his thigh, but it was stiff
and throbbed for the effort. It had tightened overnight.
He needed a poultice and more balm. When he prodded
the swollen skin, he winced. There was nothing more he
could do but clean it. What he would not give for a cool
stream in which to lay his burning body and let the water
ease the fever from him!

Once again, with supreme effort, he raised himself
up from the ground and rested upon the log. The sight
that greeted him in the light of day would have shocked
most men, but he had seen looters before. Swarms of
them picked over the dead soldiers, taking every stitch
of usable clothing and weaponry from their bodies, as
well as from the fallen destriers. Hundreds of naked

bodies gleamed white and swollen beneath the high afternoon sun, hundreds more lay fully clothed and armed, too much booty for the craven scavengers. An all-too-common sight for a seasoned warrior. Yet it was the great black buzzards, hunched over the dead, tearing at the bloated flesh and innards, screeching at the looters who came too close, that turned Stefan's gut.

There was no honor for the fallen warriors who lay prey to the human and feathered scavengers. He looked up at the gray sky and prayed to a God he rarely spoke to, begging him to spare his brothers this travesty.

Stefan's impulse was to rush out onto the field, to find his brothers and bring them safely to the wood. But he could not help them unless he helped himself first. Prudence cautioned him. In his black mail he would be known, for only he and seven other men wore it—a gift from the Conqueror to his most trusted guards. As quickly as he could, Stefan divested himself of his mail. He pulled his short dagger from his belt and hacked at a thick branch from the log he'd slept beneath. Gingerly, he rose, and tested his leg, using the oak stick for support. Awkwardly, he moved along the inside of the forest line looking for a dead Saxon or Welshman close enough for him to strip and not be seen by the looters.

Abruptly, he stopped and looked up and across the wide field, staring at the smoldering castle. It had fallen. Completely destroyed. Cold anger infused him. He dragged his gaze from the defeating scene back to the fallen that littered the field. Cautiously, he made his way through the carnage, and with each pained step, his fury mounted. The Welsh and Saxons would pay dearly for the attack. When William heard of the loss, he would come himself to see them pay with their blood upon his sword. And Stefan would be riding beside him. Revenge was sweet when it was served upon a silver platter. He could almost taste it. So intent was he on his thoughts that he stumbled upon a body. He twisted in the air to keep the brunt of the impact from his thigh and face. Landing with a loud thud, he lay perfectly still as wave after wave of pain coursed over him, so intense that it pulled the breath from his chest. He dared not move lest someone close heard the commotion. But the voices were farther off, taking advantage of the easy pickings.

Once the pain had subsided to manageable, Stefan evened his breaths and sat up.

He was in luck: the body he stumbled upon was that of a fat Saxon. In short order he stripped the man, donning his leather gambeson and silver mail. It fit well enough, though not like his own custom mail. Stefan kept his own sword belt and dagger, but grabbed the pike lying beside the dead man to use as a walking stick. He scanned the area for a sword, but found nothing but a broken bow.

He would find what he needed on yonder field. The thought turned his stomach. Never had he gone onto a field after a victory and turned into a buzzard preying on a dead man's weapons. Now he had no choice. To survive, he must. And survive he would. Fortified with the clothing of the Saxon, he did not give too much concern to his clean-shaven face. His hair hung down to his shoulders in the Saxon mode, and if questioned about his bare face he could easily blame it on a Norman pig. 'Twas common practice amongst them to shear any defiant Saxon. Stefan limped out onto the littered battlefield, intent on getting to his horse and locating his own good sword.

He kept his head low and his eyes open, searching the face of each fallen soldier in his path, praying none of them were his brothers'. Rhys had been right beside him when he fell, the others ahead. It took considerable effort to navigate over the heaps of bodies, and as he passed each one his gratitude grew. None was familiar. He found a sturdy bow and slung it over his shoulder, then several quivers full of arrows. From a Norman, he pried the man's sword from his stiff fingers. 'Twas not nearly as worthy as Thor, his own good sword, but 'twould do until he reclaimed the weapon. Slowly he moved to the spot where he had fallen. As he approached, Stefan growled low.

A Saxon whooped in glee. Buzzards scattered. In his hand, Thor. The soldier held it high in the air, showing those nearby his treasure. Stefan's anger grew when another Saxon dog pulled his saddle from his cherished destrier's back and rifled through the bags.

In slow painful steps, Stefan moved toward them, all the while scanning the blood-soaked ground for Rhys.

A commotion broke out. A fight between the two Saxons for the good sword. Stefan stood and watched, hoping they would kill each other. The one who had picked his horse clean fell to his knees, Thor buried deep in his gut.

"I warned you, Edwin, I would have the sword!" The victor of the spoil kicked the body from the blade and set about stripping Fallon clean of his bridle and mail. The greedy Saxon stopped when another man, a Welshman, from his quality attire a noble, stopped to watch the Saxon wrestle the saddle onto his shoulders.

He reached down and picked up Stefan's black helm that had come loose from under Fallon's bloated girth. He traced his finger over the back slope and what Stefan knew was the engraving of a skull and plunging sword through it." 'Tis the same mark on the same type of helm as the knights Rhiwallon captured," he said in thick English to the Saxon. Stefan's heart lurched against his chest at the news. His brothers captured? The Welshman looked across the sea of dead men, as if searching for the owner of the helm. For a breathless moment, his eyes locked with Stefan's before they moved past him to the others who picked the carcasses clean."Legend says there are eight. My liege captured six. The other two must be here amongst the fallen."He speared the Saxon looter with a sharp glare."Have you seen another helm such as this one?"

"Nay, but should I, 'twill no doubt fetch a handsome price. The knights you speak of are the Conqueror's finest. He will pay a king's ransoms for their return, eh?"

"He will pay with more than gold for their release." The Welshman tucked Stefan's helm under his arm. "Should you discover the other helm, or any other man with black mail, bring it to me. I am Morgan ap Cynfor, my tent is just past the crest. I will see you well fed and well paid for your effort."

Stefan did not know whether to laugh or cry. His brothers lived! But, as Rhiwallon's captives, for how long? He scanned the field, certain that Rhys, who had been close to him when he fell, was the other Blood Sword who managed to avoid capture. Did he live? Or was he buried beneath the spoiling corpses? Keeping to himself, Stefan scoured the field for Rhys until his leg was so swollen, and pained him so greatly, that he did not know if he had the strength to return to his place in the woods. But somehow he managed. Collapsing on the loamy ground, he lay on his back and closed his eyes.

When he awoke, it was not to the glare of the sun, but to hot wet breath upon his cheek. He started and moved away but in the low light of sunrise he burst out laughing. 'Twas Apollo, Rhys's horse! He was fully tacked and stood patiently, as if awaiting Stefan's command.

"Hello, my good friend," he softly said, rubbing Apollo's velvety nose.

Barely able to rise, Stefan pulled himself up by the stirrup. He rummaged through the saddlebags and found a pouch of venison, a skin of wine, and another smaller pouch of herbs and balms, more thread and another needle.

He sank to the ground, pulled off his mail chauses and tended his wounds. Though they pained him greatly, once cleaned and with fresh balm spread upon them, the throb eased enough for him to sit back against the log and take several long breaths, then eat and drink. Fatigue overcame him. He closed his eyes, wondering if he would find Rhys, if he lived, and how he would free his brothers from the greedy hands of Rhiwallon.

When he next awoke, the sun was behind him to the west. The air had cooled and the field of corpses had quieted. He decided to give himself one more night of rest before he made his move. Apollo was content to munch on the greenery surrounding them; hidden as they were and the fields now void of looters—though the buzzards still feasted—he was not over-worried about being discovered.

With nothing but his thoughts to keep him company, Stefan's mood turned morose. The deep void in his heart widened. Without his brothers, he had no purpose. They were as much a part of him as his hands, his arms, and his legs. They accepted his lot in life with no judgment. Indeed, they all suffered the same damned fate. Bastards all of them, mercenary knights who had found a sovereign worthy of their loyalty in the Conqueror. And he would not let William down, nor his brothers. He would find a way to free them from Rhiwallon even if he had to single-handedly deliver them.

With those final thoughts, he closed his eyes, gave in to the pain of his body, and slept.

The next morning, after tending to his wounds and taking his meager meal, with great effort Stefan stood. He ventured out onto the field one last time for a change of clothing. And from the man whose sword he stripped the day before, feeling like a craven but with no other choice, Stefan lifted a wicked seax from the dead man's sword belt, then stripped him of his leather-studded gambeson, undertunic, and other clothing.

While the clothing and weapons were not his own, they would more than do for a change. He hobbled back to Apollo and rolled his own mail and the borrowed clothing up into Rhys's prized wolf pelt. The knight had killed the beast with his own bare hands, and used the soft pelt to sleep upon when they were on the road, which was often. Then he tied the full pelt to a saddlebag. With great effort, Stefan mounted the destrier and carefully navigated the dense wood, keeping to the thicker brush to avoid Saxon and Welsh, who he was sure roamed the forests looking for men such as he, lone Normans. In four days' time, for he traveled slow, he came upon an old Druid monastery where he had spent a night not so long ago. He tried not to smile but could not help it. 'Twas the place Wulfson had tracked down his lady, one night.

An ease began to settle over him in this familiar ground. He would go to Wulfson's estate where his lady awaited word. From there, they would strategize and find a way to bring the Blood Swords home. He would not rest until he saw each of them alive with his own eyes and returned to English soil. 'Twas he who was responsible for their capture; therefore it would be he who, at all costs, would secure their release!

Just past the ruin there was an old Druid trail, and he knew it led to a stream that filled a hidden pool farther in. He stunk of blood, sweat, and dirt, and he could not bear to be so unclean. As the small oasis revealed itself to him, Stefan let out a long breath. The cool water would feel good upon his skin, and his wounds, though healing, could use a thorough cleansing.

He dismounted and allowed Apollo a long drink, then moved to the back of the inviting pool and through a copse of fern and bush to a small clearing. There he tied the horse to a branch and stripped. Taking only his sword with him, Stefan waded into the cool water.

For a long moment, he closed his eyes and reclined against the edge, allowing the water to cool his body. Though the wound in his thigh showed no signs of festering, such was always a concern. And despite the savagery of the wound to his face, it did not pain him as much as his thigh. With no soap, he grabbed a handful of springy moss and scrubbed his skin clean. He broke off a sapling branch that hung over the water, splintered the end and vigorously cleaned his teeth. He rinsed and spat, and once clean, he climbed to the bank and lay upon a large flat rock, to dry himself naked beneath the warm rays of the afternoon sun.

He closed his eyes, and allowed the fatigue of his wounds to rock him into a deep sleep.

He dreamt of days gone by, of his time in the Saracen prison fighting for his life with his brothers, of his troubled boyhood in Normandy and of the one bright light in his dark life, of Lisette, the maid who stole his heart, then tossed it in a dung heap when a better offer came along.

"Stefan!" Lisette laughed, dragging him by the hand toward the stable he had just come from. "You promised to show me the foal." Her cheeks were flushed with the excitement of a young girl in love, and her eyes did not deceive him. 'Twas not the foal she wished to see.

"Your father has forbidden our meeting. There are servants with loose tongues in the stable," he cautioned. But he could no more resist her than not breathe. Ducking behind a tree, he pulled her into the circle of his arms. "Come with me to the creek," he whispered. "I will go ahead now, meet me as soon as you can." He released her and ran as fast as ten-and-six-year-old legs would carry him, to their secret place. The place where they had spent idle hours professing their love for the other. The place where he had learned the secrets of her body.

When she came to him much later, he knew from her red eyes and tear-streaked cheeks something terrible had happened. "Lisette, what troubles you?"

She threw herself into his arms. "Papa says I must choose between that old Saxon Overly or the even older Robert de Sax-Barre. I choose neither. 'Tis you I love." She cried as if the woes of Normandy rested upon her slender shoulders alone. "When will your father publicly acknowledge you, Stefan?"

He pulled her into the circle of his arms. "My sire, the great Comte d'Everaux, heir to the de Lyon holdings, right arm of the Duke, richest man in the realm. Why should he acknowledge me, Lisette? No son am I in his eyes when my legitimate cousin Ralph is the apple of his eye."

"Because you are more worthy than Ralph could ever hope to be! And I deserve to be your countess!"

He kissed her, but when his lips withdrew from hers, he had to know the truth. "Does it matter I am not heir to the de Lyon fortune?"

"Nay! I would love you regardless!"

"But would you marry me?"

"Of course!" She'd moved back then and slowly unfastened her kirtle, exposing every soft creamy curve of her body. She was not the first damsel he had lain with, but she was the first, and last, he thought he loved. "Stefan, it matters not that the Comte does not acknowledge you now. He will, eventually; then you will have everything we ever dreamed of!"

She *was* everything he dreamed of. A beautiful, titled lady who loved him, not for what he could bring her, for he had nothing but love to give, but she was the only woman who saw past his place in the world and saw him for who he was, and did not judge him for what he had no hand in.

Stefan groaned, his heart tightened. Aye, he had taken her

not once but thrice that warm afternoon, and the next day when his foster father presented him once again to the man who was responsible for his birth and demanded he publicly acknowledge what all of Normandy knew to be true, the Comte refused. When Stefan broke the news to Lisette, she turned coldly from him and walked out of his life, and into the marriage bed of the rich Saxon, Lord Overly of Scarborough.

He woke to the soft laughter of a woman and instantly stiffened.

FOUR

Stefan grabbed his sword and rolled over, prepared to do battle, but instead found nothing. Had he dreamt the low sensual laugh?

He heard it again, closer now. His blood warmed as he conjured up a face and body to go with such an exotic sound. He hurried to Apollo as fast as his damaged leg would allow, and pushed the huge horse back farther into the thick wood. He warned him to silence, knowing the horse would stand still until given the command to move. Stefan turned and made his way back to the edge of the thick copse of foliage he hid behind. For long moments he stood, wondering for the second time if he had dreamt the voice. The light sound of footsteps crunching along the rocky path to the secluded pond heralded a visitor. He crouched, wincing at the pull of skin and muscle on his damaged thigh, and rethought his position. As he made to adjust, he stopped all movement.

"Jane, hurry, I must get out of these mud-caked rags!" called a melodic female voice in Welsh.

Stefan crouched lower. Not moving a single muscle, he watched as a wood nymph danced into view. His eyes widened. She was tall, slender, and, as his gaze raked her body, buxom. He smiled. She was undressing in a most uninhibited manner as she hurried toward the inviting pool. And he could see why. Her emerald-colored gown was covered in mud on one side, as was her long sunburst-colored hair.

When she yanked the kirtle from her body, he held his breath. The soft linen of the chemise beneath molded against her full curves in the soft breeze. "I cannot believe I fell from my horse!"

"You have become too arrogant, milady," an old woman said, hobbling into the clearing holding a cloth bundle. "'Tis time someone brought you down a peg."

A noblewoman? A *Welsh* noblewoman? He grinned wider, and silently thanked Rhys and Wulfson for their tutelage of the language. He would repay them handsomely when next they met.

The eager lady did not wait for her maid to help her undress further. She sat upon the stone he had himself just lain upon and unlaced her soft leather boots, untied her garters, then rolled down short white chauses. His body tightened when she stood and pulled the chemise from her body. Heat filled him as he slowly stood, unable to turn away, indeed, could he have. Transfixed, he took in every sensual inch of her body. She was tall for a woman and majestically golden. Golden hair, golden skin. Her breasts were full and rose high upon her chest. His hands opened and closed, wanting to feel the soft firmness of them beneath his fingertips.

He envisioned his large callused fingers gently brushing across a pink nipple and feeling it come alive beneath his touch. His cock filled as his eyes traveled down her flat belly to her rounded hips and to the blush-colored triangle between her thighs. He hissed out a low breath. She was breathtaking, and at that moment Stefan knew what it meant to want something so badly that he would give his right arm to possess it. His cock lengthened at the spectacular sight, and had she been alone he would have been so bold as to show himself, Adam to her Eve. He wanted to join with her, and mate.

"You are shameful!" Jane scolded. "What if there are bandits in the wood?"

"Keep watch, Jane, I will only be but a few minutes. We have been riding hard for days; the dirt of the road clings to me and you know I have not bathed since we departed Dinefwr."

Dinefwr? 'Twas where Prince Hylcon resided. This he knew, for the Dinefwr-Castile bloodline was amongst the finest; not only in all of Christendom, but even the Saracens of the Holy Land traveled to Dinefwr to breed their mares to Hylcon's stallions.

Intrigued, he watched the lady gingerly stick a toe into the cool water. She gasped in a breath at the chill, and when she did her breasts rose higher, as did he. He smiled despite the pain it caused him, as she slowly glided into the pool. Her golden skin puckered and her blush-colored nipples tightened.

"Go, Jane, and leave me. Go down the path and make sure that letch Dag keeps his distance."

The errant lady slid the rest of her long body into the cool, clear water, gasping at the coolness. Stefan squirmed where he stood, the tension between his thighs overriding the tension of his wounds.

The servant set her bundle down on the rock and untied it, then spread out clothes and a long linen towel. "Here are your clothes, you will have to dry yourself. I cannot guard the path and dress you at the same time. Do not dally, milady, we must be back on the road."

The lady splashed water at her maid and scoffed. "Dag has lost his way, and because of it, we have lost time. I fear we will never get to Yorkshire."

"He is not the most intelligent of men," Jane admitted, then, reluctantly, the old woman moved back down the path they had come.

Stefan knelt on the soft loamy ground and watched, captivated, as the wood nymph swam in the small pool, and as he had done, she grabbed a hunk of springy moss from beneath a fern. When she stood and the clear water sluiced down her breasts to her belly, glistening like pearls under the sunlight, Stefan stifled a groan.

She reached over to the bundle and grabbed a bar of soap, and when she lathered it he held his breath. Her slender hands smeared it across her breasts and down her belly to her thighs. She tilted her head back, her back arched, those luscious breasts pointed to the sun. Her hands slid across her body with brazen familiarity. He wanted to touch her so. She had no modesty, and he could tell just from the way she touched herself she would be an adventurous lover.

She sank deeper into the pool, allowing the water to carry the lather away. When she completely submerged and shot up, her body glistening in the sun, Stefan slowly stood and took a step closer. She put the soap to her hair and vigorously washed it. She went under again, and this time when she erupted from the water, like Venus herself, the erotic image was too much for Stefan. He groaned. She gasped and turned, crossing her arms over her chest. "Who goes there?"

Stefan grinned, ignoring the pain it cost him. How badly he wanted to show himself, and how badly he wanted to lose himself in all of that gold and honey, he could not measure, but even had he the time for a dalliance, he doubted he possessed the strength. 'Twas a shame, for it had been months since his last woman, and none could he recall as comely as this one frolicking in the water before him. He was just about to move deeper into the wood when he heard another voice. A man's voice.

"Would you like some company, Princess?"

Princess? Stefan's interest suddenly went from his cock to his head. A *Welsh* princess? Mayhap Hylcon's daughter?

"Dag! How dare you trespass! Turn your back and return to the others!" she commanded.

Stefan eyed the intruder as he emerged from the path into the clearing. Nearly as tall as Thorin, bald, but sporting a full blond beard, hard narrowed eyes, and dressed in the manner of a Norseman complete with battle-ax. A Viking. What was a Viking doing with a Welsh princess in the middle of battle-fatigued Mercia? She had mentioned Yorkshire. An area, despite Hardrada's defeat last year, still heavily populated with Norse.

"I cannot do as you command, Princess Arianrhod. As you have so thoroughly done to my uncle, so too you haunt my every waking thought." He continued stalking her, as a fox would a plump hen.

"Stop now, Dag. Stop before you do something we

will both regret," she warned, and though she tried to keep her voice strong and sure Stefan heard the fear in it.

Dag laughed as if every day he plucked an unwilling maid from the water, and continued his slow, deliberate pursuit. "*I* will have no regrets. I want you as I have never wanted anything in my life. I will have you."

The princess backed up to the rock she had undressed on and grabbed the linen from where the maid had set it. She started to stand, to wrap it around her, but thought better of exposing herself to the unwanted intruder. Instead she dragged it into the water, soaking it, then wrapped it around her body. Stefan shook his head. 'Twould only weigh her down and show off every curve.

She dragged herself from the water on the side of the pond closest to where he hid. He swallowed hard at the display. As forethought, she was a vision, to be sure, in the thin wet cloth. It clung to her full curves, and despite the position she found herself in, the princess's royal nipples were hard and strained mightily against the cloth. Slowly, Stefan moved closer to the edge of the foliage that hid him. And, as was his instinct when trouble brewed, he reached for his sword where it lay on the ground beside him.

The Viking nimbly hopped from the shore to one rock, then another, then to the one she stood upon. The princess opened her mouth to scream, but the Viking was quick; he grasped her and slapped his hand across her mouth. The little hellion bit him and punched him with her fists. The damp linen clung to her between them, but now it covered less than it had a moment ago.

Stefan's impulse was to defend the lady's honor, but too much was at stake for him to show himself.

For a woman she had spunk, and a considerable punch. Had she a weapon, the Viking might find himself looking at serious injury. But she did not. The Viking was bigger, stronger, and most intent on breaching the lady's thighs.

When she twisted in his grasp, Dag grabbed her flailing body and flung her upon the flat rock Stefan had so recently napped on. He clamped his hand across her mouth again, and drew his short knife, pressing it to her throat. "Scream and I will give the command to snap your maid's neck."

Ah, threaten a loved one for compliance. Stefan watched to see how much she loved her maid. She nodded vigorously, and Dag grinned. He slowly removed his hand from her mouth, but kept the blade to her throat. "Let me see what my lucky uncle will have when he is wed." He yanked the rest of the damp linen from her trembling body, revealing those creamy breasts. "God's blood, but you are magnificent!"

Crudely, he grabbed her. The princess cried out, but bit her lip to keep the sound to a minimum. "Magnus will geld you when I tell him of your trespass," she said bitterly.

Dag grinned wider and slid his hand down to her waist. His gaze trailed across her long supple body, and Stefan could well understand his admiration. But, so enamored with her, Dag did not see her right hand grasp a rock. "He will not believe you, nor will he keep you as wife," he breathed, and pressed his lips to her right breast. Her body stiffened and she squeezed her eyes shut, arching into him as if succumbing to his ardor. Stefan's body nearly snapped from the tightness of his muscles.

When the trespassing Viking swept his fingers across her downy curls, the princess stiffened and slammed her fist with the rock into the side of his head. But he moved his head away just in time, so that the blow, though solid, was glancing. Roughly, he pushed her flat onto her back, and with his right hand he pressed the blade to her throat while with his left he hiked up his leather-trimmed tunic and unlaced his braies.

"Do not do this, Lord Dag!"

"I have wanted you since the moment Magnus described you. 'Twas I who made sure the king summoned him, and 'twas I, his loving nephew, who volunteered to bring you to him in Yorkshire." Dag slid the dagger across a taut breast. "When I saw you, I knew you had to be mine." He chuckled. "My gift to the groom, a breached bride."

"You would do such a thing to your kin?"

"Aye, my sweet Arian," Dag breathed, "and when he rejects you, I will have you as my own wife."

"Never!" she cried, and punched the dagger from his hand. She rolled out from under him when he reached for it, then caught himself from falling into the water. She darted from him, the linen dragging behind her, as she valiantly tried to run and wrap it around her nakedness at the same time.

But the Viking was wily and he was quick. He threw a long arm after her and grabbed the corner of the linen, yanking her back toward him. She shrieked and let it go. Naked, she ran straight for Stefan. He braced himself for the impact of her, and as she broke into the green, he grabbed her arm, spinning her around, then thrusting her behind him. She let out a long shrill scream that sent the birds flying from the trees.

He did not attempt to reason with her. Instead, he trained all of his focus on the livid Viking wielding an ax, stampeding directly at him. Stefan pushed the screaming princess away from him as hard as he could, and as she hit the ground with a loud thump, the Viking cleared the thick foliage that hid him, skidding to a stop in the small clearing when he saw the naked man holding a very naked sword.

"Is she worth your life, Viking?" Stefan menacingly asked, in English.

"No woman is worth my life," the Viking answered in stilted English.

Stefan laughed, the sound rough and caustic. "I would have to agree with you there, Viking, but truth be told, I abhor a rapist. Come, raise that ax higher so that I can be done with you and clothe myself."

The Viking narrowed his eyes, and though he had a sword barely an arm's length from his gut, the craven lout could not help but take another look at the naked woman behind him. Stefan could feel the lady gather herself at his back. She hissed in a deep breath, but made no move. She was as wise as she was beautiful. He could not run with his leg in the condition it was in, and if she bolted and the Viking went after her, then she would indeed lose more than her modesty this day.

Despite his great discomfort, he smiled. 'Twas a most unusual situation to be found in. A naked Norman knight defending a naked Welsh princess against a fully clothed Viking.

Dag smiled, his wet lips twisting in perverse glee. He nodded in the direction of Stefan's ravaged leg, then looked up to his equally torn face. "For one so unencumbered, Saxon, and 'twould appear gravely wounded, I doubt you will find yourself clothed any time soon." The ax rose just an inch. "Move aside and hand over the lady, and I will spare you. If you do not, her betrothed will turn over every rock on this miserable island for the man who would keep her from him."

"Mayhap you should have thought of that yourself before you attempted to force yourself upon the lady," Stefan said clearly, growing weary of the talk. He was a man of action.

Arian pressed her naked body up against Stefan's back, placing her hands upon his shoulders as she rose on her toes to peer at her attacker from behind him. And despite the tenuous position they were in, he could not help but respond to the breasts pressing into his back and the soft thrust of her hips against his buttocks. From behind him, the princess menacingly said, "Magnus will cut your black heart from your chest when I tell him of your actions this day, Dag! Leave me now! Go back to the train and await me!"

"Nay, I will have you, Arian, just as soon as I remove this petulance!" Dag roared, and in a swift, practiced move, he dipped the ax, then with both hands swung it up. Stefan thrust Arian from him, turned and parried the strike with his sword, his arms high in the air. The Viking brought down his brawny arms with such force that Stefan's sword rattled in his hands. Planting himself firmly in the soft forest floor, he swung his sword back up, and caught the ax just below the steel head. The blade dug into the wooden handle. Stefan kicked the Viking in the gut with his good leg, but the weight on his bad one took most of the force from the kick. The Viking stumbled back only a half step, and Stefan nearly toppled.

Arian gasped, not knowing what she should do. Who was this naked man? Would he force her as Dag had tried to? Would he—

"You are weak, Saxon!" Dag bellowed, and raised his arm. The Saxon half-turned toward her and thrust her further away from him where she hovered near his back. She slammed into the hard trunk of a nearby oak, her head snapping back with a loud thunk.

Instant pain speared behind her eyes, radiating forward. Indignation at being handled in such a brutish manner quickly dissolved: Dag's handling was far worse.

The Saxon dropped to his knees beneath Dag's deadly ax, barely able to withstand the attack. Arian looked wildly about for some weapon. A rock, a stick, anything! She spied the black destrier, and the Saxon's sword belt hanging from the high pommel of the saddle. She cried out in relief. The hilt of a dagger protruded from a short scabbard secured there. She grabbed it and hurried back to him.

In a great sweeping motion from his ankles up to his shoulders, Dag swung at the naked man. The wound on her champion's thigh bled bright crimson, sweat glistened on his tan skin, and he labored greatly. He could only parry each swipe of the ax, but with each swing, the ax came closer and closer to splitting open her protector's gut.

Arian panicked, never having been remotely exposed to such brutal men and unsure how to aid her champion. Dag raised his long arms high over his head, and with a resounding force, he brought the great ax down on the man. Arian screamed and watched in horror as he rolled away just in the nick of time; as he did he looked up at her, and grabbed the dagger from her hand, and in a turn so fast it blurred her eyes he crouched, then lunged, jamming the dagger deep into Dag's throat. The Saxon twisted it, the sound of crunching bone and tearing tendon sickening. He yanked it out, then hopped backwards, bloody dagger in hand, crouched and waiting.

The sharp hiss of escaping air combined with Dag's guttural scream sent the hair on the back of her neck standing straight up. Then he stood as still as the surrounding oaks, shock clearly written across his face. All at once, blood spurted in a high arc over them, warm droplets spraying across her chest and arms. Dag dropped his ax and grabbed madly for his neck.

The Viking sank to his knees and looked up at them, his eyes wide and incredulous. With each beat of his heart, blood flowed in thick waves from between his fingers. He opened his mouth to speak, and gurgling blood bubbled from his lips. He coughed and seemed to be trying to say something. Arian stepped closer but the Saxon flung his hand back and stayed her.

Dag spit blood from his mouth. "The stag," he gasped, spitting more blood from his mouth. Dag closed his eyes and drew a deep, wheezing breath. Arian cringed at the sharp hiss of air as it rasped in and out from the hole in his neck.

The Saxon reached down and picked up the great ax. "What of the stag?" he demanded.

"He runs north." Dag coughed more blood.

"Who do you speak of?" the Saxon demanded.

Dag grinned a macabre leer and looked at Arian. Even in the twilight of his death he was lecherous. He coughed up more blood, but managed to say, "Betray Norway."

"What do you speak of, Dag? *Who* betrays Norway?" Arian demanded.

Dag sneered. "*I* will *not* betray Norway."

"You betray your uncle!"

He spat a wad of blood at her feet.

"There is no more reason for your stay here on earth!" the Saxon ground out, and in one mighty heave, he separated the Viking's head from his shoulders.

Arian screamed as the head toppled to the ground and in a bloody rush rolled toward her resting upon her bare feet. Dag's ice-colored eyes and twisted sneer gaped up at her in deadly accusation.

"You slew him!" she gasped, turning to the deadly Saxon. And as her eyes clashed with his brilliant blue ones, she shivered hard, and realized they both stood no more than an arm's length from the other and neither wore a stitch of clothing. But more than that, with the removal of Dag's head, so too had he removed any hopes of her reaching her betrothed a happy bride. The recriminations for what just took place would be far-reaching. That she had been nearly raped by the dead man mattered not: he was cousin to King Olaf of Norway, and her betrothed's trusted nephew.

Her shock at what had just occurred turned to horror

when she looked harder upon the Saxon's ravaged face. From the crease of his right eye down along his hairline to the outer edge of his cheek was a long fresh gash, sewn in a most terrible way. Even with a most skilled hand he would be horribly scarred from the wound. 'Twas a wonder he had not lost his eye, the cut came so close to it. And just as ghastly was the horrific red imprint of a broadsword burned in his chest. His eyes narrowed dangerously. His full lips thinned into a sneer and she knew a deep-seated fear she had never experienced in her entire life. Not even when Dag attempted to rape her.

Her belly roiled when ugly visions of what this man would do to her burst into her thoughts. So terrified was she, Arian gagged back the bile that rose in her throat, then doubled over and coughed as one heave chased another. Her noon meal spilled upon the ground, yet even then she could not stop the relentless twisting of her belly. Finally, with nothing left to spew, she spat to the ground. Humiliated and sure she was done, Arian slowly tried to right herself, but when their gazes clashed, another heave roiled up from her belly. She retched again and again, the pain of the spasms overriding her fear. Finally, with nothing left, she wiped the back of her hand across her mouth and slowly stood. Through bleary eyes she watched him. He had not moved a hand to assist her. He stood rooted to the ground as if he were a statue, his ravaged face twisted in fury.

If she were to die at his hands, she would not make it easy for him. She was not so foolish not to fear the man, but the outrage over what Dag had attempted to do, and now what she was sure this man would do, forced her to straighten her back. Her long hair hung in heavy damp curls down her chest, giving her some modesty, but not much. With that small comfort, tilting her chin up, Arian glared at him. His lips curled back from his teeth. She shivered hard, her bravado taking flight. Cold, wet, and terrified, she was more fearful of this man than of any other soul on earth. He was dark and violent. He had no compulsion in killing, and she was as vulnerable as a downy foal was to a pack of wolves. Her body trembled violently, and her belly roiled again.

He threw the ax to the ground next to Dag's corpse, and stepped with a noticeable limp through the glade to the linen that lay damp on the ground. He reached down to pick it up. When he slowly stood, barely able to bear his weight, her eyes lifted to his, and instead of violence, she saw raw pain. He quickly masked it. He hid it behind a slow, crooked smile. His shockingly blue eyes glittered. "Are you lost, milady?" he asked in English.

He did not attempt to hide his nakedness from her, and she was all too aware that he was all male. Heat rose in her cheeks, and she felt a flush spatter across her chest.

"I—we—I—" She abruptly stopped and realized she was looking directly at him, and that he was moving! She dropped her eyes to the ground and Dag's head. She cried out and turned farther around, now facing the forest. Her skin heated, her modesty sorely tested, for she knew he looked upon her with open want. She flinched when he placed the damp linen upon her shoulders, then wrapped it around her, turning her to face him.

She opened her mouth to protest his touching of her, but it seemed ridiculous. He had seen every inch of her and he had saved her from certain rape. As far as the flesh went, there were no secrets between her and this stranger.

She looked up to him. He was as tall as Dag and as muscled. He was as violent, but she cocked her head to one side and looked hard into his intense gaze. There were dark stormy shadows in his eyes. A man with painful secrets? "I am Arianrhod, daughter of Prince Hylcon of Dinefwr. I demand you return me to my train immediately."

He turned away from her, ignoring her demand, and grabbing his braies and chauses from the shrub he began to dress. She could not help a glance at his muscular back and tight buttocks. He was long of leg and muscled there as well. Rough scars crisscrossed his back from the top of his shoulders to the back of his thighs. Arian cringed, and imagined his suffering. When he turned to face her, she felt the heat rise higher in her cheeks.

"Are you Saxon?" she demanded.

He smiled a crooked, knowing smile, but the gesture froze when loud voices called from the path. She gasped and darted past him. He grabbed her arm, pulling her hard against his chest, his lips inches from hers. "Not a word."

Wide-eyed, she shook her head, struggling against him, and opened her mouth to scream. As Dag had, he slapped a hand across her mouth. She bit him and he cursed, but he did not flinch. He pushed harder, forcing her down to the ground; he splayed upon her and grabbed for his sword.

Breathing heavily, their breaths mingling hotly, he

hissed, "One word and I will slice your tongue from your mouth."

She tried to bite him again, and he forced her head back into the soft ground. "Do not be a fool! After they slay me for the Viking's death they will look upon you for sport."

At his last words, Arian stopped her struggling. His eyes narrowed but he kept his attention focused just ahead to the pool where Vikings and Welshmen alike scoured the area, calling for her and Dag.

When they moved to the east side of the pond, their backs to where she lay, he hauled her up from the ground, still keeping his hand firmly across her mouth and his sword to her throat, dragging her naked back to the huge black. As his intention became clear, Arian twisted and screamed against his hand. She would take her chances with Dag's men, knowing her own men would champion her. If this ruffian absconded with her, she would be lost forever!

As he moved to hoist her up upon the horse's back, he had to let go of her mouth and she did scream. He cursed and shoved her up and vaulted behind her. Arian flailed against him, shoving her elbows into his ribs, but he held fast. When she dug her nails into the wound on his thigh, he groaned in pain. He smacked her hand away, and when she went for him again he brought the sword tightly to her chest. The long blade rested across the top swell of her breast. "Touch me again there and I will slice you open."

"Lady Arian!" called Cadoc, her captain.

"Lord Dag!" Ivar, Dag's man, shouted.

"I am here!" she shrieked, pushing away from her

captor. Her outburst cost her. The hot sting of the blade sliced into her tender skin. She gasped, not believing he would do such a thing.

Cadoc and Ivar burst into the clearing, stumbling over Dag's body and looked up at her and her captor in horrified shock.

The Saxon called out in French to the horse. It rose up on its hind legs, then pirouetted around, and in a burst of muscle and sinew, it lunged into the thick forest.

Arian could hear her men calling for her in the swiftly receding distance, but what had her attention more was the warm, sticky flow of blood as it worked its way to her belly. She gasped as she looked down. On the swell of her left breast, a thin neat slice. Outrage infiltrated every inch of her body, and yet she feared if she lashed out again he would do more damage.

As they thundered through the forest, she naked as the day she was born and he clad only in damp braies and chauses, white-hot terror and a sudden hopelessness consumed her, as the fear she would forever be at this man's disposal engulfed her.

FIVE

They rode for hours. Up through the rolling hills, down into wide green valleys along streams and across a river. Instinctively Arian knew her captor was covering his tracks, and though she was no expert, she suspected he knew well how to do it. As the final ray of sun dipped beneath the western horizon, he turned off the path they had been on and into the thick wood. Branches grabbed and snagged at her hair, her arms, and her legs, leaving bloody scratches and bruises in their wake. She was beyond feeling pain, her mind and body gone numb from the day's events.

A small clearing opened up, and he reined in the great horse. With no gentleness, he dragged her from the saddle. She stumbled, and he grabbed her by the arm, steadying her. She yanked it from his grasp and hissed."You are a brute!"

His brilliant eyes speared her where she stood. "Aye, and do not forget it."

He turned his back on her, and she noticed he favored his right leg to the point he could barely put the weight of his body upon it. A woman of action, and one terrified of spending one more moment with the devil, she darted for the wood, knowing he did not possess, the strength to give chase. Blindly she ran, naked and terrified, deeper into the dark wood, as far away from him as her legs would carry her.

Stefan's instinct was to give chase. But he did not. Even had his leg been steady and secure he would have let her fly. He knew what the darkening wood held in store for the naked princess. Had he the strength he would have scoffed at her desperate flight. But he did not. Instead, he pulled the change of clothing from the saddlebag and dressed, then slowly set about tending the black. After he built a small fire, he stood unmoving and listened to the silence of the wood. After several long moments, he nodded. There, to the west, the soft babble of a stream. Leading the horse, he followed the sound to a small brook. Apollo drank, as did Stefan. Once satisfied, he filled one of the skins before returning to the fire. He pulled the sack of venison and healing pouches from the saddlebags and lowered himself to the ground. With a long sigh, he rested against the saddle and closed his eyes. His thigh throbbed like the devil and his face burned. He grit his teeth and cursed the little hellion for further damaging him.

But 'twas worth it. He'd take it again and again, for the princess was the key to his brothers' cell in Powys. Aye, she would serve very nicely for what he had in store for her.

He cast his gaze to where she had disappeared into the wood. And as he stared the thud of footsteps rapidly approached from that direction. He grinned despite his great pain. He laughed when the errant princess burst naked into the camp, her eyes wide, her long hair flying about her like a golden shroud.

"Did you not like the forest?" he mocked.

Hands fisted, she strode up to him with blood in her eye and kicked at his thigh. He grabbed her foot before it could do more damage and yanked her toward him. With a hard thud, her naked bottom landed on his belly, her breasts bobbing directly beneath his nose. He instantly responded. He yanked her hard by the hair and drew her face down inches from his. She squirmed back from his chest, only to sit upon him in a most provocative way. His cock swelled behind her, and she gasped, her silvery eyes widening. Stefan groaned, his blood quickening at an alarming rate. If she so much as moved back another half a hand he could not be held accountable for what would follow. Even he had his limits. Sensing his mood, she stilled. "Please," she gasped. "Do not assault me."

"Then return the favor," he gritted between clenched teeth.

She nodded vigorously. Slowly, he smiled again, diffusing some of the heat in his loins, and not minding the pain the gesture caused him. His fingers loosened on her hair and though he meant her no harm, he could not help his hands as they slid down her arms. Though her bracelets had protected her somewhat, small cuts and scrapes marred her smooth skin. She sat perfectly still, her nostrils flaring, her body tense. He brushed a heavy lock of hair from her breast, and she gasped, biting her lip but not moving. The wound from the sword oozed crimson. He pressed a callused fingertip to it and she flinched but made no other move. The palm of his hand rested upon the swell of her breast, and because of the cold or from fear her nipple pebbled beneath him. He clenched his jaw, and his cock grew longer and heavier. *Jesu!* He was not made of stone!

Stefan cleared his throat, and hoarsely said, "You are bleeding."

"No thanks to you!" She pushed off him and hopped to her feet, moving to the opposite side of the fire. "Do not touch me again!"

Stefan swallowed hard. She stood in naked fury, glaring at him with full-blown hatred. Her high breasts heaved up and down upon her chest, her smooth thighs quivered, and she made no move to shield from him what made her so different from a man. His gaze fixed there on the soft downy covering the color of candle-light. His eyes rose to hers, and in the soft light of the fire hers burned hot.

"Had you any honor, you would take the tunic from your back and give it to me," she said.

Stefan slowly shook his head. "I have no honor when it comes to women."

She gasped, crossing herself several times. "You are the devil's spawn!"

"I am."

For a long moment, she stood staring at him as if gauging for herself if he truly was. He would not convince her otherwise. "God will see you burn in hell!"

He nodded. "I have already been to hell, my lady, and did not find it to my liking."

When she lowered her body to the ground and curled up into a ball she gave him one last warning. "Be sure, Saxon, to sleep with one eye open, lest you find your sword in your other eye!" She rolled over, and, wrapping her arms tightly about herself, presented her back to him.

Stefan fought back the laughter that rumbled deep in his chest. Never had he come across a woman with such pluck. His mood soured when he thought of the last woman he admired. His mood soured more as he watched her shiver naked in the dirt. He sighed and pulled the woolen tunic over his shoulders.

Arian awoke to cool water and gentle pressure at her breast. She started, her eyes flashing open to find the scarred Saxon beside her, a wet linen in his hand. She slapped it from him and backed up into the dirt.

"Do not touch me!" she cried, fisting her hands. He scowled, and she noticed his hair was wet, his eyes sharp, and his tunic gone. Her eyes hurried down his muscular chest to his clad bottom. Squeezing her eyes shut, she thanked the saints for that one small favor.

"Your wound needs tending," he said huskily.

Arian looked down to her breast and gasped, remembering what he had done to her. The cut, the length of her forefinger, gaped open and ugly just above the swell of her left breast. "You have scarred me for life!"

"Hardly. Only your lover will see it and if he is worthy 'twill not matter to him."

Her head shot back and she eyed him coolly. "I have no lover! But my betrothed will not find it so comely!"

"Then he is a knave."

She shut her mouth and looked harder at this man, this marauder. "Who are you? Why have you taken me? What do you want?"

He pointed at her trembling breasts. "I am the knave who wishes to tend a lady's wound. It needs to be sewn so that it can knit properly and not be such a blight on such a—" He smiled and his gaze swept her breasts that had the nerve to pebble beneath his hot regard, then lower to her belly, and then lower still to—

"Cast your eyes away!" she said, crossing her arms over her chest and bringing her knees up. His smile widened, and she realized she had given him a perfect look at her nether parts. She shoved her legs down.

"Milady, I have seen more of you than your nurse. You are beautiful, do not be ashamed."

"I am not ashamed!" She was embarrassed to her core!

He reached out a hand to her knee and moved toward her. She backed up farther in the dirt until the rough hardness of a tree stump halted her retreat. He inched up closer to her. "I have no intention of ravishing you, unless you wish it."

She slapped his hand away. "Never!"

" 'Tis unfortunate."

"For you, sir, never for me."

He nodded and pointed again to her breast. "It will fester. Allow me to sew it."

" 'Twill hurt! And how do I know you are skilled?"

"I sewed my own thigh, and if you had noticed, despite your attack on it, 'tis a perfect line with small, tight stitches."

Her gaze rose to his mangled cheek. He scowled heavily. "Your handiwork leaves much room for improvement."

"Does it offend you?"

"The wound or the man to whom it belongs?"

"The wound."

"Aye, 'tis most unsightly."

"Then do not look upon it," he bit off.

Arian gulped in a deep breath. As much as she did not want this man to touch her in any capacity, she knew she needed to be tended and she knew that as brave as she was, she could not do it herself. She shook her head, dreading the prick of the needle. She had never been one to endure pain of any kind. She was miserable each month when her courses came, taking to her bed even with Jane's elixirs, and the few times she managed a cut or a bruise, one would have thought her legs had been chopped off.

He moved closer, and though she did not want his touch, she knew if she allowed the wound to stay open, if it did not fester, it would heal ugly. Vanity trumped her pride.

"Tell me your name," she softly demanded.

"Stefan."

"You are Norman?" she asked tensely, now more afraid than before. Would he take her to Normandy?

"Nay, only a Norman name."

She eyed him suspiciously. His English was good and his Welsh passable. "Do you speak French?"

He nodded, and pulled her toward him, closer to the fire. "Enough questions. Come closer to the flame so that I can see."

Arian resisted, but with his relentless pull, she gave in. Dragging the saddle close, he set her against it. Once she was settled, his brilliant eyes caught hers. " 'Twill hurt."

Swallowing hard, Arian whispered, "I survived Dag, your brutish attack, and a day riding naked in a saddle with a demon behind me. The needle is child's play."

When he smiled, she caught her breath. Despite his ravaged face, the gesture, not one of mocking this time but of admiration, transformed his features from demon to . . . something else.

When he pressed his left hand to her hip and bent slightly over her to minister to the wound, Arian bit her lip. His hand was hot, and rough against the smoothness of her skin. As she watched him gently wash the area around the cut, to her horror her nipples puckered. She closed her eyes rather than see his taunting gaze. She bit her lip harder and pushed her head back; in so doing, her back arched and her chest thrust toward him. She heard a slight groan, and her eyes flew open, she caught her breath. Heat flushed her cheeks at his hot regard of her. His eyes lifted to hers and at that moment, something deep inside her warmed. "I cannot do this," she breathed.

"Aye, you can, and you will."

Vehemently she shook her head." 'Tis not decent that you touch me that way or look at me with such—such want."

His fingers caressed the flare of her hip. Nervousness she had never experienced shook her resolve. "I cannot help that I crave you. I am a man, and you a beautiful woman. 'Tis natural."

She looked down at his large hand and long thick fingers. They were the hands of a man who was used to wielding weapons and killing. Yet they were capable of gentleness. He moved back from her. "I give you my oath, and my oath is my word; I am not like Dag." He pulled a needle and thread from a leather pouch beside the fire. His eyes caught hers. "Sit back, princess, and do not move. I will work as quickly as I can."

Stefan had sewn many a wound in his time, not only on his men but as horse master to the destriers. And never once did his hand tremble as it did now. He looked up into her terrified silver-colored eyes that glittered with tears, and found he did not want to inflict pain on her for any reason. He swallowed down a curse and pressed the needle to her skin. "Close your eyes."

As trusting as a child, she did as he told her and when he pierced her skin, she cried out. The needle jabbed deeper into her flesh and she cried out again. "Be still, my lady, be still or 'twill hurt more."

She choked back a sob. He pressed his left hand to her breast, to steady her and to push the two sliced pieces of her skin together, and felt her heart leap against his palm. Her nipple followed, and he swallowed hard. "Steady," he said softly. As he pushed the needle through her skin, then pulled up the thread, she bit her lip, but she did not flinch. The next stitch earned a hard flinch, the third and fourth a low moan of pain and the fifth and sixth a teardrop. The entire time her eyes were squeezed shut and her body taut. He caught the teardrop with his fingertip, and softly said, "I am done and yet you live."

She expelled a long breath and opened her eyes, catching his gaze. At that moment, he wanted to lose his fingers in her thick hair and bring her full lips to his and offer some comfort, but he did not. What he had in store for her would garner no affection, and he was not a man to play with a woman's emotions. He moved back from her and handed her his tunic. "Here."

He stood staring down at her as she tried several times to raise both her arms over her head and don the garment. But the wound was sore and she could not raise her left arm. He refused to assist her. He did not want to touch her, he did not want her to need him for anything large or small. He wanted her to be ugly and waspish, not looking lost and helpless. He let out a long breath when she tossed the garment to the dirt in frustration. He bent to retrieve it, and when he did, his cheek flared in pain. He stood with the garment in his left hand and extended his right to the naked princess.

Her wide silvery eyes glittered with unshed tears. He scowled when she placed her slender hand into his much larger one. Carefully he hoisted her up, then spun her around. He groaned as his gaze traveled the long length of her creamy back. The dimples just above her rounded bottom teased him, daring him to touch. He slammed the tunic over her head and grasped her left arm, gingerly working it through the arm slit; he was not so gentle with her right arm. Stepping to the other side of the fire, he said angrily, "There is venison in the pouch there by the saddle, and water in the skin."

He settled against the log she had vacated and crossed his arms over his chest with his legs extended before him, watching her daintily pick at the dried meat. As she drank from the skin, he watched the smooth column of her neck move in slow waves as she swallowed. He groaned and moved in the dirt. His entire body was on fire and it was not from his wounds. Nay, his groin burned with an intensity he could scarce remember.

"Does another wound bother you?" she quietly asked, watching him from across the low glow of the flames.

"Nay."

"Then why do you look as if you are in so much pain you will come undone?"

"What pains me is of no concern to you."

"You are quite right." She turned from him, pulling her knees to her chest, and settled against the saddle. A small squeak of pain escaped her lips, and he steeled at the sound. The pain of others had never bothered him before, why did he want to ease this woman's discomfort?

Bah! He had only one purpose for her, and in a few days' time she would hate him more than she did now, when she learned of his plan to exchange her freedom for his brothers. Let her be in pain. 'Twould be good practice for her.

Arian could not get warm. She moved closer to the fire, and still the chill of the night air infiltrated her skin. When she ran her hands up and down her arms, the pain from her wound intensified. Her teeth chattered and she felt the beginnings of heat in her breast. She drew closer to the fire and looked across it to find two brilliant eyes staring at her. She caught her breath but extended her hands over the glowing embers.

"Sir? More wood?"

Slowly he shook his head. "The flames will cause more smoke, and if there are any marauders in these woods they would find us. We risk much with just that small pile of embers."

Her teeth chattered, but she nodded understanding. Though she was captive of a demon Saxon, she was not so silly to think others would be less brutal than he. As the embers died, her chill increased. Her body shook as it would in the snow. She settled back against the saddle and fought to stop the quaking of her limbs.

She dreamt of demon knights and demon horses and Dag with fangs chasing her through dark castle halls. She dreamt of Magnus falling upon his sword, his pale eyes staring past her. In her dream, when she turned to see his killer, she screamed. 'Twas the Saxon, Stefan, but he was different. Darker, stronger, more powerful.

The pain in her limbs woke her. Her body spasmed in the cold and her head felt heavy and warm. Strong arms gathered her trembling body to a hard warm chest. "You shiver with fever," a deep voice softly said in her ear. She nodded, and drifted back into a troubled sleep.

When Arian woke, her skin was warm but not from the fever. Nay, 'twas from the body that surrounded her. She stiffened, and so too did the long arms and hard chest around her. "You were shaking so violently I feared the trees would fall upon us," Stefan's husky voice whispered against her ear. Her body warmed hotter.

The strong arms loosened, and she instantly felt the chill of the early morning air swirl about her. She stared up at his retreating back, wondering what he had in store for her. "Come," he called. "There is a stream nearby to wash in. Then we fly."

She hurried to her feet and followed him.

Arian was used to the saddle, but her body protested when he hauled her into it again. She noticed at the stream that his face had swollen, his wounded flesh pulling at the stitches he had sewn. When she questioned him about it, he waved her off and made no effort at further conversation.

They had been astride not more than a candle notch or two when loud voices erupted from the road ahead of them. Arian stiffened, her heart beating wildly against her chest. Could it be Cadoc? Or perhaps a noble's train?

Deftly Stefan steered the horse into the thick forest. His right arm clamped around her waist, tightened. "Not a word," he hissed in her ear.

As the voices approached, the French words became clear, and she felt the hard thud of Stefan's heart slam against her back.

SIX

Normans! His elation was quickly squashed with caution. Stefan curbed the impulse to greet them on the road. He could not. Yet. As the voices became clearer, he strained his ear to recognize even one of them. Tucked deep enough into the wood so as not to be seen from the road, Stefan watched anxiously for the first sight of them. The woman in his arms trembled, and he read her thoughts. He moved his arm up from her waist to her mouth, noticing how warm her skin was, and clamped it tightly there. "Do you think those Norman pigs care that you are a princess? A *Welsh* princess, a royal of the same blood whom they just fought and fell to at Hereford castle?"

Vigorously she shook her head. But he did not trust her. She was too impetuous, and though they were his countrymen, he did not think for one moment they would not have sport with her.

Cautiously he waited, and when they first came into view, he scowled when the mocking voices he had not heard in nearly a decade came back with as much bile as rancid meat in his gut. 'Twas Ralph du Forney, his cousin, his cousin who could not bear the sight of his bastard kin. Stefan's lip curled. And beside him, Philip d'Argent, the lovely Lisette's devoted brother. The devoted brother who shouted to any who cared to listen that the bastard de Valrey was still an unacknowledged bastard and would remain so. Stefan gently pulled the reins, and Apollo stepped back deeper into the forest. Silently they watched as more than twoscore Norman knights approached.

Perplexed, Stefan wondered what the patrol was doing so far from Hereford. Why were they not with fitz Osbern? Had he sent them out to quell further uprisings? The reason for them being here didn't matter. 'Twas their mere presence that disturbed Stefan so greatly. A lone knight on the road with a disheveled princess was an easy target, and he was not so churlish to believe that his own countrymen, his own kin even, would not see her value for themselves.

He scowled. Now their travel would be even slower, for he would have to keep to the wood and avoid the roads except when absolutely necessary.

After long-drawn-out minutes when there was no longer a trace of voices, Stefan moved his hand from the princess's mouth. She let out a long hot breath. He frowned and pressed his palm to her brow. It burned. Without asking, he slid his hand between the tunic and her skin to her left breast. She gasped, but it was not with conviction.

"*Jesu*, your skin burns."

She turned slightly to look up at him, and he caught his breath this time. Her silver eyes looked hollow and sunken deep into her skull; they burned bright with fever, her cheeks flushed crimson. He wrestled with pushing ahead to Draceadon, the home of Wulfson and his lady, who would aide him in his cause, or find refuge for the ailing princess. In the end, her health trumped his urgency to see to his brothers' release; after all, were she to die he would have nothing to bargain with for their lives. Stefan lowered his head to her and softly said, "Turn around so that I may find a safe place for you this night."

Slowly she did, and losing all decorum, her body went limp against his chest. He gathered her close with his right arm and cued Apollo to the road, and instead of a brisk walk, he urged him to a faster pace. Not only did he want to put as much distance between the two of them and his cousin as he could, he also wanted to find a secluded spot with a swift stream. As the day wore on, the body he held up with one arm became increasingly warmer and heavy against him.

As the sun made its trek far west, Stefan spied a suitable spot near a clear, swift stream. The body in his arms burned as hot as an ember. He knew of only one way to cool her. Dismounting, he carefully pulled the princess from the saddle, leaving the black to find his own meal. Stefan ignored the pain in his leg from the added weight and moved to the edge of the gurgling stream. Deftly he stripped down to his underclothing, then pulled the rough tunic from her body.

She cried out and swung at him. "Nay, Arian, be still."

With her naked in his arms, he waded out into the chilly water. It came only to his knees. With her still in his arms, he sat down, and submerged all of her that he could, then slowly scooped water upon her chest and shoulders.

She gasped and clawed at his neck to be out of the cold water, but he held her to his chest, and had to admit the chill felt good on his leg. It too had warmed, and he knew his face must look hideous. However, there was nothing to do for it. Not this night. Mayhap tomorrow.

Arian's body went rigid as the shock of the cold water assailed her hot skin. She thrashed and flailed, but he held her firm. "Let the water cool the fire, Arian, do not fight it."

After several long moments, she stilled. He held her close with one arm and smoothed her hair from her face with his free hand. Her breathing was rapid, her skin still too flushed, her flesh too warm. In a slow loose wave, she went completely limp in his arms. Gently he shook her, "Arian?"

Her eyelids fluttered open and he saw great pain in their silvery depths. "Allow me to die," she whispered.

"You disappoint me, princess. I gave you more fight."

"I am scarred and my reputation destroyed, no man will want me for wife. Let me go and I shall float away."

"Nay."

She closed her eyes, and for a long time Stefan sat on the pebbly stream floor, a naked, feverish princess clutched in his arms. Several times, he splashed the cool water on his own face. It took some of the sting from it, if only for a moment.

When Stefan hauled Arian from the water, he set her upon her tunic and allowed the cool night air to dry her. Once sure she slept, he changed into dry clothes, then set several snares along the forest edge, with hopes of meat for supper. He was not disappointed. When he checked later, one held a fat hare. Quickly he skinned and gutted the animal, skewered it with an ash branch, then set it to roast over the small fire.

He was surprised to see Arian's eyes following him about the small camp some time later. In the low light of the fire, he could not see her color, but when he approached he could see that the flush in her cheeks had lessened. But he could also see that the last two days had taken their toll. Instead of healthy and robust, she looked ill and exhausted. And as hardy as he was, he too was beginning to feel the effects of his wounds and hours in the saddle. Because of the slow pace, they had to keep to stay close to the wood; Draceadon was at least another two days' hard ride from where he thought he was. But he knew of a hunting lodge a day's ride in the direction of Draceadon from where they now were. There, they could rest before heading southwest to Draceadon.

His mind set, Stefan turned his attention back to the princess. "How farest thou?"

"Hungry."

He nodded, and tore a hind quarter from the hare and handed it to her.

Arian ate slowly, just picking at the meat. Her belly told her she hungered but her spirit did not. She had never been so exhausted or felt so lifeless. So destitute. So unsure of her future. She had never considered that the life she was expected to live would disappear like a puff of smoke in the wind. All because of one man's uncontrollable lust. She nearly choked on the piece of meat she swallowed.

How dare Dag! And how dare this one keep her captive? From beneath lowered lids, she looked across the fire to her captor. She fought back a cringe at the man's face. If left untended, the skin would blacken and he would lose half of it. A cold hand of apprehension gripped her like a fist and shook her. Where was she bound? What would become of her? And what of dear Jane, her man Cadoc, and the rest of her train? Did they search for her or return to Dinefwr? Did Ivar and Magnus's steward Sir Sar ride east to give Magnus the news of her abduction? Would he still want her should she escape? Despair filled her with each question she had no answer to. What little appetite she had disappeared. Extending her hand, she offered what was left of her meal to her captor.

His eyes widened in question. "I have had enough, take the rest.".

Slowly he took it and munched thoughtfully, his eyes on her the entire time.

Arian did not back down from his intense gaze. Instead, she studied him. The sword scar upon his chest was most gruesome, as was the mess on his face and thigh. The other scars on his back, though faded, were noticeable. He must have been most handsome at one time, but the scars ruined him. She had never beheld such a man, and was glad that Magnus was most handsome of face and spirit. Nothing like this dark angry man who refused to release her.

"How came you by the sword scar on your chest?" She softly queried.

"A reminder."

"Of what?"

He eyed her caustically and tossed a bone into the fire. "Of the savagery of men."

Shocked by such a barbaric response, she demanded, "Who would do such a thing to you?"

"A Saracen jailer in an Iberian prison."

She gasped, thoroughly horrified. She had heard tales of the savagery of the Saracens. "And you survived?"

"Aye, and my brothers as well. 'Tis our bond, it cannot be broken."

"Do they all still live?"

"I do not know, but understand I will do anything in my power to save them should they live."

The hard conviction in his eyes, but also his voice, set her back. She nodded, "I would do the same for my brother."

He moved toward the fire and stoked it with the skewer.

As it had with the sword scar, her gaze now kept returning to the ravaged side of the Saxon's face. She sighed heavily and ripped a strip of cloth from the bottom of her tunic and slowly stood then moved to the stream and dipped it in the water and withdrew it. She lightly wrung it and made her way over to the surly Saxon. She pressed it to his cheek. He flinched, grabbing her hand.

"Stefan, if you allow the wound to fester you will have no face left."

He turned away from her. "Then your worries will be over."

"Aye, and for that I would be glad. You have no right holding me captive. Why do you?"

"Because it suits me."

"There is more to it than that," she scoffed. "And only because I am as fatigued as you, I will not push. But be sure on the morrow you will have your hands full." Grasping his chin with her hand, she turned him back to look at her and pressed the cloth to his face. "Come with me to the stream edge so that I can keep the cloth wet and cool."

He snatched it from her hand, rose slowly, and proceeded to do it himself. Stubborn man! As he tended himself, Arian took a good long look at their surroundings. The clearing was small and the horse close. If she could get to the stallion while the knight slept, she could be gone before the man could limp his way to the camp's edge. She looked up as he walked slowly back toward her. Fatigue lined his face, and she could see from his slow gait and haggard look that he was as exhausted as she. He would sleep well tonight with a full belly. And, despite her own fatigue and lingering fever, she would fly. And as they had these past two days, she would keep to the wood and bide her time.

He motioned for her to return to her side of the fire. He handed her the strip of cloth, and reluctantly she took it.

"The swelling has gone down some," she commented.

"The pain eases. Thank you," he said gruffly, then moved to where he had been sitting.

A lone wolf howled at the high moon. Arian shivered where she lay curled up in a ball near the fire, and refused to think of the furry beasts running wild in the forest. If she did not escape, she was good as dead. Gazing up at the star-studded sky and silver moon, she thanked the Goddess. 'Twas high and full and would light her way. Soft snores from across the fire gave her courage. Rolling onto her side, Arian grabbed a small stone and tossed it toward her captor. It bounced off his knee and she squeezed her eyes shut, praying he did not wake. When she heard no sound, she opened one eye, let out a long breath, then opened the other. He slept.

Keeping low to the ground, she moved to the saddlebags and drew his short dagger. Having nowhere to sheathe it, she bit down on the blade, the sharp edge facing out, and hurried to the great black horse whose ears perked up at her approach. He snorted, shaking his head. Arian stopped short when she realized his bridle was nowhere to be found. Only a slack rope looped around his thick neck and tied to a nearby tree stayed him. She turned and peered at the slumbering knight. There, tucked beneath his left leg, the bridle! She did not waver. Setting the dagger down on the ground, she took another deep breath.

Noiselessly she moved toward him, praying with each step that he would not open his eyes. Biting her bottom lip, she crouched beside him, touched the brow band, and slowly tugged. Her heart beat like a drum against her chest, she could feel her blood pulse through her limbs, and she could scarce breathe. As the last inch of the reins slipped from beneath his weight, she almost cried out in joy. She grabbed the metal bit tight in her fist so that it would not jangle, and as quietly as a mouse she took a step backward, then another, never once taking her eyes from the sleeping knight.

She backed into the horse's head and he nipped at her back; she squeaked out in pain and immediately focused on the two angry eyes fixed on her. Guiltily she pushed the bridle behind her back, and like a child who had stolen a tart from the kitchen, she looked down at her feet. She would not run blindly into the forest as she had the night before, nor would she attempt to mount the horse and flee, because despite his injuries and fatigue she knew in her gut he would stop her and then there would be the devil to pay. And with those thoughts, anger overrode her guilt. Her head snapped back and she glared at him.

He drew up onto one arm and speared her with his own hot gaze. "You sorely try my patience, princess."

"You try mine as well! You have no right to keep me half-clothed and captive! I am not your property. Let me go!"

"Nay."

Angrily, she stripped the gold and silver bracelets from her arms, and the gold ring Magnus had given her in Dublin from her finger. Thrusting the small fortune at him, she said, "Here, take these, they are a worthy ransom!"

But he was not so inclined. "The bridle," he said softly, his voice low and deadly, his hand extended palm up.

Furious, she threw the bridle at him, the ends of the reins catching the right side of his face. He flinched at the impact. Arian winced. 'Twas not her intent. His eyes narrowed menacingly. He sat up, then slowly stood, his great height intimidating. His attempt to hide his pain was feeble. He took a half-step toward her with his good leg, threw a long arm, grabbed her by a hank of hair, and yanked her toward him. She cried out, stumbling against his chest. His free hand snaked around her waist and he lowered his head to her. "I have shown great restraint when it comes to you, milady, and my patience is at its end." He reached down and grabbed the bridle. In a quick deft move, he snaked the reins around her neck, cutting off her breath, then yanked her toward him.

"You will lie beside me this night. Every time you move, we will both feel the bite of the leather."

He stepped back and drew her with him. Grasping at the leather, Arian pulled it until it loosened enough for her to breathe. Stefan sat down where he had lain, pulling the reins toward him. She glared, rearing back, refusing to submit. He yanked her down with a short hard jerk, causing her to sprawl across his chest.

Arian lashed out to dig her nails into his face. He smacked her hands away and rolled over, pinning her to the ground. She flailed, trying to roll out from beneath him, but he was too big and too strong. He pinned her where she fell. As the leather wound tighter around her neck, her breath began to fade. Her fists stopped pounding his shoulders. As she lessened her attack, he eased up on the leather. Her chest heaved as she gasped and coughed for breath. He lowered his face to hers again, their breaths warm and mingling. "'Tis past time I was rewarded for putting up with you," he whispered.

Arian arched, and had opened her mouth to scream when his lips descended upon hers, silencing her. Instantly she stilled, terrified he would go where Dag had tried but failed. Cruelly his lips assaulted her, taking her fight from her. She could not breathe. She dared not move.

When he pressed his hips to her, she squeezed her eyes shut tighter. His passion thrust hard against her belly. Arian struggled against him, turning her face from him, gasping for air. He let go of the reins and dug his fingers into her hair and forced her to face him, then kissed her again, this time not so cruelly. Her body trembled, her blood quickened, and she did not understand the sudden heaviness in her breasts. His hot lips traveled from her lips to her chin across her jaw to her neck, where he nipped at her skin. She arched at the primal action and he moaned.

Her limbs felt heavy and afire, and her head buzzed. She could feel him inhale her scent, as his hot breath branded her skin. "Please," she whispered, "do not violate me."

"Nay, princess, I will not, I gave you my oath."

He drew slightly away from her, so that when she opened her eyes, she could clearly see his penetrating gaze in the low fire. "But know that each time you thwart me, you will suffer another kiss, or"—he laughed low, the sound sending the hair along the nape of her neck on end—"mayhap more."

She gasped, and he smiled wickedly, the pull of the wound along his cheek twisting his lips demonically. "Aye, I thought that would get your attention. Not only am I terrifying to gaze upon, but I am a bastard knight with no possessions to my name except yonder steed and saddle. You could do worse only if I were a field slave." He moved from her then, but pulled her toward him as he lay down against the saddle. "Until I can trust you, you will sleep beside me as if you were my sword."

"Nay!"

"Aye. Now shut thy mouth so that we both may sleep."

The next morning Stefan made haste to break camp. The fire in his face had lessened some, but he noted that the lady's body, which had repeatedly found itself pressed against his chest, had begun to warm again. In quick fashion, they tended their wounds and were ahorse before the blush of the sun peeked over the eastern forest.

Much later, as the sun made its final descent into the Black Mountains, they broke through a thicket that in actuality was a hidden passageway to a well-marked trail. The burden in his arms had long since given him the chore of keeping her a-saddle. He admitted he did not mind so much. But his concern grew as the day waxed. Her teeth began to chatter as they moved along the trail, but her body burned once more with fever. He pushed the collar of the tunic down to reveal the sword wound. He frowned. Though it was swollen and red around the threads, there was no trace of poison. He slid his hand up the slender column of her throat, liking the way it felt against his callused hands. If the wound did not fester, why then the fever? Was there something more wrong?

His concern rose. He told himself it was because if she died she was useless to him, and he had a great use for her. But . . . he gazed down at her face. She was comely, her long black lashes spiked out across the golden skin that had lost its luster. Her chest rose and fell almost in cadence with Apollo's steps. His arm tightened around her waist, and he admitted he wanted her to live, for if she died the earth would be a little less bright.

He snapped his head back at such a ridiculous notion. Bah! Women were useful for but two things, sport and bearing sons. Nothing more.

Apollo threw his head and neighed as they broke through another copse of wood and his pace quickened. Stefan grunted as the small lodge came into view. He reined the horse to a stop just before they broke clear and exposed themselves to anyone abiding within. For long minutes, he sat astride and listened. Only the sounds of the forest spoke. No wisps of smoke from the hearth, no sound of conversation or laughter. The windows were shuttered tight, and no hounds bayed at the intrusion.

"Allez," he softly commanded. Apollo moved forward.

Cagily, always on guard, Stefan's gaze crisscrossed the small estate grounds. It was as he remembered it when he and several Blood Swords spent a night here. He knew the lord to whom it belonged and knew he had fought against him at Hereford. He doubted that, had he survived, he would return so soon to the hunting lodge. Indeed, he was most likely scourging the northern part of Herefordshire with countless other defiant Saxons.

Behind the low structure was a small stable, and beyond a thick forest. Stefan halted the black at the door to the back of the structure near the cookhouse and the well. Cool water against his parched throat was tempting, but first he wanted to get the ill princess to a bed. He dismounted, bringing her with him. She struggled for a moment in her delirium, but that was all. With no other option, he slung her over his shoulder and groaned at the added pressure on his leg. He moved to the strapped door and pushed hard against it, expecting resistance.

The door easily opened. Cautiously he made his way in and immediately stopped.

The great room, though empty and covered with a thin layer of dust, looked as if the habitants had hastily departed. Goblets and moldy trenchers of food sat upon the trestle table. Flies swarmed the area, the stench most odious.

Arian moaned, stirring in his arms. He turned left to the only private chamber in the structure. He pushed open the door with an elbow, glad to see it free of flies. The bed was unmade but he doubted she would mind. Carefully he laid her upon the rumpled linens, then set about opening the high shutters to give the room air.

He moved slowly from the small chamber into the large gathering room and proceeded to fling open the shutters there to clear the odor. Then he set about removing the rancid food from the room. Mayhap when Edric sent out the call to arms against Normandy earlier in the month, Lord Alefric, whose holding this was, and his men had hastened to their master's bidding.

Though it had been only weeks, there was a thin film of undisturbed dust everywhere, the only marks in the dust the small footprints of rats. There was a small cauldron hanging from a swing bar in the large hearth, dried foodstuff hardened at the bottom. Outside, he inspected the small cookhouse to find it sufficiently stocked with utensils and crockery; in the small secured larder were seasonings, a barrel of turnips and some other rotten vegetables, and an untapped casket of what he guessed was wine.

In the stable, he found several bags of oats that the forest creatures had yet to devour, and a good many tools in one of the stalls. So provisioned, Stefan had no reservations staying here. As much as he did not want to lie low in one place, for in doing so he presented a greater chance of discovery, and it would be that much longer for his brothers' release, he could not deny that his leg needed the rest and the princess needed to get stronger. Dead, she was useless to him.

He turned the black loose in the small paddock and filled the manger with oats and hay. He set several snares along the forest edge, wanting meat for his meal, not boiled turnips. As he limped back to the lodge, he nodded to himself, satisfied for the moment. But as soon as he was able, he would take flight south to Draceadon, where he would be welcomed and not condemned for kidnapping a princess.

He scoffed. Indeed, he would be hailed a hero. But to be a hero he must first see to his hostage's health. Stopping at the well, he pulled up a full bucket of cool water. Before he entered the chamber, he lit several tapers in the great room and brought one with him into the chamber, where he lit several more. As he lit the last one, the princess softly moaned and writhed upon the sheets. Setting the taper down on a small table near the bed and the bucket down on the floor, Stefan felt her brow. It burned. He dug through the drawers in the corner and found several drying linens. He ripped two of them in half and submerged them in the cool water.

Deftly he stripped the dirty tunic from her body and inspected the wound on her breast. It swelled but not overly so. As he had done for himself when he was feverish, Stefan pressed the cool cloths to her hot skin and repeated as they warmed. She fought against him, mumbling incoherent words in Welsh.

Much later, when her soft moans subsided and her body quieted, Stefan left fresh damp linens upon her naked body. He checked the snares and smiled when he spied a grouse fluttering in one of them. Snapping its neck, he pulled it from the snare and reset it. In the kitchen he dressed the bird, set a cauldron of water to boil, then refilled the bucket from the well. The dirt and grime of the day in the saddle itched his skin. Since his time in the Saracen prison, bound and gagged, lying for days, sometimes weeks, in his own urine and feces, he had an aversion to dirt and grime on his body. He was an aesthete in his daily bathing.

As he thought of that unholy place and the terrible torture he and his brothers had endured, his frustration mounted. They had survived the beatings, the whip, the breaking of their bones, starvation, and the final act, the seared imprint of their own swords burned into their bare chests. The bond they forged in that cesspool was unbreakable, and as he thought of what his brothers might now be suffering at the hands of the Welsh king, it served to renew his vow to see them freed at any cost, even his own life!

He swiped his hand across his face. He could not set the wheels of his plan into motion until the princess was able to ride. He teetered on whether to take her as she was and pray she endured the rest of the journey to Draceadon, or take the more prudent route of giving her time to heal. For each moment they stayed here, 'twas another agonizing moment of torture for his brothers.

Irritated, he bathed, then tended his wounds. He walked naked back into the lodge. For a long moment, he stood and stared down at the feverish princess. Her slender body looked small in the large bed.

Pulling the warm linens from her body, he could not help but admire her. Even the damage to her breast did nothing to detract from her uncommon beauty. Aye, she was a most exotic bird amongst the simple sparrows of England. As he dampened fresh linens in the bucket of cool water he brought in with him, Stefan could not help a smile. If she knew how he looked upon her now, those silver eyes of hers would turn molten in outrage. He liked that part of her. She was no ninny crying at the first sign of danger. He wagered if properly trained she would be a force to be reckoned with on the battlefield. He pressed the linen to her chest, and felt her nipples pucker beneath his fingers.

His blood quickened. She was not shy, but bold and courageous—he would venture she would be the same as a lover. His hand trailed down her waist to the cradle of her hips, marveling at the smooth, velvety softness of her skin. He longed to press his lips to her belly, then to the soft down that shielded her. She would be sweet as honey. He itched to go where he knew he should not. She moaned softly, and when she did, her hips moved, pressing into the palm of his hand. Cursing, he stepped back from her, doused another linen, and placed it over the lower half of her body.

The heat in his body subsided somewhat when he donned the sturdy pair of woolen chauses and worn braies he found in a trunk in the great room. As he dug deeper, he pulled out several rough tunics such as one would don for the hunt. They were clean and would do. Once dressed and his sword belt secured around his waist, Stefan felt more like himself. Spitting the grouse, he set about securing the small dwelling.

Later, he pulled the bird from the spit, filled a goblet with wine, and made his way back to the small chamber. He settled into the lone chair, ate the meager meal, and drank heartily of the wine, never once tearing his eyes from the woman who would set his brothers free.

SEVEN

Heat swirled about her, as if she were in the depths of hell. Dark laughter filled her ears. Foreign words murmured in the hot shadows ebbed and flowed as if an audience observed her from behind a heavy curtain. She lay naked, spread-eagled and tied down upon a cold stone altar. Arian cried out when she realized there was no escape. Harsh laughter filled the flaming chamber. Craning her neck to see who taunted her, Arian's heart stopped. Through the swirling smoke and livid flames, Dag emerged naked, his jutting rod menacing and smeared with blood. She swallowed hard. Horns protruded from his bald head. His teeth were long and sharp, his lips full and red as if he had drunk blood. Arian could not breathe. She dared to look down her naked body and screamed. The same blood smeared the inside of her thighs. Desperately she fought against the bindings. "Nay!"

From the thick acrid smoke, Magnus appeared, with her father beside him, the two united as one against her. "I will not have you to wife!" Magnus bellowed.

"You shame the house of Dinefwr, Arianrhod. No daughter of mine are you!" her father roared.

A gentle hand appeared from the swirling gray smoke, touching her shoulder, followed by a coolness that settled her.

Dag laughed, coming closer to her, and nodded, acknowledging the hand that soothed her. "He cannot help you now, princess, he is weak and I am strong! My seed has been sown!"

Arian struggled against the gentling hand. Soft French words soothed her; she wanted desperately to trust the voice that went with the hand, but she feared Dag more. She twisted away from the hand, yanking hard at the rope binding her wrists to the slab of stone.

Dag's claw-like hand touched her foot, his nails digging into her tender flesh. Arian kicked at him, but he held her legs down with his hands. When he sank his teeth into her thigh, Arian screamed again and arched, fighting desperately for her freedom. Hands pressed her shoulders back to the slab. She twisted and flailed. When she opened her eyes, she screamed again. Brilliant blue eyes flashed at her with the intensity of summer lightning. His face was a ghastly blend of perfection and deformity. But the eyes—they would not release her from their fierce hold.

His voice, though, was gentle. "Arian, wake up," he called from far away. She flung her arm up to ward him off, and to her amazement, the ropes vanished. She was free! Hurling herself up, she fought strong arms that pulled her back.

"Arian! Wake up!" the voice shouted. The hands shook her so violently she thought her head would snap from her neck. " 'Tis a dream, you are safe!"

A dream? Nay, a nightmare. Wildly she looked about

her, not knowing where she was. Gasping for breath, she began to settle as the hands that grasped her loosened, giving her room to collect herself.

"Stefan?" she whispered.

"Aye, I am here."

She turned and threw her arms around his neck, pressing into him, and sobbed. She cried as if the ills of the world were hers alone to bear. She was not accustomed to such things as rape and being captive. But her captor was the only thing keeping her alive at the moment. And, she sniffed hard, he did not force himself upon her. Her spine stiffened. But he did not free her either!

Pulling away from him, Arian narrowed her eyes. "Did, you—did you touch me?"

His savage face darkened. "Nay."

She let out a long breath as muddled thoughts swirled about her. Her body no longer burned, but she felt as weak as a lamb. "I—thought . . ." Her gaze rose to his. "Would you cast your wife away if she were not pure?" she blurted out.

She could see the question caught him completely off guard. When he did not answer, she pressed him. "If she were raped and could do nothing to prevent it, would you hold her accountable?"

"I have no intention of taking a wife."

She grabbed his rough hands. "But if you were, would you refuse her for a deed she was powerless to prevent?"

Slowly he shook his head. "Nay, I would not set her from me. I would kill the man who violated her."

Arian slumped against him and nodded, swiping tears

from her cheeks. "If you were a prince and your daughter was violated, would you set her aside in shame?"

He brought her chin up with two fingers and looked hard at her. Again, he shook his head. "Nay, I would never condemn her for that over which she had no control. I would bring her closer for comfort, *after* I killed the scourge who shamed her."

A hard lump gathered in her throat. Arian tried to swallow it down, but it would not move. "Thank you," she said softly, then moved back into the bed and pulled the sheets up to her chin. "Thank you," she murmured again, then closed her eyes and let exhaustion claim her.

Stefan stood for a long time in stunned silence. A wash of emotions he did not welcome welled up inside his chest. But more than that, the thought of a child, of a daughter, *his* daughter so abused as what Dag had intended, soured the wine and food in his belly. He had witnessed many inhumane acts. Jubb had been the cruelest testament to what a man could do to a man. The day he and his brothers escaped was the day they were condemned to die—to be plunged into a cistern of flesh-eating bats, to be eaten alive, only their bones left as a gravestone. Aye, he had nearly died at the hands of a maniacal Saracen in Iberia, and, he was ashamed to admit, he had on more than one occasion promised a maid more than what he intended to give if she were to but lie with him.

Never once after a coupling had he given thought to a child born of his seed. He had no doubt there were bastards with his unusual blue eyes littering Iberia, France, Wales, and mayhap this ungrateful island, but he had never felt the stirring of emotion for a child. He looked down at the troubled princess and something more stirred in his gut. In her fitful slumber, the sheet had fallen to her waist. Her high breasts rose and fell with each breath. The blush-colored nipples puckered as if they knew they were being watched. His gaze swept lower, to the indentation of her smooth belly, to her softly flaring hips. He swallowed hard and pressed his hand to her belly, a fingertip sweeping the soft down that shielded her. Would she die giving birth? For as tall as she was, she was slender, and though softly flared, her hips were not as wide as he thought they should be, to hold, then pass, a child.

She moaned softly and pressed her hips against his hand. He froze. She moaned again and swept her hand down to rest upon his. Stefan's gaze raked her taut body, and he fought the urge to press his lips to her downy mound and kiss her there. He wanted to touch her breasts, to taste them, to make them plumpen. He wanted to hear her cry out to him for more. His cock filled and lengthened.

"*Jesu!*" he swore, standing up, then pulling the linen up to her chin.

He hurried from the chamber, fearful he might not be able to control his craving. He strode out to the cookhouse and filled another skin with wine, then limped down to the stable where he told Apollo, in great detail, of his frustration. The stallion snorted and tossed his head in understanding.

The skin was empty and Stefan exhausted, and though he did not want to return to the chamber, he needed rest, and he was not going to sleep on the ground again.

The bed was big enough for the two of them, and after all that had transpired between them, if the princess had issue with him sharing the space, *she* could sleep on the floor.

When he returned, he was glad to see her cheeks were only slightly flushed, and that her breathing had settled into a deep, even pattern. He let out a long breath. The fever had broken, and she would no doubt be a handful when she awoke. His bleary eyes rose to the high window. The sky was just barely gray now, the sun making its way up across the forest. He moved around to the other side of the bed and lay down fully clothed and armed upon the sheets.

Closing his eyes, Stefan told himself 'twould be only until the sun fully broke. He was young, and though not at his best, he was used to days with no sleep. But it eluded him. For a long time he stared up at the mud-cracked ceiling. The body beside his tossed and turned, her soft moans keeping his body on high alert. Each time she kicked the sheet from her naked body, he hastened to cover her. Finally, when he could no longer endure her thrashing about, he rolled over and took her into his arms. She fought him, but he shushed her with soft words as he stroked her long silky hair. As her body settled against his, a new tension flared within him. He was damned either way with her.

Lying on his back, as rigid as his sword, her soft breath against his cheek, Stefan was nearly at his breaking point. His hands fisted and unfisted. He was tired, hungry, irritated and so full of lust for the woman in his arms that he felt as if he would come apart at every seam. Carefully, so that she would not touch a part of him that would set him off, Stefan rolled her over onto her back. Her arms slid up around his neck. "Nay," she breathed, "do not leave me."

His blood raced like quicksilver through him, his body tightened, and he rose to capacity against her. Her naked body pressed to his, her soft lips were parted, and her breathing had increased, causing her full breasts to move in a most erotic fashion. He could not help himself when he lowered his lips to one taut, tempting nipple. Her body arched in a slow undulation beneath him. He opened his lips wider to take more of her soft succulent flesh into his mouth, his fingers dug deep into her thick hair. Fire consumed him.

His lips trailed across her chest, to her throat, up to her waiting lips, he molded into her as his tongue swirled in her mouth, tasting the sweet surrender. He knew the moment she realized she was not dreaming. Her body stiffened, her hands upon his back tightened. Gasping for breath, she pleaded, "Please, leave me."

Most reluctantly he did, putting a wide space between himself and her warmth. He lay on his side and watched her collect herself, pleased to see it was not so easy for her. She lay on her back, her firm, rosy breasts trembling, her nipples dewy from his kisses. She brushed back her hair from her face and gulped for a breath. He watched her hand trail down her belly to her mons. When she pressed the palm of her hand there, she gasped and arched. The tension in Stefan's groin tightened at the wanton sight. She turned her head and stared at him, her lips full and pouty from his assault on them, her eyes a deep smoky gray.

"What did you do to me?" she breathed.

"Gave you what your body asked for."

She turned to look up at the ceiling and closed her eyes, then licked her lips. She did not remove her hand from herself, nor did she attempt to cover her nakedness from him. Fascinated by her boldness, he moved closer to her. "Does it ache still?" he queried softly.

She licked her lips again and slowly nodded. "In a terrible way."

He kissed her bare shoulder. Her body stirred. "I can make it go away," he cajoled, wanting nothing more than to take her there.

She turned then and faced him, the intensity of her eyes jarring him from his quest to show her all the ways possible to quell the ache. She looked upon him with frank openness, and a naïve wonder that snared his hard heart. "I have no doubt. But I am promised to another."

Stefan smiled. "He does not have to know."

"*I* would know, and if there is no blood on the marriage sheets then he has sworn to annul the marriage but keep my dowry." She pulled the sheet up to cover herself. "I fear I am at a most vulnerable place, sir, and you have me at a severe disadvantage. Please do not take advantage of me again." She pulled the sheet over her shoulders and rolled away from him.

Stefan stared incredulous at her back. Most women would have spit, screamed, and fought him, claiming righteous indignation. Not so the princess. She did not run like a frightened milkmaid beset by the big bad lord; nay, she indulged herself in the wonder of her body and the sensations a man's touch could evoke. Despite her innocence, she embraced the sensual part of her being. He had known she was a child of the senses as he had watched her bathe in the pond, the way she was so familiar with herself, and her body's reaction to her own touch. He grinned like an idiot, thoroughly intrigued by her.

Whilst her captor slept, with one hard jerk Arian pulled the sword from the Saxon's scabbard. Before she had full control of it, he popped up in the bed, grabbing for her. She heaved the blade up and cried out. The pull on her wound from the weight of the weapon shot with hard jabbing pain across her chest. He snatched the blade from her and pushed her back into the pillows, sprawling atop her much as he did three days ago, but this time he did not press the blade to her. He tossed it to the floor and grabbed her up to him and shook her. "Are you trying to get yourself killed?"

"I would be happier dead than here with you!" she spat.

He shoved her away from him and rolled from the bed, and stood. He grabbed the sword from the floor and sheathed it. "Be careful what you wish for, princess. Out here in the wilds of Mercia anything can happen."

"Are you threatening me?"

He shook his head. "I never threaten what I intend to stand and deliver."

"I demand to be escorted to Yorkshire!"

He smiled, and through her anger and indignation, most especially at what she had allowed him to do to her in her delirium, she noticed that the wound on his face needed tending. 'Twas worse.

"In good time, princess. In good time." His eyes swept her person in hot regard.

Arian grabbed the sheet from the bed and yanked it up to cover herself. Her hand swept her wounded breast and she gasped in pain. When she looked down upon it she gasped again. 'Twas a most ghastly sight. Her head snapped back and she narrowed her eyes at her attacker.

Holding the sheet to her body with one hand, Arian lashed out with the other at the Saxon. "You are the foulest of men! How dare you touch me as you did?"

"You did not complain."

"You took advantage of my weakened state!" she shrieked, lunging at him, unwilling to hear the truth in his words.

He threw out a brawny arm and pushed her away. She flew backwards in a most unladylike position, landing flat on her back on the dirt floor. His eyes widened as he caught sight of all that lay between her thighs. She kicked at him and he laughed, moving farther away from her.

Wrapping the sheet tightly around her body, Arian stood. As she worked to cover her nakedness, a sudden terrible thought occurred to her. Had more happened to her before she awoke to his kisses? "Did you have your way with me in my delirium?"

He threw his head back and laughed heartily. "Had I, you would not be able to stand."

She grabbed a pillow and hurled it at him. "Return my tunic!"

"I burned it."

"Burned it! What am I to wear then?"

He smiled again, and his hot gaze swept her warm body. This time she did not pull up the sheet, which had dipped to hang from the tips of her breasts. Instead, she stood tall and regal, daring him to break his oath to her.

"I for one do not mind you walking about as you are."

"Leave this room at once," she commanded, "And do not enter again without my permission!"

Stefan's blood quickened. He heard her words but his thoughts were nowhere close to complying with her command. Visions of her last night, the feel of her soft skin and the way she responded to him, were prominent on his mind. If she had any idea what she did to a man's imagination she would not be so bold. Were he a lesser man, he'd toss her impertinent bottom back onto that bed, sink into her, and ride her into the next sunrise.

She threw another pillow at him, and dragging the sheet with her she stomped over to the large chest against the far wall and began yanking out one item after another, until finally she pulled out a long white garment. "I will wear this!" She held it up and flinched. "A man's chemise, no doubt, but clean. Please leave the room so that I may dress."

Visions of her naked and wanton filled his mind. Stefan slowly shook his head and said, "I think we are beyond modesty."

"Mayhap you, but never me." She stood glaring angrily at him. "Do not think because of a weak moment of my own, it gives you the right to act less of a gentle-born man."

"I never claimed to be gentle-born."

"I am a princess! A royal! I am betrothed to a great jarl. You will not treat me as some whore on the street!"

"I will treat you as you treat me."

"Then show me some respect."

"As you have shown me?"

Frustrated, she huffed, "How do you expect me to show you respect when you have kidnapped me?"

He shrugged. She had a point.

"Would you, at least, turn around, then?"

He nodded, and did so. She moaned slightly in pain, then he heard the slight rustle of fabric. "You may turn around," she said.

And when he did, he laughed again. The garment puddled at her feet. She would most definitely need a girdle but what amused him more was the way she stood holding his dagger, which he had set on the table, in her hand as if she could actually do him damage.

"Come near me and I'll geld you."

He strode toward her. She raised it. He strode closer and in one swift move, he slapped it from her and it clunked onto the dirt floor. He grabbed both of her hands and yanked her toward him. She cried out in pain, but his temper soared. "Do *not* try my patience. You have learned the hard way I am not a man to be denied. If you continue to thwart me, you may find more than your breast wounded."

"Would you torture me then?"

"Nay, I would never do that, but if you continue to refuse my commands, the only recourse I have is to threaten violence, or"—he yanked her harder against him—"suffer through another of my kisses. 'Tis up to you if I carry out the threat or not."

"You are a bully! A man who assaults women is no man at all!"

Stefan nodded. "There are shackles in the great room used to leash the hounds. Would you prefer to be chained to this bed?"

"You would not dare!"

"I would. And if you would like to test me, do it now so that I may take care of other chores without having to constantly look over my shoulder."

"I demand you return me to my train! I am the daughter of a Welsh prince. He will not stand for me to be treated thusly!"

Stefan grinned. "Aye, I am counting on it."

"You would hold me for random?"

He shrugged. " 'Tis a common enough practice."

"You are despicable."

"Aye, and do not forget it." He moved to the open door and turned to face her. "Take advantage of the bed whilst you can. We will be back ahorse as soon as possible."

Stefan strode from the lodge out to the forest edge, where he'd reset the snare hoping to catch a hare or two. No hare, but two plump grouses. He was hungry and could devour a full boar. But hens and turnips would have to suffice. When he went back into the lodge, to find the lady lighting several floor sconces, he scowled. He tossed the birds onto the table. "I assume you can dress these and not burn them?"

She straightened, and though the chemise was large, it was thin, and standing in front of the candlelight as she was, her soft rounded curves were clearly outlined. He scowled as his desire awakened again.

"I do not cook!"

"What exactly does a princess do?" he asked sarcastically.

"A princess manages her husband's estates and bears him sons."

"But to manage sufficiently should you not know how to accomplish those things you manage?"

Arian frowned. "My stepmother saw to the running of the castle. I was more involved with the horses and archery."

"Do you even embroider?" he mocked.

Her eyes narrowed. "I am skilled with a needle, I can best any man at the chessboard, and I can fashion a bridle from an ash sapling."

Stefan strode toward her and grabbed up the birds. "Come, princess, I will teach you how to dress and season this fowl. The next time, I expect you to see to this chore without supervision. 'Tis not a man's work."

"I am not your servant!"

"Do you think I am yours?"

"Nay, but—"

"Then come learn so that we will not die of starvation."

Grudgingly, she followed him into the small kitchen just outside the lodge. Expertly he plucked the bird, chopped off its head, slit it down the belly, and removed the innards. He drew water from the well and poured it into a small bucket that he doused heavily with salt, then submerged the bird. He washed his hands, then handed her the table knife but before he released it he said, "Do not attempt to use this on me. You may get the first strike, but I will get the final one."

Arian nodded, and he had to admit she did a good job plucking the second bird. She chopped off the head and had difficulty slitting the belly. He guided her hand and she shook him off. In a few moments, she had the bird plucked, dressed, rinsed, and in the bucket with his.

"What does the salt do?" she asked.

"A brine. It draws any poison from the flesh and tenderizes it."

Sometime later, they sat down to roast grouse and boiled turnips. With no trenchers, they ate from bowls. And for a well-mannered princess, Arian ate with relish. She was literally famished, and when her bird was gone she looked about for more.

Stefan handed her a leg of his, and she took it. "Thank you," she murmured. She drank more wine than she should have, but cared not. She was still tired and it eased her mood. Not remotely sated from the slight meal, she washed her fingers in the bowl of water near her and then wiped her hands dry on a linen towel.

"When are you to marry the Viking?" Stefan asked, as he too washed, then dried his hands.

She stiffened. "That is of no concern to you."

He made an attempt at a grin but the pull of the gesture twisted the right side of his face. Arian felt a stab of compassion for him. The wound looked painful. It was red and swollen and would leave a most hideous scar. Her eyes dropped to the crescent-shaped scar on his chin she just noticed for the first time. She pointed to it. "How did you come by that?"

He shrugged. "I have many scars, from many battles, I do not keep track."

His reticence irritated her. "Why must you hold me

for ransom? My father will gladly reward you for saving my life."

"I did not save your life, only your maidenhead—if 'tis still intact."

Arian drew up in a huff at the insult. "How dare you?"

"Princess, I am a man who has seen all in my short time here on earth. It matters not to me if you are virgin or no."

"Why do you have such a low opinion of women?"

"Why do you assume that I do?"

"A man of noble heart would not have spied on me as I bathed in the pond. *And* he certainly would never threaten a lady with violence and then carry out such a terrible act, as you did slicing me. And the way you treat me as if I were some gutter wench when I am a high-born lady lends itself to my suspicion."

"I never said I was a swain. The threat of violence is a deterrent to greater violence. As far as your wound? 'Twas your own fault for trying to escape me. If you remember the event as it actually occurred 'twas you who forced yourself against my blade in your haste to be gone from the saddle. Do not blame your actions on me."

Arian knew exasperation as she had never known. " 'Tis just like your kind to blame another for your wicked deeds."

"Aye, and do not forget that *my* kind give no thought to others unless there is something to be gained from them."

"So, I will have your attention until such time that my ransom is delivered?"

He nodded. "More or less."

Arian sat back and pushed her empty bowl from her. "My betrothed will hunt you down and kill you."

"Do you think, princess, that he will still want you after you slew his man and spent intimate time alone with a Saxon bandit?"

She stiffened, as the realization of the far-reaching effects of her situation hit her. Cadoc and Ivar had seen her naked running from Dag's body with a half-naked man. Would the finger of blame point to her?

"You just now think of the implications of the Viking's death?"

Icy cold trepidation shimmied along her spine. Would Magnus believe her? Would he still want her with her reputation ruined? Rumors would swirl, and he would be a laughingstock. "I have pushed the thoughts from my mind. I cannot bear to think of what would become of me should Magnus hold me responsible for Dag's death."

"I'd wager 'twill be his pride that will suffer most."

"Is a man's pride so blind?"

"Sometimes, my lady, pride is all a man has."

She looked up at him, and as physically close as they had been up to this day, she saw him for the first time. A proud man with nothing but his horse and sword. If it were not for the ragged scar that was barely healing along his face, he would be most handsome. His thick blood-bay-colored hair hung just to his shoulders, and the way it softly waved away from his face gave him a predator look. The shadow of a beard stubbled his jaw line. His eyes were a brilliant lapis, his nose strong and defined, as were his stubborn chin and cheekbones. She swallowed hard. There was nothing soft about this man.

"You slew the nephew of the man I am to marry."

"He challenged me, 'twas he or I. I have no remorse."

"The remorse is mine."

"Aye? Then the next time I see you set upon by a craven knave I will continue on my way."

Arian opened her mouth to defend herself, but how could she? Dag would not have been stayed by her. There was only one way to handle one such as he, and that was with violence.

"Sir, my thanks for preserving my virtue, it is worth more than you know. I am just sorry the price paid for it was the life of a man."

"He was not worthy of you. Give him no more thought."

Arian shook her head, unable to understand his callous disregard. "I do not dismiss a life as easily as you."

"Do you think Dag cared?"

She shook her head again, unable to argue the truth. "The wound on your face—how came you by it?"

"A gruesome reminder to pay closer attention to my enemy," he said.

"Aye, 'tis most gruesome," she agreed, holding his stare. She swallowed, and asked a question that plagued her. "Do—are you—" Heat flushed her cheeks. "When the ransom is met, do you plan to harm me before you release me?"

His brilliant eyes held her gaze, and for a long time she thought he would not answer. He growled low in his chest, and said, "I have never laid a hand upon a woman in anger or revenge."

"Your oath then," she pressed.

The Saxon nodded. "For the second time, I give it."

Arian let out a long relieved breath, then offered a small olive branch. "I would return your favor and sew your face. It needs to be lanced, cleansed, and resewn, or you will have a most unsightly scar."

"Scars do not bother me. Do they you?"

Her impulse was to confess that they did but, for some ungodly reason she did not want to appear so shallow as that to this man. "I can live with them if you can."

"Then do so."

"But it reddens and is festering. If left untended, the flesh will blacken and you may have less of a face then you do now. No woman would want you."

He laughed bitterly. "What makes you think they do now? I am a bastard. A mercenary knight, Lady Arian. I buy women with my blood coin. They are content with that and so too am I. 'Tis enough for me."

And by his simple admission, Arian began to understand this dark, angry man. She felt a stirring of compassion for him. Her emotion must have shown on her face, for he scowled heavily. "Do not pity me!" he snarled. Abruptly he stood and strode angrily from the room, slamming the studded front door behind him.

Stunned by his sudden mood swing, Arian sat quietly for a long moment, trying hard to understand the ways of men. From her father to her brother to Dag and now this man, she had not the slightest understanding of them. Should Magnus take her, sullied as she was, would he too prove to be as complex? She shook her head, too tired to contemplate the male sex more than what she knew. Men were guided by what hung between their legs. 'Twas the same with the stallions she bred. They were zealous in their lust for a mare in season, their mating sometimes violent. Many a mare had been injured beneath an aggressive stallion, but when they were through, they abandoned their mate.

Silently she cleared the table; suddenly exhausted, she turned to the chamber and climbed between the sheets. Though the lodge was dark and quiet, and she was more tired than she could remember being, sleep was elusive. The cry of a hawk, followed by the terrified scream of its prey, sent her skin crawling. Arian shivered and pulled the sheet up tighter to her chin. Long moments later, she heard the outer door open, then shut, followed by the thud of the bolt.

She stiffened, wondering what the Saxon had in store for her. She could hear him moving around the great room. Quietly she slipped from the bed and listened at the door. His soft curses piqued her curiosity. Carefully she opened the door and moved down the short hall and peered around the corner. Gasping at the sight that greeted her, Arian pressed her hand to her lips. The angry knight sat at the table with a knife in his hand, staring into a crude mirror. Blood dripped down his cheek.

EIGHT

Arian watched, horrified, as Stefan sawed each stitch from his face.

Shaking her head at such butchery, Arian moved into the room. "You will cause more damage. Let me do it."

His head snapped around, and his eyes narrowed in the halo of the light from the sconces he had pulled close around him. He flung his hand out, slapping hers away. "Let me be."

She was not deterred. "Your pride will kill you! Give me the knife."

"Then you should be pleased."

Arian stood with her hand out, palm up. "Give me the knife."

He sat rigid, the blade grasped tightly in his bloody fist. Her gaze moved to his cheek, and she cringed. "It bleeds and it looks feverish. Give me the knife."

When he did not move, she took it from him and set it down on the trestle top. "I will open the shutters closest so that I have better light." Once she had them open she turned to the surly knight. Placing her hands against his chest, she pushed him back into the high-backed chair he sat in. The hard planes of his muscles bunched beneath her fingertips. The hard thump of his heart reverberated against her palms. He was warm. Quickly she withdrew her hands, and pulled the sconces closer so that she could see from all angles. Taking his chin into her hand, she tilted his head back, then side to side. "You have made a mess of your face. While I am a skilled embroiderer, I do not know if my skill is sufficient to make you whole again."

He did not say a word, but his hot gaze bore into her. She took the cloth he had soaked in wine and wrung it out, then wiped the blood and ooze from his cheek. Once it was cleaned, she reached for the knife, and as she did, he grasped her hand. Slowly wrapping his fingers around hers, he pulled her close, his warm breath mingling with hers. "Give me your oath you will only tend the wound and not slit my throat."

She smiled and leaned into him, her gesture rewarded by his narrowing eyes. "Does the fearsome Saxon mercenary knight fear the helpless princess?"

He pulled her closer so that their lips were parted by only an inch of air. "There is nothing helpless about you."

Her body trembled in a way that was most disconcerting. It tended to do that when he touched her. "I give you my oath I will not slit your throat, sir knight. But do not hold me to other body parts."

He tried to smile, but the gesture was too painful. He pushed her carefully away from him. "Do your worst. It cannot hurt any more than it already does."

And she did. The cutting of the old threads was the worst of it. But once the wound was lanced open and cleaned, she could see there was healthy tissue beneath. More than grateful that his knife was deadly sharp, she was able to cut away all of the decaying skin. Finally, it laid open, free of yellow ooze. She turned her eyes up to his. "Where is the balm you used on me?"

"There in the pouch," he said, pointing to the table.

Arian cleaned her hands in a fresh bowl of wine and water, then opened the pouch and dipped her fingers into it. Gently she smoothed it inside the open wound. Stefan released a long breath and rested his head against the chair back. "It eases already."

"You were foolish to tend it yourself. The poison would have killed you."

"Why then did you not leave it?"

She regarded him honestly. "Because I could not live with myself if I allowed you to die when I could have saved you."

"Even if it meant you escaped me?"

She nodded. "Even if it meant I escaped you."

He handed her the needle he had threaded. Arian nodded, and as their fingers touched when she took the needle from him, something akin to lightning struck. She gasped, the sensation catching her off guard. He hissed in a sharp breath, his rough fingers tightening around hers. She dared to look up into his hot gaze and her heart thudded like a drum against her chest. She did not see his wounded face, or his full lips pulled back in a snarl; nay, she only saw a man who despite his ravaged body was all too aware of her as a woman. Slowly, Arian pulled her hand from his grasp, breaking the thick tension.

"See to it," he said roughly.

And she found it a most difficult chore, for flesh and

muscle were not nearly as easy to work with as silk thread and linen. She swallowed down the bile that rose in her throat and told herself 'twas but a simple stitch and nothing more. And with that in mind, she proceeded to neatly sew the gash that ran from the edge of his right eye down the outer edge of his cheek to just above his jaw.

" 'Tis bad," she said softly, gently wiping the blood from his cheek.

He took the mirror from the trestle top and held it up to his face. For a long moment, he stared. Arian held her breath. 'Twas better by far than his effort, but it was so damaged she was not sure it would not fester again. He set the mirror down and looked to her, his eyes dark and steady. Slowly he stood, his tall muscular body filling the small space between them. He reached a hand down to her and drew her to him. Her legs trembled and warmth skittered across her skin. As she had done to him, he took her chin into his hand and tilted her head back, and as he did his lips lowered to hers. "You are very brave, princess—a trait I admire."

When his lips touched hers, she started. They were warm and surprisingly soft. Not hard and cruel as the time before. More gentle than during her delirium. And more shocking was what they did to her when she was clear-headed, and very much in control of herself. Warmth infused every inch of her body. Her skin tingled in the most private places. Her belly tightened, and the ache returned. He slipped a strong arm around her waist, pressing her closer to him, holding her steady, deepening his kiss.

He was all around her, tall, hard, and making her

feel things she had never felt. And it scared her. She trembled, never having been held so intimately by a man. She had allowed Magnus to kiss her but she did not recall feeling so warm or so weak. Arian opened her lips wider to tell him to stop when his tongue slid slowly against her lips. She stiffened, fighting the wanton sensation it provoked. It seemed as if her entire body had lit up, and she could not control it.

"Please,"she softly said against him.

"Please what?"he softly queried.

She closed her eyes, and for a very brief moment wondered what it would be like to lie with a man such as this. He would be dominating and insatiable. She caught her breath—and possessive—and she knew he would never let her go.

"Please, unhand me." And he did, immediately. But he did not move away from her. His eyes had darkened to the color of a moonless night. Fire burned hot in their depths."I think, sir, you should not do that again."

"Not even if you wish it?"

"*Most especially* if I wish it."

He smiled a genuine smile, and his entire face transformed from that of a haunted demon to that of a joyous angel. She gasped, and felt once again a tightening in her lower parts. She stepped away, wanting physical and emotional distance."It seems to me, sir, that I am in somewhat of a predicament."

"And that is?"

"Lord Dag is dead and I am not without blame. The soldiers I traveled with will not rest until I am found."

"In time they will know of your whereabouts."

"In your time?"

"Aye, my time."

"I fear Magnus will be angered beyond repair."

"Your devoted husband-to-be?"

She narrowed her eyes. "Aye, my betrothed. 'Tis to him I travel."

"To Yorkshire?"

"To Moorwood, his holding just south of York."

"Pray he holds you on such a high pedestal he will look past your indiscretion."

"*My* indiscretion? I have done nothing wrong! 'Twas Dag who trespassed. Magnus will see that. He is a man of honor and will wed me, of that I am sure."

"Do you think when he hears that you rode off naked with the man who slew his nephew he will welcome you with open arms?"

"He will!"

"The Vikings that accompanied you, are they the Jarl's men or Dag's?"

Arian swallowed hard, as her nightmare of Dag's attack and what followed reared its ugly head. Doubt filled her. *Would* Magnus reject her? "Dag's, mostly."

"Were you so precious to him, your foolish betrothed would have sent his own men to keep guard."

"You are wrong! Magnus is a good man. He chose me over all women. I am sure he had utmost confidence in his nephew. Love blinds, sir."

Stefan snorted and nodded. "Aye, as does the promise of gold and glory."

Arian watched his features twist and a scowl erupt at his words. "Did your lady love fly for the promise of gold and glory?"

Long-buried memories surfaced with a force so

powerful Stefan's chest heaved. The princess was too smart for her own good. Her question struck deep into his heart and twisted it as surely as if she had taken his dagger and done the deed.

"My past is none of your concern. But it seems our present is destined to intertwine. We can be of use to the other."

"I do not wish to help you. I want only to be released." She grabbed his hands, moving toward him. "I have gold! I will pay you for safe passage to my betrothed. He will give you more upon my delivery!"

Stefan silently agreed. 'Twas his intention, but before that, the princess would be his trump card with Rhiwallon. He extracted his hands, not liking the way his body flared at her touch. "I do not seek your gold or that of your betrothed. I have a different price in mind."

Her eyes widened, and he had to smile. "Nay, princess, I do not seek what Dag would have forced from you, though I would not turn it away if freely given."

She gasped and stepped back. "You are too bold! Even if I wanted to give you that most precious gift, I cannot. Part of my marriage contract with the Jarl is that I be delivered a virgin to his bed."

"That was before. The question begged now is will he have you now at all?"

Vigorously she nodded. "Why do you say these things? Do you wish to plant doubt where there is none?"

"I speak as a man. Pride can cloud what is set clearly before us."

"Magnus will have me! I will tell him the truth, and the bloody sheets will prove I do not lie."

"Not all maids bleed their first time."

Once again she gasped. "I—I—then how would he be sure?"

Stefan shrugged, and wondered why he goaded the maid. Not that what he said was not true. Nobles held the ladies they chose to bear noble sons to a much higher standard than would a common man. He looked hard at her stricken face, and felt a stab of compassion for her. She was as intelligent as she was beautiful, if not naïve. But he would not lie to her to spare her feelings. "There is an old trick of using lamb's blood to smear the sheets, but the Viking may well insist on witnesses to be sure there is no sleight of hand beneath the sheets."

He watched her color darken. "You mean our coupling will be witnessed?"

"Aye."

She swallowed hard, chewing her bottom lip. "I had heard of this, but hoped it would not apply to me."

"Under the circumstances, I would think it would be most applicable to you, princess."

She narrowed her eyes and glared at him. "No thanks to you!"

Stefan took the moment to pause and watched the furious play of emotions wage war on the lady's lovely face. And she was most comely. Thick golden hair intermingled with deep amber strands. Her skin, creamy golden as if she spent a part of her day beneath the full sun. Her nose was small and regal, her chin softly firm, but 'twas her full russet-colored lips and those huge silver-colored eyes that when she was angry, like now, carried a hue of lavender, and were framed by the thickest longest blackest lashes he had ever seen, that gave him most cause for pause. She was an extraordinary combination of defined features that when put together created a most beautiful relief. His blood warmed and he had the overwhelming urge to kiss her again. She had been soft and sweet against him then, and he knew she would be a softer and sweeter ride.

He put his hands up as if to defend himself, then moved around the table and doused all of the sconces but one. "Do you regret my intervention?" he asked.

"I regret you taking Dag's life."

He stood beside her again and looked down at her. Women did not understand the ways of a man. There was no other way to deal with a man such as the Viking. "When you understand there was no other way, mayhap then you can accept it."

Her shoulders slumped then, and suddenly she looked fatigued. "I am exhausted, and wish to retire for a spell."

She hurried away from him to the small chamber and soundly closed the door.

Stefan smiled and poured himself a goblet of wine from the wineskin he had filled. He sat down on the great chair and slowly enjoyed the brew. 'Twas good. And for the first time since he awoke on the battlefield in Hereford, his face did not throb with pain. The princess had a gentle touch, and he was most grateful for her ministrations. He touched his fingertips to the wound on his thigh. The ache there had lessened as well. He had cleaned and dressed it earlier. He would see to it again before he took to bed, and then decide if they should travel on the morrow or wait another day. He wanted to be on his way sooner than later, before word got out to every village and hamlet that there was a rogue Saxon on the run with a Welsh princess. There would be a price on both their heads, and he was determined not to be captured. If that occurred, his brothers would be lost forever. And that was not an option.

Startled for a moment, not realizing where she was, Arian held her breath. Slowly she exhaled as the deep breaths beside her infiltrated the darkness, reminding her of the past days and her forced captivity. And who she was with. Conflicting sensations intermittently battled along her limbs, her back, her belly, her womb. Heat, cold, warmth. Desire, anger, fear, and the urge to run. Run from what she knew would be her undoing if she remained with the man who meant to sell her to the highest bidder.

Carefully she turned to face the man who had turned her life inside out. In the low glow of the candlelight, she could clearly see that he lay on his back, one arm bent, his hand beneath his head, the other arm straight, his fingers wrapped tightly around the hilt of his sword. Even in slumber, he was a warrior. Her gaze rested upon his face, noticing the wound she had sewn earlier had begun to settle. The swelling was noticeably down and the coloring not so angry. Her gaze traveled down the thick column of his throat to his wide chest and the scar there. She moved closer. He was a most magnificently created man, despite the scars. Where once she had found them objectionable, now she did not mind them so much. They were as much a part of him as his astonishing blue eyes and his surly disposition.

Swallowing hard, Arian allowed her gaze to dip lower

to his flat belly, then lower still to the bulge in his braies. He was generously endowed there. Her fingers toyed with the linen sheet, wanting to touch him but daring not to. He would awaken, and know she had reached out to him. Yet she did not pull her gaze from him. Her mind took flight and wondered in vivid imagery of his taking of her, here, now, in this bed. Of the passion that once tapped would unleash into a wild reckless inferno. A passion that once unleashed would be her undoing. Arian groaned and rolled from the bed. She must flee, go before her imagination became a reality.

Taking the candle from the nightstand, Arian carefully trod to the door Stefan had left open. She looked over her shoulder to find him still in sleep, then she did fly. She hastened from the lodge and hurried under the high moon to the stable. She did not try to lift the heavy saddle; instead, she slipped the bridle onto the black's head and the bit into his mouth. She walked him to a low stump just outside of the stable and mounted, wincing at the pain of her wound. Her heart beat like a battle drum in her chest, and she could not help but repeatedly look to the lodge, praying for divine intervention. Once astride Arian softly kicked the horse, expecting him to take off. He did not move.

"C'mon, boy," she urged, kicking him harder this time, softly clucking to him. He tossed his head, but did not move otherwise. Her frustration mounted. Why did he not move?

A soft whistle from the lodge stirred the beast. His ears perked up, and with no command from her, he trotted directly to whence she had come. A very angry and very haggard-looking Saxon stood at the doorway, with a long chain and manacles in his hand. "Did I not warn you?"

He reached up to her leg and snapped an iron manacle around her ankle, then yanked her off the horse. She screamed and tried to kick his bad leg, but he was ready for her. He scooped her up and tossed her over his shoulder, then limped back into the chamber where he tossed her onto the bed. He took the other end of the chain and secured the shackle around the leg of the bed. "Your freedom is as far as the chain is long."

She shrieked at him, throwing the pillows at his back as he limped from the chamber. Several moments later, he returned and lay back down on the bed. "If you disturb me one more time, I will shackle you to the trestle so that I may get some much needed rest."

Arian rolled away from him, presenting her back, and for the first time since her capture, tears of frustration welled in her eyes. And for the first time in her charmed life she was unsure how to wheedle what she wanted from a man.

Sun streamed through the only window in the room. For a moment Arian did not know where she was, only that sunshine pricked her eyes and her head throbbed. She closed her eyes, shutting out the sun. Her head lay upon something hard and warm. Her hand rested lower, on something also hard and warm. She opened her eyes to two dark-blue ones and opened her mouth to scream. Stefan pressed his lips to hers, stifling her. Immediately, she stopped her struggle, fearful her movements would whet his desire more. His hands trailed down her arms, pressing them into the soft mattress, his body moving over hers as his kiss deepened.

She opened her lips wider to tell him to leave her, but instead she found herself unable to speak. Fierce heat swept through her with such force that it terrified her. 'Twas as if her body had a mind of its own, for all that she could control it. Part of her wanted to luxuriate in the primal sensations he evoked in her, but the other part, the pragmatic part, knew that to do so would be her undoing. She broke free of his lips, gasping for breath. "Nay!" she cried, afraid more of herself than of him.

"Shhhh, princess, you have no cause to fear me," he said against her ear. He nibbled the spot behind her ear on her neck; her eyes rolled back and she nearly gave in to him. Her entire body thrummed with sensation. She wanted to go further, to feel more, to experience more, because in the deepest darkest reaches of her being, she knew she would never experience the scorching passion with Magnus that she felt at the hands of this mercenary knight. She also knew if she allowed the knight to sweep her away, she would lose more than she could ever regain.

She stiffened and pulled away from him, angry at herself, angry at him, angry at the events leading to her capture.

"You killed Dag! You cut me, then kidnapped me! You tie me up with a bridle and now you shackle me to this bed! You seduce me at every turn, and you tell me I have nothing to fear from you?"

He chuckled and traced a finger across her bottom lip. "You are not guiltless of seduction, my little princess. You are shameless, flaunting your rosy breasts under my nose, waking me in the middle of the night pressing your warm body to mine. I am a man who finds you most difficult to ignore. Do not blame me for wanting you to the point where I take action."

"You lie! I never seduced you!"

He shrugged. "Believe what you will." He sat up and stretched his long limbs. "The day is half over and we have lain like lazy churls abed the entire time. We must make ready and leave this place."

He rolled from the bed and stood. She saw him wince as he tested his bad leg. He strode from the room, and Arian sat up in a huff. "Unshackle me!" she shouted. His answer was the heavy thud of the front door.

Long moments passed, and her anger mounted. She needed to use the chamber pot, and wash. She needed to flee! She hiked her leg up and examined the manacle, and her anger subsided somewhat. There was no lock to it! All she had to do was turn a screw. She did, and her leg was free of the steel band. As she came from the chamber to the great room she collided with the knight. He carried a bucket of water and a smaller empty one. He handed them both to her. "Your chamber pot and your bath, milady."

Arian grabbed them from him, wincing in pain from her wound, and behind a closed door took care of the necessities of her body. Once she had washed her face and rinsed her mouth, she went outside to strip a small branch from a sapling and shredded the end, then scrubbed her teeth. She rinsed her mouth with water again and felt somewhat clean. She watched Stefan check the snares he had set along the forest line and come up empty.

"I have reset them. Whilst we await our meal I must tend to Apollo; he has thrown a shoe and his hoof is tender."

"Do we not leave today?" Disappointment filled her. Wherever it was he was taking her, it would be better than this hovel.

"I will see how he responds to the poultice and new shoe."

"You can forge a shoe here?"

"Nay, I have one in the saddlebag, prefitted."

His preparedness did not surprise her. She guessed Stefan was a man who would be prepared for anything. Except to ease her hunger.

"There are berries and nuts in the cookhouse," he called to her as she walked away.

Berries and nuts would not suffice. Her belly growled and she decided she would see to their next meal. But she could not hunt in the large garment.

She combed through the many chests in the great room and discovered an odd assortment of clothing. None of it was meant for a woman, but two tunics were not too large and would offer her more mobility than the huge chemise she wore. There were wool chauses, and several pairs of leather boots that were three times as large as her feet. She found a very short tunic that fell just at mid-thigh and she knew it to be a child's. She tore the fabric just below the arm slits so that she had more room. Donning the garment and feeling rather saucy in it, she debated whether to go outside with it on, but decided her hunger was more important than her modesty. Knowing Stefan was busy in the stable, she grabbed his bow and quiver of arrows and set out for the wood. She didn't ask his permission, knowing he would not give it.

The wood was dark and ominous, the earth soft and loamy beneath her bare feet. Birds twittered overhead and sunlight filtered through the heavy copse. As she kept low and notched an arrow, ready thoughts swirled in her head. She could not help but wonder if she should flee now. She could keep to the wood and follow the sun west each day until she reached the Welsh border. She looked down at her scant clothing. A wolf howled off in the distance, and her thoughts went to the band of Norman knights that roamed the countryside. She swallowed hard. She was not a fool. She was safer, for now, with the Saxon.

She had not gone too deep into the wood when a rustling up ahead caught her attention. The soft grunt of a pig, followed by several squeals, alerted her. Though she tried to hasten up the nearest tree, her wound slowed her. Using her good arm, she managed to pull herself up and perch upon a sturdy limb where she watched, and waited. Her patience paid off; a sow with a litter of fat piglets worked their way toward her as they foraged in the soft earth, upturning roots and grubs. Carefully Arian took aim at the largest piglet and waited for it to get closer. She released the string; the high squeal of the pig as the arrow tore into it sent the birds flying from the trees. In a furious fit, the sow turned up earth with her hooves and tusks. She rushed toward Arian, but the wind was in the girl's favor, carrying her scent away from the pack.

The sow sniffed the dead piglet, then squealed loud, calling to the remaining ones, and stampeded away deeper into the wood, away from the unknown predator.

Making sure she did not return, Arian waited before she leapt down to the ground, grabbed the piglet up by the hind legs, and hurried to drag it back to the lodge.

Stefan stormed from the structure, his face a twisted mass of fury. He stopped short when he spied her. "Did you think I had left you, milord?" she taunted.

He remained silent, his gaze never wavering from hers. But she saw the relief there. Her heart thudded wildly against her chest. Was it because he felt something for her and feared she was truly gone, or did he worry that the coin he hoped she'd bring was now out of his reach? With some effort, she lifted the pig. "One of us must provide supper, so I took it upon myself to do just that."

It was only then that his gaze left her face and traveled down her body. A soft breeze blew against her, molding the tunic's fabric to her body. When their eyes met again, she saw fire in his. A slow smile crossed his handsome lips, and as it did when he looked at her thusly, her body warmed. "Do not look at me so! 'Tis not decent," she cried, but did not mean it. The thrill of the hunt, the thrill of his reaction to her coupled with her own hunger, all sent her senses catapulting.

"You are most indecent in that small scrap of fabric." He stepped closer to her. His nostrils flared. "I find myself most smitten by a woman who hunts dressed as the Goddess."

She thrust her bow and quiver at him, then turned for the cookhouse. He followed her, and the wantonness she felt in this man's presence intensified.

She heaved the pig upon the stone counter, and turned to him to tell him she did not require his help. He was there. He dropped the bow and quiver, his eyes held hers, and he slipped his arms around her waist, pulling her hard against him. "Arian," he breathed, "you make me forget why I am here."

Not trusting herself, she pushed him away, flinching at the soreness in her chest. She had over-used it and it throbbed in pain. "Stefan, I am hungry—"

He caught her chin in his hand and tilted her head back to look at him. The hardened planes of his face bespoke the tension in his body. It emanated from him like a bonfire. "I hunger too," he said softly, then reluctantly stepped away from her. "Dress it and I will build the fire and ready the spit."

Glad for something to take her thoughts from Stefan, Arian set about dressing the pig. She gave no mind to the blood soaking into her tunic, or the blood on her hands. Her hunger drove her to hurry. She would bathe later whilst it roasted on the spit in the great room.

Triumphant, she grabbed it up by the hind legs and though her wound stung from the day's chores and the weight of the pig, she hurried from the kitchen to the great room. She was glad to see the fire roaring, and Stefan greasing the spit. "Hurry, and let it cook. I am famished."

He laughed, and when he turned to her, his eyes widened in horror.

"What?"

His gaze traveled down her garment and her eyes dipped. The blood of the pig had dampened her so thoroughly that the curve of her breasts and nipples were

clearly visible." 'Tis the blood of the pig. I will wash it."
She thrust the animal at him. "Spit it now, before I devour it raw." When he did so, she nodded and hurried
from the lodge.

The day had been warm and sunny, but now dusk
settled in a soft shroud over the forest, and the air had
cooled. In what light was left, Arian hurried to fill several
buckets of water from the well and poured them into an
empty half-barrel in the small kitchen. Then she filled
several more and set them to the side. She lit several
candles from the one burning on the small counter.

She grabbed bunches of aromatic herbs from a
cracked earthen pot. With no soap, she would cleanse
herself with the sweet-smelling stuff. Arian turned to
close the door but scowled when she remembered it
was open-ended.

She chewed her bottom lip, fearful Stefan might come
upon her. But to her horror, a warmth spread across her
chest at the thought of the angry Saxon's hot eyes upon
her naked body. Though she was not naïve, he stirred her
in a way she never imagined a man could stir a woman.
She had never been shy about her body and its cravings.
She was very aware of the beauty of nature. The sounds,
the scents, the textures, and the tastes.

And she was curious. She had peeked on her brother
more than once as he seduced a maid in the high straw
beds of the vast stables, her body warming as they lustily
mated. When Magnus had been so bold as to kiss her
the day after they met, she had allowed him, wanting to
experience the same thrill. She had been disappointed
that his gentle touch had not elicited a more passionate
response from her.

She knew from the stories Jane told her that her parents were a lusty pair who were prone to slip from the hall at all hours of the day and night to couple. She was not embarrassed when she stood to the side of the paddocks and watched the hot-blooded stallions mount the mares. She admired the way the mares played coy, swishing their tails beneath the stallion's nose, teasing him into a sexual frenzy before finally allowing him to mount. Aye, it was nature, and her body was young and craved such a natural union.

And though she did not want to fall in love with her husband, she prayed that once wed he would prove to be as lusty as the stallions of Dinefwr. Or . . . her mind wandered . . . as lusty as the Saxon.

Arian pulled the bloody garment from her body and stepped into the barrel. It was not quite wide enough for her to sit, even with her knees to her chest, so reluctantly she stood. When she grasped the heavy bucket and tried to lift it over her head, she cried out. The wound to her breast was compromised by the raising of her arm. She looked around for a bowl to scoop the water out and could not locate one. The few there were, were on the trestle table. For a long moment, Arian debated on darting into the room and grabbing a bowl or just making do. She chose to make do. And that meant scooping handfuls of water from the bucket and pouring them over her head, but still the raising of her arm pained her.

"Would you care for assistance, milady?" a deep voice asked from the open doorway.

NINE

Arian crossed her arms over her chest, half turning to Stefan. "You are too bold!"

"As are you," he said, stepping into the small area. "As well as covered in blood, and also you are wounded. At the pace you are bathing you will see the full rise of the sun on the morrow before you are clean." He grabbed up a full bucket, and slowly poured it over her head.

Arian gasped. The well water was cold but it felt good against her skin. She stood rigid, not wanting to give in to the erotic pleasure of this man pouring water down her body. 'Twas not right! But had not her reputation already been destroyed? Aye, it had, and the sluice of the water across her sensitive body was too tempting to say no to. Besides, he had given his oath to her, and would not force her to do anything she did not wish to.

She bowed her head and allowed the water to pour into her hair. With no soap on hand, all she could do was rinse it with the herbs. She grasped a handful and rolled them between her hands, then dug her fingers into her hair and lifted the thick strands so the water could infiltrate.

She tried to ignore the man behind her and the way the triangle between her thighs flared with heat, but 'twas a battle lost before it began. Her nipples pebbled hard and her breasts trembled. And it felt good and exciting, and she wished 'twas her betrothed who stood so close. Then she could give in to her carnal cravings.

The bucket empty, she did not dare turn and face him. When he put his hands upon her shoulders, she trembled violently. "Please—" she whispered.

He moved closer to her, so close she could feel the heat of his body. "It seems, princess, we are destined to repeatedly meet each time you bathe."

He rubbed something hard across her damp shoulders. His large hands slid easily across her warm skin. Soap? She turned, and his hands in motion slid across the fullness of her breasts. Arian gasped and stiffened. So did Stefan. When he did not remove his hands from her breasts but instead gently kneaded them, Arian felt the earth move beneath her. She was a wanton to allow him to touch her so, yet she remained beneath his touch.

His lips lowered to her ear and he softly whispered, "I gave my word I would not breach you, milady, but I never promised I would not touch the rest of you."

Warm shivers from his breath scattered across her skin, down her body, and yet she stayed motionless. She looked up into his dark blue eyes. They burned hot. She gazed hard at him, trying to read his thoughts. And Arian could not clarify her signals, for she was as confused as he. He reached down and lifted the rough tunic over his shoulders, letting it drop to the floor.

Mutely, she nodded her head, wanting more than she

had a right to. Despite the ugly scar that marred him, his muscles were well defined, his belly flat, his hips narrow, his manhood—she swallowed—large, and growing larger beneath his braies. Before she got herself into deeper trouble, Arian whirled around, presenting her back to him.

Stefan lathered up the soap between his hands. When he dug his long fingers deep into her hair Arian sighed, the sensation so sublimely sensual that she felt as if her body was liquefying. He stepped closer to her so that his chest pressed against her shoulders. The thick lather trailed down her neck to her back, slickening their skin.

Warm breath caressed her shoulders, followed by large strong hands massaging the velvety lather into her neck and shoulders in slow circular motions. Arian rested her head against his right shoulder and arched her back wanting his hands to slide lower to her heavy breasts and touch her there. His hands slid down around her waist, swirling the lather into her feverish skin, bypassing her sensitive breasts. Biting her lip to keep a moan from escaping, Arian gasped when the tips of his thumbs brushed the edge of the down shielding her mons. A hunger pulsed deep from within her womb outward, radiating through her entire body. With each swirl of his hands, with each breath he breathed upon her neck, with each soft thrust of his hips against her back, her hunger grew.

Her body did liquefy, and had he not slid his right arm around her waist to steady her, Arian would have melted into the floor. Pressing his left hand to the left side of her face, he pushed her head toward his shoulder, exposing the tender flesh of her neck. His fingers slid hard against her skin, moving the lather away. Hot lips pressed to her vital vein there. Heat shot to the apex between her thighs and her skin flashed hot. Arian moaned and hung heavy in his arms. Her eyes half-closed, she let herself revel in the pure carnal experience of him bathing her.

He lathered her more, and this time his hands traveled in slow up-and-down motions, finally cupping her full breasts. She arched into his palms, his lips pressed to her neck. Hot desire speared down her flat belly. She arched more, wanting the buildup of pressure to ease.

He rubbed her nipples, pressing her harder into his hips. Voraciously he kissed and nibbled her neck. Breathless, she pressed her head into his shoulder, her lips parted, the air forced from her chest. She reached around and grasped his buttocks, digging her fingers into the linen of his braies.

Stefan moaned as his body tightened and his hips thrust against her back. Their bodies strained for one tense indefinable moment, knowing there was nowhere to go yet desperately wanting to go there.

He grasped the cradle of her hips, and she could feel him fight the tension in his body. She did not dare move lest she be the one to cause him to break his oath. He lathered her thighs, his big callused hands moving so wantonly slow along her smooth skin she wanted to scream. With one hand he drew her tighter against his bare chest, and holding her like that, he slowly poured water over her body, his hand sliding across her skin helping wash away the lather. He repeated several times, and with each rinse she felt him grow and tighten against her back. Arian arched back, and her right arm wrapped around his neck, pulling him tighter against her. He sucked in a sharp breath.

"You are a wanton, Princess Arianrhod. You would tempt the saints with your touch."

She half-turned and looked up at him, her breast pressed against his bare chest. The sensation sent jolts of hot desire through her. His eyes widened and she felt him surge against her. Swallowing hard, she closed her eyes for a long moment, composing herself. She was on fire and fought a tenuous battle with her body. Finally, she was able to speak. "But you are a demon."

He turned her all the way around to face him, her breasts dragging across his skin in agonizing want. He dug his fingers into her hair, tilting her face up to his, and then lowered his lips to hers, and just before he kissed her he said, "I am."

The contact was liquid fire, her body straining for something she could not have against his. His lips, hot, firm, and demanding, sent her senses reeling. He was all things manly, his leather and sandalwood scent, his hard muscles, his dominant possession of her wreaking havoc with everything that made her a woman.

Her hands pressed upon his chest, marveling at the hard play of his muscles beneath her fingertips. She slid her hands up his chest, then around his neck, the pain of her wound long forgotten. His arm tightened around her waist, his long fingers splayed upon the top swell of her buttocks, his other hand pulling her hair so that she arched harder into him. He tore his lips away, pressing his forehead against hers, his breath warm and hard against her cheeks. "Ari," he breathed, "my body cannot stand more."

She hung in his arms, wanting desperately to allow him to proceed, but knew she could not. Slowly she nodded, and lowered her arms from his neck, but she did not remove them from his body. Nay, she could not help but trail her palms and fingers down the hard planes of his chest and follow the line of the sword to the top of his raised braies. He grasped her hands.

"Do not torture me so." He reached over and poured the last bucket of water over her, rinsing the last vestiges of lather from her body, then he drew the linen she had set on the rough counter and wrapped it around her. When she would not step from the tub, he scowled. "Go dress, before I cannot honor my oath."

She opened her mouth to protest, suddenly feeling rejected, but he put two fingers to her lips. "Go." His voice was tight, his face drawn, and she looked down at his braies. She knew what lay beneath and as much as her body burned for more of his touch, she knew if she were to remain chaste, she could not repeat what had just happened.

Arian hurried to the chamber and suddenly found herself very angry. Not at him but at herself. She had given in to her carnal craving with a man whom she did not know. A man who had kidnapped her! Why had she allowed him to touch her as he had? She was a princess, and he a self-proclaimed mercenary! A notch above a common churl. She was betrothed to a powerful jarl, her uncles were kings, her aunts queens! And she had just allowed a commoner to touch her in a way only her noble husband should. Was she under some kind of spell? She had heard of captive Saxon women falling deeply in love with the Vikings who kidnapped them. Was this the same?

Nay. She was not willing to give her heart over to any man, least of all a mercenary. Magnus would be her husband; of that she was sure. Even if he had doubts and thought her impure, she would convince him differently. She was born to the noble house of Dinefwr, the daughter of the great Prince Hylcon! Had not Magnus turned away the bluest blood in Norway, England, and Denmark, choosing her above all others? Aye, he had, and he did so because he found something in her the others did not possess, and he would not foolishly cast her aside because of rumors. She would explain to him that Dag had not been what Magnus had thought he was and that the Saxon had saved her from certain rape; then she would prove to him she was a virgin in front of all of Norway if he insisted! Arian cringed at the thought of spreading herself before an audience, but she could well understand the reason for it. Magnus would want irrefutable proof in front of those who would challenge him. So be it. Arian dressed with confidence, sure her betrothed would not cast her aside.

But as she drew the brush she had found in the drawer through her damp locks, her body thrummed with heat. Her skin felt hot, then cold, then hot again. Gooseflesh shimmered along her limbs when she thought of the bath and the sensual way Stefan had kissed her. The way his fingertips brushed her most sensitive spots. Her back straightened. Arian pressed her hand to her breasts and gasped when her thumb brushed across a turgid nipple. She closed her eyes and pressed more firmly against it. She warmed, and that spot between her thighs tightened.

What was wrong with her? *What had he done to her?* But more importantly, how could she stop it?

Stefan watched her glide into the room, a golden angel, a princess, a woman whom he craved above all others, and a woman who was out of his realm of ever possessing. She was a royal, and he a bastard. She was betrothed, and he a knight of William, she a lady who under normal circumstances would not give the likes of him a second glance. Indeed, she would look down that pert little nose of hers at him and demand he hang for desiring her.

His eyes narrowed as she approached. The green tunic she wore was too large and it hung down low over one shoulder, exposing the creamy smoothness of her skin. He wanted to press his lips to her there and feel her heat. Her body was firm and supple. His cock thickened in his braies at the sight of her. Her breasts were sweet and the treasure between her thighs burned for a man's touch. He wanted to be that man.

"My hunger is ravenous, sir knight," she said.

Stefan's blood quickened. He was ravenous as well. " 'Twill not be too long."

She nodded, but made no move from him. He moved past her and slowly turned the spit, ignoring her soft fresh scent, and the way it lingered in the air, beckoning him to come closer.

She regarded him with a quiet gaze and he would have given his right arm to know her thoughts. "Do you desire me?" she asked.

Stefan choked and looked hard at her. "What kind of question is that?"

"One that requires an honest answer."

He nodded. "Aye, I desire you."

"Why? Because I am handy?"

Stefan let go of the handle and squarely faced her. "I would desire you under any circumstance."

"Again, I ask why?"

He smiled and touched her hair. His blood, already heated, quickened. The soft thickness felt like spun silk beneath his callused fingertips. "Because you are brave, and passionate, and beautiful."

"What if I were not brave, nor passionate?" She yanked her hair from his grasp. "What if my face were that of a hag but I had this body. Would you still desire me?"

"I would desire your body."

"What is the difference?"

He smiled slowly. "A man can find release between any willing thighs."

"Is it the same for women?"

"I can tell you that the whores I buy scream that I am their one true love and I know they lie. I know some women who soften only for one man's touch and no other will do."

She peered at him hard, and slowly said, "I am confused. Magnus's kisses were warm and tender. I did not mind them. But you?" She pressed her hand to his chest, and his heart slammed against it. "You do something else to me entirely, and I do not understand why. It distresses me that your touch evokes wantonness from me when my betrothed's does not." She chewed her bottom lip. "Do you think it is because he feels only a friendly warmth for me as well?"

"Mayhap. I do not know."

She moved closer to him, the soft floral scent of her turning lethal. Stefan steeled himself. More than anything he wanted to touch her again. "Do you think, sir, that in time I could make him want me the way I want you?"

Very little shocked Stefan, but the princess's question, then her innocent declaration, did. "I—I do not know."

"Can it be taught?"

His blood caught on fire. "What exactly are you asking me?"

"I wish to know if it is possible to teach the thing between us."

Her big silver eyes, almost black in the low light, looked innocently up at him. Stefan fought hard to keep from grabbing her hard to him and showing her without delay just how much a man could crave a woman. Instead, he laughed, breaking the tension in his body. "One cannot teach what only Mother Nature can give."

Her arched brows furrowed. "You speak in riddles. What can the Goddess give that one cannot learn?"

No longer able to resist, Stefan traced a fingertip along the full bloom of her bottom lip. "Natural attraction."

"Natural attraction? Is that what is between us?"

He nodded, wanting to show her just how naturally attracted to her he was. "Aye. It cannot be denied."

Her frown deepened. "But even so, 'tis possible to become attracted to someone else and hold that attraction. If one is diligent and willing, there is a chance a couple can learn to be attracted to the other. I have seen many arranged unions blossom into love. 'Twas the way it was with my mother and father. They first met on their wedding day, and twenty years after her death my father still mourns her as if he lost her yesterday."

"Why do you ponder this?" Stefan asked softly.

Arian sat down on the bench and let out a long breath. She looked up at him and said, "If I am to be honest with you, then I would ask for your honesty as well. For what I am about to discuss causes me some embarrassment."

"I will be as honest as I can."

"First, I must know, when my father gives you what you ask for my release, *will* you release me?"

"I give you my oath I will release you."

"And you have given your oath that anything that transpires between us will remain only between us."

Stefan nodded. She let out another long breath, and for a long while stared at the flames. Only the sizzling of the roast pig interrupted her thoughtful silence. Without looking up at him, she slowly said, "I find myself in quite a quandary, and do not know how to extract myself from it without losing something precious."

"What do you stand to lose?"

She looked up at him. "I have already lost my reputation. I stand to lose my pride, but worse, my betrothed. I wish to marry him. I do not want go back to Dinefwr under any circumstances, and if Magnus rejects me for Dag's death and what he thinks happened while I was your captive, I will have no recourse but to return to Dinefwr."

"Go on."

"So, I would need a foolproof way to make Magnus not change his mind."

"You said proof of your virginity was required. He will accept that."

"Mayhap, but what if Dag's men get to him before we wed and tell him of what they saw at the pond? Me naked in the arms of a half-naked man who killed my husband-to-be's nephew, then kidnapped me and demanded ransom. Magnus is a powerful jarl and full of pride. I could not bear it if he cast me aside."

"He chose you above all others. Why do you now think different?"

"I—I don't, but—" She whirled away and slammed her fist into her palm, then whirled back to face him. The soft planes of her face tensed in anxiety. "He *will not* cast me away like some soiled garment! I am daughter to Hylcon and come to him a virgin! That is enough!"

"Your pedigree is impressive, my lady."

Her face folded and she crumpled upon the bench. "But I fear his pride is more so." She turned to look up at him, and he saw raw desperation in her eyes. "What," she whispered, "must a woman do to make a man forget everything but her?" She raised her chin and locked gazes with him. In a stronger voice she asked, "What must a woman do to make a man set aside his pride and not care what vicious rumors swirl about court, and see only her?"

Stefan slowly swallowed. His eyes swept across her. Pride was a fragile thing. Many a man was ruled by it. He had seen noble houses crumble because of it. But there were some men who would move mountains to possess one specific woman. 'Twas an obsession that drove them mad. He had seen it recently with his brother Wulfson, and before him Rohan. And even Rhys to an extent. 'Twas a place he had sworn, after the heartache of Lady Lisette, that he would never go.

"He must be consumed by her," he said slowly.

"How?"

"She becomes the one and only thing he must have, for to not have her, he would not be whole."

"How, Stefan? *How* do I make Magnus see only me?"

"I do not know how to recreate Mother Nature."

She stood and grasped his hands. He flinched at their heat. "Would you try?"

"Try what?"

Her cheeks reddened. "Tell me what a man desires of a woman!"

He scarcely breathed. Anger flashed in her eyes; she dropped his hands and whirled away, but stopped and turned to face him again. She stood proud, haughty, her chin raised, her shoulders back. Clothed in a man's tunic with more moth holes than he could count, she was the most beautiful thing he had ever beheld. Heat speared his groin as a sudden vision of her naked and willing beneath him flashed in his mind's eye.

"Will you force me to say it?" she demanded. "Will you force me to swallow my pride?"

"What do you want from me, Arian?" he asked huskily.

"I want—I want you to show me the ways to keep my husband abed so he forgets everything but me!"

"I will not touch you in the way you ask and not have you."

"Nay, you will not touch me! You will *tell* me," she lamely ended.

Heat flared in his face. "I will not touch you because you would be ashamed of your actions or ashamed of your tutor?" When she looked away, she gave her answer. And that dark demon coiled inside of him reared its ugly head. He set his jaw and turned back to the roasting pig.

"Stefan, I cannot change the blood that flows through my veins, any more than you can."

"Aye, your royal blood as opposed to my common blood," he snarled over his shoulder.

"Please, let this not come between us."

He whirled around and faced her. "You have put it squarely between us."

He grabbed her to him and snarled. "The lofty princess has no other choice but to allow the lowly bastard to tutor her in the ways of love so that she may live happily ever after with her royal jarl." He shoved her way from him. "What do I get?"

She looked at him, stunned. "You—you will have my favor."

He threw his head back and laughed. "I will have your *favor*? Will you grant me a hide of land, a sow, and a boar as well? And then am I to be forever grateful to the great and beautiful Princess Arianrhod of Dinefwr?"

"Nay! 'Tis not like that."

" 'Tis exactly like that."

He swiped his hand across his face and flinched when he touched his cheek. He was scarred, he was a bastard, he did not even have his own horse or sword to call his own! Now he knew how the whores to whom he tossed a silver piece felt when they performed for him. He stormed from the great room, the sight of her sickening him.

TEN

Arian sat still for a long time on the bench, staring at the fire. Dejection, anger, frustration, and a longing she could not name, all wreaked havoc in her heart, and she did not know what to do. But she knew she wanted marriage to Magnus, and when she realized that he might very likely refuse her now, she cursed her choice not to marry him by proxy. He had been most adamant she come to him a virgin; would he look past what had happened? Could he? She let out a long breath and was grateful for the fact 'twas a Saxon and not a Norman who held her captive. Though Norway cast a covetous eye on the island, they were not at war with the English. And though Norse roots burrowed deep into Norman blood, they were not allies. Yorkshire teemed with rebellious Vikings; Magnus, half Saxon himself through his mother's line, was a most staunch supporter of remaining independent of Norman rule.

The sizzle of burning meat assaulted Arian's nostrils, jerking her out of the pall that had settled over her. She jumped up, grabbed the spit handle, and cried out in pain. 'Twas hot! She grabbed a nearby cloth and grasped it, then turned the pig over. 'Twas done, and though her belly made noises she had no hunger. But she knew the Saxon did. For a man so large as he, he must be famished.

She hacked off a hindquarter of the pig, placed it in a bowl, then strode out to the stable, where she found him removing the poultice from his horse's hoof. He ignored her, so she set the bowl down on a mound of straw and returned to the lodge, where she forced herself to eat. After wrapping the leftover meat and placing it into an earthen jar, she set it in a cool corner. Arian left a lit sconce in the great room, then made her way to the sleeping chamber. Setting the candle down on the table beside the bed, she lay down fully clothed, wondering what it was about the angry man in the stable that intrigued her so.

Her last thoughts before sleep found her were not of the honorable man she was to marry, but of a most dishonorable man who sulked in the stable.

A small noise from the bedside startled Arian awake. Her eyes widened when the hard shadow of the Saxon materialized before her. As her eyes focused in the soft light of the candle, she caught her breath. Like a hammer on an anvil, her heart thumped furiously against her chest. He stood fully clothed beside her, his gaze hot and penetrating in the low glow of the candlelight.

"Do you wish to know what it's like to want something so badly you will do anything to have it?" he asked, his voice so low and hoarse she barely understood his question.

A hard shot of fear stabbed her belly. Her mouth was

suddenly dry. And wild excitement ripped through every inch of her body. "Yes."

"Then tonight learn your first lesson."

He moved over her, forcing her back into the pillows to keep from touching him. "As I am forbidden to touch you, princess, so too are you forbidden to touch me," he whispered against her throat, only the warm caress of his breath touching her skin. The tunic had pulled down onto one shoulder, exposing the high swell of her right breast. Her nipples puckered beneath the thin fabric, eager for attention. He reached out as if he were going to touch her, but he did not. " 'Tis the anticipation of contact, the subtleties of a caress, a smoldering look, Arian, that makes a person want more."

In the soft glow of the candle, her skin glowed warm. He dipped his head to her lips as if he were to kiss her. She closed her eyes, anticipating his kiss. Her lips parted, her breasts trembled. But all he did was caress her with his breath. "There are bonds between a man and a woman, Arian, that cannot be explained." He dipped his nose to her neck and softly inhaled. Her scent inflamed his blood, and like molten steel, it burned. "Like your natural essence of honey and rose." He moved down to her breasts, where he could see a pink nipple peek out from a worn spot in the fabric. Stefan dug his fingers into the sheet, not trusting himself, then he breathed on it and watched as it pebbled beneath his eyes. She moaned softly, moving her hips in a gentle undulation. Lower still, he moved to her belly, then to the place between her thighs. He closed his eyes and inhaled her womanly essence. His blood coursed hotter through him, and he felt his control slip. Huskily he said, "There, that is the true essence of a woman."

Arian's body trembled beneath his and yet he had not laid a finger upon her. Lowering his head, he opened his mouth as if he would take her, but blew hot breath against her soft mound.

She cried out in a long low rasp of surprise. His hands bunched the sheets, his control slipping more. Never had he wanted to touch a woman as he wanted to touch the one so close to him now. Her fresh, clean scent toyed with his senses and he knew if he pressed his lips between her thighs she would taste sweeter than heaven. Stefan lowered his lips to just hovering about her sultry body; he could feel her heat, smell her desire, and his control slipped more. He breathed upon her mons again. Her hips arched against him, brushing his lips. She hissed in harsh desire, his body stiffened to stone.

In that one tense moment of time, Stefan could not see, he could not breathe, he could not move. In that one tense moment of time, he knew what it meant to be so consumed with desire that he would offer his soul to the devil to sate it.

Slowly, for every muscle in his body raged with desire, Stefan moved away from her to the far side of the bed, and stared hard at her. She rolled over to face him, and in the candlelight, he could see a mist of moisture glossing the high color in her cheeks and the shallow rise and fall of her chest. If she but looked down, she would see that he too was affected by what just transpired. Indeed, still the battle raged within him, 'twas all he could do to keep from pulling her into his arms and taking her.

"Is your body hot, Arian?" he whispered. "Does it ache?"

"Yes," she breathed. She moved closer to him, her dark silvery eyes ablaze. "How do I make it go away?"

"I would have to touch you for you to know."

She sighed and closed her eyes, licking her full lips. The erotic sight nearly sent him over the edge. "I would give almost anything for you to touch me, Stefan." She opened her eyes and stared at him. "But I cannot."

" 'Tis a double-edged sword, Arian," he bit off. He rolled from the bed and left the room, soundly shutting the door behind him, before he broke his oath to them both.

For most of the night, Arian tossed and turned, her body on fire, her thoughts aswirl as desire and confusion reigned supreme. Each time she moved, and the air stirred, she was acutely aware of the cold place beside her in the large bed. How easily she missed his presence. How easily he had managed to work his way into not only her every waking thought but her dreams, as well. She could not explain what had happened, or why. She did not even try. Even if she understood it, it mattered not. It *could not* matter.

She rolled over and stared at the indentation in the mattress his large body had left. Letting out a long breath, she accepted what had happened for what it was: two people thrown into a terrible circumstance and for whatever the reason God chose, he threw them together for some small comfort. And it would never happen again. It could not.

Exhausted, sleep claimed her somewhere between the darkest of night and the gray hours of dawn. She woke with a start, the pale fingers of the new day brushing across her face through the high shutter. Without looking, she knew that Stefan had not returned. The room was cold, as if the life had been sucked out of it. Quickly she tended her needs and dressed, expecting to find Stefan in the hall, but it, too, was empty. The jangle of a spur and the solid cadence of the destrier's hooves drew her attention outside to see Stefan leading the great black toward her. He and the horse were fully mailed.

"Your mail, 'tis unusual in that it is all black," she noted, as he stopped before her.

His dark brows tightened. "A gift from my king."

" 'Tis an honor, he must have valued you highly."

Stefan's jaw clenched. "We must go," he said, looking hard at her.

Exasperation fluttered through her at his reticence. He was a most complex man! Yet despite his surliness and everything that had happened since she first laid eyes upon him, Arian could not help but wonder if things would not be different if he was not who he was and she not a princess. And that thought alone should have made her realize she was treading on very dangerous ground. He was her enemy, not her lover. Was she mad to forget that? Aye, she was a foolish girl with foolish notions! He would ransom her and then be off on his merry way, counting his coin while she was left putting the pieces of her ravaged life back together. She stiffened, angry with herself and feeling like a ninny.

"A moment, then, to collect my meager belongings."

There was not much to collect: a few borrowed rags she bundled up along with the brush, before she hurried back to him.

Without a word Stefan hoisted her up into the saddle,

then hopped up behind her. He grasped the reins, gave the horse a soft nudge, and they were off. When they had gone several leagues and with no word spoken, the tension was too much for her to bear. Forgetting her anger for the moment, her pride wrestled with a question she must know the answer to. "Do you think less of me for my wanton behavior?" she blurted.

"Nay."

She let out a long breath, realizing his opinion of her mattered. Why, she did not know. "Nor do I think less of you for yours."

She felt his chest rumble with laughter. "Princess, you are a most unusual woman. I fear your husband will have a terrible time keeping you under his thumb."

At the mention of Magnus, she stiffened. She did not wish to speak of him. "Where are we bound?"

"Draceadon, in southwest Mercia."

"What is there?"

"A safe place."

She would welcome a safe place. And she knew, without feeling the least bit naïve for thinking it, that Stefan would see to her safety until she was reunited with her father. Mayhap that was why she let down her guard, forgetting he was her enemy, because despite it he would not harm her. Suddenly fatigued, Arian yawned and settled back against Stefan's chest. Immediately he stiffened. She half-turned and looked up at him, squinting against the eastern sun. "Why do you stiffen? Do you find me undesirable now?"

He did not look down at her, but kept his eyes on the path ahead. "Nay, that will never change, but rest assured, there will be no more lessons."

In her heart, she knew there would no more, but she asked the question anyway. "Why not?"

"Because we are headed for trouble, and it is trouble I can ill afford."

"But there *is* more, is there not?"

He shook his head. "Nay. Take what you learned last eve and apply it to your husband, and he will be a most happy man."

She turned in a huff. "I do not understand your sudden reluctance." But she understood perfectly.

"You will, later this eve."

ELEVEN

Stefan pushed the horse hard. By midday he dismounted and led him, alleviating some of the weight, hoping the swollen tissue in his hoof would hold until they reached Draceadon. But at the slower pace he doubted they would be close enough to the main road to Dunloc by nightfall. He dreaded spending another night alone lying beside Arian. He grasped the reins so tightly that his knuckles whitened. He set his jaw and ignored the pain it caused his cheek.

Urgency pushed him to walk faster, despite the heaviness of his mail. The fate of his brothers, combined with his sexual frustration, strained his raw nerves. He had nearly broken his oath to her and to himself, not once but twice. And while his honor when it came to women could be questioned by many, he was not that much of a knave to put the lady's best interests aside for a momentary pleasure.

She would serve her purpose in freeing his brothers, and what she did afterwards was her choice, but he would not take what chance of happiness she had from her because he was selfish. And he knew his limits, and last night he had reached them.

Despite the slowed pace, they did not make bad time, but he was not close enough to risk making a run for it in the darkness should they meet up with renegades or patrolling Normans. Were he alone he would have ridden through the night, allowing Apollo to find his way back along the road, but he would not chance losing Arian. She was critical to his plan. So, reluctantly, Stefan made the decision to stop for the night. By mid-morning the next day they would reach Draceadon. He cast a weary eye to the rumbling sky. The skies had been dark and turbulent all day, but he prayed the rains would hold at least 'til morn.

He found a suitable spot not too far from the road. As Stefan helped Arian dismount, he noted her closed face and somber mood. They had spoken nary a word to each other the entire day. For that he was glad. He had already begun to push her from his thoughts, not wanting to dwell on her.

Silently she helped him untack the horse. When he turned to rub down the destrier, she scurried off into the wood. He let out a long sigh. They would need to eat. He built a small fire to heat the leftover haunch of the pig. 'Twould have to suffice.

After some time he glanced into the darkened wood, his concern growing when the princess failed to return. Mayhap she needed time to herself. God only knew he did. A solitary man even with his brothers, he did not do well in forced social situations. He knew not words of love and humor, as did Warner and other swains. He was quiet and serious, always watching the goings-on around him rather than partaking in them.

Just as he stood to fetch her, she emerged, holding the hem of her tunic to her belly, and, in so doing, exposing her long shapely legs. Heat flared in his groin. "Berries!" she announced, spreading her bounty on a big supple leaf before him. "Lots and lots of berries!"

Stefan shook his head and turned from her. He removed his mail hauberk and sword belt, but kept his mail chauses on. Mostly to keep as much metal as possible between his cock and the vixen sitting down on a rock before the fire.

He fitted the leg of pig onto the spit he had carved and propped it over the meager fire. Arian walked to the nearby stream and washed her hands, then wandered back toward him and stood staring at him. He returned her gaze, but did not speak. She raised her chin and set it—a look he was beginning to know meant trouble.

"When we arrive at this safe place you speak of, I demand to immediately send word to my father and to Moorwood that I am alive."

He spoke carefully. "Word will be sent to those who need to know you are alive and in my care."

Her face drained of color. "Must you say I am *your* hostage? Assumptions will be made! Does this Draceadon have a lady? Say 'tis she who holds me. My reputation is blighted as it is. Cadoc and Ivar will flap their jaws; indeed, my father is probably already aware of my shame."

His muscles tensed. To occupy them, he turned the spit above the low fire. "You insult me with your words, princess."

She knelt down beside him. "My apologies, but 'tis the truth."

He scowled. "Would your reputation be less blighted if you had been found naked in the arms of a magnate?"

Her head snapped back and her eyes narrowed. "You misunderstand me, sir. My shame is the same regardless of the man."

Her explanation took some of the sting from his pride. He nodded. " 'Tis most unfortunate for a woman. A man abed with a bevy of beauties is applauded for his prowess. But if a woman, most especially a royal such as yourself, finds herself in a compromising position not of her own making, she is scorned."

"Nay, 'tis not fair. And for that reason alone I must get to Magnus before Ivar and his steward Sir Sar do. I cannot go back to Dinefwr!"

Her adamant tone caused him to wonder aloud. "What happened there?" Her cheeks flushed and she looked away. The urge to reach out to her and comfort was strong, but he resisted it. "Who hurt you?"

Without looking at him, she said, "No one." She turned to face him and some of the despair fled her eyes. "Not like you think. 'Tis just better for everyone in my family that I no longer reside amongst them."

"Tell me of your family." His question surprised him. Since he took up the sword, he had never been interested enough to ask a woman of her life.

She poked at the embers with a stick casting them from the rock enclosure like fireflies. "My mother died giving birth. Each year on the anniversary of her death, my father walks the castle grounds, calling for her. These last few years, his bouts of sadness have taken longer to go away. Too many times, he has called out to me thinking I am her. It sends my stepmother Morwena into fits of madness, and my brother Rhodri into fits of rage."

"I have met your sire. He struck me as a walking dead man."

Her head snapped back in surprise. "When did you meet him?"

"My liege sent me several years ago to breed his mares to that devil of a blood bay stallion. He nearly killed them!"

Arian threw her head back and laughed. "That is Beli Mawr. He has lived up to his reputation. He is the greatest stud at Dinefwr, and my father's constant companion. His son Belenus, out of my mare Fahadda, will prove to be even more potent. 'Tis my gift to my husband," she said softly.

"Where are the horses?"

"I will assume with Cadoc. My maid Jane, who is as ancient as these oaks, rides with the train. I fear for her health." Taking up the stick, she poked at the embers again. "I could not bear to lose her, she is my only link to my mother. She brought me into this world. No one understands me as she does." She crushed an errant ember beneath the stick. "I have lost much on this journey."

"But you did gain a few things, did you not?" He chuckled when her cheeks pinkened.

"Last night was wrong."

He shook his head, not wanting this argument with her, but he could not resist reaching out to her. He lifted her chin with his fingers so that she could see he meant his words. "For me there are no regrets."

Her eyes searched his face, for what he was not sure. "Have you ever loved a woman?"

His hand dropped from her. He laughed harshly. "I do not even understand the meaning of the word."

"Have you ever wanted a woman so badly that nothing else mattered? Wanted her so badly you would give up your life for her?"

As she asked the questions, his heart suddenly did not feel so closed, because he realized that as much as he thought he had loved Lisette, he had never loved her enough to give up everything for her, least of all his life. 'Twas his pride that suffered the blow of her rejection, not his heart. And with that realization, some of the hardness left him. "There was a maid once. I thought I loved her."

"What happened?"

His face tightened. "She had a better offer."

"Stefan, I am sorry."

"Do not be. 'Twas meant to be, and I am happy with my life." He scooped up a handful of berries, popped them into his mouth, and thoughtfully chewed. "Have you ever loved a man?"

"Nay. Nor do I wish to. I see the heartache my father lives with each day, and the misery of Morwena knowing his heart will never be hers to share."

"You do not love the Jarl then?"

She shrugged and picked at a few berries. "Nay, but he pleases me. He is a good man and we are suited."

"No hopes for love?"

Vigorously, she shook her head. "Nay! I do not want the heartache of eventual loss, or worse, rejection. I will be a dutiful wife, raising my children and seeing to my husband's estates. For myself I will breed my horses."

Stefan grinned and grabbed more berries. They were sweet and juicy in his mouth. "Aye, one day I will have hides of land to do the same. But I will also train them for battle."

"At least we have that commonality."

He grinned over at her. "There is that other thing we have in common."

Her cheeks flushed crimson. "Do not remind me of it, Stefan."

His heart thudded hard against this chest. Aye, the thing between them was ever present, like the storm now brewing above. One day soon, if they were not careful, it would burst open and rain thunder down upon them, and there would be no stopping what the Goddess chose to give.

Stefan nodded, and turned to the meat. " 'Tis done." He gave her the bulk of it and himself drank the bulk of the wineskin. He sat with his back against a large rock, his wounded leg straight out, his good leg bent at the knee with his elbow propped upon it, and watched her from beneath hooded eyelids. He watched the way her hips swayed and the way her full breasts pushed against the thin fabric of her garment. He watched the way her lips, glossy from the meat, pursed as she stoked the fire, and the way her slender fingers pushed back her thick, glorious hair. Aye, he watched everything about her, and his cock lengthened.

When she returned from washing her hands in the stream, she stopped short when she caught his brooding gaze upon her. He watched the spark of desire flare in her eyes' deep silver depths. Her cheeks pinkened and she looked away, and hurried to a spot across the fire from him where she had laid down on Rhys's wolf pelt. She rolled over, presenting her back to him.

He watched her twitch and turn and move about, finding no position comfortable. He watched her roll over now, facing him, feigning sleep. In the low light of the flickering flames, he watched her cheeks pinken from the low heat. And the slow rise and fall of her bosom. Her nipples beaded beneath the fabric and he knew she thought of him. He refused to set the skin aside and go to her. He refused to go to the edge again. He refused to break his oath to her, and to himself. But more than that, he refused to destroy her life. For if he breached her, all would be lost for her, and he would hold himself solely responsible.

When she moved again, this time to lie flat on her back, he called to her in his mind, and watched mesmerized as she turned onto her side and faced him, her eyes dark and filled with naked desire. "Do you understand now why we cannot continue?" he softly queried.

Slowly she shook her head.

"We can control this craving that is between us—now. But if we continue, the craving will control us."

Morning broke dark and ominous, thick moisture filling the air. 'Twas a bad omen. He tacked up Apollo, donned his mail and sword belt, then roused Arian. "Come, the sky is full. If we hurry we can make Draceadon before it unleashes."

Quickly she hurried into the forest. She returned as quickly, and just as he swung her up into the saddle the first big drops of rain plopped down upon them. He vaulted up behind her, grabbed the reins, and urged Apollo home. He held her tightly against him as the rain slickened the leather turning it treacherous. 'Twas torture holding her so close, but he did not want her to fall. The rain mixed with her natural scent created a most hypnotic potion.

With each step closer to the old Roman fortress that was Wulfson's home—and for a time had been his—Stefan felt his excitement mount. By the day's end his messengers would be on the road delivering his demands, and soon he would be reunited with his brothers.

Arian shivered hard in his arms, jerking his attention that had not really strayed to focus solely on her. With every gain there was a loss, and he could admit to himself he would miss her. Most women feared him. They did not understand what drove him, and he did not care enough to ever enlighten any one of them. But with Arian it was different. He had spoken more to her these last few days than he had to his brothers in a year's time! He did not question the whys; he was not the philosophical type. He was more basic. If he liked a certain wine or horse or sword, he just accepted it; he did not delve into the reasons why. 'Twas the same with Arian.

"We are almost there, Arian," he said softly against her ear. As the words left his mouth, they rounded a sharp bend on the well-traveled road. Stefan's heart stopped. Arian gasped and he felt her chest rise, then fall, as the scream left her mouth.

'Twas Ralph, his nobleborn cousin, and that sniveling fool Philip d'Argent. They were just as surprised to see him, and instinctively Stefan knew that should he approach them he would lose the princess.

Whirling the black away from the Normans, Stefan spurred the steed, and prayed the tender hoof would hold until Draceadon was in sight. Grasping Arian tightly to his chest, they burst headlong into the thick forest. Shouts and thundering hooves followed close behind. God's blood! He ran from his own countrymen! But he would not take even the slightest chance and risk losing the key to his brothers' release. Arian ducked low in his arms, branches and brambles tearing at her arms and face. He pulled her closer, leaning over her to protect her, and found himself the recipient of the vicious lashes.

Stefan knew if they kept their pace and direction they would come out on the main road to Dunloc, if they could make it that far. Then Draceadon was but two leagues south. He chanced a look over his shoulder and scowled in the thickening rain. Only a handful of Ralph's men pursued. That meant the others had gone ahead. On the open road, they could come out before them. Stefan urged the horse faster, determined to break the road ahead of them and charge up the steep hill to Draceadon and to safety.

Arian held on for her life, as her fear raced at the same breakneck speed as the mighty destrier. Fervently she prayed that the Normans would not catch them. Not only were they her enemy, but enemy to all of Wales. She had heard the terrible tales of how they raped and pillaged all who stood in their way. They were vicious, arrogant and not to be trusted. Gruesome images flashed in her mind's eye, terrifying her. Holding on to the high pommel to keep from slipping off as the horse beneath her careened through the dense foliage. She kept her head low and tried to be as still as she could. One wrong move could send them both toppling to the ground below, ending the chase, and perhaps their lives.

They broke into a small clearing, with a swift flowing river on the other side. The cold rain came harder now, soaking her tunic, prickling her face. Continually she pushed back her wet hair from her face. Arian chanced a look over her shoulder and nearly died on the spot. Through the gray driving rain, she saw at least a score of mailed knights hotly pursuing them. Stefan urged the horse faster. They plunged into the cold water. With strong sure strides, the black moved them across and toward the far bank. As they slipped up the muddy slope, Arian took another look behind them and thanked the Goddess and God for the small reprieve.

"The Normans' horses balk!" she cried to Stefan. He did not look but urged the horse once again into the forest, their reckless pace picking up. The race continued, and with each twist and turn in the wood, she clutched tighter to the pommel and prayed they were one more step from the gaping jaws of the terrible Normans. They broke through the forest edge onto a muddy well-worn road. Stefan reined the horse south and the mad pace continued.

"We are almost there, Ari, hold on," Stefan whispered in her ear. She pressed back into him. Small spatters of blood dripped on her cheek, she looked up to see that the bottom part of his wound had ripped open. Biting her lip, she kept silent, knowing that to speak would only distract him.

It occurred to her then at that very second, despite their perilous flight, this man, this mercenary Saxon, had saved her from disaster not once but twice, and come what may she owed him more than her life. She also knew that this thing between them, whatever it was, bound her to him, and no matter what course their lives took, it could never be severed.

It gave her great comfort to know that this man would, for reasons unknown to them both, lay down his life for her. The realization stunned her, but it also gave her great confidence. He would keep her safe from the Normans and he would see her safely returned to either her father or Magnus.

"*Jesu!*" Stefan said under his breath, and kicked the lathered horse faster. Ahead, coming straight at them at a furious pace, more riders, two score at least, flying a standards she did not recognize. Arian steeled herself for the ultimate collision as she watched one of the knights break from the group and gallop toward them. Stefan grabbed her tighter to his chest, if that were possible, and as they approached Arian made out the sapphire-and-gold standard of a dragon on the end of the knight's lance. She scowled. 'Twas a small knight, but he rode with the fury of one possessed.

"Stefan!" A woman's scream tore through the damp air. Arian stiffened. As the name reached them, the garrison of knights behind the small leader charged forward.

Stefan did not slow the black, but kept the furious pace. "Tarian! Normans behind! To Draceadon!"

"We shall hold them!" the knight returned. A woman knight? Dumbstruck, Arian watched the huge gray that the lady knight rode rear up as the sea of knights they rode into parted for them to pass. She looked over her shoulder, completely baffled by this sudden turn of events, and watched the lady's knights regroup and charge toward the pressing Normans. Confused but keenly aware that the immediate danger of being captured by Normans had lessened, Arian kept her silence as they continued their mad gallop. The landscape blurred behind them before they broke into a wide meadow. It spread out like a glistening green ocean before it swooped up, and at its peak, the high dark walls of a fortress rose up from the hill like a dragon of yore, wings raised, poised to strike his enemy. Arian gasped. " 'Tis like a dragon's wings!"

"Draceadon," Stefan whispered hoarsely above the thundering hooves.

As they approached the wide studded doors, Stefan called up to the lookout, " 'Tis Stefan, allow me entry!"

Slowly the heavy gates swung back. A sudden thought hit Arian amidst all of the turmoil: was the lady knight Stefan's lady love? 'Twas obvious by their quick exchange she held his word dear. And the lookout? Stefan was known to him; had he not been, the gates would have remained firmly closed. A prickle of some emotion she had no experience with jabbed at her belly.

As they passed through the narrow opening, Arian dared another look over her shoulder, and saw that the entire Saxon garrison stood at the bottom of the steep hill, facing the Normans.

She dared not breathe a sigh of relief. While she felt Stefan would protect her, now they were at the mercy of the lord of the manor. Would he help? Or would he too hold her for ransom?

They rode through the forebidding gates of the menacing fortress and into a bailey, then farther on to a courtyard. Stefan grabbed her from the saddle and handed her off to a golden-haired girl who stood wide-eyed, out of the rain, just inside the wide doors to the hall. "Lady Brighid, see to her until I return with Lady Tarian."

He reined the horse around and to Arian's utter astonishment; he rode back toward the Normans.

Stefan charged down the hill to the standoff, pushing the destrier to the limit. When he reined his horse up beside Lady Tarian's gray, he nodded to her, then to her stalwart captain, Gareth, who broke into a smile beneath his helm. Slowly he turned to his cousin, who, despite Stefan's torn and bloodied face, immediately recognized him. He watched Ralph's eyes, so much like his own, narrow behind his helm. Feeling at home with Tarian and Gareth and her loyal men at his back, Stefan grinned.

"Lady Tarian of Dunloc, my cousin Sir Ralph du Forney." Tarian nodded her head but Ralph did not return the respect. Stefan grinned wider. "Lord Wulfson de Trevelyn's bride."

Ralph's eyes narrowed, and this time he bowed from the waist. "My lady," he said, his voice barely civil. There was no love lost between any of the Blood Swords and those who held themselves and their noble blood above them.

Stefan kept his gaze focused on his cousin. "What brings you so far south, Ralph?"

"We patrol the lands for armed Saxons." Ralph sneered, then demanded, "Why did you run like a coward from us?"

Stefan reached down and patted Apollo's slick neck,

then looked up to the clearing sky. "You are not privy to my motives, dear cousin. Now stand back so that I may have a private word with Lady Tarian."

"You dare speak with such airs!" Philip sneered, nudging his horse closer to Stefan. Twenty swords behind Stefan were drawn in unison, the lady lowering her short lance, brushing the noble's mail. She jabbed him hard.

"A warning, sirs," Tarian said levelly. "My husband is earl of this shire, and well you know he has the ear of William. Trespass against Stefan and you trespass the king!"

"Are you so craven to put a woman up to champion you, Stefan?" Ralph scoffed.

Stefan's anger seethed, but he would not allow his cousin to bait him. "Bray like the ass you are, Ralph. I have most urgent news for William and my lady. None of which concerns you."

Ralph bowed in his saddle. "My lady, as my bastard cousin has told you, I am Ralph du Forney, heir of the great house of de Lyon. My uncle, the great Comte d'Everaux, also has the ear of William, I can assure you." He smiled like a snake before it swallowed its prey. "My men and I are battle-weary, and in dire need of food and pallet."

Stefan stiffened even more in his saddle. His narrowed gaze swept the men who sat silent behind their leader. Some he remembered from his youth growing up in the shadow of a man who refused to acknowledge the obvious. His gaze briefly touched on Philip, who regarded him with open hostility.

Yet, despite the contempt he felt for his cousin and

cohorts, the lot of them looked as exhausted as Stefan felt. It would be of utmost rudeness for the lady of the manor not to extend the hospitality of Draceadon to them.

"We have pallets aplenty in the stable, the hall is most spacious, and our stores are full. You and your men are welcome to share Draceadon's hospitality for one night," Lady Tarian invited. She looked to Stefan. "Sir knight, would you ride alongside me to the hall?"

" 'Twould be my honor," he replied softly. They turned their horses, and as they broke from the group, Apollo pulled up lame. Stefan cursed, and immediately dismounted to inspect the hoof. A sharp rock had embedded itself between the shoe and the sore spot he had tended. He pulled the seax from his belt and dislodged the stone. One of Tarian's men dismounted and handed Stefan the reins to his own horse. "I will walk him to the stable."

Stefan nodded and mounted, but said, "Be gentle with him, he has been ridden hard. Rub him down and do not feed or water him until after the noon meal."

Once more ahorse, as Stefan and Tarian made their way up the steep hill, Stefan said softly, "Tread lightly, milady. Ralph is as cunning and as secretive as a fox, and that lout Philip will shift alliances twice a day should it prove a benefit to him."

She nodded and looked ahead, her eyes focused on the great fortress. "I pray you have word of my husband," she softly said.

A sudden knot in his throat prevented him from answering, so he nodded. She cast him a grave look, and he could see the glisten of tears in her eyes. She sat sword-straight in her saddle and his heart went out to her.

She swallowed hard, and just barely above a whisper she asked, "Does he live?"

Once again not trusting his voice, Stefan nodded. Lady Tarian made a noise half sob and half laugh, but when he looked at her, she sat regally composed upon the gray.

TWELVE

From the threshold, having refused to go into the hall with the Lady Brighid, who eyed her with open curiosity, Arian watched for Stefan's return. Arian knew she looked a fright, standing in her bare feet, the sodden oversized threadbare tunic stuck to her, her hair plastered to her dirt-smeared face and arms. But she didn't care. She wanted to know that Stefan was unharmed, and only then would her anxiety lessen.

A hard tremor of fear ran through her limbs as she watched Stefan come through the gate beside the lady knight. She squinted. He sat upon a different horse. Her eyes widened when the Normans, mingled with the Saxon knights, filed through behind him. What was this? Stefan did not seem to care that they were behind him? But—? He appeared to be completely consumed in conversation with the knight who rode the great gray horse beside him.

"Why are the Normans permitted within the walls?" Arian, in Welsh, asked the young lady beside her.

"I do not understand, your tongue, my lady," Brighid

said in English, coming out despite the drizzle to stand beside her.

But Arian could not repeat the words, so captivated was she by the sight unfolding before her. The Normans turned toward the long stable at the far side of the bailey, followed by the lady's men; only she and Stefan turned their horses toward Arian. A squire ran up to both horses and took the reins. Stefan dismounted and she watched him limp to the lady's side.

"Dear Lord, what happened to him?" Brighid gasped beside Arian.

She cast the girl a scowl, then turned her attention back to the knights. Arian's jaw dropped when the lady knight pulled her helm from her head. Long thick black hair tumbled about her shoulders. She tossed the helm to her squire and dismounted the high steed, with Stefan's careful assistance. To Arian's amazement, the dark-haired woman threw herself into Stefan's arms. Despite his wounded state, he pulled her into his embrace and hugged her close, whispering soft words into her ear. When they broke apart, Stefan offered his arm, and thusly they came toward her. Arian felt suddenly faint.

Jealousy pricked her hard, its nails gouging into her belly. She shook her head at the absurd emotion. Stefan was nothing but a lowly knight, a knight with no land, no title, a knight with only his horse and sword. *A bastard.* Yet her belittling him in her mind did not quash the hurt feelings.

Frustrated and feeling out of place, Arian watched him guide the lady up a wide step to stop several paces from her. When he looked to face her, Arian caught a small gasp. His expression startled her, for she did not think the man capable of a joyous look, but there it was before her. While fatigue lined his face, and to be sure that face was torn and bloody, there was a calmness about him that transcended his pain.

"Sir Stefan!" Lady Brighid gasped. "What happened to your face?"

He smiled at the girl and yanked a braid. " 'Tis nothing."

She giggled nervously, then asked, "Sir Rhys? Does he come with you?"

Instantly Arian watched Stefan's face flash to furious. "Nay, he does not, but rest assured he is alive and will come to you as soon as he is able."

The girl grasped his hands. "Is he wounded? Have you seen him? Did he ask about me?"

Gently he set her from him, "In truth I do not know his whereabouts, but in my gut I know he lives."

Brighid broke away, and in a flood of tears ran into the hall. Arian let out a short breath she had been holding. She caught the brief, intimate exchange between Stefan and the lady and her anger rose.

"I am Arianrhod, daughter of Prince Hylcon of Dinefwr and Lady Branwen of Powys," she said to the lady. "Your man holds me against my will. I demand to be released at once!"

The lady smiled, and when she did it was as if the moon rose. Arian could well understand any man's smitten heart. She was breathtakingly regal. For one so petite, she walked as if she were the queen of the realm. As she approached Arian, eyeing her disheveled appearance cautiously, she said, in a commanding voice, "A princess? Really?"

Arian nodded, her chin high, her spine straight, ignoring those who lingered in the courtyard trying to catch a word. She may look a waif, but she knew by the lady's tone and approving eye she was aware she spoke the truth.

Lady Tarian nodded. "I am the daughter of Sweyn Godwinson and the Abbess Edith."

Arian caught a breath. "An abbess?"

Lady Tarian nodded, her dark eyes snapping. "Aye, an abbess." She strode past Arian and said over her shoulder, "Your train was here two days past in search of you. Should I send a rider after them?"

The news stunned her and gave her hope. "I demand you allow me to go to them at once!" Arian commanded.

"All in good time, princess," Stefan said, taking Arian's arm and escorting her into the hall. "All in good time."

She balked, yanking her arm from his grasp, halting their stride. "Nay! Now! I have spent these last days chained to a bed, tied to you half-naked, my person bruised and scarred by your hand, and nearly starved, and you tell me all in good time? Nay. My time is *now*!"

Lady Tarian turned from the doorway, sweeping Arian's disheveled person with a nonchalant gaze. "Your clothes are not fit for a field churl, most unbecoming a princess."

"Indeed, Lady Tarian, your man would not allow me to clothe myself!"

The lady looked up at Stefan, her eyes twinkling at some hidden secret. "Chivalrous knight, do you forget your lessons so soon?"

Stefan grinned and bowed. "There were extenuating circumstances, my lady."

The lady glanced back at Arian, and said, "I cannot wait to hear the tale. But first your wounds must be tended and the lady bathed and clothed."

When they entered the hall, Arian gasped in surprise. Compared to the forebidding exterior, it was beautiful. Large, intricate wrought-iron sconces lined both sides of the long stone walls, and in between them large colorful tapestries adorned the walls. Suspended from thick oak ceiling beams in the middle of the hall, a huge round black iron candelabrum with intricate scrollwork hung, adorned with scores of blazing candles. There was a large fireplace built into the front end of the hall—it was cold—and at the far end another fireplace, easily twice the size of the forward one. Above it hung an ornate standard, a golden dragon on a sapphire field, and beside it hung another standard, one of a gruesome white skull with a sword plunging through it, on a black field, crimson drops of blood dripping from it, but in between both was the standard of two golden lions on a scarlet field.

Arian stiffened and halted. She looked to Lady Tarian and Stefan who walked with them.

" 'Tis the lion of Normandy. Why does it fly here?"

"My husband, Lord Wulfson, is William's trusted vassal. Why should it not?"

Arian's jaw dropped. So she was not Stefan's lady? Then her eyes narrowed as a startling realization stung her. She looked hard at Stefan, who stood tall and all too arrogant before her. *Why did she not see it?* All Normans were killers with more arrogance than any other men on earth! "You are not Saxon!" she accused.

"I never said I was."

"But you—you led me to believe it was so!"

He shook his head." 'Tis what you wanted to believe, so I allowed you."

She looked to the lady. "How could you marry a Norman?"

Lady Tarian smiled tolerantly. "My mother is Welsh and my sire Saxon. I married my Norman husband because I could not survive another day without him."

"Why did you flee from the Norman knights?" Arian asked Stefan.

He eased against the hearth. Deep pain lines etched his face. "Ralph du Forney would have snatched you for his own pleasure, and you, dear princess, would not command the high ransom I demand if you were no longer a virgin."

Arian strode to where he stood and struck him with her open palm upon on his good cheek. Lady Tarian gasped, as did the servants who bustled by. Stefan grabbed her by the wrists and yanked her hard to his chest. "Does the truth bother you?" he ground out.

"You are heartless, Sir Stefan, and I would expect nothing less from a Norman." She spat to the floor.

"If I were heartless, you would have been raped at the hands of your guard. Do not talk to me of what I cannot do. You are in no position to order."

Arian yanked her hands from his grasp. "Do not touch my person again."

His eyes had darkened to the color of a moonless sky. His nostrils flared, and she could see the muscles work in his jaw. "So, as a Norman I am completely beneath you?"

"As a common bastard you are beneath me. As a Norman you are not fit to breathe the same air I breathe!" Arian whirled and faced the lady of the manor. "What of your husband? Does he play the same despicable games as his brethren?"

Lady Tarian smiled tolerantly.

"Do not ask questions that do not concern you, princess," Stefan bit off. He turned to Lady Tarian and said, "Milady, once I have bathed and Edith has seen to this face of mine, we will talk more."

"I never should have allowed Wulfson to insist I stay here to defend Draceadon! I should have been by his side!" Lady Tarian burst out. Her fingers played with the hilt of the broadsword that hung from her leather belt.

Stefan placed a hand upon her shoulder. " 'Twas a slaughter, Tarian, you would be buzzard food. 'Twas the right choice to make. Those craven Welsh and that crazed Edric have been scourging all of Herefordshire. You are safer here, and 'tis what Wulf would want above all else."

Lady Tarian choked back a sob, and turned from them to what looked to be the lord's chair by the great hearth, leaving Stefan and Arian alone. He cast a glance down at her and scowled. Arian scowled back. "I do not appreciate being lied to, Sir Stefan. Is there anything else you wish to tell me?"

"Nay," he said, and strode from her to Tarian, where they shared a few words before he moved past her and through an archway, then disappeared.

Lady Tarian rose slowly from the chair, her eyes misty and far off. Arian knew that look; she had seen it a hundred times on her father's face. 'Twas the haunted look of one who had lost their beloved. Trancelike she turned to Arian, and softly said, "Forgive me my manners. I worry for my husband and his brothers." She motioned toward the wide stone stairway. "Come, allow me to show you to the lady's solar, where you may bathe and rest. I will send fresh clothes and a tray for you."

Stubbornly, Arian hesitated not wanting to accept this woman's hospitality. She was a hostage. Was she expected to walk behind her like a leashed lamb? Happy for a morsel? Arian cast a furtive glance over her shoulder to the far door to the hall. It swung open wide, and Norman and Saxon knights filled the great hall like locusts on the wheat fields.

Arian spun around. A hot bath, fresh food, and clean clothes did not seem such a bad thing after all. The chamber was open and airy, and the bed large. "Here is Annis; she will tend you until your own maid arrives," Lady Tarian said as a girl of no more than fourteen entered the chamber.

When the lady turned to leave, Arian called out to her, "A word, please."

Slowly she turned.

"I would know the true character of Sir Stefan."

Fine dark brows knitted in confusion. " 'Tis above reproach."

"I would not know it by his actions."

"Nor have you walked in his boots. He has seen horrors we could never imagine."

"He is a liar and a knave!"

Lady Tarian shook her head. "You will come to under-stand Stefan in time, should he allow you to. There are few men such as he. You are fortunate he was close by."

Arian nodded, and for the moment, her fears were allayed. But she would be wary of this beautiful half-Welsh lady married to a vicious Norman lord, and all whom she called friend.

"Did Cadoc say which direction they traveled?" Arian asked, stepping closer to the lady. "I implore you, send word to him on my behalf. I will reward you with gold! My sire and my betrothed will also reward you."

Lady Tarian shook her head and moved toward the door. "Your fate is not in my hands." And soundly she closed it behind her.

THIRTEEN

W hat have you done, Stefan?" Tarian demanded, barging into the small chamber down the hall from her own. He winced as Edith bit off the last stitch she had resewn. He did not know what balms she concocted, but the right side of his face had gone completely numb before she began her repair. A much-welcomed respite from the last week of pain.

He looked tiredly up at Wulfson's lady. "What *have* I done?"

"Aye, what have you done indeed? She is a princess, for God's sake! A royal Dinefwr!"

He scowled.

"Ah! Do not look at me so, I did not mean you are not worthy of her, but she is betrothed!"

Stefan laughed, and dragged his fingers through his hair. "I asked Wulfson the same thing about you."

Her face crumbled at the mention of his name. She grabbed his hands and sat down beside him on the short bench. "Tell me of my husband. Tell me all."

Edith moved from them, giving them privacy. Stefan

took a long, deep breath, then exhaled. "We were out-numbered. The battle was lost before it began."

"Why then did you engage?"

Stefan's head snapped back and looked hard at her. "Normans do not turn tail!"

"Aye, God forbid your pride should suffer!"

" 'Twas not like that, Tarian. We had the cavalry, we had the castle, we had the archers. Once we had engaged, we had to send more men onto the field, or it would have been a complete slaughter."

"Where are the Blood Swords?"

"All but myself and Rhys, whom I have not yet found, reside in the dungeons of your dear ex-uncle Rhiwallon."

"He would slay Wulfson!"

"He may wish to, but he has grander plans."

"Tell me!"

"I overheard a Welshman speak of your uncle's glee in capturing six of the Blood Swords. He means to taunt William with their lives."

"He will only bring the wrath of Normandy upon his head!"

"Aye, but he does not seem to care. Methinks he will use them as leverage to keep us from his borders and, I suspect, to make a treaty on behalf of Edric."

"For what?"

"Herefordshire."

"William will not give it up!"

Stefan smiled slowly. "Rhiwallon is wily, to be sure, but I have a golden snare."

Tarian sat silent for a long moment as his words penetrated her mind. "How came you by the princess?"

Stefan grinned and told her, leaving out the more intimate details of their encounter.

Tarian smiled knowingly. She knew him too well.

"What do you plan to do with her, Stefan?"

He grinned wider. "Fate delivered her into my arms. We must use her wisely."

"I understand your fascination with the lady, but my concern is how to restore my husband and your brothers."

"The answer lies abed just down the hall. A princess for the Blood Swords."

Tarian gasped. " 'Tis brilliant!" Just as quickly, her brows knitted together in thought. "How do you know they will trade for the princess?"

"She is to meet and marry Magnus, a great jarl of Norway, Olaf's cousin in Yorkshire. Olaf, milady, is Thorin's half-brother. The Norse desire allies to the west. 'Twill put William in the middle. Give Olaf his brother, Magnus his bride, and William the Blood Swords."

"And what for my loving uncles?"

Stefan laughed low, "A king's ransom, and a most gracious alliance with the Norse that they so desperately desire, and William's gratitude."

"And you think the princess is the answer?"

He nodded. "I am sure of it. As you heard, she is the daughter of Prince Hylcon of Carmarthenshire, and her mother Branwen is blood aunt to Rhiwallon. Arian is his cousin. For his blood, he will make the trade, for if he does not, he will not only find an enemy in Hylcon and Magnus but we both know how vindictive William can be. 'Tis a combined fight Rhiwallon does not want, and one he cannot win."

"How will you orchestrate this?"

"Dispatch your swiftest messenger now. Instruct him to find the captain Cadoc and give word of his lady here, but give no other information. He will come running. When they arrive, offer the hospitality of Draceadon. Once inside the gates they will be disarmed, and guards set to watch that they do not make trouble. We allow the princess to see her man, but not speak privately. Once he is assured she is safe and no harm has come to her, he, along with Gareth, will go to Rhiwallon and offer our terms."

"And you will give her up?"

Stefan's head snapped back and his eyes narrowed. "Of course. Why would I not?"

Tarian smiled a knowing smile. He shook his head. "Nay, 'tis not like that. Besides, even if I desired the maid, you saw her dislike for my station. I would see her gone from here and married to her Viking as soon as possible."

"There is more, Stefan," she said quietly.

"There can never be any more, and not with my brothers' lives at stake!"

Tarian pushed. "Would you see her to her betrothed?"

Stefan's heart lurched against his chest. "Nay."

"A Norman escort would not be a bad thing."

"Nay, when the trade is made I will return to Normandy."

Stefan stood and moved past Tarian. Turmoil swirled in his belly. The thought of never seeing the princess again roiled with his emotions. He did not like the feelings. "We must send word immediately to Hylcon," he said, moving past the subject of the princess.

"He will bring an army here!"

"Nay, he will send it to his dead wife's cousin, who holds the key to his daughter's safety."

She grabbed his hands. "Think of what I just proposed, Stefan. Promise the Welsh a full Norman garrison, take Ralph and his men with you, as well as the Blood Swords, to see the princess safely to her betrothed. Allow her men and those of my uncle to accompany you. Do you think for one moment they will attempt another crossing in this war-torn land? With such a show of power, promise her safely delivered as part of the bargain"

"Do you think the Welsh so foolish to think she will be safe in Norman hands? What would prevent them from thinking we would demand another ransom?"

"A guarantee. A hostage. A person the Blood Swords value highly, and because of that would be sure the exchange was made."

Stefan scowled. "Who?"

"I would give myself to Rhiwallon as hostage."

"Nay! 'Tis too risky. He would keep you! Wulfson would never permit it!"

" 'Tis logical. Strike the deal, and when the Blood Swords cross the border into England I will pass to their right into Wales. My uncle will not harm me, of this I am sure. If the men are able to ride to Yorkshire with you, so be it. Upon your return and that of the lady's captain bearing Magnus's seal that he is delivered of his bride and wed, I will be released."

"I do not like it."

"Nor do I, but there is no other way." She turned to

look up at him. "Stefan, what if they act as if they are in agreement, but choose to attack us here and take the lady back by force?"

Stefan's face tightened, the memories of the bloody battlefield erupting in his mind's eye. "Many Welsh and Saxon were lost at Hereford, my lady; the rest scourge north. With Ralph's men and your garrison, we have a sufficient army to repel them. I will send William a message immediately, and if the tides are in our favor he will know soon enough. He will be sending more men to fortify Herefordshire as it is. And if we are attacked? With the fortifications you and Wulf have made, and full stores, we will be able to wait them out."

Tarian nodded, the deal struck.

Arian woke with a start, sitting up in the darkened room. Where was she? Immediate realization hit her. Draceadon. A hostage. She glanced across the wide expanse of the bed. Soft snores from the other side filled the room. Squinting in the low light, she could barely make out the soft silhouette of the lady Brighid curled up in a ball, slumbering soundly beside her maid. More snores filtered up from the foot of the bed, no doubt the girl Annis on the pallet there on the floor.

And with that recognition more realization crashed in her head. Stefan! For a long moment Arian sat there in the bed, the only light the soft glow of the candle on the table beside her. Her stomach made low roaring sounds. She swallowed and winced. Her throat was dry and despite the small meal she had eaten earlier, she was now famished. Hunger drove her to move from the bed, but more than that, her desire to extract from the Norman knight her fate. He as well as the lady of the manor had been tight-lipped. Fear gnawed at her. Had Stefan lied to her? Had his plans changed? Would she ever see her betrothed?

Arian slipped from the bed, and quickly pulled a borrowed tunic over her soft chemise. As she carefully opened the heavy door she stopped all movement. A large guard snored at the threshold. Peeking up and down the well-lit hall, she lifted one leg then the other over him, and hurried down to the hall.

As she moved silently down the wide stairway, Arian could see the hall slept. At the far end gray shadows outlined scores of men, sprawled out on pallets. At the base of the stone stairway, she stood silent for a long moment, debating whether to return to her chamber or brave the kitchen for food. Her hunger held sway. The warmth of the low-burning hearth drew her like a moth to a flame. Silently she walked to it. There was an alcove just beyond that led to a hall that most likely led to the outer kitchens, and, she realized, to escape!

" 'Tis not wise to be about the hall at this late hour, milady," a deep male voice said from behind her.

Slowly Arian turned, and though the tall Norman was several paces from her, his blue eyes glittered with a predatory gleam. Fear coiled tightly in her belly. He bowed, sweeping his arm across his chest, then stood. When he smiled, the hair on the back of her nape spiked. "I am Ralph du Forney, heir to the great lordship of de Lyon. I am at your service."

Regally, Arian nodded her head, acknowledging him. "You speak English well, sir."

He smiled again, and stepped closer. "I am well traveled and spent much time in Edward's court."

Arian moved a step back for each step he took toward her. "You have nothing to fear from me, milady. I can assure you I am not the savage my cousin is."

"Your cousin?"

"Aye, that knave de Valrey. He has the manners of a boar."

"Stefan is your cousin?" she stuttered in disbelief. He was a bastard mercenary.

"Unfortunately, he is."

"But—I thought he was a bastard?"

"In heart and soul and name, he is. And though my uncle Robert refuses to acknowledge him, he is the mirror image of that great lord."

"Who bore him?" She asked still not believing the Norman.

Ralph chuckled softly and moved in closer. She had only the wall to offer her refuge. "Ah, that is the great mystery. Some say 'twas the Duke's own sister-in-law, Alyce. But if that were true, she being a married woman, her husband would have grounds for divorce, would he not?"

Arian looked harder at the man, and for the first time realized that while his blue eyes were not nearly as brilliant as Stefan's, they were much the same. The information slowly sank in, and as it did, shame filled her at her treatment of him.

The news stunned her. He was a noble! But she should have realized it, for as much as he spoke of his humble heritage, he spoke as a noble, he carried himself with the confidence of one, and though he had the hardness of a mercenary, he knew well how to handle himself in a way that bespoke of courtly life.

Ralph touched her shoulder, his fingers sliding across the lock of hair that rested against her breast. She slapped his hand away. "Do not touch me, sir!"

"I but admire you, milady." He moved in closer and inhaled her scent. "You smell sweet." He pressed the palm of his hand to her breast. Arian twisted away from him.

"You are too bold, sir! I am spoken for, and even were I not, I give you no permission to touch me so!"

"But you allow a bastard to pant atop you?"

Arian gasped. "You speak untruths." And despite it, her anger seethed not at the insult to herself, but to Stefan. She stepped toward the arrogant Norman. "And even had I, *noble* sir, your bastard cousin for all of his faults is five times the man you could ever hope to be! Do not slander him in my presence again. Now, be gone before I scream so loud the entire shire will come running to my defense!"

Ralph threw his head back and laughed. Arian wanted to strike him. He sobered and looked closely at her. "He has gotten to you too? 'Tis his way, milady, he is the master of seduction. He leaves a trail of broken hearts and bastards littered from one end of the continent to the other. He will do the same to you."

Ralph's words struck deep. A sickening feeling, like poison, spilled into her heart. Ralph moved closer. "I do not tell you this to slander but to warn. His heart is black with hatred of women."

Arian's fury mounted. "Are you so ignoble yourself, Sir Ralph, that you would have me lift my skirts here and now for your amusement?"

"Nay, fair lady, I would woo you as a lady of your station is due." He reached out again to touch her, and when he did the unmistakable sound of a sword sliding from a scabbard sliced through the quiet.

"Touch her, Ralph, and you will find your innards on the floor," Stefan said, emerging from the shadows.

"Do not challenge me, cousin. You will lose," Ralph growled.

Stefan glanced at Arian, making sure she was not injured, then gave his full attention to his cousin. He pressed the tip of his sword to the man's chest. "As wounded as I am, you are no match for me. If you would like to prove otherwise"—Stefan stepped back and pointed to the sword in Ralph's belt—"draw your steel and let us clear this up here and now."

Ralph's fingers toyed with the hilt of his sword, his eyes narrowed to slits, and a twisted smile played upon his lips. "When I lay you low there will be more to witness it than the lady." He bowed to her, then turned on his heel and stalked back toward the front of the hall.

Stefan sheathed his sword, then held out his hand to her, palm up, an invitation for her to take it. Instinctively her hand twitched, wanting to touch him, to place her hand in his, and to trust him. But she resisted. To touch him again, she feared she would succumb to more if he pressed her.

"I will not bite you, Arian," Stefan said softly.

She looked up into his somber eyes for a long moment before she placed her hand into his. His long warm fingers closed gently around hers, and he drew her farther away from the hall to the small alcove just beyond. When they stopped, she withdrew her hand

and squarely faced him, a tumult of emotions sparring in her chest.

Despite all she had learned of the man before her, Arian had warmed first at the deep, familiar timbre of his voice and second, to his gentle touch. The feeling angered her. "Would you slay your own cousin? Is violence your answer to every misdeed?" Whirling away, she moved to the edge of the deep alcove. He did things to her heart and body she did not understand, and, moreover, did not like.

He came to stand close behind her, so close she could feel the heat radiate from his body, and she could smell the clean manly scent of him. 'Twas of spice and sandalwood. She closed her eyes and set her jaw, warding off the warmth he stirred in her.

"That is the second time you have chastised me for preserving your virtue." The soft percussion of his breath when he spoke caressed her ear.

She straightened her back. "You are wicked," she breathed.

"Aye, I am more wicked than you will ever know, princess."

She whirled around and caught her breath. His cobalt-blue eyes burned hot and bright under the low light of the wall sconces, and she noticed his wounded face had been tended. And tended well. There was no swelling and the redness had gone. The stitches were clean and neat. Without realizing what she did, Arian raised her hand to his cheek. He grabbed it and squeezed.

"I wish you no harm!" she cried out. Immediately he dropped her hand.

"Nor I you, so to that end do not touch me."

Confused, Arian demanded, "Do I repulse you now?"

"Nay," he said softly. "You forget, I have seen all that God gave you the day you were born." He moved a step closer. "I have touched you in a way only a lover true should. The memories stir fire in my loins."

Heat flushed her cheeks at his admission, and she felt it deepen when she envisioned him as she first saw him. Tall, muscular—hard. "As I have seen you, sir," she whispered, not trusting her voice. Her knees quivered and her fingers twitched. A familiar warmth spread from her belly to other body parts. She realized it was a feeling unique to her proximity to the man before her.

He grinned, and Arian almost mirrored it. The gesture lit up his austere face, humanizing his demon features to handsome.

"Aye, you did, and a most unusual introduction was ours."

Ralph's words of Stefan's amorous affairs prickled at her. "Have you seen many women as you saw me?" Arian bit her bottom lip, embarrassed she spoke what was on her mind.

Stefan's smile widened. He reached out a hand to touch a lock of her hair. "If I am honest, I would say too many to count."

Indignant, she gasped, but he moved a little closer, and brushed the tendril from her cheek. "But if I am truly honest, I will admit, I have never beheld such perfection as I did that morn."

More heat spread through her veins at the knight's bold confession. And though she had never been a woman who looked for compliments, she found his most welcome. And knowing that he made her feel as warm as if she were wrapped in furs in front of a roaring fire, Arian knew she played a game she was not permitted to. She was betrothed to a good man, and not only would her honor not allow her to dally again with the demon Norman, her heart could not bear the burden of loving him.

Swallowing hard, Arian moved to a safer distance.

Stefan shrugged and reached past her to a small table there, and filled two goblets with wine. He handed her a cup and took a long draught from his own. He drained it and set it down on the small table. "Drink up, milady, and I will see you back to your room. As you just witnessed, 'tis not safe for you at this late hour with so many men about."

Stefan offered his arm, and when she placed her tiny hand upon his skin, heat flared. His groin tightened, and he fought the battle that raged within him. As they mounted the stairway, Arian's sweet scent played with his senses. Dirty, she had been beautiful; clean and garbed in rich clothes that fit, she glowed with ethereal beauty. He fondled the hilt of his sword, wanting a release. Arian looked up at Stefan, and asked, "How did you know I was in the hall?"

"You are under lock and key, milady; my man came to my chamber to alert me of your movement."

"But he was snoring!"

"A ruse."

As they approached her door, he maneuvered her against the wall near a sconce. The flame burned nowhere near as brightly as her eyes. "Beware, Arian. There is nowhere for you to hide, and if you should manage to slip past the guard, you will find more to fear outside the castle walls than here within them."

"What are your plans for me?"

He placed a hand on either side of her head, against the stone. "At the moment, my plan is to steal a kiss."

"How many women have you seduced, then left with child?"

Stefan started, her outburst halting him. "What kind of question is that?"

"One to which I would like an answer!"

He grinned and lowered his head to hers. His eyes trailed across her heaving bosom, the nipples taut beneath the thin fabric. He fought the urge to press his lips there. Instead, he lowered his lips to hover just above hers. "I do not keep count."

"You are a lout," she breathed.

"Aye, a lout who cannot help himself." His lips brushed across hers, her breath warm against his cheeks. When she did not resist, his body swelled. He kissed her again, deepening it. Her soft lips parted beneath his. Stefan moved closer, his chest brushing against her full breasts; he smiled against her lips when her silvery eyes widened. Gently, he pressed her back into the wall. He kept his hands off her, knowing if he touched her he would want more than he did now.

But when she pressed her hands against his chest, then slid them up and around his neck, he grasped her to him. She moaned softly, capitulating, and he took full advantage. Starved for her, he kissed her hard and deep. Thoughts of her naked and willing beneath him swirled in his mind, of hearing her cries of pleasure as he thrust into her, firing his blood.

Frustration mingled with lust was not a good combination. As if reading his thoughts Arian pushed away from him. He peered hard at her, wanting her more. She was a vision of all things innocent and carnal. Her hair cascaded in wild disarray about her face and shoulders, her pink lips were full and swollen from his kiss, her silvery eyes dark with desire, her breasts, *Jesu*! How his hands ached to caress them, rising and falling in quick shallow gasps.

"Arian . . ."

She shook her head, ducked under his arms, and pushed open the heavy door before slamming it soundly in his face.

He stared at it for long moments, while conflicting emotions crashed in his head. "*Jesu!*" What was wrong with him? He swore to her and himself he was done, but just the thought of her had him crawling back like a whipped dog to his master.

"Bah!" he said, throwing up his hands. She was just a woman, one of thousands. He would find refuge in more willing thighs.

He strode angrily to his chamber down the hall from hers, to the guard there. "See to the lady's door!" he bit off, flung open the door, then slammed it shut. He flung the bolt and stripped naked.

For more candle notches than not he lay naked on his back with his hands behind his head, staring at the ceiling, painfully aroused. His frustration and worry over his brothers, his disgust at himself for allowing them to be captured, wrangled in a wild tussle with his lust for the woman beyond the stone walls of his chamber.

He made to roll over but the pressure on his thigh

was too much. When he flung himself onto his back, his cock slapped against the smooth linens. He groaned louder, gritting his teeth, resisting the urge to relieve the pain in his groin. He wanted her gone, married to the Viking, away from his sight. Away from his senses. Away from his thoughts. Then she could be forgotten.

But the vision of her golden thighs and plump breasts toyed with him. He could almost feel her soft fragrant skin beneath his rough fingertips. He wanted to press his lips between her thighs and taste her honeyed sweetness. He wanted— *God's blood!* If it were his choice, he would ease himself between those golden thighs and end the craving of his body for hers.

He bit down on his jaw so hard he feared his teeth would crack. At his limit, he squeezed his eyes shut and grabbed that demon between his thighs.

FOURTEEN

Arian spent the next two days under heavy guard. At every turn, she was met with a wide mailed chest and a scowling Saxon. She was permitted freedom in her chamber, the hall, and, under very heavy guard, the courtyard for a stroll. She seemed to be quite an oddity amongst the churls. Each time she stepped outside the hall, they would gather in small groups and stare at her. Several attempts to bribe servants to aide her in her escape were discovered. Her punishment? She was forbidden to speak to all servants save Annis. Arian could not put her anger and frustration into words, so volatile was she. She felt like the caged tiger she had once seen when a traveling circus passed through Dinefwr many years ago. The animal paced the small barred cage, growling at any person who ventured too close. Even his master stayed clear of the sharp teeth and claws.

And try as she might to engage the lady of the manor and her sister Lady Brighid in conversation, they tried just as hard to avoid her. 'Twas only at mealtimes they were forced to converse, and she found them most unwilling to offer a word. But even more than their reticence, Arian found Stefan's distance most annoying. Nay, more than annoying. 'Twas unbearable. He was her only familiar in this hostile land. By nature she was a social creature, craving interaction. She watched him move about, clad in noble garb, his limp nearly gone, his face healing. He cut a most handsome figure. But there was a haughty reserve about him that intrigued her more than his handsome face and powerful body. He did not commingle with his countrymen, he did not chatter nor did he partake in games of chess or dice. He kept mostly to himself, his brilliant eyes sharp and observant.

Several times she found his brooding stare upon her, and when she smiled, he scowled, then stalked off as if she committed a grave offence against his person. 'Twas only when the beautiful Lady Tarian or her guard Gareth approached him that he seemed to relax.

His easy camaraderie with the lady disturbed her on a most basic level, and though she knew the lady's heart belonged only to her husband, Arian sensed the deep regard she had for Sir Stefan.

The more Stefan stayed away, the more Arian wanted his attention. A word, a soft gesture. Acknowledgment that she was more to him than a pawn in his deadly game.

His Norman cousin Ralph, however, was not so reticent. Nor was his lap dog Sir Philip. At each turn, she found one or both of them lurking nearby. At the lord's table, one of them always found his way to her, and she detested sharing a trencher with either. Whenever she cast a glance at Stefan, he was otherwise engaged in conversation. Yet it seemed whenever Sir Ralph became too familiar, the guard Gareth or, most reluctantly, Stefan would steer the bold Norman away.

So Arian spent endless hours sitting in the bustling hall, her head obediently bent over her embroidery, her eyes and ears open and ever vigilant, hoping for an opportunity to slip quietly from the hall and make her escape.

As it happened, on the third morning Arian found herself quite alone in the hall after the noon meal. From beneath her lashes she saw that the main doors to the hall were crowded with churls and knights. She cast her gaze toward the small alcove off the hall and frowned. More men. She was not as alone as she thought. Her frustration wore hard on her nerves. Stefan's avoidance and his reluctance to discuss the terms of her release frustrated her beyond reason. She had a right to know her fate! She had a right to expect something, *anything*, from him in the way of news. He would not tell her even if a messenger had been sent after Cadoc.

She stood from the chair she sat in and tossed her sampler into the fire. As the flames gobbled it up, she turned to the stairway and looked up. She would go to Stefan's chamber, await his return, then demand he disclose his plans to her. But as she pushed the heavy door open, she realized she had no leverage. What could she threaten him with? His life? Hers? Take Lady Brighid as a hostage and threaten her bodily harm should he not release her? Arian laughed at the absurdity. She could no more inflict pain on the girl than take her own life, and Stefan knew it.

The moment she entered the room, his manly scent engulfed her. The strength of it halted her in her tracks.

Even gone from the room, Stefan dominated it. Quietly she closed the door and leaned her back against it. Closing her eyes, she stood still, allowing his essence to fill her. Sandalwood mingled with leather, and then there was his unique scent she could never, as long as she lived, forget. It haunted her in her dreams, it called to her now. Her limbs warmed, and her nipples tightened with just the merest image of him in her mind.

Arian's belly slowly tumbled. Her life was in the hands of a single Norman. What would he demand for her return? Land? Gold? A title? Had he dispatched a rider to locate Cadoc? A messenger to her father? What of Magnus? Would he demand riches from him as well? Was she truly just a means to accumulate a fortune?

Stefan was a man without possessions, a man without a name; of course he would use her to gain what he so desperately wanted. 'Twould raise his byblow status. All of his careful tending of her when she raged with fever was not because he cared for her, but to secure his future! Thoughts tumbled wildly in her head, and Arian realized at that exact moment she had created a rosy image of the man who gave no thought for her but only for himself. She was a fool to soften for him as she had!

Angrily she moved to the middle of the room, wondering what she would say to him once confronted. He did not care for her, she had no leverage. Why did she bother? *Because*, a small but defiant voice said from the very depths of her soul, *he is a man like no other, and you cannot stay away.*

Arian inhaled sharply, then slowly exhaled. A noise, then a deep voice from the hall startled her. Stefan! She turned to face him, but another voice caught her attention. Lady Tarian! What would she think of her—a princess awaiting a bastard Norman in his chamber? Panic overcame her. But just as quickly it flew. 'Twas a perfect opportunity! She would hide and listen, and learn.

After a quick scan of the room, she saw that there was no place to hide! The bed was too low to the ground. There was no furniture to hide behind. She darted to the tapestry hanging on the wall and slipped behind it, praying neither would look down and see her silk-slippered feet.

The door opened. "Tarian, this is not necessary. I can see to the stitches myself!"

"Hush and drop your chauses."

" 'Tis not decent!"

"Then you should have allowed Edie the chore."

"That old woman prattles on and I have no patience for it."

"Sit, then, and let me do it."

Arian heard a grunt of resignation, followed by the sound of Stefan moving about the room.

Lady Tarian snickered and said, "Would you have me call your princess? Would that get you undressed any faster?"

"She is not *my* princess!"

"So you keep saying."

"I may be many things, milady, but I am not a man to dishonor a lady betrothed."

"But if she were not?"

Arian held her breath and waited a long moment for Stefan's response. "A dalliance at most. You know I have no yearning for more."

His words stung. Did he think so little of her?

"Wulfson thought the same thing, and look at him now? Heavy with the chains of matrimony dragging down his every step."

"Milady, please would you cease this talk? I have no yearning for a wife."

"Not even one with hides of green pastures for your horses?"

He chuckled low. "Now, with that as part of the package, I may be persuaded to take on that yoke."

"Ah, so your true heart's desire rests with the destriers?"

"Aye, and in that the princess will see my dream come true. With the money I will demand from her husband and her sire, I will purchase my land."

The sound of him unhitching his sword belt, followed by another grunt as he no doubt untied his legging, then the sound of him sitting on the bench not more than one pace from her, caused Arian's heart to beat so hard in her chest her noon meal churned in her belly.

"It has knitted nicely. How does it feel?"

"Still sore but strong."

The scrape of the stool was so close, Arian feared to breathe lest she be heard. "You will only feel a pinch or two."

"Just be done with it. I plan to ride to Dunloc today and offer more gold for word of Rhys."

"Aye, Brighid is beside herself with worry."

" 'Tis for naught. He will not wed her."

"Why do you say such a thing, Stefan?"

"He has nothing to offer. He is young still. By the time his fortune is made, she will be long married to a noble, with a half score of children."

"My foster father would never allow it, even if Rhys came with a title."

"Aye, 'tis the lot of a bastard is it not?"

"What of you, Stefan? What plans do you have?"

"Once the Blood Swords are delivered, I await my king's command."

A heavy sigh permeated the room. "Do you tire of warring?"

"Nay, 'tis my calling."

"Wulfson is the same."

"We all are, Tarian. It is as much a part of us as the scars we bear."

Another pensive sigh fluttered through the quiet of the room. Arian held her breath, afraid to breathe.

"There, 'tis done. The ones in your face can come out in a few days' time."

The creaking sound of the bench as it was relieved of Stefan's weight cued her to his movement. "My thanks, milady."

"You are most welcome, sir knight. I will take my leave, and if you have no objection I would ride to Dunloc with you."

"I take that knave of a cousin with me, and his constant shadow Philip. It would please me if you stayed here and kept watch. My hostage will bolt at first chance, and she is the key to all of our futures."

"Aye, I will see she does not fly."

Arian's blood fairly boiled, so angry was she. How dare he speak of her so casually after all they had shared?

The sound of the door opening startled her from her thoughts. And as the door slammed shut her heart hardened. She would find a way to escape this place, and in so doing take the arrogant knight's hopes and dreams with her. She was no mewing lovelorn maid. Nay, she was Princess Arianrhod, daughter of Hylcon, and she would no longer stand to be treated with anything less than her due!

She flung the tapestry from her and strode into the room, then abruptly stopped. Stefan stood glaring at her from the threshold.

"Did you find what you were looking for, princess?" he casually asked. But his eyes were narrowed and sharp, belying the tone. She strode toward him and slapped him with all her might on his wounded cheek. He did not so much as flinch. She raised her hand to slap him again, but this time he caught her before she could do more damage.

He yanked her hard against his chest. "Did you not like what you heard?"

"You are not fit to feed the swine much less touch my person! Release me now, you black-hearted bastard!"

He did not. He pushed her hard against the wall, his fingers digging deep into her hair, disrupting the intricate braidwork. "I was good enough to save your virtue not once but twice. I was good enough to save your life, but because you cannot stand the truth, I am now not good enough to touch you?"

"I hate you!"

He laughed and lowered his head. "Do you really?" he mocked.

"With my heart and soul."

"Prove it." Then his lips crushed against hers and Arian realized he would know she lied.

FIFTEEN

Though she fought him, Stefan felt her body soften. The soft rush of her breath against his cheek when he raked his lips down the smooth column of her throat to the bend of her neck and shoulder. The way her breasts plumpened beneath his hands. The breathless moan of a woman whose body wanted more than a token caress.

His body swelled in response, his cock thickened, his breaths as hard and forced as hers. Sliding his hand down her waist to her hips, he pressed into her, and she did not resist. Heat flared in his loins, desire slammed through him like a sword. He would go mad if he did not have all of her.

In handfuls, he pulled up her kirtle and chemise beneath it. When his rough hand pressed to the silky smoothness of her thigh, they both moaned. His lips broke from hers, their breaths hot and moist. He opened his eyes and his heart leapt into his throat. Her silvery eyes blazed molten. He slid his hand up higher, his gaze never breaking hers. He could feel the sultry moistness of her, waiting, wanting.

He had gone too far, lured too deep into her seductive waters, but he could not stop himself. Arian pressed her hips against him and Stefan groaned. Unable to control himself he brushed his fingertips across her moist lips.

Arian's lips parted when she gasped, her eyes closed, the vision of her submission spurred him. Stefan closed his eyes, savoring the moment, and sank a finger gently into her. He felt the air leave her body as she melted into him. He pulled her tighter against him, and his lips found hers. In a slow circular slide, he moved his finger in and out of her hot wetness. In wicked undulation, her hips followed him.

She grasped his shoulders and pressed closer to him, but he resisted pressing all the way into her. His lips broke from hers, and he fought the battle of his life when he resisted untying his braies and sinking his cock deep into her. He squeezed his eyes shut.

"Stefan." She gasped for breath. "My body aches as if a fever consumes me."

He pulled her close and withdrew his finger from her. "Nay," she cried out. He smiled down at her but did not release her completely. Nay, he could not. He brushed his fingertips across her stiffened mound. Arian gasped again, wide-eyed, in wonder. He swallowed hard. "There is more than one way to bring the body to release, Arian," he whispered into her ear. He pressed more firmly against her and moved his fingers in a steady quick fashion. He clenched his jaw as her wetness increased and her body tightened.

He kissed her parted lips, his tongue swirling against hers as a hard wave of passion overcame them both. She cried out, but his kisses silenced it for his ears only. Her body spasmed and jerked and he felt her go liquid in his hand. Slow and easy, he rode out her release with his fingers, and when she was done he felt her knees weaken. He scooped her up into his arms, her limp body hanging, her chest rising and falling in a quick staccato, her eyes closed.

The sight of her stirred something deep and primal; but more than that, a wild possessiveness rose in his heart. When her eyes fluttered open and he saw the raw desire still lingering, he moved her to the bench, gently sat her down, then moved away from her.

He turned halfway to the door but an invisible string yanked him back. She half-reclined on the low bench, her face flushed, lips full and parted, her clothing disheveled. He set his jaw, fighting the devil in him that wanted to finish what he had started.

"Do not come near me again, Arian, for I cannot promise that I can resist my desire for you the next time." He turned and moved as quickly from the room as his legs would carry him.

Once at the end of the narrow hallway, Stefan stopped to collect himself. His body burned, his heart thudded like a smith's hammer in his chest, and his mind raced crazy with wild reckless thoughts of carrying her off to a secret place and making love to her until the world forgot about them both. He threw his head back, clenching his hands so tightly his nails bit into his skin, fighting the urge to yell out his frustration to the world.

"Stefan?" Tarian asked, slowly approaching him from the stairway. "What is wrong?"

He let out a long breath and slowly unfisted his hands and looked at her. "Nothing."

She looked past him, knowing what he would not say. "Riders approach, Stefan. They fly the colors of Dinefwr."

"The lady is in my chamber. Send Brighid to watch her." He moved past her gaping face and hurried down the stairway, glad for the interruption. "Call the guard to arms!" Stefan shouted as he hurried into the hall.

"Gareth and Ralph are positioned in the courtyard," Tarian answered, catching up to him.

Brighid rose from the chair in front of the hearth. Tarian pulled her aside and had a private word with her. The girl's eyes widened as she looked to Stefan. He scowled heavily at her. She swallowed hard and hurried past him. The vestiges of his frustration had not lessened. He took a moment to compose himself, grateful for Lady Tarian's silence. He turned to her and offered his arm. Together they strode out to the courtyard.

Gareth and his men, backed by Ralph and a full showing of his men, sat upon their destriers, mail-clad and lances down. Stefan nodded in approval. They had planned their reception of the Welsh and Norse down to the last horse.

As the red and gold boar standard of Dinefwr came into view, followed by the blue stag on a white field standard of Magnus the Tall, Stefan scowled. Emotions he did not want to acknowledge warred a vicious battle with his duty to his brothers. He pushed all thoughts of Arianrhod of Dinefwr aside. His only yearning, he told himself, was to see his brothers safely returned.

The captain of Arian's guard, Sir Cadoc, he presumed, galloped ahead of his men coming to an abrupt sliding halt before Gareth and Ralph in the courtyard.

Stefan strode toward him. "Disarm yourselves!" he called in Welsh.

Cadoc looked past the guard to Stefan. He watched dark eyes narrow behind his helm. "I demand to see my lady!"

Stefan continued toward the knight, and as he did the rest of his company followed closely, and though Stefan had complete trust in Tarian and her captain Gareth, 'twas not the same as knowing that his brothers had his back. Easily Stefan moved between Gareth and Ralph, and though he was at a disadvantage, he showed no fear. Indeed, he would gladly take on any man at the moment. Mayhap it would ease the fire in his blood.

"You will see your lady in good time, and that will depend on how quickly you and your men drop your weapons to the ground."

Cadoc looked past Stefan, hoping, Stefan was sure, to catch a glimpse of his lady. "I assure you, sir, she is alive and well. Disarm yourselves so that we may *parle* and proceed with the most urgent business at hand."

Wordlessly Cadoc dropped his sword, threw his bow and quiver of arrows and his dagger to the ground. His men, along with the Jarl's, followed suit. Once they were disarmed, Stefan said, "Now dismount and hand the reins over to my men."

Slowly they did so. Once divested of all but the clothing on their backs. "I demand to see my lady this instant!" Cadoc cried.

"Who here represents Magnus of Norway?" Stefan demanded, ignoring the Welshman.

The standard bearer stepped forward. In very broken Welsh, he said, "I am Sar, my lord Magnus's steward." He looked over his shoulder to a hulking blond giant who sneered at Stefan. "Sir Ivar, the late Lord Dag's captain, and his men."

Stefan nodded and looked past him to the other Norsemen, who stood with defiant sneers across their faces. "Are these men Lord Dag's?"

Sar bobbed his head, and said, "Most, sir, but several are from my lord's household."

To Cadoc Stefan said, "Come to the hall, sir captain." He turned to Sar. "And you as well. We have grave business to attend."

As they entered the hall, Arian came flying down the stairs, her face alight with happiness. "Cadoc!" she cried. As she came closer, Stefan grabbed her by the arm halting her before she met her man.

"Nay, princess, there is time for greetings *after* your man hears and agrees to my terms."

She yanked her arm from his grasp and stared hotly at him. Her cheeks pinkened when his gaze swept the length of her. He could not help it. At the first sound of her voice, his body responded, and he knew she too relived what had transpired such little time ago in his chamber.

Cadoc made a move toward them. Stefan's sword, as well as Lady Tarian's, stayed him. "Stand back, sir, or find your innards on the floor," Stefan warned. Cadoc's eyes bounced from Arian's to Stefan's but he stepped back.

"I seek only to learn my lady's welfare."

"As you can see, she lives and breathes." Stefan stood back, his eyes scanning the servants and townsfolk. "Be gone from the hall!" He turned back to Sar and Cadoc, motioning to the lord's table. "Sit, so that we may *parle*."

When Arian moved to sit beside her captain, Stefan drew her to his side and gently but firmly pushed her down on the bench, then took the seat to her right. Lady Tarian was to his right, Cadoc and Sar across the table, Gareth and Ralph, behind them. Once the hall was clear, he spoke. "Sir Cadoc, King Rhiwallon and his brother Bleddyn have something I want. Six of my fellow Norman knights. Your master, Prince Hylcon, and"—he looked at Sar—"your master Lord Magnus want something I have." He inclined his head to the princess. "My lord King William will be greatly vexed when he learns of his knights' capture. I am sure your respective masters will be greatly upset when they learn of the lady's capture. I therefore propose a trade. The lady for the knights."

Arian stiffened beside him.

"But, sir," Cadoc erupted, "why would Rhiwallon give up the knights for my lady?"

Stefan leaned forward. "Because if he does not, *your* master will come after him, Magnus of Norway will come after him, and my lord William will come after him, but not before I get a piece of him first."

Cadoc sat still for a moment, soaking it all in.

Arian cleared her throat. "If I may speak?"

Stefan nodded.

"When I accompanied my father to Dublin earlier this year for the great summit, emissaries from Denmark, Sweden, Wales, and Scotland attended, their sole concern Normandy." She looked hard at Stefan. "My betrothed spoke for the young king Olaf, just returned from Orkney. He spoke passionately of wanting peace with Normandy as well as all of England. Magnus has interests here in England as well, and desires only peace. 'Tis one of the reasons he chose me as a bride. He wishes no enemy of the Welsh." She swallowed, "But I suspect he wants no enemy of William more."

"What else was discussed?" Stefan asked, his curiosity piqued. 'Twas unusual that such magnates gathered on foreign soil to discuss peace.

"King Murchad of Dublin's pirates are more savage then the Vikings of yore. They cause much damage to the trade routes; my father has suffered great losses by their hands. Murchad needs allies to the east to squelch the uprisings in his own land, so a bargain was struck."

"Hah! 'Twas Irish pirates who destroyed my lord's fleet!" Sar said. " 'Twas not safe to return by longboat, so we had no choice but to cross England."

"It does not matter right now," Arian said. "With such concern for peace, my father and my betrothed will agree to any terms in an effort to stay the Conqueror's wrath."

"But Rhiwallon is stubborn! His hatred for William is deep," cried Lady Tarian. "*He* is the key! What if he does not relent?"

Stefan calmed her. "He will, with pressure from his cousin's husband to the west, William from the south and east and Magnus from the north. He will be squeezed until he releases them. He would be a fool not to. He cannot manage to stave off all of us."

Cadoc looked to Arian. "My lady? How dost thou fare?"

His question was not lost upon her.

"She is a virgin still, if that is what you mean," Stefan said harshly. And as he did, he watched both Cadoc and Sar breath a sigh of relief.

" 'Tis well, she is," Sar said. "For my lord Magnus would not take a sullied bride."

Arian coughed beside him, and when Stefan looked down at her, he saw that her cheeks had pinkened considerably. "I take my vows very seriously, Sir Sar. I am a virgin still."

"Be prepared to show proof. As this is a union of great significance and under such—questionable circumstances, my lord will demand an audience of witnesses."

Arian nodded. "I will do whatever my lord asks of me."

Stefan's hand fisted around the hilt of his sword.

"My lady?" Sar ventured.

Stefan felt the tightness in his belly, knowing the question that would follow, and he decided he would allow the princess to give the answer she wanted.

Arian nodded, and Stefan noticed the flush in her cheeks had flown.

"So that I am fully informed, please, tell me of Lord Dag's demise and your"—he dropped his eyes to the table before he looked to Stefan, then to Arian—"reason for being here."

Stefan felt Ralph's interest increase. Arian took a deep breath and slowly began, "As you know, I fell from my horse that day. And since we had been on the road for over a week I desired a bath. While Jane"—Arian's head snapped back. "What of Jane? Is she well, he did not harm her before he—"

"She is well, and on her way here with the other servants, the carts, and the livestock, my lady," Cadoc offered.

Arian expelled a long sigh of relief. "Whilst I bathed, Lord Dag approached me. I commanded him to leave. He refused. He was so bold as to touch my person. I broke from him and ran into the wood." Arian looked up into Stefan's gaze. "'Twas there, I— When Lord Dag further attempted to force himself upon me, Sir Stefan championed my honor. They fought, and Lord Dag lost."

"Why did you flee?" Cadoc demanded.

"Would you, sir, have given me quarter?" Stefan demanded.

"I—I would have—" Cadoc stuttered.

"Dag's man would have slain me where I stood. Besides, I knew then whom I had, and knew how she would be of use to me. My safety aside, 'twas for this exact purpose I fled with your lady. I am willing to return her, intact, for the lives of my brothers."

Arian's hands fisted, and he felt the hard tremble of her body beside him. He knew if he looked upon her face he would behold a storm. But 'twas better this way. Fate would see her married to her Viking, and he reunited with his brothers.

Sir Sar shook his head and looked solemnly up at Arian. "I fear, my lady, when milord Magnus learns of his nephew's death he will be greatly troubled."

Stefan pounded his fists on the table. "His anger will turn on the knave when he learns what he meant to do. I bear witness: Dag was of the lowest of character and was bent on breaching his uncle's betrothed for his own gain. If Magnus is a man of honor, he will see the maid had no hand in the events that followed."

Stefan stood and looked to Cadoc. "Quench your

hunger, for once you have, you will ride to your master with word of his daughter and our demands, whilst Gareth rides to Rhiwallon." He turned to Gareth. "Demand to see that my brothers live before you give Rhiwallon my demands." Stefan looked to Sar. "You will ride east to Yorkshire with word to Magnus."

Sir Sar bobbed his head, but looked as if he wished to speak. "Is there something else, sir?" Stefan demanded.

Sar bobbed his head again. "My lord Magnus will not be in Yorkshire for at least another month. 'Tis his cousin Lord Overly of Scarborough who he has asked to receive the lady and see to her welfare until his arrival. I will travel across the sea to my lord with all haste."

Ralph drew in a sharp breath. Stefan did not look up at him, but asked, "Lord Overly of Scarborough?"

"Aye, his Saxon kin by way of my lord's Saxon mother, Lady Rowena of Covington."

Anger coiled in Stefan's gut, like a noose on a hanging man. "Does Lord Overly have a lady?"

Sar smiled and bobbed his shiny head. "Aye, a most lovely Norman, Lady Lisette. Are you acquainted?"

Ralph chuckled. "More than acquainted, eh, Stefan?"

Stefan shot him a glare. "Aye, we have met." He felt Arian's sharp stare on him but refused to look at her. Instead, he turned to Tarian, and said, "Send for Father Dudley so that he may scribe the missives."

"Sir Sar," Arian said, slipping the knotted gold ring Magnus had given her in Dublin from her left hand and handing it to him. "Give this to my lord Magnus, and assure him I am well." She slipped a silver bracelet from her right arm with the boar insignia of Dinefwr engraved into it. Reaching across to her captain, she said, "Give this to my father with my wishes of his good health and assure him I await his support." She inhaled slowly, then exhaled. "Should he still be unwell, assure my brother I await his support."

And so, only two candle notches later, two companies of men rode west with urgent news while one rode hard east.

When the hall thinned, Arian found herself standing alone in the middle of it. One thought she could not ignore raced in circles around her: Stefan had not used her for his own personal gain. He had used her to save the lives of his men. Some of the sting of her capture left her. But just when she caught herself softening toward him, she remembered the conversation she overheard in his chamber and her heart closed. The emotions drove her mad. She could well understand why some women ran through the village tearing at their hair, screaming for the demons to leave their bodies. She felt much the same. She was at the end of her emotional rope. The only thing she wanted was the normalcy of her life to return. And for that to happen, she required Jane. Her constant. Never had she been so relieved as when she heard her nurse was well.

The lookout shouted from the hall tower. A train approached.

SIXTEEN

The dam of emotions Arian had been holding inside broke the minute her nurse's familiar loving arms wrapped around her. But their reunion was short-lived.

"Lady Arian," Stefan said curtly, standing on the front step of the hall, "I would have a private word with you."

"I am busy."

He stepped down toward her. Jane trembled in her arms. Arian stiffened at his indifference. "You scare Jane."

"She will have more to fear if you do not give me a private moment of your time."

"What is so pressing you cannot wait until I see her to bed?"

"Milady," Jane said softly, "I can wait."

Arian shook her head and moved past the surly knight. "I will be but a few moments." And she hurried as fast as Jane could move past the knight into the hall. Once Jane was settled and her trunks brought to the solar, Arian sucked in a deep breath, squared her shoulders and nervously walked to the chamber door. She opened it, expecting to have a moment to compose herself, but instead Stefan's wide chest and brilliant blue eyes awaited her. She cried out and stepped back into the room, but he grabbed her hands and pulled her down the hall to his chamber. "Nay!" she balked. "I will not go there again with you!"

He did not hesitate in his step, but dragged her over the threshold and into the room, bolting the door behind them. He whirled around to face her, and she caught her breath. A stormcloud of emotion ravaged his handsome features, and she realized he was showing great restraint; of what she was not sure.

He opened his mouth to speak, but no words came forth. Swiping his hand across his mouth and chin, he whirled from her to the tapestry, then whirled back to face her. "I want your oath you will do nothing to interfere here. There is too much at stake!"

Wide-eyed, she stared. How dare he demand anything from her after—after his kidnapping and treatment here? "You ask much and give little, sir. Why should I do anything for you after what you have done to me?"

"I saved your virtue! Mayhap your life! Had I not interfered, you would not be a virgin still! And your precious Magnus would toss you out with his morning piss!" He stepped closer. "Would you like me, Princess Arianrhod, to take from you what you almost lost to Dag? Will you then stop throwing my rescue of it in my face?" He grabbed her upper arms and shook her.

Stunned by his outburst, she could not move.

"Would you?"

She twisted out of his grasp, and moved to a safer

distance. His question shifted something inside her, something she could no longer deny. Slowly she raised her chin. Her anger thinned, then vanished. How could she be angry with him for saving so much? But more so, how could she be angry with him for feeling as frustrated as she? "If I could, I would," she whispered. His eyes narrowed. "You evoke wanton thoughts from the very depths of me, Stefan. I yearn for something with you I will never have with my husband. But I will not shame my father, nor myself, nor Magnus. I cannot give you what we both so desperately want."

He moved closer, slowly, in long, sure strides. "I asked you here, in private, to tell you not show yourself to me again. Do not come near me, Arian, until it is time to travel to Yorkshire, for I cannot promise you I will not take from you what we both so desperately want you to freely give me."

He was close enough for her to touch, and though she knew she should not, she could not help herself. Softly she laid her open hand against his chest. The hard thud of his heart beat strong beneath her palm. His handsome face twisted in agony, his blue eyes, so full of fire, begging for what they could not have. "You may be a man of the sword, sworn to slay your king's enemies, Stefan. But—" She moved closer and looked up into his hungry gaze. "You are a noble man, true, and I trust you would never force yourself on my person." Dropping her hand, she stepped back. Drawing in a deep breath, Arian nodded, then slowly exhaled. "I will do as you request, but I ask a promise of you in return."

He nodded.

"Promise me, sir knight, you will see me safely to Moorwood in Yorkshire, and there we will say our farewells." She swallowed hard and looked up at him through misty eyes. "Promise me you will not look over your shoulder, and I promise I will not look over mine. 'Tis best for us both."

"Arian," he said hoarsely, and she almost succumbed to the ache in his voice. Clenching her jaw, she remained rigid, unwavering.

Stefan grasped her hands and dropped to one knee. She caught her breath, and for the first time in her life, Arian felt a deep raw unrestrained desire to put her own needs and desires aside for another. Bringing her hands to his lips, he kissed them. She moved closer, wanting to draw from his power and strength. His arms slid around her waist and he drew her to him. Her fingers sunk into his hair and she pressed his head to her breast. "Stefan," she whispered, her voice mirroring the ache she heard in his. "I do not understand this thing between us. It terrifies me. I fear one day soon I will no longer have the strength to fight it."

He looked up at her, his eyes blazing with desire, but behind the fire she saw raw pain. He pulled her down to her knees. Sliding his hands into her hair, he brought her lips up to his. "It terrifies me as well," he said softly, then lowered his lips to hers in a deep passionate kiss that left her breathless.

Her world spun out of control. Never had she wanted anything more than she wanted this man before her, and never had she been so miserable knowing he could never be hers. Stefan tore his lips from hers and abruptly stood, bringing her up with him.

He extended his arm and smiled softly. "Come, my lady, let us go our separate ways."

Moist heat welled in her eyes. Hastily, she nodded, and allowed him to escort her down to the hall, where he left her at the lord's table and walked away from her, never once looking over his shoulder.

In the ensuing days Arian caught only a glimpse of Stefan when she visited the stables to tend her mare and to Belenus, the stallion she had bred and raised from a foal. To her surprise, she found a friend in Lady Tarian. She was drawn to the woman's quick wit and sage running of the manor. By simple observation, Arian learned what she had never bothered to learn in Dinefwr. Lady Tarian allowed her to accompany her in minor dealings with the churls and the many servants assigned to duties in the hall. 'Twas enough to keep her occupied and to keep mind and body from thinking of Stefan.

Eight days after Gareth had ridden off to Powys, he returned not only with Cadoc but, to her delight, her brother, Rhodri, and word from the Welsh king.

Rhodri strode into Draceadon's hall as if he were lord and master. Arian ran to his open arms. "Rhod!" she cried. For one so young, his face was stern to those who watched, but he could not help a smile when he embraced his sister, lifting her off her feet.

"Arian, you have worried a score of years off my life! Father is fit to be tied. I fear Rhiwallon will have a full-scale war on his hands if the lout double-crosses the great prince of Dinefwr!"

"Then he has agreed to the terms?" she asked, and lost much of her happiness when Stefan strode into the hall, followed by Ralph and that rodent lackey of his, Philip.

Everyone turned at his entrance, and Arian's heart leapt high in her throat.

"Gareth?" Stefan called. "Does Rhiwallon agree to our terms?"

"Pray he does!" Lady Tarian said breathlessly, coming to join the group.

In a short span of time the, hall was cleared of all but those who had a stake in the trade.

"Rhiwallon is furious," Gareth admitted. "But he relented when young Rhodri here arrived with an ultimatum from Prince Hylcon and his cousin Cynfyn in the northern kingdom. There would be hell to pay. Still the stubborn king refused, until he was assured that the Viking would sent a flotilla of longships to regain his bride." Arian watched Stefan's face tighten. Gareth grinned. "I of course informed him William was prepared to cross the Channel with two thousand strong, more than willing to breach the Marches if his men were not returned."

"What of Wulfson, Gareth, did you see him?" Lady Tarian demanded.

Gareth's smile waned. "He is alive; and though not in top form all of them will survive."

Lady Tarian and Stefan let out a sigh of relief.

"This all sounds too easy, Gareth. What twist does the Welsh king put on the trade?"

Gareth scowled. "He wants not only Lady Tarian, but the Lady Brighid as well."

"Nay!" Tarian cried.

Stefan reached to her and pulled her close, and softly

but firmly said, "He will not harm the girl. She will no doubt be reunited with her father." He looked to Gareth. "I agree to his terms. We will set out at first light."

"There is one more thing, sir," Gareth said.

Stefan nodded.

"He requires seeing the princess with his own eyes before the exchange is made."

"He is free to come to Draceadon."

"He insists she be present at the meeting place."

Stefan laughed, the sound cold and calculating. "Does Rhiwallon think I am a clod? The lady stays here. Out in the open, too much can go awry."

He looked to Rhodri. "You are her brother?"

He nodded, standing tall and unyielding before the Norman. Pride swelled in Arian's chest. "Aye, and I will kill any man who lays even one finger upon her person."

Stefan's lips twisted into a nasty smile. "Ride ahead and assure your kin that you have seen your sister with your own eyes, that she is alive and well. She will not leave this place until my brothers are safely returned. We will set out tomorrow and meet. I expect you to convince Rhiwallon he has no other choice." Stefan stepped closer to the young prince. "For if he does not agree to my terms, you will never see your sister alive again."

Rhodri drew his sword. Arian screamed but it was for naught. Stefan kicked the lad from him, drew his own sword, and pressed it to her brother's throat. "Do not begin a battle you can never win." Stefan stepped back and waved his sword toward the door. "Go."

Rhodri looked to Arian, and she slowly nodded. He

turned stone-faced from the group, calling for his squire and his men, then disappeared through the hall door.

Stefan turned, sheathing his sword, and bowed to Arian. "You are excused, my lady. What we have to discuss now is of no interest to you."

Anger at his rude dismissal boiled just beneath her skin. Haughtily she raised her chin, spun around, and turned to the wide stairway to her chamber.

SEVENTEEN

Two days later found Stefan, Lady Tarian, Lady Brighid, Sir Cadoc, and their respective companies high upon a ridge, overlooking a small clearing in the thick woods along the Welsh and English border. They watched as the dragon standard of the Welsh king Rhiwallon broke through the thick forest on the Welsh side, behind it a battle-ready accompaniment of mounted soldiers. Rhodri of Dinefwr also rode with them.

Stefan's heart leapt high in his throat with happiness as his brothers emerged under heavy guard, their hands bound behind their backs, their horses roped in a train, each upon their own good steeds, looking no worse than what a good night's sleep and a hot meal could not cure.

"My love," Tarian said softly, as she leaned forward in her saddle to see her husband, Lord Wulfson, leading the group of them. "He lives," she said between tears.

Stefan nodded. "Aye, Rhiwallon is no fool. Had he harmed them he would face William here or in hell."

Stefan gave the signal for his men to follow, and very carefully, they made their way down the steep hillside.

Stefan felt Tarian's excitement beside him as they approached. "Steady, my lady. Steady," he cautioned.

When only thirty paces separated each side, Stefan called out to Morgan, Rhiwallon's captain. "So we meet again, Morgan."

The Welshman nodded. "I fear, Sir Stefan, it will not be the last time."

"Pray that it is," Stefan said, as he urged his mount closer. He made eye contact with Wulfson first and saw raw fury in his eyes. Did he know Tarian was to be traded for him and their brothers? Next to him, Rorick, whose lips quirked in a smirk. Then to Ioan, the big Irishman, stoic as always, to Warner, who nodded, and to Rohan, whose jaw twitched with anger. And finally he looked to Thorin who sat towering over most of them, his cool pale eyes ever watchful. Only Rhys was absent, and that gnawed at Stefan's gut. With him gone, they would be much like a hand without a finger.

Stefan looked to Gareth, who escorted Lady Brighid to the other side. When Gareth made to escort Tarian, Wulfson shouted out, "Nay! She is not part of the bargain."

Immediately Tarian was surrounded by armed Welshmen and moved further away.

"Wulfson!" Tarian cried, valiantly trying to retain her composure. " 'Tis only until you deliver the princess to her betrothed."

"Nay!" he roared, and urged his horse forward. Morgan drew his sword, backed by several others. Stefan spurred his destrier and rode interference between the raging Norman lord and the king's captain. He grabbed the bridle of Wulf's steed and yanked hard, bringing him around. "Think, man," Stefan hissed in his friend's ear. "Rhiwallon will not harm her for fear of retaliation! Leave with me now so that we all may live tomorrow!"

Morgan smiled a nasty smile. "You may all go, but the Viking returns with us."

"Nay, 'twas not part of the deal," Stefan said menacingly.

"Rhiwallon insists. Should Wulfson fall, there will be no urgency to carry out the exchange, and return for his lady. Thorin is kin not only to Olaf but blood brother to all of you. For him, any one of you who lives will see the exchange made to save his skin."

"I will stay, Stefan, and keep watch over the ladies." Thorin's deep voice boomed over them all.

Angry, Stefan glared at Morgan and nodded. A man cut Thorin's horse from Rohan's and pulled him into the thick protective fold of soldiers.

Morgan motioned to another man, who nudged his horse forward and dropped a large satchel to the ground; it clanked when it hit. "Your swords," Morgan said. He looked to Rhodri. "You are free to return with us."

Rhodri spat and spurred his horse toward Stefan, crossing sides; his handful of men followed his lead.

Morgan sneered in contempt at them all, reined his horse around, and thundered into the woods; his men followed, surrounding Tarian, Brighid, and Thorin.

"I will kill him!" Wulfson yelled to the wind. "I will kill him!"

Stefan's heart tightened for his friend. He was beginning to understand what he must feel. He would feel it soon enough when Arian married Magnus. Deftly, Stefan dismounted, and cut them all loose from their bindings. He handed each brother his sword, then remounted.

"Come, let us go to Draceadon. I will explain all on the way."

"Explain now why my wife is in the hands of that cur Rhiwallon!"

Stefan waved his brothers over, and as they circled around him he could not help a smile. "I cannot explain my joy. I have worried like a milkmaid over you these past weeks."

"Aye, we thought you dead upon the field, Stefan," Rorick said grimly.

"Where is the lad Rhys?" Rohan demanded. "And why do you ride his horse?"

"I fear he is mulch at Hereford. His horse found me as I lay wounded myself, and I searched the field for him. 'Twas there I heard a Welshman speak of your capture. Once I was able to ride I came upon Prince Hylcon of Dinefwr's daughter on her way to marry a Norse jarl." Stefan grinned. "I saw an opportunity and seized it. Her for you six, but before Rhiwallon will release Tarian, we must deliver the princess to Moorwood, south of York, to her betrothed."

"Tarian, the girl, and now Thorin, are the guarantee the princess is safely delivered and no other ransom demanded?" Wulfson asked.

"Aye, Wulf, 'twas your lady's idea. Though I argued with her, it made the most sense. That Rhiwallon sent for Lady Brighid as well was a surprise but understandable. Alewith no doubt cavorts with the Welsh and that blackguard Edric."

Wulfson seemed to lose some of his anger, though

he looked as if he had not had a decent night's sleep in weeks. "Then let us get this princess of yours to York! I have a yearning for my wife!"

The Blood Swords, united save for two, thundered from the thick forest toward Draceadon.

Wulfson refused to wait one day for Yorkshire. Stefan understood his urgency, though he himself did not feel it. The sooner they reached the eastern part of the island, the sooner he would turn away from Arian and not look over his shoulder. The reality of never seeing her again began to gnaw at his gut.

But Wulf was adamant, and Stefan could not argue. The men, though tired and hungry, were fit for the journey.

As they entered the hall, Stefan hurried straight for the dungeon. The dank smell of urine and feces that would forever permeate the hellhole assaulted his nostrils, as it had months before, when Wulfson had rescued Lady Tarian from the same place. But this time, though a princess was held in the bowels of the fortress, 'twas not to keep her prisoner but to keep her safe. Safe from his own kind.

He grabbed a torch from the wall sconce and shoved the key into the lock, then hurried down the slick steps. When he approached the cell that held Arian, he was met with a fierce glare. He challenged it and quickly unlocked the door, and swung it open.

"My lady?"

She stalked past him without so much as one word, and regally crossed the cistern center and walked slowly up the stairs. He cursed and followed her, giving her light lest she fall and break her neck.

Her maid Jane met them atop the stairs, her hands a ball of nervous flittering. "My lady? How farest thou?"

"I am well, Jane; please see to my bath." Arian said staunchly, as she made her way past her and into the hall. Stefan caught the nurse's eyes. He did not expect the softening in them.

She bobbed her head and said, " 'Tis well you kept her under lock and key as you did, sir, Sir Philip has tried everything but burrowing under the castle to get to her."

Stefan nodded. "I entrusted the other key to Father Dudley for her release, should I not have returned today."

Again, the maid bobbed her head. "My thanks, sir." She hastened from him then.

Slowly Stefan made his way to the hall, to find his brothers seated at the lord's table, eating and making plans.

"Stefan!" Ioan boomed, raising a skin of wine. "Our thanks!"

The others joined in, even Wulfson, raising their cups, bellowing their thanks to him.

Stefan scowled, but drew closer. When their voices died down Warner asked, "What eats at you other than the obvious, brother?"

Stefan poured himself a full goblet of wine. " 'Twas my mistakes that caused your capture and Rhys's death. What is there to thank me for?"

"How can one man be responsible for that slaughter?" Rorick solemnly demanded. "We were outnumbered eight to one, and while the Blood Swords are the mightiest warriors in the realm, even we have our limitations. That we survived is the true testament to our skill!"

Warner took a long pull of his wine, and said, "Had you not devised such a wily plan with the archers in the field we would all be burning in hell at this very moment!"

Rohan slapped Stefan on the back. "We shall find Rhys. My instinct tells me the lad is lying in some nubile maid's bed as she lavishes attention upon him. He will milk it as long as he can, then return to us. Have no doubt!"

Despite their dark mood, Stefan smiled at the image of the young knight lying abed as a beautiful maid clucked over him like a mother hen over her chicks. Aye, he would accept her ministrations until he was well enough to travel. He looked to Wulfson, who stared at his feet. Emotion he could not put a name to clogged his throat. He cleared it, and softly said, "Wulf, if it is the last thing I do, I will see your lady returned to you."

His brother's deep green eyes lifted to his. Slowly he nodded. "I have no doubt, but her safety is my responsibility. I will not have her taken from me."

"We will ride hard each day, Wulf," Stefan said. "With the large contingent of men and show of arms no one will dare accost us along the way. Upon the Jarl's arrival the vows will be said. Accompanied by the young prince Rhodri to bear witness to the nuptials, you will ride to Rhiwallon. I have sent word to William; he will send more men to accompany you."

"I do not trust Rhiwallon," Wulfson gritted. "He smiles like the fox after swallowing the hen."

"He is not daft," Ioan said. "He will not stand to lose everything just to smite William."

Warner stood and raised his cup. "To finding Rhys alive and well in the arms of a nubile maid! To Lady Tarian returning to soothe the savage wolf, and the safe return of our brother, Thorin, who were it not for his sage guidance we would all be mulch!"

Grimly the Blood Swords raised their cups, and drank.

Arian was roused before the break of dawn to ready herself and her train. They would depart for Yorkshire after the breaking of the fast. A short time later, when she descended into the hall, dressed for travel, she found it a wild blur of activity. Taking advantage of the chaos, she slipped from the hall to the stable, where she found Cadoc's squire readying her mare Fahadda.

"I will see to her, squire. Find another chore to busy yourself," Arian commanded. The boy bowed and hurried from the stall. She looked to the next stall and recognized Stefan's black beast. He shook his great black head and snorted at her, as if laughing. "You will not think it so funny should I geld you!" she hissed.

"Pray do not geld him, milady." Stefan said from behind her. "He will lose his fire for battle."

And though she fought it, her body instantly warmed and her hands shook.

Slowly she turned and faced him. He was close. So close she could see the silver spokes in his brilliant blue eyes. So close she could smell him. So close she could feel his warm breath upon her cheeks.

"Is the thirst for battle all that drives him? Does he

not look forward to green pastures with a mare and foals and to live out his days in harmony?"

Stefan snorted. "He is a horse!"

Arian turned from Stefan to Fahadda. Smoothing her hand down the mare's sleek neck she said, "He is a horse, true, but when he is old and broken down from too many battles, what will become of him? Will he be slain and used as dog meat?"

Stefan pressed close to her back. "He is a fine stallion, with a long noble lineage; he will sire many like him." Stefan reached past her and placed his hand upon hers that lingered on the mare's neck. The contact was warm, and cracked like lightning between them. "He will mate with mares such as your Fahadda, to be sure. She is noble, mighty, and strong. They would produce a great line for generations to come."

Arian stood perfectly still as her emotions ran rampant with thoughts of a child of Stefan's. He too would be noble, mighty, and strong.

Slowly, she turned to face him, holding her breath fearful he might press her, but more fearful that she would allow him. "When your warring days are behind you, Stefan, will you see a green pasture and begin your legacy?"

He brushed his knuckles along her cheek. "Nay. I will be too old and broken to offer comfort to any woman. My life is in the saddle."

"But there is land to be had!"

"Aye, there is, but I have no name, no family."

"But Stefan! You could build your line. A proud, mighty line. Why would you choose not to?"

He scowled, and dropped his hand, moving away

from her. "I would be no comfort to a wife or child. I am a solitary man. Even amongst the Blood Swords I find myself on the outside looking in. 'Tis no life to share with any woman."

Deep sadness for this man, this good man who risked all to save his brothers, gripped Arian's heart. "You do yourself a grave dishonor, sir. You are more worthy than you know."

His eyes narrowed and his head snapped back. "You misunderstand, princess. I am worthy of many things, but I am not so arrogant to think that what I have to offer a woman would be enough to keep her content. Women want a noble husband, riches, land, and status. Not a mere soldier who would lay down his life for his own true love. Even you, dear princess, have made it clear that as a royal you would marry only one of your own station, and you scorn all others."

"Nay! 'Tis not true!"

"It is, and I do not hold it against you. You are who you are, just as I am who I am. Long ago I accepted my lot in life. You should do the same."

He turned from her and went into the stall beside hers and led his horse from it, leaving Arian standing in stunned silence. With each passing moment, she realized he spoke the truth. And it was ugly. Were she free to marry any man, she would never look lower than her station. And that made her very sad, for she thought she was more worthy than that. She had never thought herself like the other noble ladies at court, who walked the halls with their noses so high in the air one could not see their faces.

But in the last weeks she had realized there was more

to a man's character than his bloodline. And though Stefan de Valrey was bastard-born and bastard-raised, he was a man who stood above all others in her eyes. She wished to tell him her feelings, but she could not. She turned to the mare and readied her for the journey ahead.

EIGHTEEN

As they turned their horses to the road, Arian felt a nervousness she could not define. 'Twas not fear of the impressive accompaniment of knights and soldiers, nor fear of what lay ahead. She had no cause to fear her betrothed. Magnus was a good man who had the respect of his king and vassals. He was a man she could proudly stand beside. But 'twas the other, Stefan de Valrey, who caused her such torment. His presence made her belly flutter wildly, her heart tighten, and her blood warm.

She looked ahead to the man who had changed so much about her. Gone was a silly girl who thought life was but trivia and feasts. Gone was the girl who did not consider the responsibility she was born to. And gone was the girl who vowed to never open her heart to have it broken. If she were honest with herself, she felt more than admiration for the proud knight.

Arian was acutely aware of the special bond Stefan shared with his men, and though he may have felt an outsider amongst them, he was not. Their bond was complete. Unwavering as the earth was solid. He was relaxed and easy in their presence. 'Twas only when Ralph or Philip interfered in a conversation that his reticence returned. She understood his love for his brothers, and moreover, his determination to free them.

On the first night on the road, beneath the lavish tent from Dinefwr, Arian watched Stefan relax against his saddle and lift a goblet to his lips. Lord Wulfson said something and Stefan threw his head back and laughed. Her longing grew deeper. While he had made every effort to see that her train was protected, and that she was comfortable, he did nothing more. He kept his distance. And while she understood, she did not like it.

When they broke camp the next day, Arian made several attempts to steer her mare toward Stefan, but he was always just out of her reach. As the day drew to a close, the knights ahead came to an abrupt halt. She spurred her mount to the front, despite Cadoc and Rhodri's calls to return. Her blood curdled at the sight before her. The outrider who had left that morn to scout a manor for them to spend the night lay dead on his back in the road, a sword with the gold and red dragon standard of the house of Godwinson whipping in the harsh wind, taunting all who stood witness.

Stefan dismounted beside the dead Norman and drew the sword. He ripped off the standard and threw it to the ground. Turning to his men, he said softly, "I have had my fill of unruly Saxons. From this moment forward, any man, woman, or child who stands in our way shall be cut down at the knees."

His hard gaze caught Arian's before moving past her to her brother and Cadoc. As he mounted his horse, he said to his squire, "See that he is buried."

The young man hurried to the task.

"Tighten the flanks," he called back to Ralph and Philip, then to his men, "We will stop at the first manor we come upon, and God help them if they refuse us."

Just as the sun sank behind them, an impressive wooden and stone structure rose ahead. Arian sighed in relief. Until several moments later, after Stefan and several of his men stormed into the place and the inhabitants ran shrieking from the structure. Stefan strode up to Arian and gave her a short bow. "'Tis called Worthington. Your lodgings for the night, princess." He clicked his heels, then turned from her.

His surliness irritated her already drawn nerves. But she allowed her brother to help her dismount and accompany her into the structure. In a sharp wave of revelation, she stopped on the threshold. In all but size, it was an exact replica of the hunting lodge they had spent such intimate time in. Her skin warmed as she remembered the moments spent there. Heat spread across her cheeks down to her chest. She could well understand Stefan's mood.

Once settled in a small but comfortable chamber, Arian returned to the main room, and was surprised to see the large trestle shoulder to shoulder with knights. When she entered the room, Stefan stood and the others hurried to follow. He nudged Wulfson aside so that there was a spot for her on the end.

She smiled and sat, but not before she said," 'Tis customary for the nobles to sit first."

He scowled. "Here we are the same."

Arian did not argue with him as she sat looking for her brother.

"A-wenching," Stefan muttered.

"I detect a note of envy in your tone, Sir Stefan."

His blue eyes bored into her. "Aye, would that I could find the release I so desire. My mood would be greatly soothed."

Arian took a deep breath and slowly released it. "Why, then, do you sit here when England's thighs await?"

Stefan nodded and stood. "Aye, why not." Then he stalked from the hall.

When the door slammed behind him, Arian turned to find his brothers' eyes solemnly regarding her.

"I ask on behalf of all of us, Lady Arian, that you set Stefan free," Rorick said carefully.

"Set him free?" Arian asked, confused. "But there are no ties that bind us!"

His deep sea-colored eyes narrowed as he fought for control of his next words. "Invisible though they are, the bonds are strong. Make the break, marry your jarl, and give my brother back his heart. He has suffered more than you will ever know. I do not wish to see him suffer more."

She looked at each and every one of them, and saw the same closed look. She understood clearly: she was the enemy. "I—I do not know what to say to you, sirs. I am on my way to wed. Stefan's heart is his to give. I do not have control of it."

"You do!" Rorick ground out. He leaned closer. "He is no good to anyone when you lead him along by the leash of hope. Make the break. Make it permanent." His eyes narrowed to slits. "Or I shall."

"Do you threaten me?"

"Nay, I do not. I have no quarrel with you. I state only

that if you do not sever the ties I will do it myself."

Feeling like a deer caught between two bows, Arian defended herself. "Stefan is a man of his own mind and heart. He understands I am promised to another, as I understand he is wed to his king."

"Then make it clear," Rorick said. Shaking with anger, Arian stood, having barely touched her meal. How dare he threaten her? Did he expect her to lie to Stefan and tell him she no longer cared for him? She could not do that, any more than he could say it to her. Such cruel words would tear her heart in half. But then— then she could turn all her attention to her betrothed . . . and not pine for what could never have been. 'Twould force her to look ahead and not behind.

Her shoulders slumped. 'Twould tear her apart to hurt Stefan. But it would also set him free. "Excuse me." Slowly she made her way down the hall. As she entered the chamber, Jane raised her deep brown eyes from her stitching, and Arian knew she read her heartbreak. She sank to her knees at Jane's feet. "After all these years, Jane, I begin to understand my father's heartache."

A loud thud, followed by the scrape of metal, roused Arian from sleep. She shot up in the bed, Jane shielding her from the intrusion. Deep voices in French and English clashed in the hall. Stefan's voice was close, just on the other side of her door. Arian moved from behind Jane and reached for her short dagger on the side table. Grasping it to her breast, she moved to the door.

"Nay, milady! 'Tis too dangerous!" Jane cried.

The clash of steel upon steel told the story of what transpired on the other side. More Saxon voices erupted. Dread filled Arian's heart. They were under attack! Did Stefan fight alone? Where were the Blood Swords?

She threw the bolt and heaved the door open. Stefan stumbled in backwards, fighting off two Saxon swordsmen. Arian jumped back and watched horrified as Stefan lost ground an inch at a time under the harsh attack. She dared not scream lest she distract him. More fighting sounds came from the hall and Arian realized they were under attack from all sides.

The two men had pressed Stefan back into a corner when a third man burst into the room. Frozen with fear and not knowing what to do, Arian stood rigid in the room. She could barely make out Stefan's large form from behind the three men. He lost more ground. When he went down on one knee, fending off the violent thrusts of the three swords, Arian snapped.

"Nay!" she screamed, and lunged at the closest man, who turned in surprise. She plunged the dagger deep into his chest. The other two shifted their attention from Stefan just long enough for him to impale one with his sword; the other he kicked forward. Arian pulled her dagger from the dead man and turned on the other, ready to see him to hell. But Stefan did the honor. He hacked back with his sword, stopping the man in his steps. His dying eyes widened and in a slow fall forward he hit the floor dead.

Stefan stepped over the carnage and pushed her back toward the bed. "Stay here. Do *not* leave this room!" Then he flew from her, slamming the door behind him. Jane threw the bolt. Arian stood in stunned silence, the bloody dagger in her hand, and stared aghast at the three dead men on the floor. "I have slain a man, Jane," she whispered. "I have taken a life."

And with shattering realization that kicked the breath from her chest, Arian knew she would do it one hundred times again to save the life of the man she loved.

When Stefan ran into the small hall, he was met with the cold stares of his men and a floor littered with bodies. Fury seethed in his gut. "How did they gain entrance?" he demanded of Ralph, who stood guard at the main door to the manor.

Ralph pointed with his bloody sword to a hole in the floor near the short hallway leading to the chamber where Arian had slept. "A secret passage? Why was it not discovered when we swept the hall?"

Rorick wiped the blood from his sword on the tunic of one of the dead Saxons, then glared at Ralph. "Next time we will not leave the chore to the inept."

Wulfson strode through the door, followed by Warner and Ioan. "There were at least thirty of them. The stables run wet with their blood."

Rhodri came bursting in behind them. "What goes on here?"

Stefan snarled, "If you were not so bent on repopulating the island, you would know we have been attacked!"

"Arian?" he gasped, stepping past Stefan, who grabbed his forearm, halting him. The younger man yanked his arm from the Norman's grasp.

"She is safe in her room. Barely."

Rhodri faced Stefan, anger twisting his face. "She

would not have been in such danger had you not kidnapped her for your own gain!"

Stefan turned on the young man. "Would you have her raped then? Would you have her bring shame upon your house because she was no longer a virgin and her chances of a royal marriage gone?" He stepped closer to the upstart. "Would you, Prince Rhodri, have forgiven her for what she had no control over?"

The young man stood, silently furious. "She is *my sister*! I would have stood by her no matter what."

"You have an odd way of showing your loyalty, lad. Had you not been so enamored of the milkmaid you would have been the one sleeping on the pallet by her door, not I." He fondled the hilt of his sword. "Mayhap it was best you were not there. I doubt you would be alive now."

Rhodri drew his sword. Before it was fully free of his scabbard, the Blood Swords, with the exception of Stefan, drew on him. Stefan smiled and walked into the sharp point of Rhodri's blade. "Do you challenge me?"

"Aye! I call you out."

Stefan threw his head back and laughed. In a move so swift no one expected it, he flung his brawny arm against the blade and half-turned, kicking the young prince onto his royal arse. He caught the sword before it hit the floor and stepped on the lad's chest, bringing the blade down to his throat, pressing the point to the vein there. "I refuse to fight an unarmed opponent." Stefan dropped the sword to the floor next to Rhodri's head. Turning to his men, he said, "Let us clean up this mess, then prepare to depart at first light."

He turned and strode down the hall to Arian. He pounded on the door." 'Tis Stefan."

The door flew open, and with a sob, she flung herself into his arms. For one tense moment, he stood stiffly, but he could not resist her warm softness. His arms slid around her waist and he brought her gently against his chest. Something warm and wonderful filled his belly. She clung to him and his arms tightened around her. He pressed his lips to her hair, inhaling the flowery scent of her perfume. "The danger has passed, Arian. You are safe."

Her body shuddered in his arms. "Stefan," she said, tears clogging her throat, "I—I killed a man."

He smoothed her hair from her face and pushed her head slightly back so that he could look into her eyes. "My thanks. Had you not, 'twould be he standing here with you in his arms, not I." He looked to the ground where the dead men lay sprawled upon the bloody rushes then back to her deep silvery eyes. Lowering his lips to her cheeks, he kissed away the tears. Then he kissed her moist lips, drawing her harder against him. Emotion swelled in his chest, clogging his throat, making it difficult for him to breathe. "Come," he said, his lips hovering above hers. "Let my men clear the bodies."

When he turned with her in his arms, Wulfson and Rorick stood silently watching. Neither seemed pleased with his handling of the princess. He scowled, narrowing his eyes, daring either one of them to say a word.

He guided her past them all, out to the front steps of the manor, where he sat her down on a bench. Quietly she sucked in the fresh air. Her hands trembled, as did her shoulders. After several long moments she looked up at him, her eyes glittering like steel. Gone was the terrified girl; in her place stood a furious woman. "Who were they and how did they gain access to the manor?"

Taking exception to her curt tone, he scowled. "From the wood, there is a trapdoor with a tunnel, leading to the hallway just outside your door."

"Why was not a guard posted at my door?"

"I slept across your threshold, princess. They were silent and deadly. Two were upon me before I heard a sound."

"Why did you even sleep if you suspected trouble?"

"I am human."

"You gave your word you would see me to Yorkshire! I was nearly slain this night! Because of your laxness I was forced to take a man's life!" She stood, and began to pace in front of him.

Confused by her sudden mood change and her attack on him for yet again saving her life, Stefan lashed out. "Once again, you chastise me for saving your skin. If your life is so unimportant to you, then it is to me as well." He curtly bowed. "Find another champion, Princess Arian, one who does not mind your constant nettles and barbs. I am through with you."

"Nay! I am through with *you*! You have seduced me with your gallant words and courtly manners all in the hope of ruining me! I have been blind to your ways, thinking you truly held me in high esteem. Be gone from me, Stefan de Valrey, you are beneath my station and not worthy of my time!"

Speechless at her harsh words, Stefan watched her

whirl away from him and stride back into the manor, brushing past his men.

Arian ran back to her chamber. Tears blinded her eyes. Her heart was shattering into a thousand pieces. Abruptly she stopped when she hit a hard wall. Rough hands grabbed her arms, steadying her from falling. She looked up into the piercing eyes of Sir Rorick. "I have done what you asked!" She yanked out of his grasp and continued her flight.

Bursting into the chamber, Arian slammed the door shut, pressing her back against it. Her gaze caught that of Jane's as the maid threw a bloody rag into a bucket— the last remnants of the bodies gone.

"Jane!" Arian cried. "Jane, I am weak like my father. I have done what I swore never to do! And now my heart is breaking and there is naught I can do to stop it!"

Jane rinsed her hands in a bucket of clean water, then wiped them dry. The old woman, hunched with age, moved to the bedside and smoothed the hair back from Arian's damp cheeks. "When you were born, your mother was delirious with joy. She had lost six daughters before you came. I knew before you greeted the world that Branwen would leave that day. She knew it too, poppet, and she was brave. She loved you with all her heart and she knew she would never see you grow into the beautiful lady you are today."

Arian gazed up at the old women through tear-filled eyes. Jane smiled sadly. "Hylcon was devastated. He refused to allow anyone near her body for almost a week after she died. He refused to see her buried, even. Instead, he ran. He was gone for nearly a year."

Arian's heart constricted with such tightness she could scarce breathe. She now knew how her father felt. When she thought that Stefan would die before her eyes, Arian realized that her emotion for him ran far deeper than she suspected. 'Twas love. Pure, simple, and unshakable.

"Prince Hylcon did his people a grave injustice when he left, and though he returned in body, he never fully returned in spirit. He was forced to wed Morwena and to produce an heir. The morning she announced she was with child, he never set foot in her chamber again. We have all suffered from his broken heart."

Jane pulled Arian into her thin arms. "Do not continue his legacy. Wed the Jarl, bear his children. Become a great lady. Give him all of yourself that you can, and know that a tiny piece of your heart is safely tucked away for another. But do not howl at the moon, do not neglect what you were born and bred to do. You are a princess, Arian, and you have much to give your people."

Jane's words, though meant to inspire, did the opposite. 'Twas Stefan she wished to marry. 'Twas Stefan whom she wanted above all other men.

"You are young. You have a lifetime to fall in love with your husband. But you must be willing, Arian. Close your heart to him and neither of you will find joy in the union."

Arian slumped against the woman, not wanting to admit the truth. "Jane, let me sleep." Arian closed her eyes. "Let me sleep." Gently, the maid laid her down, then pulled the covers up to her chin.

"Sleep, poppet. Tomorrow the sun will shine and you will see the world in a brighter light."

Arian nodded, knowing that as long as she could draw breath her world would remain dark without Stefan at her side.

Two days later found them on the fringes of Yorkshire and two days out of Moorwood to the southeast. Along the well-worn roads, they repeatedly met with sullen Saxons, and on three separate occasions found themselves recipients of rotten fruit and vegetables launched from the thick forests. The Normans did nothing to avoid altercations; indeed they seemed to live for them. They arrogantly flew their black skull and bloody sword standard below that of the Conqueror's double lion standard.

Word of the massacre at Worthington had preceded them, and for once, Arian was glad of the protection of the Normans. But with each step east, her heart crumbled more. The thought of never seeing Stefan again ate at her with each stride of her horse. Since she had so insulted him, Stefan had not even looked her way. The tension amongst the men was palpable, and no one, not even his brothers, engaged his black mood. He rode point from sunrise to sunset, daring anyone to challenge him.

On what was their final day, an outrider with an armed escort was dispatched to Moorwood. As Arian watched the riders crest then disappear behind a hill, trepidation scurried sharply along her back. What should have been a day greeted with excited anticipation was instead mourned with terrifying foreboding. Would Magnus know of her change of heart? Could she conceal her love for another man? She looked ahead to

Stefan's straight back and the proud set of his shoulders. Rorick's words came back to haunt her, and she knew in her heart she had done the right thing, forcing Stefan from her with her lies. What could they have together? A few stolen moments? Nay, she would not belittle her love for him that way, nor would she shame her husband.

Resigned to her lot in this life, Arian squared her shoulders and looked ahead, beyond Stefan, to Magnus, where her life would be.

As the sun began to sink behind them, Stefan shouted that riders approached. Arian breathed a long sigh of relief when Magnus's blue and white stag standard crested the hill. Just as the elation of no attack rose, it subsided. Was Magnus in residence already? He was not expected for at least another week.

Stefan, flanked by his Norman brothers, rode forward to meet Magnus's contingent. With Rhodri at her side they urged their horses forward to the sound of angry French words.

"I will not release the lady from my care until she is wife to Lord Magnus," Stefan bit out.

The man he spoke to looked past Stefan and caught Arian's gaze. 'Twas not the noble who coolly regarded her that held her interest, nor was it Stefan for once. Nay, Arian's gaze traveled to the beautiful woman ahorse beside the indignant Saxon lord. Her thick, intricately braided golden hair shone, and her bejeweled clothes were rich in color and fabric. And she had eyes only for Stefan. Arian stiffened in the saddle.

"Sir Stefan," the woman purred. "Surely you trust us to see to the princess's welfare? My Lord Overly is cousin to Lord Magnus, and has been given the honor of entertaining her until he arrives three days hence."

Stefan removed his helm, his long thick hair falling around his shoulders. The lady gasped. "Stefan! Dear Lord, what happened to you?"

Jealousy ripped though Arian at the lady's familiarity. Stefan's jaw tightened and she saw a small tic of the muscle along his cheek. "Since when, Lady Lisette, has my health mattered to you?"

Overly looked from his wife to the Norman, his brows drawn. "My lady, you are acquainted with this man?"

"She was once betrothed to him," Ralph offered.

Arian gasped, and all eyes turned to her. Quickly she recovered from the shock. So this was the woman who had broken his heart? Anger swelled, followed by the undeniable urge to protect Stefan. Arian spurred her horse closer and inclined her head.

"Princess Arianrhod, daughter of Prince Hylcon of Dinefwr," Stefan introduced. Arian sat straight in her saddle as the lesser nobles bowed their heads. She nodded to her brother, who came slowly up behind her. "My brother, Prince Rhodri."

"Princess Arianrhod, Lord Overly and Lady Lisette of Scarborough," Stefan said in a clipped voice.

Lady Lisette smiled, but her eyes glowed molten, and with a shattering realization, Arian knew the woman knew her secret, and in that, she would be never be an ally.

"I can see, Sir Stefan, why you are loath to let her go," Lady Lisette said, looking Arian up and down, as if she were a mare to be purchased at market.

"I gave my oath to her father and King Rhiwallon that

I would see her wed before returning to Wales. Lives are at stake." He turned to Lord Overly. "Do not question my intentions again, sir, or you will find yourself *and* your lady removed from Moorwood."

Overly, a man in his early fifties, nodded, but Arian detected anger there. His lady, however, smiled and nodded at Stefan. "I shall do my best to see to, your, er, Lord Magnus's lady to be." She fluttered her long black lashes.

Arian smiled sweetly. "My thanks for the offer, Lady Lisette, but I have a most capable staff. But I would ask that you make haste to have the lord's chamber readied for me upon my arrival. I fear I am travel-weary, and would like to bathe and rest before the evening meal."

The Norman beauty's eyes iced and her lovely jaw set into a hard line. "Of course."

As their train progressed toward the manor, numerous Saxon and Norse lined the well-worn road. Their contempt was painted plainly on their faces.

Arian took comfort in two things: one, she was not Norman, and thus innocent of the events of last year; and two, she was marrying a great jarl whose relatives were settled not only here in Essex but Norway as well. Nervous apprehension swirled in her belly as they came closer to the town and more people lined the road.

As the great wooden and stone manor that was Moorwood rose beyond a great meadow on a small dirt motte ahead, the villagers pressed closer. The Blood Swords drew in around her and Cadoc in a precise square formation, their shields raised, their lances lowered. They were a most fearsome sight in their black helms and black mail, astride fierce black destriers as well-armored as their masters.

She had serious misgivings about allowing the Normans to provide escort to Moorwood, but now she was glad for their protection. Looking ahead, she saw Lisette cast several furtive glances over her shoulder, not at Arian but in concern for the knight who rode behind her. Hostility laced with jealousy grappled in her chest. Arian breathed in slow and exhaled slower. She had no claim to the knight. Each time her longing for the Norman became unbearable, she remembered Jane's words of wisdom, and told herself duty and honor came before love, even at the expense of a broken heart.

NINETEEN

The next two days passed in relative calm, yet Arian found a Norman guard at her elbow at every turn. The only time she caught sight of Stefan was at the late meal. He and his men took up the lord's table, making it plain that they were in charge, not the Saxon lord and his lady. Indeed, Moorwood was Magnus's home by way of his late mother, and Overly and Lisette only his host and hostess to see to his betrothed's needs until his arrival.

Arian found her appetite waning each time she sat down to take a meal, and though she knew she should, she had no interest in the running of the manor or viewing the surrounding countryside. There was no warmth in the cold stone and wood manor, nor amongst the villagers. The heavy pall of doom hovered above them all.

The Saxons' thinly veiled civility toward the Normans she could understand, but they were equally reticent with her. They followed her with their scornful eyes, believing the rumors that swirled about her and the Norman leader, Stefan de Valrey.

Arian could thank Sir Philip and Lady Lisette for stoking that fire. The assembled nobles waited, like a stable cat for the mouse to stick his nose out of his nest. The uneasy feeling that treachery brewed amongst those abiding in the hall gnawed at her. So she kept to herself, refusing to make even a feigned attempt to befriend these sullen people. 'Twas better that way. Until she was rightful lady here, she would keep silent and not rock the cart.

Philip and his sister Lisette, who had a most unnatural relationship, were the brunt of many caustic stares, not only from the servants but from the gathered Saxon nobles. The way they fawned over each other, one would think they were long-lost lovers. Overly didn't seem to mind, but on several occasions when Stefan was in the hall Arian caught his scowl as the two prattled on.

On the third morning, Arian slipped from her chamber earlier than normal and stopped at the soft laughter of a woman. Lisette. Pressing into the small alcove outside her chamber, Arian listened.

"Philip, surely you jest?"

"Do you think me so unworthy?" he asked, his voice low and petulant.

"Ah, my sweet, you are a most worthy catch for any lady, even a princess, but do not think for one moment you have a chance with that frigid Welsh bitch."

"I swear upon our mother's grave your lover has breached her. Magnus will annul the marriage and I will step forward! Think of the dowry and the power she will bring us!"

"Darling, you know not of what you speak. Stefan de Valrey is many things, but he has an indomitable honor that is most annoying. If he says he did not breach her, then he speaks the truth. The man will not lie even to save his own skin."

Arian held her breath as long minutes drew out.

"Then all is lost," Philip sighed.

"Nay, brother, there is still time. Magnus's outrider arrived just a short time ago; the Jarl will not arrive until later this eve. The marriage will commence in two days' time from his arrival."

"De Valrey no longer has interest in her. He refuses to allow her name spoken in his presence. She will see the Jarl a virgin bride," Philip whined.

More laughter infiltrated the hallway, sending the hair on Arian's neck spiking. "Come to my chamber, Philip, I have a plan that will guarantee no blood upon the marriage sheets."

Arian released a long breath. When the voices trailed off down the long hall, she bolted the opposite way, to the hall and to her brother.

She found him speaking with Gareth and Cadoc by the great hearth. She looked past him to Stefan, who strode into the hall, his men falling in behind him. Her heart leapt high in her throat and beat with such an intensity she felt she might choke on it. Stopping in her tracks, Arian fought the urge to run to him and express her fears. Rhodri was strong, but he was young and inexperienced. Her chest rose and fell hard when Stefan refused to release her gaze. His face tightened and his hands fisted at his sides, but he made no move to break the stare.

She moved a step toward him. His dark brows drew down over his brilliant eyes. Breaking his gaze, he turned away from her until the door slammed shut behind him. Her chest clogged with emotion. What did she expect from him? That he would come crawling on his hands and knees just so that she would throw him a bone? She had done her job too well. Stefan de Valrey held nothing but hatred for her.

Slowly she turned and walked back toward the lord's table, and caught Sir Rorick's eyes. She swallowed hard. He nodded, and indicated she sit beside him at the table. Not wanting to, but wanting to be close to Stefan through his fellow knights, she did so. She would speak to her brother after the meal. When Arian sat, the rest of the men present did so as well.

The priest said a hasty prayer, and in a sudden eruption, voices swirled around her as the men ate heartily and spoke of the coming of the Jarl. Arian nibbled at a crust of bread.

"I have noticed, milady, that you have not eaten more than a sparrow these past days," Sir Rorick said softly from beside her. She raised her eyes to his deep blue ones, so different from Stefan's but just as compelling.

"I have no appetite, sir."

"What you did in Worthington was for the greater good. In time Stefan will forget."

His words stung, but Arian nodded her head. "Indeed, if he does forget, then I suppose I am the one who loses all."

Rorick scowled in confusion. Arian smiled sadly. "I

will never forget him, Sir Rorick. My feelings run too deep for him, but if he does, as you say, forget me, then his feelings were not as true."

"Mayhap that is best then."

"Mayhap," she said softly.

The meal concluded without further exchange. Toward the end of it, a beaming Lady Lisette, hanging on her brother's arm, descended into the hall. Grudgingly the men stood. As she sat across from her, Arian nodded, then stood and said to her brother who sat to her right, "Rhodri, a word please."

As they meandered down to the other end of the hall, he looked at her, concern tugging at the crease near his eyes. "You do not look well, Arian. The Jarl will be most displeased to discover his bride so forlorn."

She let out a long breath. "Is it that obvious, Rhod?"

"Aye, it is. You wear your love for the Norman on your sleeve for all the world to see. Rumors run rampant of you and he in the village and the household here. Pray they do not reach Magnus's ear. I know you pine for the knight, but I beg you to stop. Nothing good can ever come of it. You are a princess, Arian, a royal; he is a bastard mercenary."

"But I have done nothing—"

"It matters not. The circumstances of your meeting have been painted and repainted until there is no resemblance to the original picture. As it is, I have defended your honor twice amongst the lesser lords who have traveled to witness the marriage. I will be glad when the bloody sheets are hung for all of Yorkshire to witness!"

Arian set her jaw, angry that her virtue was questioned, and, in so doing, Stefan's honor also. Only an eyewitness and the bloody sheets would prove her chastity, and though the Norman might be a bloodthirsty killer, he was not a rapist.

"Rhod, I overheard Lady Lisette and her brother Philip talking in the hall. They concoct some type of plan before my nuptials to discredit me in front of Magnus. 'Twould appear, from what I hear, Lord Philip has his eye on my dowry."

Rhodri threw his head back and laughed uproariously. Arian grabbed his sleeve. "I find no humor in their plot!"

Rhodri wiped his eyes. "Nay, 'tis not that, but that the little Norman thinks he is worthy to even consider wedding a princess of Wales!"

"Nothing surprises me, anymore, Rhod. This last month has been most unusual and unpredictable."

He hugged her close and kissed the top of her head. "Keep your dagger on your girdle, and I will keep close to you until you climb the stairway to your marriage bed. Never fear, you will see Magnus a virgin. I stake my life upon it!"

Foreboding swirled in her belly at his words, but Arian kept her eyes open and allowed no one to come too close, and for once was not irritated with the Norman guard that shadowed her every move.

When the sun had set behind the western horizon and still the Jarl's train had not arrived, Arian felt a niggle of apprehension. What if he had heard the rumors and he chose to stay away, refusing to ask her if they were true?

Nervously she paced before the lord's table. The

gathered nobles who had come to witness the marriage
grew as restless as she. Finally, having no other recourse,
Arian called for the meal to be served. Just as she sat at
the table, the lookout shouted that the Jarl's standard
had been sighted.

Arian felt her stomach drop to her feet. She looked
up straight into Stefan's eyes. Swallowing down the
lump in her throat, Arian looked away and allowed her
brother to escort her to the stone entryway of the manor
house. Nervousness feasted on her insides as the wait
for Magnus grew interminable.

When the standard bearer broke through the wide-
open gates to Moorwood, Arian's knees wobbled. When
Magnus appeared astride a great white destrier, his
long blond hair flowing behind him like a cape, his tall
muscular form sitting proud and square, she leaned on
Rhodri's arm for support. He patted her hand, steadying
her. The trumpets blared as the train came up behind
him, adorned in the blue and white colors of the house
of Tryggvason. Arian wanted to feel pride, but dread
engulfed her.

Magnus drew his great horse up in a flurry of fan-
fare. He smiled beneath his helm. He pulled it from
his head, his hair spilling around his great shoulders,
and his pale blue eyes, so much like Dag's, glittered
in excitement. He tossed his helm to his squire, dismounted and strode toward her. He dropped to one
knee and took her hands into his and kissed them.
"My lady," he said in his thick accented Welsh. "How
farest thou?"

She curtsied and said, "My lord, I am well."

A flicker of pain scattered across Magnus's handsome features, and Arian knew he thought of Dag.

He smiled up at her, then rose. Nervously, Arian pulled her hand from his and turned to Rhodri. "My lord, please, may I introduce my brother Rhodri."

Magnus stood to his full towering height; taller than Stefan, Arian thought, and while Magnus was well-muscled he was not nearly the specimen Stefan was. She caught herself making the comparison.

"My lord, my sister has eagerly awaited your arrival. I am glad to see you safely here."

The men made short bows. Lord Overly and Lady Lisette welcomed him, as did several of the lesser nobles. Magnus waved the rest of them off, then turned, beaming down at Arian. "My lady, I cannot express to you my distress when I learned of what transpired in Mercia. I thank God you are here and safe with me now."

Her heart started. He did not question her virtue? Arian smiled. "Milord, I beg a private word with you before we dine."

He took her hands into his. "There is time for that later. I want to savor you, Arian, for I would have swum the North Sea in my mail, so great was my desire to be here by your side." He pulled her to him. "Come, let us reacquaint ourselves with each other."

With his heartfelt candor, he was making what she had to say that much more difficult. Guilt washed through her. The hall glowed with a thousand candles as they entered, the aromatic scent of fresh herbs and flowers from new rush mats wafting invitingly in the air; the tables had been cleaned and set with fine silver goblets and silver candelabra. The scent of fine roasted meats filled the air; everyone had gathered in their finery to welcome the lord of the manor, Jarl Magnus the Tall. As they entered to the cheers of many, Arian felt her opportunity slipping away. She must speak with Magnus before the rumors made their way to him, causing him to doubt her. "My lord, please a private word first."

He smiled down at her, and she could not resist a smile in return. His face glowed with love for her, and she felt as if Belenus had kicked her in the gut. "Of course, my love. Your wish is my command."

Arian looked over her shoulder to find Stefan staring hard at her as she made her way up the stairway. With her eyes she pleaded with him to stay where he was and not interfere. But that was not to be; as she and Magnus entered her chamber with Jane and Magnus's man in tow, Stefan, followed by Sir Wulfson, Sir Rorick, and Rhodri, strode into the shrinking room.

"What is the meaning of this?" Magnus demanded, turning instantly from love-sotted swain into angry magnate.

Stefan gave the Viking a short bow. "I am Stefan de Valrey, knight of William. These are my men Lord Wulfson and Sir Rorick."

Magnus's eyes narrowed. "What business does Normandy have with me?"

Stefan glanced at Arian. "I am here to see to William's interests in the east."

Arian held her breath when Magnus turned sharp eyes upon her. "What interests would those be?"

"My lord," Arian began, "did not Sir Sar explain the exact nature of my arrival here?"

Magnus's face reddened in anger. "Aye, and yet I still do not believe Dag capable of such a thing."

"What is there not to believe?" Stefan demanded, stepping closer to the Viking. "Dag was bent on breaching the lady for his own gain, knowing you would refuse marriage to her."

Magnus's pale eyes glittered. "What purpose would that serve him?"

"He desired me enough to shame me *and* you, then claim my hand for himself when you refused me," Arian softly said.

Magnus swiped his hand across his face, finding the brutal facts of his nephew's death hard to accept.

"It does not ring true to Dag's character. He has a wife!"

"We will never know what ran through the knave's head. I witnessed the exchange and can vouch for the lady's defense and Dag's transgression," Stefan said flatly.

For a long moment, Magnus stood silent; Arian could see his mind working, asking questions, putting the pieces of the puzzle together.

He turned and looked directly at Arian. "How did Dag find you?"

"He but followed the path to the pond."

"What did he see?"

"What do you think he saw?" Stefan cut in.

Magnus turned glaring eyes on Stefan. "Pray you tell me, Norman. What did *you* behold?"

"An innocent woman preyed upon."

Magnus smiled, his lips twisting into a white line. "Forgive me, sir, for having difficulty digesting the image of my betrothed being ogled not only by my nephew but by a complete stranger."

Arian felt the heat rise in her cheeks. Her eyes darted to Stefan's, then back to Magnus. "I was bathing, milord. When I came from the water, I wrapped the linen Jane had set out for me around myself."

"Were you clothed when you ran into the wood?"

More heat warmed her cheeks. "Nay, I was not. Dag had ripped the linen from my person, and I ran for my life."

When Magnus turned to Stefan, his eyes glittered in rage. "So my betrothed is set upon by my nephew, she runs naked into the wood straight into your waiting arms, you slay my nephew and then? What?"

"We rode for a safer place."

"Why did you not return her to her train?"

Stefan smiled. "I had a use for her myself."

"A true Norman. Greed first, honor second," Magnus said carefully.

"Magnus!" Arian cried. "Enough of this! If the circumstances of my meeting Sir Stefan are too much for your pride to bear, say it now, and I will return to Dinefwr. I will not stand here and be humiliated for something I had no control over. Had Sir Stefan *not* been present, there would be no marriage between us."

He stood angry and tall before her. She understood his wounded pride. More calmly, she continued. "There is more to the tale than Dag's demise and my capture. The Normans remain here because, as Sir Stefan has said, my cousin Rhiwallon holds his man hostage. He still holds Lord Wulfson's lady, as well as her sister and Sir Thorin, who I am to understand is your king's half brother. They will not be released until we are wed. I suggest, my lord, you set your pride aside and we wed with haste."

"Did you bed the Norman?" he asked, barely audible.

Arian's jaw dropped.

"The lady's virtue has not been compromised by me," Stefan flatly answered for her.

Magnus stared hard at her. "I asked you, my lady, did you bed the Norman?"

"Nay!"

He turned from them, and with his hands behind his back, he began to pace the room. Arian looked up into Stefan's stormy face, wanting some kind of reassurance from him, but not knowing what.

She turned to find Magnus's brooding stare on them both. "Then explain this thing between you."

Stefan stepped forward, but Arian placed a hand on his arm, halting him. She walked up to the proud Viking and placed her hand on his chest. Softly she said, "Is it not possible for me to be indebted to the man who not only championed my virtue but my life? And not on just one occasion but several? Is it such a small thing to be thankful?"

Magnus looked over Arian's head to stare at Stefan. "There is more to it than that. I can see it in the way you look at him and he you."

Arian stiffened. That her feelings for the Norman were so clear to all shamed her. Slowly, she shook her head, and lied. "Nay, Magnus, you are wrong. I am but grateful for his interference; nothing more."

Magnus slid an arm around her waist and drew her to him. His eyes still blazed but 'twas not anger now. "I could not bear it if you loved another," he said softly, lowering his lips to hers. Arian stiffened, then loosened under his assault. When his lips brushed across hers her body did not warm, nor did it spark with anything but mild annoyance. He pulled her tighter against him. She knew if she remained cool, he would suspect more. Her arms rose up and locked around his neck, and she opened her lips, accepting him, for in two nights' time she would have to surrender all to him. In what seemed an endless kiss, he finally drew away from her.

"Where has the fire gone, milady?"

"I—you caught me off guard, and there are"—she turned to look at the men and Jane, raising her eyes to Stefan's stony glare. She felt Magnus's gaze follow hers.

"It seems I have caught you both off guard." He set her from him and said to them all, "Are there others who know of the circumstances of Dag's death?"

Stefan nodded. "Rumors swirl."

"I have no doubt." He stepped from Arian and commanded, "Here in this chamber the night of our wedding, I demand the priest, Prince Rhodri, Lord Overly and"—Magnus smiled—"you, Sir Stefan, on behalf of Normandy, to bear witness when I take Lady Arian that she bleeds virgin's blood. Hang the sheets from the highest rooftop and let no one say she was not pure when she came to me. Should any man question her honor, they will ride my ax to hell!"

Stefan shook his head. "I will not witness your taking of her." He looked to Wulfson. "My man will in my stead."

"But I insist!" Magnus charged.

Arian kept her silence, understanding why Magnus flexed his might.

"Insist all you wish. I will not do it," Stefan said. He clicked his heels together and made a short bow. "I have matters that need my attention, but before I withdraw allow me to make several points clear to you. Until you are wed, Lady Arian's safety and virtue are in my hands. My men will continue to stand guard outside her chamber door, as well as escort her about the manor and surrounding grounds. Her own men have been included in the details as well. I have no objection to you also appointing your men to see to her well-being, but this point is not negotiable. Once you are wed and satisfied she came to you pure, then I and my men will take our leave of this place. Those are my terms."

"What right do you, a Norman, have to tell me, lord and master here in my own house, what your terms are? You have no authority here!"

"Yorkshire is part of England and William is king. By his right of conquest I have the right to speak in his name."

"I will see all Normans cast from my house!"

"Try, and you will have all of Normandy to fight."

"Magnus!" Arian cried. "Let it be. There is no harm in

the Normans' presence; they will be gone in two days' time."

"Nay, they will be gone by sunset tomorrow!"

"But we are not to wed for two days."

"We wed on the morrow."

Arian's blood chilled. Panicked, she looked at Stefan. Magnus laughed. "Pray you are a virgin still, Arian, for if you are not, the Norman will pay with his life!"

Arian pressed her hand to Magnus's forearm. "Please clear the chamber, I wish to speak to you in private."

Once they were alone, Arian looked up into the face of the man she was to marry. She took his big hands into hers. "Tell me truly, Magnus, do you believe me?"

"That you are a virgin still or that you hold no feelings for the Norman?"

"Both." Carefully, she watched the emotions play across his handsome features. She understood his anger, his frustration, and his fear. Were she standing where he stood, her heart would be breaking.

He grasped her hands. "Arian, I am a proud man, and while I do not care what gossipmongers spew of me, I care that you are caught up in the viciousness. That a Norman is tied to your good name, even one who saved you from grave peril, sickens me. They are the scourge of this earth."

Guilt assailed her. If Magnus knew what had transpired, he would cast her out like a dirty rag. "Be glad for him, Magnus. He saved my life."

He pulled her into his embrace, and kissed the top of her head. "Truly, I am in his debt. Forgive my boorish manners."

She withdrew slightly and smiled up at him. "There is

nothing to forgive. Under the circumstance you handled yourself as the noble you are."

He brought her hands to his lips and kissed them. "Come, my lady, my hunger is fierce. Let us sup."

When they descended into the hall, every person stood, and each one of them seemed to be holding their breaths. When Magnus broke out into a wide smile, a collective sigh was felt throughout the place.

As he seated her to his right, she smiled up at him. "My lord." Before he took his seat beside her, he called down the hall. "My Norman friends, come sup at the lord's table, and tell me of your king and his plans for this island."

Arian held her breath, praying Stefan would decline, but she knew he would not. 'Twould be an insult to the lord and his lady. For propriety, he would accept. As he strode toward her, the arrogance in his step could not be mistaken for anything other than it was. His men fell in behind him, each a twin to the other.

Arian swallowed hard, but met his glare. She would not give the gossipmongers more to whisper about. Stefan made a short bow. "My lady." Then he sat to her right. The others sat on the other side of Magnus, squeezing out Lord Overly and Lady Lisette. As Lisette was relegated to the next table down, Arian caught her harsh glare and could not help a smug smile. 'Twould serve her right. The lady gave herself too many airs.

The blessing was said by Father John and the meal was served.

"Tell me, Sir Stefan, does William have plans for Yorkshire?"

"I do not know."

"Will he go north of the Humber?"

"I do not know."

"I suspect he has his eye on Scotland as well."

"The Scots are a bitter lot," Rorick chimed in. "And while I have no doubt we could easily take that part of the island, methinks they are safe. For a year or two." He laughed and drained his goblet.

"What of the young Olaf?" Stefan asked. "Does he plan to take up where his sire left off?"

Magnus set aside several choice pieces of meat he had cut for Arian, then waited for a servant to fill their shared goblet with rich Burgundy wine before he spoke.

He raised it to her lips, and softly said, "Drink, my dear, it will chase away your bride's nervousness."

Arian made to take the goblet from his hands, but he would not release it. "Allow me, Arian, 'tis a prelude to my most attentive nature."

Arian smiled, deciding there was no time like the present to try and reacquaint herself with this man who only a month ago held her favor. She wrapped her fingers around his big hands, and without breaking his gaze, she brought the goblet to her lips. He tilted it, and she drank deeply of the wine. When she pushed it away, in a slow slide he wiped the dampness from her lower lip with his fingertip. "You missed some," he whispered.

Arian looked boldly into his eyes, knowing the entire hall watched the exchange expectantly. If she were to convince them all, most of all Magnus, that she had eyes only for him, there would be less tension between them. She knew his pride waged a terrible war with his heart.

Demurely, she fluttered her lashes. "My thanks," she said softly.

Magus smiled and set the goblet down and turned to Stefan, sitting to her right, as if just remembering his presence. "My pardon, Sir Stefan, did you say something?"

Arian turned slightly in her seat to face him and caught back a sharp gasp. She understood Magnus's game the minute her eyes clashed with Stefan's glacial ones. The small tic in his right jaw betrayed his fury. "Aye, I asked if your king had plans to take up the sword and claim England."

Unable to sit so close and face him just a hand's-breadth from her, Arian turned back to face her betrothed.

Magnus motioned for the servant to refill his goblet. "Olaf is young and a fervent Christian. He wants peace at all costs. Tell your king that unless he provokes us, he can expect Norway to mind her own affairs."

"Aye, but what of his kin, Sven of Denmark? He casts a covetous eye to the south."

"Sven is a fool. Should he take up arms against the Conqueror, he will get no help from Norway; of that I can assure you."

"I have ridden these last eight years with Thorin Haraldson; 'tis he who Rhiwallon holds hostage until word of your marriage reaches him."

"Olaf has many bastard siblings. He has no interest in them."

" 'Tis unfortunate. The Viking bastard has the ear of the most powerful king on the continent."

Magnus nodded. "That may be, but Olaf is strong in

his own right. He does not require Norman assistance, nor does he desire it."

"One cannot have too many allies in these unpredictable times," Stefan cautioned.

"If you have not noticed, Sir Stefan, anyone of Norman descent is unwelcome in the east. I fear that if William does not tread with care, he may very well find the area afire with revolt."

Stefan leaned across Arian, his chest brushing against her back, toward Magnus. "If one finger is raised against me or my men, there will be hell to pay."

Magnus laughed easily. "You misunderstand. I offer no threat. But do not think I would not raise more than a finger to protect what is mine."

"All that is England belongs to William."

Magnus's eyes narrowed, very softly he said, "Nay, all that you see for fifty leagues in any direction is mine. No man will take it from me."

"By right of conquest he can do it with a simple charter."

"I will kill the man he sends to take it from me."

Arian pushed both men away from her, and said sternly, "My lords, enough of politics. Let us sup in peace!"

Magnus smiled and backed down. "My pardon."

Arian settled down with his apology. She could not blame him, though; she would react the same. She could not damn herself enough for not doing a better job of hiding her feelings for Stefan. 'Twas because of her weakness Magnus acted as he did. She would do better, for peace here at Moorwood as well as peace in her marriage. She would hide what burned so fervently in her heart.

But as the meal continued on a much lighter note, Arian could not relax. She sat between the man she loved and the man who would be her husband. Once the table was cleared and the musicians began to play and the village girls to dance, her mood still did not soften. Stefan remained beside her, his warmth encompassing her like a cloak. She dared not cast a glance at him. He sat as rigid as a lance beside her.

When one of the girls twirled and gyrated before Lord Wulfson, who scowled and turned to his goblet, then to Rorick, who grinned and grabbed her swaying hips to him, the girl pretended to be afraid. He pressed his face to her bosom and kissed her there. The wench broke from his grasp and twirled to Sir Ioan, who had turned to face her, his legs stretched out before him. Agilely she stepped between them in a quick staccato. He closed his legs, catching her between his muscular thighs.

"You are not quick enough to escape me," he laughed, and brought her down into his lap. She threw her arms around his neck and kissed him soundly on the lips, then freed herself. Arian watched the wench's dark eyes twinkle in mischief as she swayed and twirled toward Stefan. The music picked up in tempo and volume, her hips moved back and forth at a frantic pace; her loose kirtle slid off one shoulder, her breasts the only support for the flimsy fabric. As she moved in toward Stefan, Warner reached out and caught the front ribbons of her garment. She twisted, and when she did her ample breasts sprang free. Roars of male appreciation hit the ceiling beams. In a wild thrust of hips and breasts, she flung herself across Stefan's lap, her back to his thighs, just as the music ended on a high note.

Arian could not look away. The woman's breasts glowed from perspiration as they heaved up and down from her heavy breaths. She smiled up at Stefan and grabbed his hand, pressing it to her voluptuous mounds. "Do I please you, milord?" she gasped.

"Aye," Stefan growled. He stood and hoisted her over his shoulder, and amidst loud cheers, he strode from the hall with the half-naked woman slung over his shoulders.

Arian felt as if she had been kicked in the stomach. But she dared not show it. She turned a smile to Magnus, to find him gazing upon her. "Tell me, milord, of Norway."

His face broke into a wide grin. " 'Tis beautiful, most especially in spring when the lilies bloom across the land."

"It sounds much like Wales when the entire region is purple with bluebells."

"Norway is a most welcoming land. I look forward to our life there."

And she would try to look forward to it too.

A short time later, exhaustion claimed Arian. The walls and eyes of the smoky hall pressed down upon her, and try as she might, visions of Stefan in the arms of the lusty wench would not go away.

"Milord, the day has been long, and I tire. Please see me to my chamber."

He nodded and stood, extending his hand to her. Slowly she rose, as did everyone in the hall. With chin high and shoulders proud, Magnus escorted her from the hall to the wide stairway, followed close behind by two Norman, two Welsh, and two Norse guards.

Before the door closed behind her, Magnus halted her. "Arian, one word before you retire."

Slowly she turned to face him, seeing the pain in his eyes. Her farce was not lost upon him. Guilt assailed her once again, and she truly did not know what to do. He cleared his throat and slowly said, "Come what may in the days to follow, know always that I had your best interest at heart."

Confused by his words, she asked. "What are you saying, Magnus?"

"Only that my heart is true." He pressed a kiss upon her forehead, then left her.

When Arian entered her chamber, even more confused by his words, she was surprised to see a chambermaid straightening the linens on her bed. "What are you doing?"

The maid bobbed her head and bowed. "Freshening your bed, milady."

Arian looked about the room for Jane. Save for herself and the maid, the chamber was empty. "Leave the bed and send for my maid Jane," Arian commanded, walking over to the small table near the low-burning brazier. The nights had cooled considerably since her arrival; soon the leaves would be in full change, and winter would find her in the cold fjords of Norway.

Arian gave the departing maid no heed as the door closed behind her. Her eyes trailed across the room to where her wedding gown hung from a high stand. 'Twas beautiful, made of fine blue and white silk, with intricate silver embroidery around the low bodice, bell sleeves, and hem. The silver undertunic, embroidered with fine blue and white silk threads, she had stitched herself. 'Twas a garment fit for a queen.

She sank to the floor, fighting the despair that threatened to engulf her. Why could she not trade places with the lowly wench and take her beloved to bed this night? But she knew the answers. She was a princess, she must marry a prince or a most powerful magnate, and Magnus was that. But Stefan was a magnate in his own right. Noble blood flowed through his veins as well. Neither his sire nor his dam was a churl, but a great count and the sister to the woman who would be Queen of England. But it mattered not. Even should Magnus refuse her, Stefan had not declared love for her. And if he did not love her, then what was there? A marriage like her father's to Morwena? Where one always held out hope for the other who would always chase a ghost? She sighed. Was it not what Magnus would endure? Would she ever wake and not think of Stefan before she opened her eyes?

Her fate was sealed. On the morrow she would be Lady Arian of Trygg. 'Twas her lot in this life, and she would be grateful for it. She stood and brushed the wrinkles from her gown, and it occurred to her she had not seen Jane since before the late meal. Arian opened the heavy door of her chamber to find six pairs of eyes upon her.

She looked to Sir Rorick, the one closest to her. "Sir, I seem to have misplaced my woman, Jane. See to her whereabouts and instruct her to come to me at once."

Sir Rorick looked stunned that she would request such a thing from him. "My lady, I am a knight of William, not a squire. Ask your man." He stepped back and looked to Pal, a young man from Dinefwr.

Pal bobbed his head. "I will locate her." He turned and hurried down the hall.

Arian made a sarcastic smile and gave both Sir Rorick and Sir Ioan a short bow. "My pardon for making such a heinous request of a Norman knight!"

TWENTY

Stefan pressed his lips to a taut dark nipple. It came to life beneath his lips. Thick arms wrapped around his head, pressing him harder into the sultry cleavage. The wench tasted of wine and sweat, but she was willing and she would make him forget, at least for a time. He hiked up her kirtle, catching a whiff of her musky scent. Stefan thrust her onto the bed of hay in the stall next to Arian's mare. The horse whinnied, as if disgusted with his choice for the night. Images of the woman who rode the steed prickled at his mind. His body tightened and his blood lit up. But not for the willing body writhing beneath him.

"*Jesu!*" he cursed.

"Who comes?" the wench cried, trying to sit up.

His hands squeezed her plump breasts, pushing her back into the hay. "No one, be silent," he commanded.

Her skin wasn't nearly as soft or fragrant as the woman's who haunted his dreams at night and every waking moment of the day. Stefan cursed again and pushed the wench's thighs apart. She arched into him, groping between his thighs, nearly ripping his braies from him. She freed him and he hissed in a sharp breath. Her callused hands stroked him to hardness.

"My lord," she moaned, "I have never had a man so large as you."

Closing his eyes, Stefan imagined that the rough hands fondling him were the soft slender ones of a princess. Wet lips pressed to his. Stefan twisted away from her, his eyes flying open.

In one swift move, he flipped her over and pulled her up by the hips, throwing her skirt over her back. He did not want to see a face when he entered her. He wanted to imagine it was another. "My lord!"

"Silence!" he hissed, grabbing her backside and spreading her full buttocks. He pulled her toward his stiff cock. He looked down at that moment and halted all movement. The sight of her body sickened him. She pressed into him, the tip of his cock sliding up between her buttocks. In a fit of anger, Stefan shoved her away from him and stood gathering his braies, tying them in short jerky movements.

She turned over, panic-stricken. "My lord, do I not please you?"

Fury tore through him. Arian had ruined him! She had made it impossible for him to touch another and not make a comparison! She had made it impossible for him to lose himself in another's body no matter how willing or comely that body was!

" 'Tis not you," he growled, then strode from the stall to the hall.

He approached his men and the Welsh and Norse

guard outside the door of the woman who had ruined him. While his men moved from the door, the Welshman and Norse did not. "I will hack you down where you stand if you do not move from the doorway," he threatened.

"Sir, no one—" the largest of the Norse began to say.

Ioan and Rorick drew their swords. The guards stepped aside, and the solitary Welshman stood aside as well. Stefan pounded on the door.

"Who goes there?" Arian called from the other side.

"Stefan," he ground out.

After a long moment, the door slowly opened. He pushed her away as he entered, then flung the door closed behind him. He did not know why he was there or what he was to say, he only knew a seething rage he could not control, and all of it directed at one person. The proud and beautiful Arianrhod of Dinefwr.

"Why are you here?" she demanded.

Gone was the innocent maid he had rescued, gone was the hostage. In her place stood a woman who knew her mind and her destiny, and who refused to allow him to be a part of it.

He strode past her and began to pace the room. "You smell of your whore," Arian spat when he passed close to her.

He whirled around and faced her. "You reek of Viking!"

Arian strode past him toward the door. He grabbed her arm and pulled her around to face him. "Nay, Arian, you will not cast me out like a soiled cloth." In a wild fit of passion he could not control, Stefan tore her kirtle down the front, exposing creamy white breasts. Hungrily he caught one in his mouth. His arms slid around her waist, pulling her harder against him. Her scent, her silky smooth skin, her voice tantalized him beyond mortal control

"Nay, Stefan." She twisted away from his grasp to the far side of the chamber. "Why are you here?" she demanded.

"*Jesu*, Ari," he groaned hoarsely. How could he tell her he ached for her? That every part of his body screamed for her and only her?

"Why are you here?"

Arian held her breath. His eyes blazed furiously, his hands opening and closing into fists at his side. He opened his mouth to speak, but words failed him. "Tell me," she whispered, hoping yet dreading, that he came to claim her.

"I—" He bowed, and when his eyes lifted to hers she knew any hope of them together was gone. "My pardon." He whirled around and left the room as abruptly as he entered. As the door slammed shut, her body jerked and her heart broke. For had Stefan pledged his oath of love to her, she would have set Magnus aside, forfeiting her dowry and all that was hers for the nameless Norman.

Just as the door closed behind him, it opened again. Arian's heart leapt in her chest, then plummeted; 'twas only the maid whom she had encountered earlier.

She bobbed and stopped in her steps, her eyes widened and Arian realized her disheveled appearance was most shocking. Drawing her kirtle over her bare chest, she demanded, "Where is my woman?"

"She—she midwifes in the village."

"There are no others to see to a birth?"

"There are complications, she left with the woman's husband a short time ago. She bade me to offer her regrets but promised to return in the morn to ready you for your marriage."

Arian let out a long breath. Of all people, she wanted Jane with her this night, but she understood there were few as skilled as Jane in seeing a new babe into the world.

"Very well." Arian let out a long, tired breath and asked, "What is your name?"

"Miriam, my lady."

"Miriam, I am weary and seek my bed. Fetch me a chemise from the wardrobe, then see yourself to the pallet."

Miriam bobbed her head and saw to the task.

For more candle notches than not, Arian tossed and turned upon the large bed. Sleep eluded her. Stefan's scent clung to her. He was all she could think of. He was all she wanted. Each time she inhaled his scent she felt his presence as if he were there, lying beside her. A deep ache clawed at her heart, so intense it pained her to breathe.

Had he just said he loved her, had he just asked her to be his, she would have given all to him. Angrily she threw a pillow across the room and sat up. But he had not. Because he did not return her love. And after what she had said to him at Worthington, she could not blame him.

She flopped back into the sheets and closed her eyes, praying for sleep. But when it came, nightmares assailed her. Visions of blood and war and fire—and death.

Arian woke with a start as the gray fingers of dawn inched through the cracked shutters. Fatigue pressed upon her as she stifled one yawn after another. The reality of what the day would bring prodded her wide awake. 'Twas her wedding day. Calmly she accepted her fate. Stefan had his chance and did not take it. And though profound sadness and an unexplainable sense of loss engulfed her, she would not cry. She would not wish, she would never beg. What was done was done. Slowly she arose from the bed.

The morning was a whirlwind of activity; as Arian sank into a hot, soapy bath, Jane hurried into the chamber. "A thousand pardons, my lady, but—"

"Do not apologize, Jane, all is well now that you are here."

As Miriam stripped the linens, replacing them with fresh sheets, she crumbled sweet-smelling herbs and flowers amongst them. Instead of settling her nerves, the overwhelming scent clogged Arian's nostrils. Her stomach fluttered when she thought of Magnus laying her upon them later that eve, touching her as Stefan had, and more.

"Leave us, Miriam," Jane commanded.

The maid bobbed her head, scooped up the basket of soiled linens, and hurried from the chamber.

"That girl irritates me with her nervous head-bobbing. She seems to be afraid of her own shadow!" Jane complained.

"I doubt she has served a lady before," Arian said.

"Then she should not be practicing on you!"

Jane set about bathing Arian, washing her thick golden-red hair and rinsing it with scented water. Once she was dried and seated before the murky mirror, the chamber suddenly bustled with females. One maid to create an ornate braided crown, another to smooth the fine lines from the silken wedding gown, one to manicure her nails and feet, and yet another to rub down her limbs with fragrant oils. Even Lady Lisette came to help, and for the first time the woman did not bait her with a snide look or sour words. Indeed, she seemed most content.

When Arian was finally dressed and bejeweled, there was a knock on the door. 'Twas Magnus's manservant. He carried a gold-inlaid willow box before him. Making a quick bow to Arian and Lady Lisette, he set the box down on the table beside Arian. "My lady, my lord Magnus asked that you honor him this day by wearing the crown of Trygg."

Arian watched as he withdrew a magnificent crown of entwined gold, silver, and shining copper, encrusted with glittering precious jewels. A leaping stag of burnished gold centered the crown. She bowed, and he set it upon her head. 'Twas heavy and uncomfortable, but she would wear it with pride.

Taking a deep breath, she caught Jane's gaze and smiled. "I am ready," Arian said. She stood, and all the ladies in the room gasped in praise.

"You are a vision, my lady," the manservant gushed. "My lord will be pleased."

Another knock at the door saw Rhodri, followed by Cadoc. Her brother stopped in mid-stride, the smile on his face nearly splitting it. "My God, Arian, you are beautiful!"

She could only smile, too afraid that the emotion tightening in her chest would be misconstrued. She had longed for her wedding day, to marry her one true love who would place her on a pedestal and treasure her over all men and women. But the one she cherished would not claim her, and the one she did not love was only too happy to.

With a will of tempered steel, Arian forced all thoughts of Stefan from her heart. On this, her wedding day, she would show Magnus the respect he deserved, and not wish for another as she vowed to be a dutiful wife.

Rhodri extend his arm. Arian looked up into his eyes, barely able to see him through the tears she could not control.

He drew her into his embrace and kissed her cheeks. "You are a vision any man would fight to the death to have, dear sister. Including Magnus. He has been pacing a hole in the hall and now eagerly awaits you in the chapel." He placed her hand on his forearm. "Come."

Refusing to bear witness to the nuptials, Stefan sat in the empty stall beside Arian's mare, along with his brothers, and emptied a second wineskin. It did nothing to ease the ache in his heart. Longing twisted with a desperate need for the woman he could not have. Emptiness filled his soul, and he felt as if there was no reason to take his next breath. For Arian was his life, and without her, 'twas as if he had no sustenance. And though he would ride, and battle, and see to his king's needs, the most vital parts of him would be missing. His heart and his soul.

The clamoring cheers yanked him from his sour musings, and he realized the vows had been sealed. If the destrier had kicked him in the gut it would have hurt less than the sound of the cheering people of Moorwood.

Despair that he had never experienced even in Jubb now consumed him. On the morrow, he would leave with his brothers and travel to Wales with word of the nuptials, and Wulf would hold his lady in his arms once again. Envy pricked at his gut as the cheers grew louder.

He threw his head back and took a long draught of wine. "I promised her I would not look back when we rode west," Stefan said, to no one in particular.

" 'Tis for the best," Wulfson said.

Stefan's head snapped back, and he eyed his brother. "Is it?" He shook his head. "I do not know if I can do it!" Misery flooded him.

'Twas easy for Wulfson. He had found the one woman in all of Christendom he would love; but Stefan had found his own one and only and now he was to stand aside as she wed another. He drank more of the wine, wanting it to numb his aching heart, but it only made him more morose. And the anger he thought he could control simmered just beneath the surface. He could not control it after all.

He clenched his jaw and stood, fury, longing, and love filling him. He punched a wooden beam. "I cannot stand the torture of her lying with another!" He threw his head back and screamed his battle cry, then dropped to his knees. "I cannot bear it."

For a long time the men were silent. Stefan rubbed the heels of his hands into his eyes, slowly shaking his head. "I cannot do this," he moaned. "I cannot sit here whilst that Viking salivates."

"Then take her," Rohan growled. "Take her and be done with it!"

"Take her?" Stefan asked, incredulous. "She is wed!"

Wulfson stood and stepped toward him, placing a meaty hand on his shoulder. "Is it lust and jealousy in your heart, Stefan, that drives you? Of having something you cannot have?"

Miserably, he shook his head. " 'Tis more. It pains my heart."

"Do you love her?" Ioan asked, stepping forward.

Sudden clarity shook through Stefan. "Aye, above my own life."

"Then go to her, man, and plead your case!" Rorick urged.

"She is wed!"

Rohan laughed, the sound demonic. "Aye, but there is still a way. An old Norman law dating back to Rollo's time."

"Tell me!" Stefan demanded.

"Jus primae noctis."

"But I am not lord here," Stefan said.

"You are captain of William's guard, and in his stead you are lord here!" Rohan shouted. "Your word is law!"

'Twould later be a matter of great debate, but Stefan did not care. He wanted only one thing, and would use an archaic law to grasp it. And even without the law on his side, he would not be denied. He pushed his brothers aside and ran for the hall.

Arian lay back on the cool linens, her teeth chattering, her knees quaking, modesty overcoming her. She could not bear to meet the eyes of Father John, her brother who could not meet hers, the Norman Sir Ralph, and Magnus's cousin Helm. All present to bear witness that she bled when her husband performed his duty. All there to bear witness that no sheep's blood was smeared on the sheets, all there to bear witness that she was a virgin until her husband breached her.

Even Magnus seemed nervous. Slowly, his man undressed him, as did Jane Arian. When her lady was clothed only in her silken chemise, Jane drew the screen so that she was at least afforded some privacy as she slid into the large bed. Arian pulled the sheet up to her chin and forced herself to watch Magnus undress. When he stood naked before her, she swallowed hard. His manhood stood rigid before him.

He pulled the sheet back and sat upon the bed as Father John came around to her side of the bed and lifted the sheet so that he could see her.

"Your pardon, Lady Arian, but 'tis necessary."

She nodded. Closing her eyes, she held her breath when Magnus's great body covered hers. She felt him hard and warm against her thigh and nearly cried out in fear. She did not want this.

He smoothed the hair back from her cheeks, and softly said," 'Twill be over soon, then they will go."

She squeezed her eyes shut tighter, and nodded, wishing he would get it over with. Slowly she parted her thighs.

A hoarse shout, followed by a hard thump in the hallway, startled her. Arian's eyes flew open just as the door burst open. Stefan strode across the threshold, his sword drawn, his men behind him prepared for battle.

"What is the meaning of this?" Magnus demanded, rolling from Arian.

Her heart beat so hard against her chest that Arian

thought she might perish from the percussion. She grabbed the sheet up to her chin and sat back in the bed. Stefan did not look her way, but kept his hard glare on her husband. "In the name of Normandy, I claim *jus primae noctis.*" Stefan said, his voice low and angry.

Magnus threw back his head and laughed. "You are not lord here! You have no right. And even were you, that law is not our law."

"You will not shame my sister!" Rhodri erupted, his hand on the hilt of his sword.

"Nay, Rhod, do not, he will kill you!" Arian screamed, coming to her knees in the bed.

"Sir Stefan," Father John said calmly, " 'tis an archaic law of Normandy, one that would never be upheld. Think of what you demand, and the consequences of the action."

Stefan nodded. "The consequence would be a child of Norman and Welsh blood. 'Tis my king's wish that the blood of both lands blend."

"But Wales is not part of the conquest!" Magnus argued. "And you are not lord here!"

"I am William's arm."

" 'Tis preposterous! Does your king mean to force Norman blood on the people of this island by raping their women?"

" 'Tis an outdated law, to be sure, but still a law," Stefan admitted, but righteous in his stand. "Remove yourself from the bed, Magnus, or I will have you tried and hanged for treason!"

Magnus stood furious and naked in the room, surrounded by Norman knights. He would get no aid from his two men, nor from Father John.

"Do I not have a say in the matter?" Arian demanded, suddenly furious. How dare Stefan?

Magnus's eyes narrowed suspiciously, as he looked from Arian to Stefan, and she understood his thoughts. "Nay, Magnus, you are wrong!"

He nodded, and turned back to Stefan. " 'Tis a ruse to hide the fact she is not a virgin."

Stefan laughed contemptuously. "Have you so little faith in your lady, Magnus? Do you think her so disloyal?" Stefan looked at Arian then, and gave her a short bow. "A more honorable lady I have not met. You do yourself and her a great dishonor questioning her virtue." Stefan moved to Arian's side of the bed, but looked across it to the furious Viking. "Dress yourself and be gone from this chamber. In the morn, you will decide if you still want her."

"Nay! She is mine now! I will not hand her over, not for one night, not for one minute!"

"You have no choice in the matter. Go now before you will not be able to."

"Nay, Stefan!" Arian cried. "I will not have this!"

He glared at her. "Nor do you have a choice in the matter, my lady."

"Would you rape me then?"

"I will have you this night. How is up to you."

"I will give you this manor and the thousand hides that go with it, if you but leave us now," Magus pleaded.

Stefan shook his head. "You offer me what is already mine." He looked to Rhodri. "Take your brother-in-law from this chamber before I make your sister a widow."

"The priest stays! I demand a witness to her virgin blood!" Magnus screamed.

"Nay, I would not shame her as you have with a witness other than myself." Stefan spoke slow and measured, so that every occupant in the chamber understood his conviction. "My word is my oath: the blood on the sheets I will produce in the morn will be her virgin blood!" He raised his sword. "Then, my lord, hang it from the highest tower for the entire island to bear witness."

Magnus grabbed his braies and chauses, yanking them on. His eyes pleaded with Arian's to resist, but she did not. Should she, blood would be spilled, and that she would not have on her hands.

Moments later, the chamber was empty save for her and Stefan. The soft candlelight cast a warm glow across his harsh features. He bowed and sheathed his sword, then turned to throw the bolt, barring anyone entry. When he turned back to her, she could not read his face, but his blue eyes glittered like molten fire in the candlelight. Dragging the sheet with her, Arian came from the bed. She slapped him hard across the face. "How *dare* you?"

"I did not plan this to happen, Arian."

Fury infused her, so blinding that she could see only white. "What have you done? *Why*?"

" 'Tis simple, Arian. I love you."

"You *love* me? You tell me now? *After* I am wed?"

"I did not realize it until now."

She laughed harshly. "What you are doing is selfish. All you have ever done has been for your own selfish reasons! Have you never put someone else's feelings before your own?" She whirled away from him, then turned, glaring at him. "I am not a conquest! I am a woman with feelings. How do you expect me to face my husband?"

"I will remove him."

"Nay, you will not! I am married in the eyes of God! You shame me to my core, Stefan."

A stormcloud gathered upon his face. "What is done is done! Tonight you will give yourself to me!"

"I will not!"

"You will. If there is no blood upon the sheets, your honor will be forever soiled."

"You speak to me of honor? What of yours, Stefan? What honor is there in raping a man's wife on his wedding night?"

"The law allows—"

"The law is barbaric and you know it!"

"It is the law!"

Angrily, she ripped the sheets from her body and stood naked before him. "Then take me now and be done with it."

"I did not wish it to be this way."

"You did not consider anyone's desires but your own. Take me, Stefan, then leave me."

Stefan stepped toward her, their gazes locked in furious battle.

"Arian, why do you hold back what we both so desperately desire?"

"I do not want you like this, Stefan. 'Tis too late for us."

"Nay, it is not. Come to me, my love." He moved closer. "Give us this one night, Arian."

She shook her head, hot tears filling her eyes, and her heart broke all over again. The one thing she so desperately wanted from him, his heart, he now freely gave, but now she could not accept it. "Should I lie with you, on the morrow Magnus will annul the marriage, and I will hang my head in shame."

With his fingers, he lifted her chin so that she could look directly into his eyes. His gentle touch and warm breath soothed her in a way she was not prepared for. "You are too proud to ever hang your head in shame."

"Stefan, if we become lovers this night we are doomed."

He brought her lips to his. "Nay, I do not believe it."

His kiss was just a soft brush of his lips across hers, but it stirred her blood. "Stefan," she moaned. " 'Tis wrong."

He slid a strong arm around her waist, bringing her against his chest. "Nay, there has never been anything so right in my life as you here in my arms."

Arian could not fight what they both knew was meant to be. The fates had conspired not just once but many times to throw them together, only to tear them apart. But not this night. This night nature would finally consummate what fate had conspired. Yet as much as her heart, body, and soul wanted him, she knew in her gut that should she go where he led her, there would be more than Magnus's pride to suffer.

Stefan kissed her forehead, then her nose and cheek. His kisses trailed to her ear, his warm breath causing gooseflesh to erupt across her entire body. Her breasts filled and her nipples stiffened. "You smell of exotic places," he whispered.

Arian felt her control slipping. He did not press her; he was giving her the choice, and she could not deny him.

"Stefan . . ." she breathed, and gave herself up to him.

"Arian . . ." he sighed. "My love."

He brushed her long hair from her shoulders, pulling back just enough to gaze upon her. "You are beautiful." He lowered his lips to the pink scar on her breast and kissed it. "Forgive me for my brutishness that day, Arian."

"I forgave you the first time you kissed me."

His lips brushed a taut nipple, bringing her up against him. Arian closed her eyes and melted in his arms, the sensations he wreaked with his mouth and tongue so wonderfully sublime that she knew she must be dreaming. That he was here with her in her bed, and in moments would be inside her as God had intended man and woman to be, terrified yet thrilled her. She placed her hands on his shoulders, then dug her fingers into his hair, pressing him harder against her breast. He laid her back upon the bed. Naked she lay, unashamed as his eyes roved every inch of her. He spread her long hair out about her like a golden shroud, his eyes devouring her. "I cannot explain how I feel at this moment, Arian. 'Tis terrifying and thrilling, and my heart—" He touched a finger to her lips, "My heart feels as if it is too full. I fear it will burst."

Her hand trailed up to his and she sucked his finger into her mouth, swirling her tongue around it. Stefan hissed, and she felt him move against her thigh.

"Remove your clothes, Stefan, my body grows impatient for you."

Grinning, he stood and quickly removed every stitch from his body. When he was naked and full in front of the low candlelight, Arian caught her breath. He reminded her of the ancient Celtic gods, warriors of great strength and power. His scars did nothing to detract from his manliness; nay, they only enhanced it.

"You are magnificent, Stefan."

He eased down on the bed beside her sweeping his hand down her belly to her hips, pressing the heel of his hand gently against her soft downy mound.

Sensation erupted, wild wanton need flashed, heating her to the extreme. Suddenly Arian wondered how she could have ever denied this man her body. So long she had wanted, and now that desire had turned into a gut-wrenching need that if not sated would drive her mad.

"Stefan," she breathed, pressing her hips against his hand. "My ache for you consumes me."

He smiled into her eyes and she nearly died—the emotion she saw there was so profound it nearly undid her. A sudden terrible fear grabbed ahold of her gut. This was love in its purest form. The joining of heart and body and soul, and she would be robbed of it forever after this night. Her eyes burned with unshed tears for what she could never again have.

"Do not cry, my love," Stefan whispered as he lowered his lips to hers. "I will never be far from you."

When he kissed her, in that moment he chased her fear far away. She melted into him, and let him take her to the place she had wanted to go for so long now it seemed a lifetime.

"Take me now, Stefan," she gasped, tearing her lips from his.

He smiled again and slowly shook his head. "Nay, I

want to savor every part of you." He kissed her cheek, her chin. "Slowly," he whispered, then kissed her neck, his lips lingering there as his hands reverently cupped her breasts, until his lips found the deep valley he had created. Breathless, she hung suspended in anticipation, wanting all now but deliciously surrendering to his slow teasing seduction.

He kissed the scar on her breast, his tongue sliding across it then down to her sensitive nipple. He gently sucked it into his mouth. Arian closed her eyes and rose up to him. His arm slid around her waist, bringing her hard to him as his voraciousness intensified. Then just as the passion reared, he let go of her and pressed her gently back into the bed.

Slowly, tasting every inch of her, his lips traveled lower. He kissed her belly. "You are indescribable," he said softly against her sultry skin. She released a long slow breath. His lips traveled to the cradle of her hips. "You smell . . ." His lips traveled lower to just above the soft down that shielded the core of her. He brushed his nose softly across her there, and inhaled her scent. ". . . like heaven."

His warm breath against her there sent delightful shivers of excitement along her limbs, and her sweet hunger for him grew. He kissed the inside of her thighs as his fingers softly stroked where he had just kissed. "Arian," he breathed, "I burn for you, with the intensity of a thousand suns." He looked up from her thigh, and smiled softly. "I do not want this night to end."

Arian caught her breath at his words. For such a fearsome knight, he was so gentle and patient with her that she wanted to cry. But in his gentle patience he had stoked a wildfire within her. "Nor do I, but for it to end"—slowly, she opened herself to him—"it must begin."

His eyes glittered. He nodded, and what he did next sent her shooting to the stars. His lips pressed to her nether lips and he gently suckled her. Arian grabbed the sheets, twisting them in her fists. A rush of erotic sensation shot through her entire body, causing her to gasp for breath. His tongue slid against the seam of her followed, his lips gently sucking. He brushed a finger across her hardened nub and Arian thought she would fall apart.

When his tongue slid across that oh-so-sensitive place, she moaned, pressing her hips into him, wanting more. He did not disappoint. He slid a thick finger against her swollen folds. Arian held her breath. In a slow delirious slide, he pushed his finger into her. Arian came up off the bed, the sensation so incredibly delicious that she could not help the cries of pleasure escaping her. With excruciating slowness, he moved his finger in and out of her, as his lips and tongue flicked and suckled the small, hardened mound that created so much sensation.

The fire in her loins burned brighter and hotter, spreading to places inside that seemed on the verge of total destruction. "Stefan," she breathed, "the fire, it rages."

He moaned, kissing her downy mound before he lifted his head to look up at her. Her moistness glistened on his lips but she felt no shame; nay, that he gave her such pleasure filled her with womanly power. Slowly he slid his finger from her. Her hips rose, wanting to recapture it, but he rose above her, covering her body with his. His lips pressed to hers in a deep soulful kiss, his tongue swirling against hers. His hardness pressed into her thigh. Arching beneath him, Arian wrapped her arms around his neck, bringing him closer to her.

Gently he pressed into her soft wet opening. Arian held her breath when he entered her. He gathered her closer in his arms. " 'Twill hurt, my love, but only for a moment," he said softly.

"Nay, Stefan, you could never hurt me."

He pushed further into her and she took him. He broke past her virgin shield, and though she felt a twinge of pain, her body was ready for him. Gently, almost hesitantly, he moved deeper into her, giving her body time to accept him. Arian held her breath until he was fully sheathed. Stefan kissed her eyelids, her cheeks, and her lips. "When you are ready, Arian," he breathed.

She looked up into his brilliant eyes and his love for her shone through like the brightest star in a black sky. Emotion rushed through her. Never had she felt so cherished, nor so safe as she did at that moment in his arms. And with it, a profound sadness filled her, that this one night would have to carry her through the rest of her life.

His lips captured hers in a rough passionate kiss. His body swelled and she felt his muscles tighten. She moved beneath him, wanting his mark upon her.

He thrust into her and she caught her breath. He lifted his hips, pulling from her, then thrust again, and again, and again, until in perfectly synchronized undulation their bodies came together as one in the primal ebb and flow of two lovers mating. His fingers dug into her hair, his lips captured hers, his tongue swirled against hers. He carried her away up into the clouds, into the sun and beyond.

Sensation engulfed every part of her body. Her skin flushed warm and moist, her blood ran hot and swift in her veins. The wave of desire rose with each thrust of his hips, raising her higher and higher until it crashed inside of her with a soul-shattering inferno. Arian cried out as hot shards of fire burned her insides, causing a cataclysmic release that shook her very soul. Gasping for breath, she clung to him, riding out the sensation knowing she would never be the same again. Stefan gathered her closer in his arms. She felt the shift in his body, and knew he too would experience in his way what she just had.

Still reeling, Arian brought her legs up, locking them around his thighs. "Arian!" he cried just as his body crashed into hers. He strained against her, his body spasming against hers as his seed filled her. When his body slowed, his breath was as hard and forced as hers.

She held him tight against her, their bodies slick with sweat. He collapsed beside her, drawing her close into his arms. She laid her head upon his shoulder, and there they lay until their breaths returned to a more regular pace.

Wild terrible thoughts raced through Stefan's mind. He tried to force them from his head, but they would not relent. Like a ravaged beast, he could not help what his primal instinct charged him to do: remove the man who stood between him and the woman he loved. He gathered Arian tightly in his arms. She cried out in protest. He loosened his hold. "Arian, where do we go now?"

"Nowhere. We have until morn, Stefan," she said softly.

He rose up on an elbow and looked hard at her. "I want eternity."

Fear clouded her smooth features. "What are you saying?"

"I am saying I want you for eternity. I will do whatever is necessary."

She pressed her fingers to his lips. "Nay, Stefan, do not say such things. 'Tis not only against man's law but God's. I am married, and Magnus is very much alive. I could never live with myself or look upon you again knowing we were responsible for his death."

"Accidents happen . . ."

"Nay! Stefan, you speak the unspeakable! Do not say these things!"

Fury raged within him that he would even think of murder! He rolled from her and grabbed a candle from the side table near the bed. He brought it to the sheets and smiled grimly. "Your virgin stains he insisted upon. If he truly cared for you, the blood would be unimportant."

"Our marriage is, as most are, an alliance of two great houses. Love is never a part of the arrangement, but for some an unexpected gift."

He set the candle back upon the table. For a long moment, he stood unwilling to accept that this woman whom he loved above all others would leave him at the crow of the cock and go to another man, never to be seen again. Fury, frustration, and longing for her before he lost her wrangled in his heart, and though he knew what he was willing to do would ultimately drive her from him forever, he could only visualize Magnus dead, his sword buried in his gut.

His gaze rose to hers. "I cannot stand the thought of him touching you as I have." He dropped onto the bed, reaching out to caress her breast. His thumb rubbed across her nipple. He smiled when it puckered. "Your skin is softer than silk," he said, as his lips replaced his finger. She arched into him. She tasted of milk and honey. Her breasts were full and plump, made for a man, but the image of her suckling his son tore at his heart. His lips tightened.

Arian gasped. Anger flared in his heart. Anger at the fates for placing her in his path only to snatch her away. Grasping her face between his hands, he pressed his forehead to hers. "You are mine, Arian! Mine!" He pushed her back into the pillows, and in one swift stroke, he entered her. A primal possession overcame him with such a force he wanted to throw his head back and howl at the moon, to let all who heard it know that he had claimed his life mate and would fight any man or beast who tried to take her from him.

Entwining his fingers through hers, Stefan raised her arms above her head as his hips rose and fell, marking her with each thrust as if a call to any man she was his. And he would not relinquish her. The fury burned deep in his loins, like a lash stroke each time he thrust into her. Their bodies strained one against the other, and like the lash he came uncoiled in one great crack of the whip. "Arian!" he cried, as he wildly undulated against her, filling her with his seed for the second time that night.

And just as he had, in a furious wave of passion her body heated to overflowing and she came in a hard wave of release, clutching his hands in hers as her body arched into him, holding there motionless for one sublime moment before crashing back to earth.

Arian fell into exhausted sleep mere moments later. Stefan pulled her closer to him, where he lay on his back staring at the beamed ceiling, his mind a raucous cacophony of plots. He could slip down the hall and slit the Viking's throat and no one would be the wiser. He could challenge him to a duel, and before the entire population of Yorkshire he could slay him without so much as a second thought. He could pay a pack of thieves to slay him on the road to Norway, or hire an assassin to stealthily strangle him.

But with each plot Stefan concocted in his mind, he knew Arian would never forgive him for murder. She valued all life, even that of those who would cause her harm. Should he kill her husband, he could not bear the recrimination in her eyes each time she looked up at him. But nor could he stomach the thought of another man's, even her husband's, hands upon her!

"Stefan," Arian murmured, pressing her lips to his chest.

His anger dissolved. Replacing it was a heartbreak so debilitating he could scarce breathe.

Arian sat fully clothed in the dark room. Only Stefan's deep even breaths disrupted the quiet, and only the sputtering candle illuminated his powerful body sprawled upon the rumpled sheets. Their time together was near an end.

Emotion clogged her throat. She would promise her soul to any deity for the power to change fate. But 'twas not to be. If he still wanted her, her husband eagerly awaited the crow of the cock to claim his wife, and she would be here for him. She refused to think of life without Stefan. She refused to allow tears of sorrow to stain her cheeks. She refused to allow her heart to guide her back into the bed with him and savor one more kiss. 'Twould be torture, and she could bear no more. She was filled to capacity and greatly feared that, if pushed any farther, she would break.

Visions of her father wandering aimlessly in the dark corridors of the castle, calling for her mother, gripped her heart. She saw herself doing the same, dressed in rags, her hair a mess, the tracks of tears permanently stained upon her cheeks. And there in the shadows her husband and child, looking upon her with great sorrow.

Nay! She would not do it!

As the first gray fingers of dawn peeked through the high window, Stefan stirred. Arian caught her heart in her throat. Like a great wild beast he stretched his mighty muscles. A smile softened his face. His sleepy eyes opened quietly, searching the room for her; he smiled a slow satisfied smile. Her body trembled. It took every bit of strength she possessed not to go to him.

When he realized she was clothed and not coming to him, his smile faded. He looked up beyond her to the window. Raising on one arm in the bed, he said softly, "Do not leave me, Arian."

She stood. " 'Tis too late for us."

He rolled from the bed and grabbed his clothes from the floor and dressed. As he strapped on his sword belt, he looked to her, as if he wished to say more.

"Please, Stefan, do not make this any harder than it has to be. Go. Now."

He nodded, but before he turned to leave he yanked the bloody sheet from the bed. "For your husband."

Arian bit her bottom lip. As Stefan opened the door, Magnus's large body filled the space. Stefan shoved the sheet at him. "Your proof." Then strode past him.

Arian raised her eyes to him, unsure where she stood with him. "Milord?"

He turned to Father John, who stood behind him, and handed him the sheets. "Hang them from the tallest spire for the entire shire to bear witness."

Arian closed her eyes as her stomach rolled in one continuous wave. When she opened them Magnus stood before her. So many emotions clouded his face. Relief, anger, pain.

He stood silent, his pride, his heart, and his emotions hanging plainly from his sleeve. Arian felt a stirring of compassion for him. None of this was his fault. Yet he paid the heftiest price of all. She made a shallow curtsey. "Magnus, from this moment forward, I will give you all that I am capable of giving you." She touched his chest with her fingertips. "My deepest apologies. 'Twas never my intention for any of this to happen."

"Did he hurt you, Arian?" he asked softly.

She shook her head, not trusting her voice.

"If you bear the bastard's bastard I will cast him from my house."

Arian's heart tightened as the vision of a son with Stefan's brilliant eyes and dark hair sprang into her mind's eye. At her silence, he continued, "I will not lie with you until your courses have come twice, so that I can be sure you carry no bastard."

A sudden infusion of anger sprang up inside her.

Bastard or no, no child of hers would be cast away. And while she understood Magnus, he would come to understand she was not a woman who would lie down like a rush mat. But that was a battle she had yet to face, so she kept her silence. "Let us break the fast, husband, and present a united couple to the gossiping nobles and the people of this shire."

Magnus nodded, and extended his arm.

Stefan strode through the hall, calling to his men, who mingled with the inquisitive nobles up at dawn to witness what they were hoping would be a duel to the death between Stefan and the Jarl. Stefan could only wish that it would be so easy, but they would get no performance from him this morning. Arian had made her choice and it was not he. Anger twisted his innards, while jealousy poisoned his mind and despair pierced his heart.

How was he to look upon her on the arm of her husband? How was he to close his eyes each night and see visions of her beneath the Viking, giving herself as she had just given herself to him this night past? He would leave by midday, and as he had promised what seemed so long ago, he would not look over his shoulder. He would ride west, and forget he had ever met Princess Arianrhod. But even as Stefan tried to convince himself he could forget her, he knew he lied. She was with him always, like his hand or his arm. In his heart and soul, where she would be until he drew his last breath.

As the thoughts settled upon him, he forced himself not to go back and claim her forever as his. He stopped in his tracks, his men catching up to him. Slowly he turned, and looked back at the wood and stone manor house, above which the blue and white standard of the Jarl flew arrogantly in the morning breeze. 'Twas ugly and dark, the house, and though he had spent the greatest night of his life within its dreary walls, he hated to look upon it.

"Riders approach," Rohan said, stepping past Stefan. Stefan turned and looked down into the wide valley that separated the village from the manor land. " 'Tis a royal messenger," Stefan said, squinting. He would recognize the gold and scarlet standard of William anywhere.

"With a full garrison accompaniment," Wulfson mused.

As a single rider broke through the wide gates into the bailey, the churls scattered. Stefan smiled grimly, recognizing William's most trusted messenger, Robert fitz Hugh. What business did the king have in Yorkshire?

"Stefan!" Robert called, urging his mount faster.

Despite his heartache, Stefan could not hold back a smile for the young man. 'Twas good to see him. "Robert! What brings you here?"

He reined his horse to a halt before them and quickly dismounted. When he pulled the helm from his head, his face changed to hard and grave. "Word from William."

"It must be urgent, for you to ride from Rouen. Tell me."

Robert pulled a scroll from the leather pouch slung across his chest and handed it to Stefan. As he broke the seal, Stefan looked past him to the accompaniment. "Why do you travel with so heavy a guard?"

" 'Tis no guard, Stefan, but a full garrison, at your disposal. Another fifty ride but a day and half behind me."

"But we prepare to take the road west this day."

"Nay, you do not. Read the missive."

Hastily he unrolled the scroll. The Blood Swords crowded around him. William's bold hand sprang from the paper.

"Sir Stefan,

"I pray this missive finds you and your brothers in good health. I have been fully informed of the treachery of Edric, and of his alliance with Rhiwallon and Bleddyn. As you have no doubt witnessed, those people of Yorkshire continue to resist my will and my claim to the English throne. My spies tell me there are even Normans amongst them who plot against Normandy.

" 'Tis not my desire to punish them but to bring them to heel. As my trusted man, I give you overlordship of York and all surrounding areas, including Moorwood to the south and Scarborough to the north, to see to the interests of not only Normandy but England. Soon enough those stubborn English will understand they are beaten, and that I am rightful king. Keep the Blood Swords with you, and the garrison I send with Robert. Offer firm and fair terms to the lords whom you now oversee, and should they refuse to kneel to you, then they do not kneel to me, their king.

"Whilst I grow weary of war, do not hesitate to draw your sword in the name of your king. 'Tis my understanding, although I have no proof as of yet, that Magnus Tryggvason plots with the cur Murchad of Dublin, who coddles Harald's two eldest sons. Even more of a threat, he sleeps with the wolf Sven of Denmark, who claims the throne by right of blood through his great-uncle Canute. Keep him close, my friend, and watch his every move. As I write this, my spies inform me that his men assemble on the north coast of Scotland, *aided by the Scottish kings who, as you know, harbor that milksop of a boy Edgar. Secure the shire, Stefan. Do not spare a life if it threatens the throne I sit upon.*

"*Treachery abounds. Trust no one but Robert and your brothers.*

"*By my command, William.*"

Shocked by the sudden turn of events, Stefan looked to Rohan, Wulfson, Rorick, Warner, and Ioan, who looked equally shocked, then to Robert, who pulled another scroll from his pouch and handed it to Stefan." 'Tis the charter giving you lordship of the shire."

TWENTY-ONE

As the morning meal commenced, Magnus held up his hand and stood. When he opened his mouth to speak, Arian's heart dropped to the floor. Stefan burst into the hall, flanked by his brothers, and behind him a swarm of mailed knights.

She felt Magnus stiffen beside her. His own guard rose from the lower trestles, and those who stood along the hall came to attention also. Tension gripped every heart in the hall.

At that moment, Father John bustled into the hall, grasping the soiled linens in his hands. He stopped short and looked about.

Stefan strode arrogantly toward the lord's table, his eyes locked on Magnus's.

"Your business here is concluded, Norman," Magnus boomed. "You have caused enough damage. I order you to leave at once."

A slow smile twisted Stefan's lips. Arian held her breath, knowing it did not bode well for Magnus. But she remembered Stefan's oath to her, and her fear for her husband's safety was allayed.

"I beg your pardon, milord, but my men and I came only to feast before we turn our horses upon the road. Do not let our presence prevent you from your speech."

Arian's eyes narrowed. What game did he play? And where did the influx of soldiers come from?

"My lords!" Father John cried, stepping between the two men. He made a short bow to both Arian and Magnus, then held the soiled sheets up for all to see. " 'Tis your oath, Lady Arian, this is your virgin blood?"

She nodded. "On my unborn children's lives, I swear it."

"My lord Magnus, is it sufficient evidence to appease the marriage contract? Or do you contest the validity without witness?"

For a long-drawn-out moment, Magnus did not respond. Arian stood still and stiff beside him, holding her breath. "Aye, I accept it," he said at last.

"Then I pronounce—"

"I repudiate her claim!" Philip cried out over the priest's voice.

Shocked at the accusation, Arian gasped, as did everyone around her. She turned to the man. Lisette stood beside him, and together they looked like twin foxes with fat partridges in their mouths

"What is the meaning of this?" Magnus erupted, on top of Father John's same demand.

Arian felt Stefan's anger behind her. "You lie!" he challenged.

Lisette flung off her husband's cautionary hand on her arm. "We have proof you were lovers before her marriage!" she spat at Stefan.

"Show it," Stefan said menacingly.

Lisette nodded to a woman standing in the corner, and when all eyes turned to her Arian held her breath, knowning she would have to defend their lies. 'Twas Miriam, the maid who slept in her chamber the night before the wedding, the night Jane was gone. In her arms was a folded sheet. Confused, Arian looked up to Stefan, then to Lisette, to Philip, then finally to her husband, whose face had flushed scarlet with rage.

Skittishly, Miriam approached them and handed Philip the sheet. He thrust it beneath Arian's nose. "Are these not the linens found only upon the lord's bed?"

Arian looked at them, noting the gold embroidery of a succession of leaping stags along the border. She nodded, as did Magnus. With great flourish, Philip flung the sheet wide, and there in the middle were several drops of dried blood.

"Where did you get this?" Magnus demanded.

"From your lady's bed yesterday morn, the night after she lay with the Norman!" Philip spat.

"Nay, we did not!" Arian cried, turning to Magnus.

"There are witnesses, including the Norman's own men who watched him go into the chamber only to come out later," Lisette hissed. Arian glared at the arrogance of the woman. Her venom was so clearly marked across her comely features that it distorted them into something very ugly. 'Twas her jealousy that drove her to the lies. So, this was how the brother and sister sought to bring her low? Arian's resolve stiffened. She had the truth on her side.

"Did the Norman come to your chamber unchaperoned?" Magnus demanded, his face twisted in contempt.

"Aye, he came to my room, true, we did but talk. Nothing more. I swear it!"

Stefan grabbed the sheets from Philip. "Your treachery is surpassed only by your foolishness." He flung the sheets to the floor and stamped upon them.

Lisette laughed, thoroughly enjoying the dramatic charade, playing out for every magnate in Yorkshire to witness. "Ask the chambermaid how she found your wife when she came into the room?"

Magnus turned to the cowering maid. "Speak!"

Miriam looked from Lisette to Arian, then to Magnus. "I—I came into the room just after the Norman left. When I stripped the linens the next morn I found the lady's clothes were ripped from her body."

"You lie!" Arian shouted.

Before anyone could move, Magnus drew his sword and turned on Stefan. "Draw your sword, you lying cur, I will kill you here and now. You will never come between my wife and me again!"

"Nay, Stefan, do not!" Arian cried, knowing though Magnus was big and strong, he was no match for the seasoned Norman.

To her great shock and relief, Stefan did not draw his sword. Nay, he did not need to: his men had tightened in a half-circle around him, their own weapons drawn.

"If you were any other man, under any other circumstances, Magnus, your guts would be on the floor." Stefan made a short bow and withdrew a step. "But, as a man who has watched his promised run to another and the pain that such entails, I will not take up a sword against you."

Magnus laughed, the sound low and menacing. He pressed closer to Stefan, the point of his sword only a hand's-breadth from Stefan's heart. Rorick growled a warning, his sword aimed high at Magnus's heart.

Stefan reached out, and with the flat of his hand, he pushed Magnus's sword away. "Should you slay me, you will lose what little chance of happiness you have with your wife."

"My wife?" Magnus roared. He turned his pale eyes upon Arian. "Choose between us now, Arianrhod of Dinefwr, and settle the matter. I will not live with you when your heart cries out for another!"

"We are wed in the eyes of God. The choice has already been made," she firmly said.

"If you will not make the choice, I will make it for you." Magnus leveled his sword. "Raise your sword, Norman."

"Do not do it!" Arian screamed.

Slowly Stefan drew his weapon.

She leapt toward Magnus and grasped his arm. "Nay! Do not do this!" she cried. "Annul the marriage, Magnus. I will give you my entire dowry, but do not do this! He will kill you."

He shoved her from him, the force of his push sending her tumbling backward into the rushes. Rhodri grabbed her up from the floor and pulled her from the fray.

For Arian, Stefan had exacted supreme self-control when the Viking first challenged him, but now, for his own reasons, he would kill him. The Viking was tall and he was strong, but Stefan was battle-seasoned. But more than that, this was not about justice or honor, or anything but that with the death of this man, Stefan would finally have the only woman who would ever matter to him.

Magnus's captain tossed him a deadly ax. Rorick growled and tossed Stefan his own sword. Both men, double-weaponed, faced each other. Stefan was a student of close hand-to-hand combat. Though it ran the risk of much damage, it also afforded him a greater chance of a fatal strike.

Magnus struck first, his long arms far-reaching. He jabbed with his sword, and with his right hand brought the ax up and around in a great slicing swath, then bringing it down in a vicious blow. Stefan crossed swords just above his shoulders, taking the brunt of the blows. He pushed upward, his arms swinging wide, forcing the steel edges away from him and sending Magnus backward. Keeping low, Stefan jabbed his swords, catching the Viking's thigh. Magnus roared in fury, and as Stefan anticipated, Magnus's rage propelled him forward in a wild reckless attack.

Stefan dropped to one knee and thrust up with one sword, crossing the other over his head, warding off the ax blow. Stefan continued his irregular attack and retreat, slowly wearing his opponent down. At one point, Stefan caught Arian's horrified gaze. He caught himself, and that momentary hesitation cost him. Magnus thrust, catching Stefan off guard, slicing open his forearm, then fell back, preparing for another blow. A hush fell upon the hall.

Stefan looked up from the wound, and smiled. "Touché, Magnus." He made a short bow and lifted his swords. "Now that I have played with you, before I kill you, confess who else amongst you plots with Sven of Denmark."

"I know not of what you speak." Magnus was suddenly not nearly as zealous in his attempt to defend himself.

"Sven's ships sail for the shores of Scotland. 'Twas it not in Scotland that you spent this last month, not in Norway as you told your wife?"

"You lie!"

"Do I?" Stefan rotated the tips of his swords in the air, then lunged, slicing Magnus's forearm as he had Stefan's. Blood dripped to the floor. "Was not your visit to Murchad in Dublin this spring past a guise to meet with Sven's captains and plan your invasion of England?"

Magnus slowly circled Stefan, who only turned and followed his movements. "Nay, 'twas a peace accord, nothing else."

"Why did you bring one hundred men with you here?"

"To rid my land of Normans!"

"Tell me all, now, and save lives. Mayhap then God will not judge you so harshly."

"William has no blood right to the throne of England!

He will fall!"Magnus roared and thrust.

Stefan smiled grimly, parrying the strike. "Mayhap not blood right, but he has a dead king's promise." He circled the Viking. "Does the young Olaf plot with his kin to the north?"

"He is weak! That boy will not survive the winter!"

"Ah, so he has refused aid. 'Tis well for him. William will be most appreciative."

While Magnus would not give up his conspirators, Stefan had a good idea who amongst them plotted against his liege. And he was most certain now the Viking was sleeping with the Danish king. It would make what he was about to do easier.

'Twas time to end this charade. In a practiced, complex set of steps, thrusts and half-turns, Stefan moved into the tight space of Magnus's reach, so close the Viking could not effectively defend himself. Stefan dropped one sword and grabbed the hilt of the Viking's dagger, pulled it from the belt, then plunged it into his throat, just as he had done to his traitorous nephew.

Arian screamed behind him, as did every other woman in the hall. Magnus dropped his sword then ax, grasping his throat. Blood oozed from between his fingers. He dropped to his knees, his pale-blue eyes staring up in shock. He turned to Arian. He reached out to her. When he removed his hand, blood spewed out in a high arc.

Arian came to him, kneeling beside him, pressing her fingers to the wound. He opened his mouth to speak but only a gurgling sound came forth. He fell forward across her lap, his blood soaking her blue and yellow kirtle.

Stefan stood staring down at the grisly sight, and marveled that Arian did not scream or cry out in hysterics with the dying Viking in her lap. When she turned cold eyes up at him, he felt as if 'twere he who had been sliced in the heart. He dropped to a knee beside her. "Do not condemn me for his death, Arian."

"Who else is to blame?" she demanded, her voice as cold as her eyes. "He would have annulled the marriage, he did not have to die."

Stefan stood, and motioned to Robert. "The charter." With the document in his hand, Stefan stood atop the nearest trestle top and held it high over his head. "This royal charter gives me lordship of Scarborough to the north and to Moorwood in the south. As lord here I claim the lady of the manor as my own. Any man or woman who interferes will be hanged for treason!"

Father John scurried up to where he stood, wringing his hands. " 'Tis not good, Sir Stefan. Nay, 'tis bad, very bad."

"Go the chapel and prepare for a wedding," Stefan commanded.

" 'Tis immoral!" Rhodri challenged.

"Nay! 'Tis not decent! I will not do it," Father John protested.

" 'Twill be done!" Stefan roared.

He looked down at Arian, who still sat with Magnus in her lap. Stefan scowled. "The widow will be no more. I will take her to wife this day." Stefan grabbed the good father's robe and pulled him close. "You will do it, or you will find yourself lying beside Magnus!"

"Sir, surely your king—"

"My king gives me title here. I am lord and I will have her as my lady."

"But—but you will set the shire aflame with outrage."

"So be it."

TWENTY-TWO

When Stefan returned to Arian, she stared up at him, her eyes showing no emotion. He extended his hand to her, as several of Magnus's men, oddly quiet, carried his body from the hall. Where to, Stefan did not care.

"Come with me, Arian," Stefan softly said, squatting down beside her.

She shook her head. "Nay, I cannot, Stefan."

"Leave her," Rhodri said, stepping beside his sister. "You have brought her nothing but pain and shame." He reached down and scooped Arian into his arms. "I am taking her home to Dinefwr."

Stefan stood, his heart torn between setting her free and forcing her to stay here with him. Blood covered her kirtle and the floor. His arm still bled. When Rhodri turned with her and took a step that would be the first of many to separate them forever, something inside Stefan snapped. "Halt!" he commanded.

Rhodri continued toward the stairway.

Stefan drew his sword. In several long strides, he reached the prince and pressed it to his back. "I will skewer you where you stand. Release her to me."

Slowly Rhodri turned to face him. Stefan did not look at Arian, afraid of what he would see. "Would you slay her brother as well to have her?"

" 'Tis not my wish."

"But you would?"

Stefan did not answer, but dropped his gaze to his beloved. His blood chilled in his bones. Hatred filled her eyes. "Put me down, Rhod," she said.

"Nay, Arian."

She pushed out of his grasp, putting herself between her brother and the man who had caused her nothing but heartache.

Stefan sheathed his sword and extended his bloody hand. "Come with me, Arian. I will not hurt you."

"I have nothing left for you to destroy." She placed her own bloodied hand into his.

Stefan looked past her to Rhodri. "Come with us to the chapel."

"I will not wed you!" she cried.

"You will."

She tugged her hand, but his fingers tightened around them, the blood, sticky, binding them. "Your time as a widow will be short-lived."

" 'Tis sacrilege!" Rhodri charged.

" 'Tis my will. It will be done!" Stefan stormed. He yanked Arian after him. She stumbled, and when she could not keep up he swept her up into his arms, her angry brother following close on their heels. He called for Ioan and Warner, who stood close, to follow.

Dazed, covered in her dead husband's blood, Arian knelt before Father John. Stefan knelt beside her, her brother,

and two of Stefan's knights standing as witness to the
macabre ceremony. She did not fight; she did not have
the strength, nor she knew, could she win. Like his king,
Stefan de Valrey took what he wanted by force. That he
forced her in the shadow of Magnus's death, she would
never forgive. He had given her his oath he would not
take her husband's life, and before her eyes, those of
Yorkshire and God, he broke his oath.

Father John's voice droned on, and with each word her
heart closed another inch. When finally he pronounced
them man and wife, Arian looked stonily to Stefan. "I am
your wife in name only." She stood and slapped him. He
stood silent, unmoving, accepting her scorn. But at least
now she belonged to him.

She turned and strode from the chapel into the bailey, for all to see her bloodstained clothes. The nobles
who had assembled for her first marriage parted as she
strode through them and into the hall. Bile rose in her
belly as she watched the maids clean the blood from the
floor. She ran past them up the stairway to her chamber,
to find Jane awaiting her with a hot bath.

Arian cried out, ripping the bloody clothes from her
body, as hysteria finally claimed her. Jane took her trembling body into her arms, calming her before she gently set her in the tub. Drawing the screen close around
them, Arian sat back in the warm suds and closed her
eyes, wanting to erase her life.

She stiffened when she heard Stefan's deep commanding voice booming below. She exhaled a long
breath and laid her head back against the high rest.
Had he commanded the nobles to gather? How would
they react? Magnus was well loved in this shire, his

subjects loyal, for he had been a fair lord. She caught back a sob, unable to believe him dead. 'Twas not because she held love for him, but she did respect him. And despite all that had transpired, up until the very end he had been willing to set his pride aside and accept her as his wife.

Her fist hit the water. Not so Stefan! His pride had caused irreparable damage! How could she live here amongst these people when they knew her first husband had been slain by her second husband? How could she expect them to respect her when Magnus's blood was still warm when she wed his murderer?

"My lady," Jane soothed, "do not be so hard on yourself."

Arian looked to her maid. "How can I not be? I marry the man who slew my husband whilst his blood is still on my hands! 'Tis because of my lust for the Norman that Magnus is dead!"

Jane shook her head and sat upon the stool beside the tub, and began to wash Arian's hair. "You shared more than lust with the Norman. Do not deny it."

"I do not, Jane, but I allowed it to show. Magnus's pride could not bear any more. I am as responsible for his death as Stefan is."

"Then do not give him the entire burden to carry."

Arian shook her head. "Jane, he gave me his oath he would not harm, Magnus. In front of us all he slew him, just as he did Dag, just as he does any man who stands in the way of what he craves!" Arian squeezed her eyes shut. "He would have slain Rhod had I not agreed to wed him."

Jane rubbed in the thick lather, her fingers digging

into Arian's scalp. "He would not have slain the prince."

Arian opened her eyes, blinking back the sting of the soap. "You are too addled to see him for the barbarian he is."

"A barbarian I might be, but I am also your husband," Stefan said, from the other side of the screen. "Hurry your bath, I would have you by my side when I address the gathered lords and their ladies."

A short time later, Stefan collected her. He had cleaned up as well—no vestiges of blood upon him. But Arian did not have to see it to know their hands were covered in Magnus's blood. "I would speak with Rhod."

"He rides with Wulfson for Wales."

"He did not say goodbye!" And suddenly she felt all alone.

"Wulf is anxious to have his lady, and Rhod anxious to announce that your marriage to the Viking took place."

"But no word of my forced marriage to the man who slew him?"

"Not until it benefits me."

"Am I just a pawn in your war games?"

Stefan shook his head as he fought for words to console her, but there were none. "Arian, my heart is yours. That has not changed."

"If what you say is true, then you would have considered my feelings. You would not have threatened to slay my brother and you would not have forced me to wed you by hanging my brother's life over my head." He opened his mouth to defend himself.

"How can I trust you with my heart, when on every turn you use force to have your way?"

"I did not force you last eve."

"You stormed into my chamber and my marriage bed demanding first-night rights! And after you threatened everyone in the room, your words to me were sly, and you were patient, but had I not succumbed to your honeyed words you would have stolen from me what you stole from Magnus."

"You lie to yourself, my lady. Do not say you did not want me as I wanted you."

"I will admit your words convinced me."

"Do you regret it?"

"I regret that I was not stronger in the eyes of my betrothed. Had I been, he would still live."

"He was a traitor!"

"To your king, not to mine!"

Stefan's cheek twitched. "Did you love him?"

"Nay! You know I did not. But I did not hate him either." Angry tears stung her eyes. "His blood is on my hands. I will never be able to look upon you, Stefan, and know it is not on yours as well."

"We will discuss this further, but first there are the assembled lords to address. I bid you stand beside me and at least pretend we are united. For divided we will fall."

The tension was so thick when they descended the wide stairway into the hall that Arian feared for their safety. Fury, outrage, and contempt reigned supreme. While Stefan seemed unaffected by it, guilt washed through her. 'Twas because of her Magnus was dead.

Norman knights stood on one side of the hall, swords

drawn, Magnus's guard on the other, Saxons between. The nobles were quiet, but on their faces, their hatred was plainly painted.

Stefan guided Arian upon the dais, seeing her to her seat beside the great lord's chair. Stefan remained standing. Sitting stiffly in the chair, chin high, Arian gazed about the crowded hall. Smoke swirled high in the rafters; the stale smell of ale and wine mixed with that of blood and body odor assaulted her senses. The air was thick and warm. Her gaze trailed down to the place on the floor where Magnus had fallen. The servants had done an admirable job cleaning the area: fresh rushes covered the stains, but still his blood cried out.

"I am Stefan de Valrey, knight of William and overlord of this shire. Magnus Tryggvason was a traitor to the Crown." Cries of denial erupted but Stefan continued undaunted, "A traitor who challenged William by challenging me."

"What proof do you have?" a voice called out.

Stefan looked over the crowd to the hall entry, where a gantlet of Norman knights stood at the ready. The doors burst open, and Ioan and Warner dragged in a most defiant and bedraggled Sir Sar. Arian moved to the edge of her chair, and peered questioningly up at Stefan, but he kept focused on the struggling man.

Ioan thrust him at the base of the dais. "The traitorous Jarl's messenger."

Stefan pointed to the odd little man, who, divested of his noble garb, looked more like a jester. "For those of you who are not familiar with this man, he is known as Sar, steward of Magnus, a most trusted position. And as steward he was privy to all of the Jarl's interests, including his interest in seeing the Danish king claim the English throne!"

Arian gasped, shocked at such evidence. She did not believe Magnus to be a traitor, she thought . . . Sar glared up at Stefan, who continued to scan the gathered crowd. "I share this information for several reasons. First and foremost, as a warning to any of you who may have the same thoughts: let it be known, William will not tolerate treason. Punishment is death." The crowd thrummed with tension. "Had not Magnus challenged me and paid for the challenge with his life, understand, he would have been hanged."

Arian sat stunned, unable to digest Magnus's hand in any kind of treason.

"Proof!" another voice shouted.

Stefan nodded. "Sir Sar was captured just this morn sneaking into his dead master's chamber." Stefan reached into his tunic and pulled out a scroll with a broken seal. " 'Tis the seal of Trygg—a missive Magnus wrote last eve for Sar, his messenger to the Scots." Stefan unrolled it and held it out for all to see. " 'Tis word to the Scottish kings and to Sven of Denmark that Lord Magnus, upon his marriage to the Welsh princess, was dispatching his fleet of one hundred ships to Whitby on the Yorkshire coast, with five hundred men to fight, as well as the one hundred he brought here with him."

Incredulous gasps echoed through the hall. Arian sat perfectly still. "As I speak to you, what is left of Magnus the Tall is on its way to Whitby. His head upon a pike will be their welcome to England!"

" 'Tis barbaric!" Arian hissed.

Stefan turned cold eyes upon her, but said nothing.

He looked back to the crowd. "William's justice is swift and it is mighty. Pledge your fealty to me this day and you pledge it to him. You will see, in time, that William is a fair man to those who are loyal to him." He looked down at Arian. "As am I fair to those who are loyal to me." He turned back to the hall. "But also know that I am a man who puts king first, country second."

A nervous twitter erupted in the hall. Stefan smiled bitterly. "Should you choose not to pledge your fealty this day, you will not leave here."

Outrage erupted, but quickly died down. They may not want to accept William, but they were not complete fools. They valued their lives and their holdings.

He looked over the sea of faces. Arian followed his gaze. Though they had quieted, she knew they only waited. They would pledge fealty this day because if they did not they would die as traitors. But on the morrow, out of earshot, they would conspire, and one day soon they would take up arms against Stefan. One hundred Normans were no match for the entire shire.

She nodded as each person, down to the servants, pledged their fealty, first to William, then to Stefan, and finally to her. When each man, woman, and child in the hall and surrounding area had promised to be loyal to the king, Stefan called for a feast of celebration.

Despite her fatigue, Arian sat quietly amazed. Loud celebrating voices shook the rafters, while music and dance filled the hall. How could they, after the events of the last two days, celebrate? But when she looked closer she noticed 'twas the Normans who celebrated, not the Saxons, though they made a good attempt to pretend. Nay, there were whispers and looks and new alliances being born—none, she would wager, to the Norman's advantage.

She leaned to Stefan and said, "Do you really believe they will remain loyal to you?"

He smiled down at her, and she could see it was forced for appearances. "Not for one heartbeat of time."

Arian sat back, thoughtful and weary. Never had she felt such hostility and scorn. She was glad Rhod had ridden out. Trouble brewed, and she did not want her brother caught up in a war that was not his to fight. She looked askance to her husband. Despite her heartache, Arian knew not what to do. So much had changed in the last few days. Yet beneath all of her guilt, frustration, anger, and denial, there in her heart her love for Stefan lurked.

"My lord," she softly said, "I am fatigued. I seek my chamber."

Stefan stood, extending his arm. The hall rose with her. As he escorted her up the stairway, she felt every eye in the place burning holes in her back. Stefan pushed open the door. As she walked through, he followed her into the chamber. Jane rose from the chair where she stitched a piece of clothing. "Leave us," Stefan commanded softly.

"I have need of her," Arian said.

"Your husband will tend you," Stefan countered.

"I do not wish your help!" Arian said, striding into the room. When he followed, she spun around and faced him. "Will you force yourself on me, then?"

He stopped at her words, his brows drawing together in a dark scowl.

" 'Tis your way, Stefan. If you cannot have what you seek with compliance, you take it. Always you take for your own end! When will you see that you cannot force the world to bow at your feet?"

"I did not force your love. You gave it freely."

"You kidnapped me!"

"Aye, and I would do it again. In the end we both benefited."

"You slew my husband!"

"He challenged me! He was a traitor to my king and his own people! You would have been a widow regardless."

"You gave me your oath, Stefan. You swore to me you would accept my marriage and not look back."

His anger mounted on his face. He stepped closer to her, and she could see he fought to keep his hands from her, not to harm but to conquer. "When I gave my oath I did not know the depths of Magnus's treachery. 'Twas only after we were together that William sent word of his treason. His missive to Sven confirms it."

Stefan waved Jane from the chamber. When the door closed behind her, he threw the bolt and turned to Arian. "Will you force yourself upon me now?" she threw at him.

"Nay, I will not touch you again unless you ask for it. But understand this, wife. I am your husband, I am lord and master here, and you will stand beside me until God strikes one of us dead."

"I will not share this chamber with you!"

"You will." With those his last words, Stefan stormed from the chamber.

It was late when she heard the chamber door open, then close. Arian feigned sleep. Moments later, the bed creaked, heavy with her husband's weight. She felt his eyes upon her back.

He moved closer to her. She could feel his body heat radiate toward her. The night was warm, and she slept in only a thin linen shift, the covers pulled down to her feet. Despite the warmth of the air and the man beside her, she shivered.

"Why do you deny me, Arian?" he asked. The quiet anguish in his voice drew a small gasp from her. A sudden wave of emotion crashed through her. Slowly, she turned over to face him. His blue eyes burned bright in the low candlelight. The flickering of the flame cast odd shadows across his handsome scarred face. 'Twas the noble face of a noble man who had to fight for everything in his life.

"The guilt eats at me, Stefan."

"You must let it go, Arian. There is more to Magnus's plots than you know, and you, my love, were caught up in the middle of it all."

"What do you mean?"

Stefan rolled onto his back and rubbed his eyes. "Your meeting was no accident. He and Sven of Denmark have been plotting since Hardrada died not far from here almost a year ago. He traveled to Dublin, knowing your sire would be in attendance as well. Your father is rich and respected by the Welsh kings. What better way to ingratiate oneself than marry a Welsh princess and have her great family of the west as ally? Do you remember Dag's last words before he died?" Arian's heart began to beat faster in her chest. She thought back to that gruesome day, and though she tried, she could not remember. "He said, 'the stag runs north.' He meant that Magnus runs north to that cur Sven. He knew what his uncle was about."

Stefan rolled over to face her, and as his words sank in, she began to understand. "Did he think the Welsh would back his plan to invade England?"

"The northern kings did, as did Rhiwallon and Bleddyn. 'Twas the only reason they agreed to the hostage trade. Without your marriage to Magnus, all would be forfeit. They had no choice."

"But they still hold Lady Tarian and your brother Thorin."

"Aye, but Wulfson and Rhod ride with news only of your marriage, not of Magnus's death. By the time they learn the truth, it will be too late."

"And what of you, Stefan? A man who wanted no wife. Now you are married to a princess. Will you use my father to your gain?"

"Arian, I married you because I love you. No other reason."

"You forced me to marry you! Do I not have a say in my life?"

"Your life is with me. You will see in time 'tis for the best."

"Nay, Stefan, you do not understand. You say you love me, but you slew my husband after you gave your oath you would not! Then you force my hand. 'Tis not love!"

"I would give you my life," he said hotly.

She grasped his hands. "Give me mine."

"Your life?"

"If you love me, let me go," she whispered.

"Let you go?" he asked, stunned.

"Aye, allow me to return home." As she said the words, her heart cracked.

For a long moment, Stefan stared at her. His eyes brightened almost as if tears glittered there, but she knew that that was nonsense.

"You are my wife!"

"Only because you forced me! I would have never willingly married you!"

"Is marriage to me so repulsive?"

She shook her head, nay, 'twas not how she meant it. She loved him.

"Because I am a bastard?

"Nay, for if you do not set me free I will never trust you," she said softly.

Slowly he nodded, and rolled from the bed. She rose on her knees. "Where are you going?'

He drew on his braies, then his chauses. "To find a place to sleep."

Stefan strode from the chamber, his mind a swirl of thoughts and emotions. He could not let her go! He would not! *She was his wife.* He strode back to the hall, which had fallen quiet. He found his men sitting at the lord's table, huddled together deep in conversation.

Rorick stood and handed him a horn of ale. Morosely, he accepted it and sat down.

"What ails you?" Warner asked.

Stefan looked over at his friend. "Other than these unruly Saxons? I have no clue to the workings of a woman."

Rorick laughed and drank; Ioan rolled his eyes and

also drank. Rohan slapped him on the back. "There is no greater mystery than what lurks in a woman's head, brother."

"She wishes to return to her father."

The men went silent. Then Rohan spoke. "Will you allow it?"

Stefan shook his head. "She is my wife!" He threw back the horn and drained it. "I cannot bear to let her fly from me."

Warner scratched his head. "I am confused, Stefan. I thought she felt for you as you felt for her."

"She blames me for Magnus's death."

Ioan laughed, the sound harsh. "Had it not been you, 'twould have been one of us. He was a marked man from the beginning."

"I tried to explain that to her, but she is angry at me for shaming her on her wedding night." Stefan filled his horn again.

"Women have to know that they have made the decision for themselves, Stefan. She needs to come to you because 'tis what she wants, not what you have forced upon her," Rohan said wisely.

"Aye, her words exactly."

"Have you consummated your vows?" Rohan asked.

Slowly Stefan shook his head.

"Then give her what she wants, brother," Ioan said.

"Annul the marriage, and release her completely," Rohan agreed.

Stefan's heart cracked in half at the notion. Pain so fierce that it caused him to catch his breath twisted in his chest. So much so, he caught his hands to his heart and pressed upon it to soothe the pain. But it did no good. His stomach pitched and swelled, and he thought he would vomit. He shook his head, denying what he knew was the right thing to do. If he forced her to stay, she would grow to hate him; at least now she still cared. But he knew Rohan spoke the truth. Stefan nodded, and stood on unsteady legs. He would do what he must do. And it would kill him.

TWENTY-THREE

Moments later, when he strode through the chamber door, he found Arian crying in the big bed. His heart broke more. "Arian," he softly said, as he approached. She turned red eyes up to him. Her chemise hung open, her full breasts peeking out from beneath the fabric, glistening from her falling tears. He swallowed hard and focused instead on her face.

Carefully, lest he scare her, he sat down on the edge of the bed beside her. He held out his hand to her; warily she looked at him as if he would bite her.

"Please, give me your hand." Tentatively, she placed her soft hand into his big callused one. He smiled, and love welled up for her. She was brave and she was beautiful, and she had been through hell with him from the first moment they set eyes upon each other. He loved her more at that moment with such passion and conviction it consumed him. And he owed her her freedom. She deserved it. She was a beautiful bird that if caged would wither and die.

He brought her hand to his lips and gently kissed it. "I have been selfish, Arian. I have been brutish and I have thought of naught but myself all my life. I have made many mistakes along the way; many I cannot undo. And while you may think our meeting was a mistake because of where it has led us both, I could not disagree more. You have shown me, my love, that I am not dead inside. That I am capable of love. If I could take back any of my time spent with you, I would be selfish and say nay. But I can give you back your life by giving you your freedom." He turned her hand over in his and kissed the palm of her hand. "I release you, Arian. You are free to return home. I will petition the Pope myself for an annulment. William will stand by it, as he has the Pope's ear."

She crumpled in the bed. Stefan gathered her up into his arms. "Arian, 'tis what you wanted. I give it, freely, but with a heavy heart."

She choked back a sob and looked up into his eyes. Hers radiated pain and suffering, and beneath it he knew she still loved him. His heart pained him as well. "I am sorry for causing you shame. I am sorry for Magnus's death, and I am sorry for forcing the marriage on you. I cannot take back Magnus nor the shame, but I can give you back your life."

He kissed her forehead. "Ask anything else of me, Arian, and if it is in my power, I will give it to you."

She went limp in his arms, her head rolling back against his shoulder. He could not resist kissing the trail of tears on her cheek. "Do not weep."

Her eyes fluttered open. "Stefan, why does my heart feel as if it has been shattered into a thousand pieces? Why do I feel that this is wrong?"

"Wrong?"

"You and me, apart."

"I know it is not right. We were meant to be, Arian, and though the road has been wrought with difficulty, I have never been so sure of anything in my life. You are the only woman I will ever love."

"What if I am with child?"

The thought of her carrying his child twisted like a hot iron in his chest; he had not given the possibility any thought. Yet he would not force her to stay because of a child. But he could not ignore a babe, either.

He smoothed her hair back from her face. "Arian, tell me now, what do you want?"

"Stefan," she moaned, "I want you to hold me, and to tell me all will be right with our world. I cannot bear to live like this."

He kissed her damp lips. When she did not push him away but opened her lips to accept him, fire enflamed his body. He wanted her so desperately he could barely control himself. But he would not lead; he would follow.

"One more night together, Stefan," she whispered against his lips. "One more night." She pressed him back into the pillows. Deftly she unbelted his sword belt and pushed it aside, then raised his tunic over his head, then his chemise. When she tugged at his braies' strings, he grabbed her hands.

"Once these are off, I am not leaving this bed until morn."

She smiled a slow sad smile, and pushed her heavy hair behind her shoulders. "I would be most disappointed if you did." When she pushed down his braies and chauses he caught his breath. His cock was already full and had lengthened to capacity. She pressed her lips to his, entwining her fingers in his, pushing his arms over his head. "You are my captive tonight, milord," she breathed against his lips. Stefan's muscles tensed, his skin smoldered, and blood ran hot in his veins.

"I am yours, milady, to do with what you will."

Arian laughed, nibbling his lips then his chin. Her kisses trailed down his throat to the sword scar. Her fingers unlocked from his. Her warm hands trailed down his arms. His muscles bunched beneath her fingertips. She flicked his nipple with her tongue, then suckled it as he had done to her. He strained beneath her, but did not reach out and touch her. Her fingers kneaded his chest, trailing lower to his belly, followed by her singeing lips; he hung on by a thread. She pressed her hands to his hips, leaning over him, her full breasts teasing his raised cock.

"Arian," he moaned.

"Shhh." When she took him into her hands and slowly moved them up and down his shaft, his hips came off the mattress. When she pressed her lips to the head of him, Stefan hissed in a harsh breath. His fingers dug into the sheets, twisting them in his fists. He was on the verge of losing all control. He grabbed the carved headboard for leverage, knowing if his hands were free he would touch her. He looked down at her and nearly came at that instant. Her long hair hung down around her shoulders in a gold and crimson shroud, but 'twas her lips upon him and her small hands wrapped around his thickness that set him off. She was in so many ways innocent, yet she had experienced so much in the last month. Stefan arched into her, throwing his head back, closing his eyes, and let her take him away. At least for this night he would forget about tomorrow.

Hunger coiled low in his belly, desire and need so excruciating that he had to force himself to breathe. When she broke from him, he caught his breath and looked down at her. She smiled shyly, and, on all fours, she crawled up his body, dragging her moist nether lips across his cock when she did. He raised against her, the head of him pressing into her warm wetness. She rose slightly, denying him entry. "Arian," he hoarsely groaned. "I cannot take much more."

"But you must, milord, I am not done with you."

Slowly she sat back upon him. Stefan's body froze, afraid if he moved he would grab her to him and sink into her, never letting her go. He watched her face as she slowly mounted him, her features changing from tentative to accepting; then, when he thrust up into her, sublime pleasure. She closed her eyes and softly exhaled. When she opened them, he caught his breath. Her silver eyes were so dark he would swear they were black. Her cheeks flushed pink in the candlelight, her full lips parted as she too caught her breath.

She arched, her full breasts bobbing against her chest, then in a slow rocking motion she moved against him. Stefan sucked in a harsh breath, keeping himself from letting go. His hands itched to grasp the cradle of her hips and rock her harder into him, but he forced himself to allow her to set the pace. And she did. Slow, deliberate, and achingly sublime. She leaned down, placing her hands on his chest, giving him more of an angle. He could feel her interior muscles clench and unclench around him; her hips swirled, and in a dance as old as time, they made love.

Slick sweat erupted upon his skin. Her lips pressed to

his. He kissed her back with wanton desire as his hips rose and fell against her. She slickened around him, her breath harsh and forced, matching his in need. As her momentum increased, she dug her fingers into his hair, her soft moans of pleasure captured in their kiss.

"Stefan," she gasped, as her body shuddered against his. He gritted his teeth and groaned as her body spasmed around his, pulling him deeper into her hot vortex. He came in a mad feral rush; his hands broke free from his death grip on the headboard, but still he managed not to touch her. In a wild upward surge his seed filled her, marking her as his. And she *was* his. Primal possession overcame him. He cried out as the last drop of him left his body, and she came tumbling down from her journey to the stars.

She collapsed against him, her sultry body twitching as the last vestiges of her release claimed her. His hands twitched at his sides, yet still he controlled his urge to take her into his arms. Her fingers trailed along his forearms, kneading his taut muscles. When finally she brought his arms around her, he let out the long breath he had been holding and clasped her tightly to him. He nuzzled his nose in her hair, inhaling the sweet essence that was uniquely her own.

"Ari . . ." he breathed, never wanting to let her go, but knowing if he was ever to have any chance of her forgiveness he would have to.

Arian lay quiet in her husband's arms. Her husband. The one man who would forfeit all for her. And had. Emotions collided in her heart. She knew the moment she asked him to stay that she would regret it. Not for what they had just shared, but because it would cloud her already wavering judgment. Her love for him was not in question. Nor his for her. There was more to it than that. On every turn of her head or in nearly every thought, the image of Magnus bleeding to death in her lap haunted her. And no matter how she tried to justify his death it always came back to her. *She* was responsible. Not Stefan. How could she live with herself?

Stefan's lips pressed to her temple. He smoothed the damp hair from her brow. "What thoughts plague you, my love?"

She smiled sadly. How could she explain to him she could not live with herself and because of *that* she could not live with him? She looked up into his brilliant eyes. "I know not what to do, Stefan. My love for you is as strong as before, mayhap more, but the guilt eats at me."

He nodded, thoughtful for a moment. "Arian, I have done things in my life I am not proud of. Things I wish I could take back. But I cannot take back the past. I can only go forward, and learn from past mistakes."

"But—"

He kissed her. "Shhh, allow me to finish." When she nodded, he continued. "Forgiveness is a most powerful balm for the heart. Both asking for it and giving it. I have asked your forgiveness, and I hope one day you will find it in your heart to grant it."

"I have already, Stefan."

He smiled, and her heart melted a little more for him. "Then, my love, you must give yourself the same quarter." Her brows knitted in confusion. "Forgive yourself for whatever hand you imagine you had in Magnus's death. You acted from the heart. Emotions are stronger than any sword, Arian. I have learned this lesson recently. Love makes a lucid person mad. Since I met you, I have experienced emotions I never thought possible. From the highest high to the lowest low and everything in between. You wreak havoc with my heart, but"—he laughed—"I would have it no other way. I cannot control it any more than I can control the rise of the sun each day. I no longer question it, either. It is what it is. I accept it."

"Stefan, Magnus knew—"

"Aye, the world knew of our love. When you accepted his offer for marriage you did so with a clear heart, Arian; yet he did not. Had he not fallen beneath my sword, do you think he would have considered your feelings if they interrupted his grand scheme? Do you think he did not have a mistress or two tucked away?" She shook her head. "Twas not the same." "You are denying what lies plainly before your face. Magnus was a traitor. Though he claimed Norse citizenship, Magnus had holdings here in England. He would have been hanged. As overlord here, I would have written the order and carried it out. He knotted his own noose. Not you, nor I."

As Stefan's words settled in, some of the guilt she had been dragging around in her heart lessened. "You know I speak the truth. Mayhap part of your anger now is knowing Magnus had other intentions, and you feel a bit scorned?"

Arian winced, admitting that at least on a small scale her pride was involved. "I will admit that when I discovered his treachery and reason for marriage, my pride stung."

"Arian, you were a pawn in his deadly game. He

would have tossed you to the wolves if it meant saving his own skin." He pushed her back into the pillows, his soft eyes searching her face. "Whereas I"—he kissed her lips—"would lay down my horse, my sword, and my life for you."

He had her then. And the knowledge that there was no future for her if this man were not by her side crashed with resounding force through her body. "Stefan," she whispered, wrapping her arms around his neck, drawing him close. "I am afraid. I am afraid of losing you, and I am afraid of these people of Yorkshire. They have blood in their eyes. I do not trust them."

"Yorkshire will be dealt with."

TWENTY-FOUR

In the day following Arian's marriage to Stefan, a dark pall hung over the village and manor. The Saxon nobles including Overly and Lisette with Philip chasing behind left Moorwood in a mass exodus. For their departure she was grateful.

Though her marriage to Magnus had been short-lived, Arian was by Norse law heir to all that was his, including command of the one hundred men who had accompanied him to Moorwood and the hundreds more he sent to Scotland.

Arian, without her husband beside her, so as not to incite more hatred from the Vikings, called the captain of her new Norse guard to her chamber. When he entered, she nodded, acknowledging his short bow to her. "Your name, sir."

"Bjorr Thorkellson."

"Sir Bjorr, how long have you been in my late husband's service?"

"Six years."

"And in those six years, was he a fair lord?"

"Aye, most fair."

"Though he is dead, you are aware that under Norse law all that was his is now mine."

He nodded, but she knew from his guarded face and short answers the news was not welcome.

"I understand your dislike for the Normans, and for myself for that matter, but we must move past that." She looked up into his eyes, and said, "I require your help, sir. The area is unstable. 'Tis only a matter of time before we are attacked."

"My loyalty is to Norway."

"Not to me—your lady?"

He slowly shook his head. "You are not my lady. Because of you, my lord is dead. My men will not fight for you or your Norman husband."

"Not even for gold?"

He shook his head. "Nay, not even for gold."

Arian stood and nodded. "You leave me no choice then, Sir Bjorr." His face turned ashen. "I will not force you to fight for me or my husband." His eyes narrowed. She smiled. "Return to Norway and protect what is mine. Once things are settled here, I will journey to your country and settle my affairs."

"What trickery are you about?"

"None, sir. You are free to return to Norway."

He stood for a long moment, unsure. "You will not set your Normans against us as we leave this place and call us traitors?"

"Nay. I do not play games of intrigue and backstabbing."

He bowed then, and was turning to leave the chamber when Stefan strode in. Bjorr continued on his way, and Stefan's eyes narrowed.

"What have you done?"

"Released my Norse army."

Her husband was not pleased. "They will join with Magnus's men to the north and return to slay us all whilst we sleep!"

"Nay, Stefan, they will not."

"Arian, I am well versed in the ways of men and war."

"You are well versed in conquering with might, my love. There are other ways."

"You are wrong."

"Nay, I am not. You will see." She closed the door to their chamber and set the bolt, not caring that the sun was high in the sky. She looked over her shoulder at him and smiled. "Come, let me show how to soothe the savage beast with just a kiss."

The next morn Robert departed west for Normandy, and Bjorr with his men set out for their homeland. As Arian and Stefan watched them depart, Arian's feeling of foreboding deepened. Yet she did not second-guess her decision to allow the Vikings to return. They were useless to her if they would not fight for her, and should she force them as her husband counseled, they would turn on her. Stefan reached down, taking her hand, entwining his fingers in hers. When she looked up into his eyes, emotion swelled in her chest. He was hard, he was savage, but he was fair. He was a man of honor, and though a man, he realized she was a worthy ruler in her own right. He had accepted her counsel, and for that, he would always have her undying gratitude.

Several hours later, just as they sat for the noon meal, the lookout shouted that riders bearing the king's standard approached.

"The Saxons demand the heads of Lady Arian and Lord Stefan!" Robert cried out as he galloped back into the bailey, followed by a handful of the men who had departed with him that morn.

Arian gasped and turned to Stefan, who stood beside her on the stone steps to the manor house. His arm tightened around her waist. He was calm, while fear turned her to stone. "Fear not, my love. We will see the day won."

He pulled her into the hall and set her upon the lord's chair. "Listen to me carefully, Arian, for our lives depend on it. Gather the servants and set them to the task of filling the interior stores. Douse the kitchen fires, prepare for tending wounded, then secure the manor and arm yourself." He pulled her to him and kissed her hard; when he pulled away, his eyes burned hot with passion. "Trust no one but your own people and the Blood Swords."

"Where do you go?"

"To secure the grounds."

As Stefan rushed from the hall, Arian called for the servants, but to her dismay and growing fear, only a handful assembled before her.

"Where are the others?" she demanded of the cook.

The woman's eyes dropped to the floor. "They have gone."

"Gone? Why?"

The woman raised her eyes to Arian, and she saw guarded contempt in them, and understood. "Go then, all of you, if you cannot stand to serve here. I will not hold you."

And to her dismay they all turned tail and fled, leaving her alone in the hall save for the ancient Jane and the few Norman and Welsh servants. Arian took immediate action. "Jane, see that the stores here are filled. Douse the kitchen fires and the fires throughout the manor." She turned then and ran to her chamber to change into the heartier garb that she wore for the hunt. She grabbed her bow and quiver of arrows from the stand in the corner, and fitted her dagger in her girdle, then rushed to close and bolt the high shutters in each chamber. She lugged in great buckets of water and food. She ran to the armory and grabbed two handfuls of bows, then returned with quivers full of arrows. As she raced about to secure her home Arian did not think twice about using deadly force to save her life or Stefan's.

The bailey was a mad rush of activity, but off in the distance she saw dark black billowing smoke from the village beyond the great meadow. She ran back into the hall and up to the guard tower to find Stefan conferring with his men. She gazed out across the crowded bailey and to the road farther beyond. Her blood iced. Off in the distance, hundreds of Saxons gathered.

They were vastly outnumbered. "What will we do?" she asked, afraid of the answer.

Stefan's face was drawn and hard. "We have already begun, *chérie*. Ralph's men have been dispatched and will come around at their flanks. Upon their charge, we fill them with our arrows, and once they are sufficiently weakened we will finish the deed with our swords. More men travel along the western road; they were several days behind Robert. They too will serve my purpose."

As he spoke, the Saxons converged on the fringes of the meadow, sending up a wild raucous battle cry. Arian's eyes widened in horror. " 'Tis Ralph!" In stunned silence, they watched as Ralph's men joined the fray, not as enemies but as allies of the Saxons.

"*Jesu!*" Stefan cursed.

Arian grabbed Stefan's sleeve. "Magnus's men, Stefan, they are but half a day away, let me go to them!"

"Nay! 'Tis too dangerous. And they will not aid you."

Stefan stood silent for a long moment, and she saw savage fury line his face. "Ralph is a fool!"

"William warned us there were traitors amongst our own kind," Rorick seethed.

"Stefan," Arian said softly, "there is much that I must attend to." She stood up on her toes, wrapped her arms around his neck, and kissed him. "Do not worry about the manor. I will see to it."

"Aye, Arian, I have faith you will."

She hurried from him then, to find Jane in the hall tearing linens. Arian grabbed up her bow and two quivers of arrows. "Jane," she said, sure there were no other ears to hear. "I go to Bjorr, and beg for his help."

"My lady! You cannot, the fields are infested with Saxons!"

"There is a back way to the wood." She hugged her nurse close then moved past her through the pantry and then to the courtyard.

As if she had every right, Arian hurried to the stable, saddled her mare, then hurried to the back gate and demanded that the guard open it. When he resisted, she drew her bow and leveled an arrow at his chest. "Open it now or die."

He did so, and she flew east, then turned on the north road to the longships that awaited Bjorr and his one hundred men. What had taken them hours to travel by foot, Arian caught up to them in a fraction of time. When she approached Bjorr, he scowled and looked past her for her escort.

"I come alone, sir. I beg a private word with you."

He nodded, and moved away from his men, who watched her with shifty eyes. They held her responsible for their lord's death, to be sure, but she was not so sure that had they known of his plot with Sven they would have defied their young king, who wished only for peace with England.

"Sir, I need your help, and that of your men. Moorwood is under attack. Lord Stefan's own cousin betrays him, allying himself with the angry Saxon lords. If you do not come, all will be lost this day."

"You ask me again to support the man who slew my lord?" he asked, incredulous.

"Your lord, my husband, was about to betray his king and his people!"

Bjorr shook his head." 'Tis hearsay at best."

"Nay, you know in your heart it is not. Sar was proof, and while your lord may be dead all that was his is mine, including you."

He drew his ax. "I can easily remedy that, milady."

Arian spurred her horse closer, unafraid of what he

threatened. "Aye, you can, or you can hear my offer, then decide where your true loyalties lie."

He regarded her for a long silent moment, then said, "I am listening."

" 'Tis reminiscent of Hereford, Stefan. We are outnumbered, and this time by seasoned Normans!" Rorick cursed. "Ralph! The craven lout!"

"He is most ambitious, but more foolish. He has sent riders ahead to stall the garrison William has sent, and knows we are thin here," Stefan mused aloud. He turned to Robert. "Strip your mail and keep the destrier light. Take your squire, slip through the back gates, and ride like the wind to the west. When you come upon William's men, expose Ralph's man and his plots. Then return. We have enough to keep them at bay for a day, maybe two, and even should they break through the outlying walls we can hold up here until you arrive with reinforcements."

Robert made a short bow, then hurried to the task. Stefan faced his men: Ioan, Rorick, Rohan, and Warner. "So here we are again, outnumbered by treacherous Saxons and a treacherous cousin. As at Hereford, let us continue to use the archers to our advantage. The Welsh up on the walls have done a good job so far keeping them at bay, but they gain ground. We retreat only when we have no choice, but we will not open the gates to engage. Let us go now and aid them with our own bows."

They all nodded, and when Stefan climbed down from the tower, he looked for Arian, but found only her ancient maid, nervously wringing her hands. Dread instantly filled his heart. "Milord," Jane cried, "Lady Arian has flown."

"Flown! Where? Why?"

"She was in a fit of agitation, but said she would beg the Viking for his assistance."

"How?"

"A horse through the back gates."

Stefan ran from the hall to the back of the bailey, near the stable where he found his guard. The minute the man looked up at him, Stefan knew he had let her past. "Where is she?"

"Gone, milord."

"You let her go?"

"She threatened to kill me!"

"Bah!" Stefan turned back to the manor to see his men, precious few that they were, alongside Arian's men set up along the high walls.

His heart tore him in half. One part wanted to stay with his men and fight to the death should he have to, and the other wanted to go after his wife and bring her back to safety. But was it truly safe for her here? He climbed the ladder to the wall and looked down upon the sea of Saxons. They were doomed. In one mad rush they could scale the walls, and they would have to retreat to the manor, and while it was sturdy, it too would fall.

Why, he wondered, had they not already done so? On closer inspection the Saxons appeared to be disorientated and unsure. Ralph did not have control, but from where Stefan stood 'twas a Saxon noble, who had pledged fealty just the day before, who led the mob of mostly churls with pitchforks and scythes. There were other nobles amongst them ahorse, but they too did not appear to have much of an appetite for a fight. Had they the conviction of their cause, they would have rushed the walls.

"They have no clear leader," Stefan yelled to Rohan. He pointed to Ralph, who watched the disarray from his horse toward the far left flank."And he seems to have no authority." Stefan pulled his bow from his shoulder and notched three arrows."Notch your bows, men, and aim for Ralph's black heart!"

Like a dark stormcloud, a score of arrows sailed through the sky, their path straight and true. Stefan watched them arc, then come together as one mighty rod and fall short several long strides from where Ralph sat upon his horse. The traitorous Norman raised his fist toward them, and Stefan knew he laughed at them. So be it.

"I'm going to circle back, and one by one, I'm going to pick off the Normans and the Saxon lords. With no leader, the churls will run home," Stefan told his men. He grabbed several full quivers and threw them over his shoulder, then ran out the back gate, where he kept to the wood and circled up and around. His going was slow, and it took him considerably more time than he had first thought. By now the sun was in full rise, and he could not help but worry over his wife's safety. When he got his hands on her, he would shake her until she could not see straight! How dare she put herself in jeopardy? There was no pleading with the Vikings. The only string that held Stefan to Moorwood was his unwavering trust in the woman whom he called wife. In the short time he had known her, she had transformed from a naïve princess to a great lady to be reckoned with. Yes, they would both survive this day, and their bond would be as unbreakable as hewn steel.

As he broke from the wood behind where Ralph and his captain had lurked for most of the morn, Stefan stopped cold. More Saxons poured in from the north road, armed Saxons, and he could see that mixed in were many warriors of northern descent. Great hulking men with battle-axes. Were these part of Sven's men? Stefan hunkered down and watched, waiting for the first opportunity to strike. Though Ralph was well mailed and wore a helm, Stefan was a good enough shot that with an opening, he could hit him in the throat and be done with his cousin forever.

He moved farther down the tree line to where the leading Saxon huddled with his men. As quiet as a breeze, Stefan notched an arrow, aimed, and let it fly. Before it hit true, Stefan turned and made his way deeper into the wood and back toward the Normans. A shout rang through the field. And Stefan knew the man lay dead on the ground. Word quickly spread, and as the Saxons thinned in their panic, he took aim at another lord who had just the day before pledged his fealty to Stefan. He dropped to the ground. Continuing to keep low and to the wood, Stefan set his sights on the huge Dane who led a small but deadly contingent of foot soldiers.

Ralph called for the archers to turn to the wood and they let loose a flurry of arrows. But they were far off the mark. With the hailstorm of arrows, Stefan took aim and brought the mighty Dane to his knees. The man bellowed in outrage and yanked the arrow from his chest.

Stefan moved back whence he came, and for the next span of time, he played a cat-and-mouse game with his enemies. His hope was that the harassment would send them all running in a hundred directions, in fear and disarray. But Ralph was smarter than that. He knew Stefan's game, and he pulled them all, Norman, Saxon, and Dane, together on the far side of the field, where they awaited his direction.

Unless Stefan crossed without cover, he could not make it to the other side and take a shot at his cousin. Stefan watched and waited, musing on his options. He had taken out a dozen men, most of them well-armed leaders. Somehow, Ralph had managed to escape him, and had also managed to renew the fighting spirit in the troops.

Angrily Stefan watched from the trees as Ralph assembled the men, setting the few archers he had to the front, then the foot soldiers, then the knights. Stefan shook his head. The man was not known for his tactics. The foot soldiers should go first to soften the walls and throw the hooks, whilst the archers bombarded the bailey, preventing those within from protecting the walls. Then the knights should come when the doors were breached, and hack at any who stood in their way.

But Ralph's idiocy would be Stefan's gain. When Ralph lit the arrows, Stefan scowled. He would burn the place and every living soul inside to the ground. He watched, furious and afraid for his brothers, as the swarm of flaming arrows rose high in the air, and was glad to see a good number of them sputtered out. But many landed along the wooden wall and beyond.

Buckets of water poured down the walls. Angrily, Stefan watched as Ralph led the men to form a thin circle around the manor. 'Twould make it nearly impossible to defend. Robert's men were only fifty; Arian's Welsh guard thirty more, and his Blood Swords who were worth three men apiece. Not one churl had stayed to take up arms in defense of Moorwood. They would be stretched to their limit. Their only hope of survival was to hold Ralph off until reinforcements arrived. He prayed that Robert had made it through Ralph's men; with more knights, the craven traitors would flee for their lives.

Stefan took up his weapons and jogged around to the far side of the wood, closer to Ralph. He watched as the walls were repeatedly engulfed in flames then doused with water. They seemed to be concentrating on several spots and the fires were doing their damage. If Stefan could not get a clear shot and take Ralph from the battlefield, he would lose his men. And he would not allow that to happen, not again!

As the sun began to set, it became clear to Stefan that part of the high walls had weakened, to a point that with a battering ram they would be easily breached. He had managed to pick off a few more of the armed Danes, and even a few of Ralph's men. Though Norman, they were traitors, and when the time came he would see each of them dead. He knew what Ralph planned: he would say they were all set upon by the local lords and the Blood Swords fell. What he did not count on was Robert breaking through his lines west.

Frustrated with his inability to get closer to Ralph, Stefan stripped off his mail. Breaking branches from the trees, he stuck them down his back and front and in his sword belt. He rubbed dirt on his face and waited for the sun to dip more to the west. When the light had shifted to his advantage, on his belly he slowly crawled out from the wood. Stealthily, he made his way toward the camp where Ralph held court, giving directions.

"We do not need a ram," Ralph boasted. "The walls will fall by sundown, and when they do, under the cover of darkness we shall spill into the interior and see the day won!"

Rousing cheers erupted. Crouched behind one of the great destriers, Stefan slowly withdrew his bow. Silently he notched an arrow and took aim.

"Men approach!" the lookout called.

Ralph moved so quickly from the fire that Stefan lost his opportunity. "Norman?"

"Nay! The Norse guard has returned and the Lady Arian rides with them!"

"The bitch!" Ralph cursed.

Stefan's heart nearly dropped from his chest to his feet. Arian returned? With Magnus's guard? How did she—

Caught off guard with word of Arian, Stefan was exposed as the men mounted their horses. " 'Tis the Norman Stefan!" a Saxon cried. Stefan let the arrow fly at the closest man and notched several more before he was overpowered by several Normans. He lay pinned to the ground as Ralph stood over him and threw his head back and laughed uproariously. "Ah, cousin, you are finally beat!"

Ralph drew his sword. "It will give me great pleasure to slit your throat. Be sure I will comfort your lady on the cold winter nights to come."

Stefan shouted out his mighty battle cry, and as he did, with supreme strength he kicked at the two men holding his feet and half-rolled from them, breaking the grip on his hands. He drew his sword and crouched backward. Normans surrounded him, and he saw doubt in some of their faces.

He rose to his full height and wagged his sword tauntingly before them all. "You may win the day here, Ralph, but Robert has made it to the garrison on the road here. You cannot kill us all. You are doomed."

"Robert never made it past the edge of the wood, dear cousin. You will be dead before the lady's guard arrives." He raised his sword.

Stefan laughed. "Your greed is only surpassed by your foolishness, Ralph. Do you think you can best me with a sword?"

"The minute I falter, my men will finish you off." He gave him a short bow.

Stefan looked to the thick circle of men surrounding him. "You will all hang from the highest gibbet for your treason."

"Nay, Stefan, we will be hailed as heroes for saving the day." He jabbed at Stefan with his sword; easily he parried it. In a slow circle, they measured the other. Ralph was tall and competent enough with his sword, but Stefan was highly trained in the art of swordplay. Ralph jabbed again, and just as before, Stefan easily parried it. He would toy with him as long as he could, hoping that Arian and her guard would get to the field in time, and when they arrived all hell would break loose. The Jarl's men were battle-hardened and bloodthirsty, and Stefan still could not understand how she had convinced them to return and fight for the man who slew their lord.

"You toy with me, Stefan," Ralph said, as the circle closed around them. "You bide your time. Fight me now or I will let them loose."

Stefan nodded, and in a short hard jab that caught Ralph off guard, he lunged, catching him on the right forearm. Ralph hissed, and returned the blow, narrowly missing Stefan's shoulder. Without his mail he was lighter, but completely exposed. Carefully he moved around the Norman and struck again, this time to his back. The velocity of the hit shoved Ralph halfway across the circle. His men began to cheer and jeer. And in the distance, Stefan watched the walls surrounding the manor go up in a sudden burst of flames. More cheers followed. Stefan took advantage of the moment. He thrust again, catching Ralph once more on the forearm. As the knight returned the strike, Stefan twirled out of his way, landing low as Ralph's blade swished across his back. Stefan popped up and kicked the knight in the knee. Ralph screamed in pain as he toppled backwards.

Shouts from the woods pierced the tight circle. "We are under attack!" a man shouted.

Stefan moved in on Ralph as he came to his feet. He kicked him in the face this time, sending him reeling. His screams rent the air, mingling with those of the others. The circle had thinned considerably, but Stefan stayed focused on Ralph: he was key to the battle; once removed the day would be won. Ralph came to his feet, assisted by his squire. Behind him, Stefan could see the manor house was aflame and the gates wide open, but pouring from the bailey were mounted knights. He dared not turn toward the wood to see where the guard was; instead, he focused on Ralph, who now had two armed men at his side. Slowly they approached, their weapons drawn.

"You will die as you lived, Ralph: a craven. Before your blood stains this ground, I offer my thanks."

"For what?"

Stefan smiled. "For all of de Lyon."

"Never!"

"There, dear cousin, you are wrong. Robert informed me of my sire's death and the missive he sent to William before he was poisoned. You did not tell me he was dead. Why? So that you could slay me and claim all?"

"Your father was an old fool. He could no longer live with himself, he said. He must atone for his sins! He would make you heir, then embark on a pilgrimage to Jerusalem. Bah! I made sure that did not happen. But 'twas too late, he had sent word to William."

"Your greed will be your end." Stefan struck the man to Ralph's left, slicing open his calf. He turned and crouched again, bringing his sword around in a low sweeping motion, finishing the job. The man howled as blood spewed from his torn leg. The other rushed Stefan, but he was prepared. He kept the crouch position, and as the man came at him, Stefan jabbed his sword into his belly, skewering him. He kicked off the body, but as he did, Ralph hacked at his shoulder, catching him off guard. Stefan grunted in pain, ignoring the rush of blood down his arm. 'Twas his left, not his right, his sword arm. He pushed up from the ground. In short hacking sweeps, he moved toward Ralph, who now had no others to back him. A battle ensued around them, the manor ablaze. In the din Stefan heard Rohan's battle cry, followed by Ioan's, then Rorick's, ending with Warner's. Ralph paled in the moonlight.

"Make your peace with God now, cousin."

"Stefan!"

He froze. Arian? Here, in the midst of a battle? He turned to tell her to go, to run for cover. 'Twas his fatal mistake. He saw her upon her horse, her eyes wide with fear. He reached out a hand to her. At that moment, she screamed, and in slow motion, he turned as Ralph's blade came down upon him. He rolled out of the way, catching the edge of his attack on his shoulder. Ralph kicked Stefan's sword from his hand as he hit the ground. Stefan now with no weapon, his cousin brought his sword down with both hands. Stefan kicked out, trying to bring himself up off the ground, but he had no strength in his left arm, and his right was numb. He fell back to the ground. Ralph's eyes burned with hatred.

"Make *your* peace, cousin," he said, and just as he brought the sword down a hiss, followed by the indisputable thump of an arrow finding home in skin and bone, rent the air. Stefan watched, shocked, as Ralph grabbed at the arrow that went clear through the side of his neck. He raised his eyes up and beyond Stefan, who followed his gaze. Arian sat upon her horse, another arrow notched in her bow.

"Stand down, Ralph, or my next arrow will cut your throat in half," she threatened.

He stepped toward Stefan, and before his foot touched the soil, another arrow ripped through his throat. Blood sprang forth, and Stefan knew he was done. Stefan rolled over and slowly stood; grabbing his sword from the ground, he moved to Arian as quickly as he could. She held out a hand to him, and he vaulted onto the back of her horse.

"My thanks, milady." He took up the reins and spurred the horse toward his men, who, with the help of the Norse guard and Arian's Welshmen, had formed a tight gantlet around the quivering Saxons and the remaining Normans, who cowered worse than the Saxons did. In the distance, the entire manor and bailey lit up the night sky in flames.

Stefan gave the signal to blow the horn. After several trumpets, eerie quiet fell over the bloody field.

"The day is lost!" he shouted to the subdued army. "Throw down your weapons, now, and I will spare your lives this day."

Metal clanked upon metal as the men dropped their swords, axes, and bows. Stefan looked beyond, to the raging fire that once was Moorwood. "You Saxons destroy well." He looked to Ralph's men—some half-score left. "Dismount." Slowly they did. The Blood Swords circled them. "You are traitors to the Crown. Decide this night how you wish to die on the morrow!"

He felt Arian stiffen in his arms, but she remained silent. For a long moment, Stefan scanned the fearful faces before him. Most of them were field churls who would follow their master to the edge of the earth, their loyalty so deep. 'Twas the kind of man he wanted.

"What you have destroyed today, we will rebuild tomorrow for William." His eyes scanned the few nobles who stood amongst them. "Cadoc!" Stefan called. "See that these men are retained." Next Stefan's eyes settled on the fearsome Danes. "Give a message to your king on behalf of mine: we are aware of his plot to invade England. Olaf will give Sven no support, nor will Sven find support amongst the Welsh kings. William's hand firmly holds the reins here. And be sure Yorkshire will see more seasoned Normans each day that I am lord here. And I am not going anywhere."

The Dane closest to Stefan made a short bow and bent to pick up his ax. "Nay," Stefan warned. "You return as you are, stripped of your fight."

The man glared at Stefan, but backed away, and was quickly followed by his men, who faded into the darkness.

Once more, Stefan turned to the large group of churls. "Return to your families this night, but at first light return to me here, and together we will rebuild a castle worthy of a king!" Wide-eyed, the churls looked at one another, unable to believe they were free to go home.

As the field emptied, leaving only Stefan and those loyal to him, he tightened his arms around his wife. He flinched at the pain in his forearm, knowing he would need stitches. He was grateful she kept silent. When they spoke, he wanted their words to be private. Slowly, they made their way to the manor that was now no more than a smoking heap of rubble.

"Jane?" Arian asked, fear lacing her words.

"She is safe in the wood behind the manor," Rohan said from beside them.

Her body loosened in his arms.

As they stopped to gaze upon the wreckage so did everyone behind them, including the Norsemen. "How did you convince the Norse captain to return and fight for you?"

She leaned back into his arms. "I offered him and his men Magnus's lands in Norway."

Stefan threw his head back and laughed. "You are a wily princess, milady."

"I am a determined one."

As they entered the bailey, there were only a few huts left unscathed. The kitchens, made of stone though scorched, still stood. Thankfully the stable held as well.

"The manor is completely ruined," Arian said softly.

"We can rebuild," Stefan said just as softly.

"I never liked this hall or this setting. There is a more protected area down the road a ways, with a river close by. 'Twould be a good place to raise our sons," Arian said.

She turned in his arms, and her eyes glowed softly in the low embers surrounding them. He lowered his lips to hers and kissed her long and deep. When their lips parted Stefan raised her chin with his hand." 'Tis a hostile area, Arian. 'Twill be difficult at best to win the hearts of these people. There is no Saxon blood in our veins."

"You are strong and just, Stefan. The people will see it as I have."

"Mayhap in time, but there is another option."

She leaned comfortably against his chest. "I am listening."

"I am heir to my father's holdings in Normandy. They are vast, and it is safer there for you."

"I go where you go, my love," Arian said, her silvery gaze penetrating Stefan's soul.

Emotion welled up in his chest with such a velocity

he thought he might die from the rush. "What do you wish, Arian?"

For a long minute, their gazes held as she pondered his question. "A new start, here, for us both."

He grinned and pulled her close to his heart. His gaze scoured the smoldering ruins settling on his brothers, Rohan, Warner, Rorick, and Ioan, as they tended the wounded. With Wulfson, Thorin, and Rhys—whom they *would* find—still absent, part of him felt incomplete. But he would survive, as would his brothers. Stefan kissed the sunburst-colored hair beneath his chin.

Princess Arianrhod of Dinefwr was not only his wife, but his life force, his heart and soul, and Stefan knew with unshakable truth that so long as she remained beside him, they would thrive in Yorkshire and build a dynasty that would last one thousand years.

Delve *into a* passion *from* *the* past *with a* romance
from Pocket Books!

LIZ CARLYLE
Never Romance a Rake
Love is always a gamble....But never romance a rake!

JULIA LONDON
The Book of Scandal
Will royal gossip reignite her husband's passion for her?

KARIN TABKE
Master of Surrender
The Blood Sword Legacy
A mercenary knight is bound by a blood oath to reclaim his
legacy—and the body of the one woman he desires.

KATHLEEN GIVENS
Rivals for the Crown
The fierce struggle for Scotland's throne leads
two women to courageous new destinies...

**Available wherever books are sold
or at www.simonandschuster.com.**

POCKET BOOKS
A Division of Simon & Schuster
A CBS COMPANY

**POCKET
STAR BOOKS**
A Division of Simon & Schuster
A CBS COMPANY

19096

Delve into a timeless passion...
Pick up a bestselling historical romance from Pocket Books!

Karen Hawkins
To Catch a Highlander
In this game of hearts, love is the only prize.

Johanna Lindsey
The Devil Who Tamed Her
He loves a challenge...and she is an irresistible one.

Jane Feather
To Wed a Wicked Prince
This prince has more than marriage on his mind...

Sabrina Jeffries
Let Sleeping Rogues Lie
Enroll in the School for Heiresses, and discover that desire
has its own rules...and temptations its own rewards.

Meredith Duran
The Duke of Shadows
Born an outcast. Raised to nobility. Only one dangerous
passion can unlock his heart.

Ana Leigh
One Night With a Sweet-Talking Man
He talked his way into her heart.
Can he do the same with her bed?

Available wherever books are sold or at www.simonandschuster.com.

POCKET
STAR BOOKS
A Division of Simon & Schuster
A CBS COMPANY

POCKET BOOKS
A Division of Simon & Schuster
A CBS COMPANY

Available wherever books are sold
or at www.simonsayslove.com.

18158

Catch up with love...
Catch up with passion...
Catch up with danger....
Catch a bestseller from Pocket Books!

Delve into the past with *New York Times* bestselling author
Julia London
The Dangers of Deceiving a Viscount
Beware! A lady's secrets will always be revealed...

Barbara Delinksy
Lake News
New York Times bestseller!
Sometimes you have to get away to find everything.

Fern Michaels
The Marriage Game
New York Times bestseller!
It's all fun and games—until someone falls in love.

Hester Browne
The Little Lady Agency
New York Times bestseller!
Why trade up if you can fix him up?

Laura Griffin
One Last Breath
Don't move. Don't breathe. Don't say a word...